Half Past Midnight

JEFF BRACKETT

DEDICATION

Half Past Midnight is dedicated to the best wife in the world. There is absolutely no way this novel would have ever been completed without her support and encouragement. She helped me bring what was only a half-baked idea into reality.

I love you, Meloney.

CONTENTS

JEFF BRACKETT

ACKNOWLEDGMENTS

This novel has been such a long time in the making, and there have been so many people who have helped me with it, that I just know I'm going to miss some of you here. Please forgive me if I do.

First, thanks to Megan, Zach, and Amber, for not laughing at your crazy old dad's dream.

And to my parents, who inspired me to begin this project so many years ago. *Half Past Midnight* is the result of a discussion with them wherein my mother jokingly made the comment, "If there ever is a nuclear war here, I hope I'm standing directly under the first blast." That single comment started my twisted mind wondering, "but what happens if you aren't?"

Thanks to Linda, for encouraging a much younger me to take my writing seriously.

And to James Husum, my "brother from another mother" who has read and critiqued various incarnations of this novel in an attempt to keep me honest.

Thanks to Lynn O'Dell and Jim Chambers of Red Adept Publishing. They are the best editing team I could ever hope for. You guys took a rough manuscript and helped polish it until it was actually a presentable story.

And to Dave, for sharing his intimate knowledge of the Abram's battle tank, and Edwin for sharing his expertise in military Chemical, Biological, Radiological, and Nuclear warfare training.

Thanks to everyone in the Dead Robots' Society, for inspiring me to get back into writing after a too-long hiatus. Special thanks to Terry Mixon, for helping to educate me on the way the biz works these days, and Justin Macumber, the head "Dead Robot", for helping me come up with the name *Half Past Midnight*, when my working title showed up on someone else's book. (See Justin, I didn't forget you!)

Last, but far from least, I would like to thank all of the men and women who serve in our military, who lay their lives on the line for all of us every day, so that the Doomsday War remains fictitious.

Any mistakes in this novel are mine. Anything I got right, is due to all the people who helped me out with this endeavor.

Thank you all.

Doomsday fell on a Saturday.

I was at work. But then, I was always at work, or at least that was how it seemed. I didn't know at the time just how easy I had it.

In those days, I was a CNC machinist and programmer. I worked in a small, family-owned, high-volume, high-precision machine shop. Quite a mouthful, isn't it? The key words there are "family owned," and the family that owned this particular business was the Dawcett family. It was, not so coincidentally, *my* family.

I was the only son of Raymond and Elizabeth Dawcett, owner and office manager, respectively. That effectively gave me the unofficial title of S.O.B., supposedly standing for "Son of the Boss," but some of the employees used it a bit too gleefully.

That particular Saturday morning, I was tweaking the setup on a CNC lathe to run an extremely close-tolerance job. It was a tricky setup, requiring all of my concentration. On a weekday, there would be all the myriad distractions that come with Monday through Friday's nine to five. So I had come in on Saturday.

My dad was also in, working in the office on a proposal for a new job. He'd been forced to cut back on his workload ever since his heart had gone bad and he'd gotten the latest model Jarvik. The doctors had restricted him to light workdays, warning that he would tire much easier for the next several months. So in his typical fashion, he'd decided if he had to work fewer hours per day, then he would do it seven days a week. We often joked about the limitations of his bionic heart, but we both knew he wasn't getting any younger. And he wasn't even close to being completely recovered.

Everything was going smoothly with my setup, and I was nearly finished when the power abruptly went out. Sudden darkness. Safety mechanisms on the lathe kicked in, immediately clamping the brakes onto the spindle, winding it down from fifteen hundred RPM to a full stop in less than two seconds.

Great! Just my luck. Try to get ahead and see what happens? Then, in my best Dangerfield voice, I said, "I don't get no respect."

I stood there a moment and considered my options. There was a slight chance the power would come back on momentarily, but I didn't think it very likely, since both the one-ten and the two-twenty had gone down together. The loss of power to either system wasn't that unusual, but I could count the number of times we had lost power to both on the fingers of one hand. On each of those occasions, the electricity had stayed down for several hours.

Lucky me. I got to add another finger to the tally.

As my eyes began to adjust to the gloom, I saw the darkness was not as absolute as it had first seemed. Far across the large machine shop, I could make out the dim outline of the door to the office area. That was my beacon as I made my way through the otherwise pitch-blackness. Stumbling over pallets and tool chests, I cursed quietly with each bump. Soon the cursing wasn't so quiet, but I finally made it into the adjoining office.

I entered the office through the door behind Dad's desk, but he didn't turn to greet me as he normally would. Instead, he remained facing forward, his attention apparently focused outside.

"What's going on, Dad? We just lost all the power in…" I rounded the desk and saw that he wasn't paying any attention to me. He just continued to stare outside with a puzzled expression on his face.

I followed his gaze and saw what held his attention. "What is…?"

For several seconds, my mind simply refused to accept what my eyes conveyed. The sky was one of life's constants, one of those things one could always count on to remain within a specific set of parameters. On a clear summer day in June, I knew I could count on seeing the blinding yellow disk of the sun in a deep blue sky. What I saw instead took me aback.

"What the…"

The sun was indeed a blinding yellow but, past that point, I had trouble comprehending what I saw. The sky was *not* the normal crisp blue of a hot Texas summer morning. Instead, it dopplered into more of a shimmering violet, with the deepest of the color centered around a second glowing orb about fifty degrees to the north. It was almost as large as the sun, though not quite as bright. In fact, it seemed to be fading slightly even as I watched. The sky around it shimmered slightly, like an aurora borealis.

In the eastern sky, a bit to the north and halfway between the sun and the horizon, burned a small, intensely bright ball of light. It seemed as bright as the sun, though it appeared to be slowly fading.

"What the hell is that?" Even as I said it, though thirty-seven years old, I realized I still wanted to flinch when I forgot myself enough to curse in front of my parents. But still, Dad didn't comment and, when I looked back at him, I saw he still hadn't moved. Not at all.

"Dad?"

Still nothing. Alarmed, I stepped toward him—and stopped. It wasn't until then that I finally realized what else was wrong. Dad wasn't just motionless—he wasn't breathing.

"Dad!"

Knocking over his guest chair, I scrambled to my father's side. I hesitated a second, irrationally afraid to touch him, knowing at the same time that I had to. My hand shook as I felt for a pulse.

"No, no, no, no, no," I chanted over and over, as if willing it not to be so would bring him back. In desperation, I dragged him out of his chair to the floor. Laying him on his back, I grabbed the portable defibrillator from the wall and ripped open his shirt. The sight of his surgical scars stopped me. *Could I use the defib on him? Would it interfere with his Jarvik?* I considered CPR, but another glimpse of the healing incision on his chest halted me yet again.

"Shit!" I opened the Portafib and ripped open the adhesive electrodes. Reading through the instructions, I applied them to his chest as shown in a diagram and glanced at the indicator on the box. "God *damn* it!" The indicator was as dead as the lights in the shop—as dead as my father on the floor before me. I flung the Portafib across the office.

"What the hell am I supposed to do?" I screamed at the ceiling. The world had gone mad, and I didn't know how to react. The sky, Dad's heart, a second sun—suddenly I knew what had happened. All the pieces abruptly fell into place, and I knew what the fireball outside was—what had killed my father. Worst of all, I knew he had died just a few minutes before, while I was stumbling around in the darkness of the shop and cursing at boxes. The last thing my father had heard had been me cursing. The shame and sorrow of that knowledge freed the tears I didn't know I'd been holding back.

Somehow I felt that I had betrayed him by not comprehending what had happened until after I realized he was dead. It was as if he had died so I would know what had occurred and, if I had caught on sooner, before I turned to look at him, he would have been alive to respond when I spoke.

I knew that was nonsense, just as I knew there was nothing that I, or anyone, could have done even if I had been right there when it happened. The electromagnetic pulse created by an orbital nuclear explosion would short out any unshielded delicate electrical circuitry, the microminiature circuits of an artificial heart, for example.

Dad's Jarvik had simply burned out at the same time the lights went out. I realized that intellectually, but emotionally, I still felt guilty.

* * *

Sobbing, I dragged my father out of the middle of the floor and into my mother's adjoining office, where I laid him out on the carpet. Knowing I would probably never return made what I was doing that much harder. This man had given me my life, taught me the fundamental values for day-to-day living. Now I was going to repay him by leaving him to lie on the floor of a darkened office without so much as a decent burial.

My next actions did nothing to alleviate my remorse, but now that I knew what had happened, I knew they were necessary. Turning away from my father, from my father's corpse, I went about gathering things to help me through all that I knew was to come. I tried to remember what I'd read.

A search through the desks yielded matches, a personal sewing kit, and a small first-aid kit. In the lunchroom, I found a coffee can full of packets of salt, pepper, sugar, and non-dairy creamer, as well as some instant coffee.

I found other odds and ends, and everything went into a growing pile in the middle of the floor near the front door.

Then, I went back out to the shop, leaving the connecting door open so the twin lights of the sun and its new companion would help push back the darkness a bit. Even with that, it became necessary to light a match as I made my way deeper into the darkness to my workbench. My hobby was knife making, a natural fusion of my career in machining and my love of martial arts.

My most recent creation was in a drawer under the bench. Fumbling a bit in the dark, I found the custom Bowie knife I'd recently finished and grabbed the unstained leather sheath I was still working on. Thrusting the treasure through my belt, I hurried back to the pile of items I'd left at the office front door.

After I'd gathered everything into a bucket, I took a deep breath and went back into my mother's office. This was the part I dreaded.

Kneeling at my father's side I whispered, "I'm sorry, Dad." Tears formed once more. "But you and I both know I love you... and you're already gone. A burial won't do you any good now, and it'd just take up too much time. And I have a feeling time's getting really short." I was torn between the need to do something—anything—to properly observe my father's passing, and the need to get to my wife and children. But, as difficult as it might be, I knew which choice had priority. Sobbing now in earnest, I closed his staring eyes. "I love you, Dad. Please understand." I bent and kissed his forehead, my final farewell.

Wiping my eyes, I stumbled to my feet and exited, closing the office door behind me. I picked up my bucket and walked out into a world completely changed. I glanced at my watch through blurred eyes. It was ten forty-one a.m., twenty-seven minutes after the lights had gone out.

* * *

Knowing it was useless, I tried the ignition on my car. I figured if I didn't at least try it, I would always wonder, "What if, by some wild chance, it had worked?"

It didn't.

I was willing to bet that very few cars in the nation ran at this point. Very few, indeed. EMP again. The semiconductors of an electronic ignition system were just too delicate. My little Toyota was now nothing more than half a ton of artistically-shaped scrap metal. I had expected it, but it was still disappointing.

At least I was better off than most people at this stage. I knew I had a few alternatives at home. One consisted of a fairly tired, but theoretically EMP-proofed minivan. Long ago, I'd had a mechanic replace the old electronic ignition system with an even older standard ignition, and had stocked up on extra parts. The mechanic was a fellow survivalist and had known exactly what I had in mind. Hopefully, my better half would be organizing the kids and converting the van into our survival vehicle.

We had long ago discussed this scenario and agreed that under these circumstances—me at work, her at home with the kids—she would begin preparations for our little evacuation and wait no more than four hours before pulling out. I would follow as soon as possible… if possible.

* * *

My parents' house was on my way home, and I wasn't looking forward to telling Mom about Dad's death. Nor was I looking forward to having to convince her to come with me and leave Houston.

In my mind, I went over various conversations. *Mom, I need you to pack a few things, just what we can carry to my house… on foot. What? Oh, well, you see, there's a nuclear war brewing, and we need to get out of Houston before the shit hits the fan. Dad? Uh, sorry, but Dad's dead. So put on your tennis shoes, and let's get going.*

I shook my head. There was no good way to do any of it.

It was just over a twenty minute walk to Mom and Dad's. As I trudged, I saw children playing in their yards, oblivious to the nervous huddles of adults glancing at the odd display in the northeastern sky, and speaking in low whispers. A family of three busily loaded a pickup truck, apparently unaware that it wouldn't start.

As soon as I came within sight of my parents' house, my heart dropped. Mom's car—her new hybrid electric car with the state of the art electronic ignition—was gone.

I let myself into the house, just in case.

"Mom? You here?"

Silence confirmed her absence, and my heart dropped. *Shit.*

I took a deep breath and turned to leave, but then remembered Dad's gun cabinet. I went to the master bedroom and to the back wall of their walk-in closet. Sliding the clothes to one side, I opened the door to the hidden cabinet. Inside were three hunting rifles and a shotgun. Dad was an avid hunter.

Or, he had been.

My chest began to tighten as I thought about him again. *Not now. No time for it now.* I pulled out his Remington pump action .30-06, a scope, and two extra clips, then slid everything into a rifle case. I found three more boxes of ammo for the rifle and dropped them into my trusty bucket.

I'd thought it over as I packed the gun and, though it seemed heartless, I couldn't wait there on the off chance that Mom would somehow return. Nor could I afford to search all over Houston for her on foot.

The best I could come up with was to leave a note and hope she made her way back to read it. It was awkward, putting pen to paper to explain what had happened with Dad—more so when I wrote what I had done, where I was going, and why I hadn't waited for her. I could only hope that she would understand. I asked that she follow as soon as she could.

Leaving the note on the kitchen table, I turned to leave. I glanced at my watch and saw that it was 11:13. On my way out, I locked the door on yet another part of my life.

* * *

I must have been quite a sight as I trekked homeward—a big man with a scraggly beard toting a five-gallon bucket and a deer rifle along with a rather large knife tucked into his belt. People stared as I walked, but no one seemed to want to question me. Hell, if I'd seen me under those circumstances, I wouldn't have spoken to me either.

I used any shortcut I could think of to save time: hopped fences, cut across fields, and followed a small creek that ran between neighborhoods. Eventually, I came to the state highway that ran near our home.

Traffic was light and slow as a mixture of diesel-powered and old pre-electronic-ignition autos wove through the maze of shiny, stalled hybrids and electronic cars. Luckily, there was enough clearance between stalls and on the shoulder to allow steady progress.

The amount of traffic told me word had gotten out that there was a nuclear war in the making, and that was good. However, it also meant every road out of Houston would very soon be choked with traffic, and that was bad. Very bad.

Despite the number of incapacitated vehicles, in a city of three-and-a-half million people, there would still be more than enough left functioning to clog the eight freeways leading out of town. I hurried home to join the chaos.

CHAPTER 2

* * JUNE 13 / 2:23 P.M. * *

Les dieux feront aux humains apparence,
Ce qu'il seront auteurs de grand conflict:
Avant ciel veu serein espee & lance
Que vers main guache sera plus grand afflict.

The gods will make it appear to mankind
that they are the authors of a great war.
Before the sky was seen to be free of weapons and rockets:
the greatest damage will be inflicted on the left.

Nostradamus – *Century 1, Quatrain 91*

Nearly three hours later, I finally made it home. I was barely through the front door when I collided with my son in the darkened interior of the house. With the power out, the only light came through the open windows. Zach carried a paper sack nearly as big

9

as he was. "Hi, Dad. Wow! Where'd you get the gun?" He grinned in childish delight.

"Borrowed it from your Grandpa Ray." I didn't figure this was the time or place to tell an eight-year-old that his Grandpa was dead.

"Oh." His attention shifted in that sudden way that only a child's could. "Well, whatcha got in the bucket then?"

His energy and enthusiasm made me smile despite my fatigue. "Don't worry about it right now. Where's your mom?"

"In the garage. She's putting a whole bunch of stuff in the van. Guess what! The 'lectricity went out, so Mama said we're gonna spend the weekend at Nanna's. Is that why you got the gun? Are you gonna shoot a deer while we're there?"

I scowled and invoked the third unwritten Law of Parenting. "Aren't you supposed to be doing something?"

"Yes, sir. I'm taking this stuff out to the garage for Mom."

"Well, don't you think you'd better get with it?"

"Okay." He paused for a second. "Dad?" He came closer and lowered his voice, his face suddenly serious. "Why is Mom so mad? She yelled at me and Megan and slammed the door and stuff. And we didn't even do anything!"

I set the bucket down and leaned the rifle against the wall. "Here, give me that." I reached for the sack he held. "Your mom is really nervous right now, Zach."

He nodded as if he knew exactly what I meant. I knelt down next to him. "Did she tell you why?"

"Huh, uh."

I thought for a moment on the wisdom of telling him what was going on. How could I explain to a child that there were people in the world who wanted to kill each other because of differing political or religious beliefs? That those people were so wrapped up in the "causes" they promoted and fought for, that they no longer cared about anything else, including the lives of their fellow human beings?

"Go get Megan, and both of you come out to the garage."

"Yes, sir," and he ran off to get his sister.

I turned and stepped into the garage. By the light of the garage windows, I could see that Debra was indeed upset, though worried seemed a more accurate term. I also saw that she had evidently been working at a frantic pace, loading the back of our minivan with any item that would be of use during the coming crisis. Nearly every bit of space from the front bucket seats to the open hatch was filled—garden tools, food, clothing, food, camping supplies, more food. Knowing my wife, I was certain she had thought of everything.

There was an area of about two feet of empty space before the hatch, and she was busily filling that with the survival books, magazines, and microfiche books I had collected over the years. The rest was totally packed. I was gratified to see some of the worry leave her face when she saw me in the doorway, relief altering her expression. Setting down the sack, I walked over and opened my arms. We held each other for a moment, needing no words, simply relishing the feel of one another. I felt her shoulders shake as she sobbed quietly, and I pretended not to notice. She hated losing control of her emotions.

"I was so scared. At first it was just the electricity, but then Megan noticed the phones were out too. So, I went outside to see if the Thompsons had heard anything, and I saw the sky." She sniffed. "I remembered what you'd said back when you were hanging out with those survivalist crazies." All of this was said with her face still buried in my shirt. "I guess maybe they weren't so crazy after all."

"I guess not." I stroked her hair.

She took a deep breath and stepped back, discreetly wiping her eyes. "You all right?"

"So far, so good," I replied dryly. "The hard part is still ahead, though." She nodded.

"I take it you haven't told the kids what's going on yet."

She shook her head. "I didn't want to scare them, but I'm pretty sure Megan's guessed anyway. She's read most of that science fiction garbage you keep around. And she's smart enough to know I'm not just packing for a weekend at Nanna's."

I smiled. "Smart enough to keep quiet about it around her little brother, too. He's so hyped about seeing your mom again that he hasn't got a clue there's anything more serious going on." I paused. "Listen, they'll both be here in a second, and I want to tell them. I mean, even if Megan's figured it out already, she deserves to hear it from us. And Zachary may be young, but it looks like he's going to have to grow up in a hurry."

She thought for a minute and nodded acceptance just as Zachary came charging into the garage, followed a moment later by his older sister.

At sixteen, Megan was every bit as pretty as her mother had been at that age, though a few inches taller. Not that her mother wasn't still pretty, but maturity brings a different beauty. Debra, despite her personal opinion, was a gorgeous woman. Megan, on the other hand, was a beautiful girl.

"Hi, squirrel bait."

She tentatively returned my grin, as well as the insult. "Hi, scum wad."

This had been a tradition in our family since she had been about seven years old. She and I had begun to derive a perverse pleasure in making fun of one another. I suppose that showed my level of maturity… or lack thereof. It had actually gotten so bad that my wife, slightly perturbed at the prospect of going through life with a daughter named "Squirrel bait" and a husband whose name changed without notice from "Scum wad" to "Scuzz bucket" or "Monkey toes"—I do have extremely long toes—had threatened us with bodily harm if we didn't curb our insanity. Out of deference to her mandate, we thereafter confined our odd pastime exclusively to Saturday mornings.

For the next few years, Saturday mornings became an endless barrage of name-calling, from the borderline offensive to the ridiculously funny.

However, as Megan got older, she became aware of the fact that she was becoming a young lady and decided our Saturday morning ritual was too childish for someone of her maturity and sophistication. The insults tapered off to gradually be replaced by the expression that only a teenage girl can give—that rolling of the eyes that asks the *Gods That Be* what she had ever done to deserve such an immature parent.

The fact that she now returned my jibe, rather than ignored it as usual, told me she was probably pretty frightened. It meant she felt more like Megan, the little girl, than Megan, the all-powerful teenager.

"Okay, you guys, we need to talk." I knelt so I would be at Zachary's eye level and looked up at Megan. "Megan, I think you've already got a pretty good idea of what's going on, don't you?"

Her striking brown eyes showed worry but little fear as she nodded. "I think so."

"Smart girl." I held my hands out to her brother. "Come here then, Zach."

He came over and sat on my raised knee. His normally cherubic face was totally serious, evidently sensing the tension that the rest of us were trying to hide. "What'sa matter, Dad?"

"You know what a war is, don't you, Zach?"

"Yeah, it's when ever'body shoots each other and stuff, like on TV."

I almost smiled. "Close enough. Okay, listen up. This morning, a real war started between another country and ours. I don't know yet who we're at war with, but we have to get to your Nanna's house so we'll be safe until we know more."

He thought about it for a second. "Why won't we be safe here?"

"Do you know what a nuclear bomb is?"

He shook his head. "Huh uh."

"A nuclear bomb is a bomb that can blow up a whole city and poison the air all around it with radiation."

"What's radiation?"

"Well, it's… uh, it's a kind of poison that works real slow so that you don't know you've been poisoned for a long time."

"Can't a nukilar bomb hurt us at Nanna's?"

"Nuclear." I automatically corrected. "And yes, a nuclear bomb could hurt us at Nanna's. But they probably won't drop one there."

"Why not?"

Could he understand the concept of priority targeting? Debra saved me from attempting to find out. "Because they don't know where she lives."

That apparently made sense to him. After a few more questions, he said he understood. I doubted it, but at least the effort had been made.

Our talk completed, Debra began telling the kids what still needed to be done before we could leave. She issued tasks like a commanding officer, and the kids took orders like two soldiers as I took care of a little task of my own.

Our backup vehicle was an old, *very* old, dirt bike that I needed to check over. I'd be riding shotgun for the van on the motorcycle for a couple of reasons. The bike was a much more economical vehicle than the van when you considered gas consumption and, since it couldn't fit in the van, it had to be ridden. Also, if the traffic turned out to be as bad as we anticipated, we could probably use it to open up a place for the van between vehicles that might be reluctant to let people in.

As soon as I completed my check of the bike, I grabbed an old military surplus ammo case from my tool cabinet. I hesitated a moment, considering my actions. As long as the case remained closed, the contents were protected from EMP. Once I opened it though, I risked losing the treasure inside if another warhead were to explode.

Well, they're not doing me any good locked away. I took a deep breath and opened the case. Nestled inside were two cloth-wrapped bundles. The cloth kept the contents from coming into contact with the metal sides of the case, which would in theory have kept them protected from this morning's pulse that had fried just about any electronic system it touched. Almost reverently, I removed the first bundle and reclosed the case. I unfolded the cloth, and held the little radio up for inspection.

It was a combination AM/FM/weather radio and flashlight that powered off of either the built in solar cells, or an attached hand crank. I cranked the handle for a few seconds and watched the charge indicator begin to glow. After a few seconds I turned the radio on. There was nothing but static, but at least it worked. I exhaled with relief, only then realizing that I'd been holding my breath for several seconds.

I carefully re-wrapped the radio, placed it back in the protective ammo box, and checked the second radio. It also passed inspection, and I grinned. I placed the case with the spare radio in the back of the van before setting its unwrapped brother in the front seat.

With that task done, I joined the "troops" in taking orders from Debra. I had been with her long enough to know she was in her element: chaos. One of her greatest assets was her organizational ability. When she finished with the mess, it would be reconstructed into an evacuation as well organized as the local library.

First, I went back into the house to retrieve the bucket and rifle. When I returned to the garage, Debra eyed the rifle with distaste. While she had always been pretty pacifistic, she'd never interfered with my martial arts training, even when I had opened a small school and taught classes every other weeknight. But she had never been big on firearms and refused to allow them in the house. I'd never pressed the matter as I had other options in the way of home defense.

"Where'd you get that?"

"Dad." The reply brought the grief back to the surface. Debra noticed immediately and started to question me, but desisted when I shook my head. I couldn't trust myself to talk about it yet, especially with the kids in the next room, and she knew me well enough to back off. She went back to the original subject.

"Is it loaded?"

"Yes."

"Can't you carry it with you on the motorbike?"

"No sling for it. It's going to have to go in the van."

She paused a moment. "Put it by the passenger's seat. And make sure the safety's on."

Then she turned away, going back into the house with Zachary. She knew the fireball in the sky heralded a momentous change in the world and was obviously willing to set aside old prejudices, but the coldness of her tone made it abundantly clear that she didn't like the new rules at all.

I took Megan aside for a crash course in basic firearm safety, showing her how to release the safety, sight, fire, and reload the weapon.

"Megan, everything's changed now. You have to understand that. If it comes down to your having to shoot someone with this, you won't have time to think about it. You'll have to remember everything I've taught you in class: put your feelings aside until later, concentrate on what has to be done, and do it. Do you understand?"

"Yes sir." She hesitated a moment. "But what if I'm too scared, Dad?"

It was completely unfair to force a sixteen-year-old girl into adulthood so abruptly, but at this point, it couldn't be helped. "Okay, Megan, what if someone was holding a gun to your brother's head? Could you shoot them to save his life?"

When she nodded, I continued, "What about your mother? Or me? Could you shoot someone who was trying to kill us?"

Another nod. "Listen, kiddo, you and I are the only ones in this family who have any kind of fighting skills. That means it's up to us to protect your mother and Zachary if anything happens. It's just like you learned in class. There's nothing wrong with being afraid. And there's nothing wrong with not wanting to hurt anyone. I'm *glad* you don't want to hurt anyone. But if there's a situation where you have to, even if you have to kill someone to save Zach, or your mom, or me, then you have to put your hesitation aside. If you don't, then one of us could get hurt, or even killed. Understand?"

Eyes downcast, she meekly responded, "Yes, sir."

I pulled her to me and hugged her tightly. "I love you, kiddo, and I wish I could put into words how very proud of you I am. You're smart, pretty." I pushed her back to arm's length, put a finger under her chin, and brought her eyes back up to meet mine. "And you could probably beat the crap out of anyone that looked at you crosswise. You're the best student that I've ever had."

"Like you gave me a choice?" She smiled and blinked away the moisture that threatened her mascara. "I'll put the gun in the van." With that, she walked away.

At this point, Debra, an aluminum baseball bat in hand, reentered the garage. I cocked an eyebrow inquisitively.

"Maybe we'll get time for some softball." Her eyes dared me to make further comment.

"Maybe we will," I agreed straight-faced. I decided it was safer not to mention the fact that she'd left the ball and gloves in the house. So much for pacifism.

She went past me to the front of the van. Over her shoulder, she suggested, "Why don't you go change? I laid some things out on the bed for you."

* * *

I shook my head in astonishment when I reached the bedroom. When she said she had laid out some things, I'd expected a change of clothes. Next to the clean clothes, boots, and denim jacket, my delicate, anti-firearm, pacifistic wife had neatly laid out some of my nastiest little martial arts "toys."

Debra was subtly telling me that she recognized and accepted the fact that the world might suddenly become a nastier place in which to live. But by not mentioning her concession in front of the kids, she was also telling me that she would appreciate it if I would keep my little arsenal hidden from them.

I agreed, no use making them any more nervous than I already had. I quickly set to the task of selecting suitable armaments.

I strapped a sheath containing an eight-inch, flat, black throwing knife to the top of my left forearm. I was pretty good with it, and could usually sink four out of five throws. Next, I hung a *manriki gusari* around my neck. A three-foot-long fighting chain, its weighted ends tapped against my ribs. I rejected the crossbow, since I could hardly expect to load and shoot while riding the motorcycle. I did grab a pair of knives in clip-on sheaths, one for each boot, and secured that custom Bowie to my belt, within easy reach.

Last, I put on my jean jacket and looked in the mirror. I felt like a reject from a low-budget ninja movie, but all of my toys were hidden, with the exception of the lower half of the Bowie hanging from my belt.

For the pièce de résistance, I had a sheathed machete hung on a web belt slung diagonally across my back with the handle within easy reach over my left shoulder.

Feeling a bit like a walking armory, I stuffed the remaining weapons into a sport bag and carried it out to the garage. Debra met me at the door.

"Do I look as conspicuous as I feel?" I shifted the sport bag to my other hand.

"That depends on how you feel."

"A little bit like Robocop's long-lost father."

She shook her head. "I'll never understand how you can crack jokes when things get so bad." She reached up and stroked my cheek before I could answer. "I know it's just your way, and I've been around long enough to realize that it's more of a nervous response than anything else." She gripped my chin and pulled my face down to her eye level. "But it drives me nuts sometimes!"

She stepped back and gave me a once-over. "Well, you look all right. Nothing too obvious, anyway. Are you ready?"

"Not quite. Is there room left in the van for my staves and sticks?"

"I already packed them," she replied quickly.

"What about my backpack?"

"Packed."

"Well can I at least grab a bite to eat?"

She smiled smugly. "Sandwiches in the front seat."

I chuckled at the sheer normality of the exchange. "All right, I give up!" I raised my hands in mock surrender. "I freely admit it. Once again, you've thought of everything!"

"Good thing, buster. Otherwise, you don't get a sandwich."

CHAPTER 3

* * JUNE 13 / 3:15 P.M. * *

L'horrible guerre qu'en l'Occident s'appreste,

L'an ensuiuant viendra la pestilence
Si fort l'horrible que ieune, vieux, ne beste,
Sang, feu. Mercure, Mars, Iupiter en France.

The horrible war which is being prepared in the West,
The following year will come the pestilence
So very horrible that young, old, nor beast,
Blood, fire Mercury, Mars, Jupiter in France.
Nostradamus – *Century 9, Quatrain 55*

Five minutes later, we were ready to pull out of the garage so we could
strap the bicycles on the back and top racks of the van. That meant

announcing to our neighbors that we had viable transportation. It also meant announcing that we were bailing and leaving them to their own devices. My conscience twinged a bit, but I wasn't about to risk my family's safety for the sake of maintaining good relations with the neighbors. For all we knew, missiles could be streaking toward Houston at this very minute, so I didn't want to spend any more time here than was absolutely necessary.

Debra and the kids got into the van, Zachary sitting on the floor in front of Megan on the passenger's side.

I walked around to the driver's side. "Don't open the garage door until you start the van. I'll put the bikes on as soon as you're in the driveway, so you won't have to get out at all. Just don't leave until you see that I have the motorcycle running, okay?"

"Afraid we're going to leave you?" she joked.

I shrugged. "Rejas *would* be a pretty long walk."

She leaned through the window and gave me a quick kiss. "Okay, let's see if this thing's going to start." She pumped the gas, turned the key and, with a whoop from all of us, the van purred to life. Grinning, she thumbed the transmitter for the automatic garage door opener.

Her grin quickly faded, as did mine, when nothing happened. With a panicked motion, she jammed her thumb on the transmitter again. I watched understanding dawn on her face at the same time I realized what was wrong. The garage door opener was such an accepted part of our lives that it took a moment for me to realize that the power outage had knocked it out along with everything else. I didn't know about Debra, but I felt incredibly stupid. We'd been looking so far ahead, we'd overlooked the obvious.

Signaling for Debra and the kids to wait, I climbed up the hood of the van and reached to pull the linking pin out of the arm on the opener. Now the door could be raised manually and, since the air was quickly becoming fouled with the van's exhaust, I hurried to open it. With a look of relief, Debra pulled out onto the driveway. I dragged two of the bikes up the side of the van and into place on the roof rack, scratching the paint in the process. If that was the worst that happened, I figured we'd be in good shape. The other two bikes went onto the rack on the back hatch. After checking to make sure they were all secured properly, I ran back to the garage, strapped on my helmet, and climbed aboard the old dirt bike.

After making sure the fuel line was open, I thumbed the choke, pulled back the throttle, and kicked the starter lever. It took nearly a dozen tries, as the engine hadn't been run in nearly a month, but it finally started. I rolled the trusty relic out of the garage, and dismounted to close the garage door.

"What are you doing?" Debra yelled. "You're worried about the garage at a time like this? Let's go!"

She was right. I shook my head. "Habit!" I climbed back on the bike to take the point position as we pulled out of the driveway.

We headed northwest on Highway 249. It was a little out of the way, but the route kept us well away from Houston's Intercontinental Airport. Major runways could be used by U. S. bombers and, in the survivalist community, were thought to be likely priority targets for surface strikes.

The traffic, though slow, was lighter and much more orderly than I expected. I had feared that the road might be packed bumper to bumper with a panic-stricken mob, ready to ram anything that got in the way. Instead, I actually had a motorist slow down to let me into the flow of traffic. I waved gratefully, then pissed him off when I opened a gap to allow Debra into the lane ahead of me. It wasn't likely that he'd been offering a package deal, but I couldn't afford to become separated from the van.

After Debra maneuvered into the space, I gunned the little motorbike and whipped into a space in the next lane. Again I slowed, momentarily creating another break in traffic for Debra. In this manner, we quickly leapfrogged into the faster inside lane, moving along at a clipping twenty-five miles per hour, as opposed to ten miles an hour in the outer lane.

Once we'd finished jockeying for position, I took the time to examine the occupants of nearby vehicles. Sitting on the motorcycle gave me a good vantage point. Most of the people looked grim and determined. I was surprised at how few appeared panicked. I had always been told to expect the worst of people in the event of an emergency evacuation. My survivalist acquaintances had assured me that in the event of such an emergency, most of the public could be expected to… well, the phrase "freak out" kept popping up.

Well, there it was, "Crisis relocation," as the government called it. Sure, everyone seemed frightened, and a very few looked seriously freaked out. But the wild-eyed, bullet-slinging maniac with the demented, insane laugh they had told me to watch out for didn't seem to be present. It wasn't for lack of opportunity, either. Nearly every other car I looked into had a weapon of some kind in evidence. From hunting rifles, to pistols or shotguns, it seemed everyone had a firearm within reach. Sure, this was Texas, but I'd never seen such a flagrant display of firepower before.

As this dawned on me, my skin began to crawl, and I abruptly lost all of those earlier feelings of being excessively armed. Instead, I felt more like the punch line of an old joke.

Just like me to bring a knife to a gunfight.

* * June 13 / 4:23 p.m. * *

After a long hour of stop-and-go traffic, we leapfrogged back to the outer lane. Our exit led to a narrow, two-lane country road that wound back through thick forest to the northeast. The traffic was sparse; in fact, it was nearly nonexistent. The road had many intersections and, one by one, all of the other vehicles eventually turned off, leaving us alone in the forest.

We had traveled for about ten minutes without seeing another car when Debra honked the horn and began flashing her headlights to get my attention. Fearing engine trouble, I immediately pulled over and removed my helmet. If we lost the van, we would lose most of our supplies, as well as our best means of transportation. I listened for any unusual clanking or clattering as Debra pulled up behind me but my fears evaporated when she yelled excitedly out her window.

"There's a station back on the air!"

I dropped my helmet in the grass and ran toward her, as she continued, "They said that L. A., New York, and Washington have been bombed."

Sticking my head in the open window, I saw Megan cranking the charger on the little radio. The volume increased as the nervous voice of the announcer pierced static-laden airwaves.

"...-trollably. Washington, D. C. has received an undetermined number of hits. There is no official comment on the amount of damage the capital has received, but we are assured that the President is safe, as well as most of his staff.

Citizens are urged not to panic, but we repeat, a state of emergency does exist throughout the United States, and citizens are advised that martial law is now in effect for the duration of this emergency."

This was followed by that irritating tone associated with the Emergency Broadcast System. A few seconds later, the message started over.

"This is KKFM radio in Houston, Texas, operating in voluntary cooperation with the Emergency Broadcast System. This is not a test. We repeat, this is not a test. Citizens are advised that a national emergency has been declared. All persons living within the Houston metropolitan area are instructed to evacuate immediately. Military and law enforcement personnel are on hand to ensure an orderly evacuation. All National Guard and military reserve personnel are ordered to report for immediate active duty. Citizens are urged to cooperate fully.

At ten fourteen this morning, local time, several high-yield nuclear devices simultaneously detonated above the United States. These warheads released a high-voltage electromagnetic pulse that has caused massive electrical and communication failures across the western hemisphere. There are unconfirmed reports of major nuclear attacks on New York City, Los Angeles, and Washington, D.C.. Both New York and Los Angeles, as well as many of their surrounding suburbs, are reported to be burning uncontrollably.

Washington, D. C. has received an undetermined number of hits. There is no official comment on the amount of damage the capital has received, but we are assured that the President is safe, as well as most of his staff. Citizens are urged not to pan..."

Megan gently shut off the radio, and we all stared at one another until Zachary broke the silence.

"Are we gonna get blowed up?"

Debra turned to where he sat at Megan's feet and smiled reassuringly.

"No, babe, we aren't. We're far enough away from the city to be safe if they drop a bomb on it."

"What about the ray-shin poison?"

"Radiation. We'll be safe after we get to Nanna's house." She turned to me and gestured back to the motorcycle. "But we'll never get there if we don't quit talking and start driving."

Her feigned confidence evidently reassured him somewhat, but a nervousness remained in his face. As I leaned through the window to kiss Debra, I saw Megan reach beside her seat and check the rifle.

I remounted the motorcycle with a feeling of disquiet. Undeniably, the world was changing. But I couldn't accept that it was changing into a place that forced my children to find comfort in weapons. I shuddered to think of the expression I had seen on my daughter's face, the grim countenance of one who truly expected death.

It was unfair, and I knew that I only had myself to blame. I had cultivated her interest in the martial arts, had taught her that she need fear no one, that each opponent had a weakness. No matter how strong he was, or how big, he was always vulnerable in some way.

In effect, I had attempted to instill some of the old spirit of *bushido*. Now, how would she react? A bomb had no weakness to exploit. We evidently had an enemy, but who was it?

You couldn't fight an enemy you couldn't see. She must have felt trapped and betrayed. Sure, she could cope, but it was going to be a rough transition.

* * *

The road was soothing, almost hypnotic—an endless ribbon winding through the deep evergreens of the Texas Big Thicket. Only occasionally was the tranquility broken by the sudden appearance of another car from over a hill, or around a bend in the road. When this happened, I found myself quickly scanning the vehicle for any sign of a threat. Was the driver in control, or was he panicked? Were there any obvious signs of weaponry?

Sure, I was a bit paranoid. I had been all day, since I had realized what that fireball was, anyway. But I had been a Boy Scout as a kid and couldn't seem to keep their motto from echoing through my brain. "Be prepared."

I wondered if any of my old scoutmasters were prepared for this. I doubted it. Last time I had checked, they didn't offer a merit badge in "Nuclear War Survival."

At any rate, a little paranoia seemed to be in order for a trip that could mean the difference between living for several years or dying a miserably slow death from radiation poisoning—something that I understood could take from several hours to a several *months.*

Well, paranoia is one thing, I thought, *but let's not get morbid, too.*

For distraction, I concentrated on watching the road unwind ahead of me and tried to will any missiles away from the area. I was beginning to relax a little, enjoying the scenery as much as possible under the circumstances. Even the grief that had constricted my chest all day began to ease as I watched the trees go by.

Before long, I was entertaining myself by searching for wildlife along the roadside. I had seen a few squirrels and a dead armadillo, when a Rabbit whipped around the curve ahead, coming straight at me. The tires and Volkswagen emblem on the hood were a dead giveaway that this was *not* an indigenous form of wildlife.

I veered right and laid the motorcycle on its side, feeling my jeans shred as I came to a stop. I saved myself from an impact with the trees, but scraped my right leg from hip to knee. The Rabbit veered to its right, hit the opposite embankment, popped up on two wheels for a heart-stopping moment, then swerved back onto the road and nearly clipped the van before running off down the road.

Struggling out from under the motorcycle, I heaped curses on the driver, his mother, and father; I even threw in a few reproductive suggestions that, unless he was extremely well endowed, would be anatomically impossible.

Debra and Megan reached me at that point, with Zachary close behind them.

"Are you all right?" my wife and I asked at the same time. We chuckled for a second. Comic relief was wonderful medicine. Then, I repeated, "Are you okay?"

She nodded. "Missed us by at least six inches. You're the one that wrecked. Are you hurt?"

"Just a little scraped up." My leg began to throb.

Debra sent Megan for the first aid kit, then she examined my leg.

Zachary tugged on my sleeve to tell me in all seriousness, "You shouldn't say asshole, Daddy. It's a bad word."

At first I couldn't wipe the stupid grin from my face, giddy as I was with adrenaline and relief, but I quickly got myself under control and agreed that it was indeed a bad word and apologized.

Megan saved me from a further lecture from the perspective of a confused and nervous eight-year–old by returning with the first aid kit and another pair of jeans. Debra sprayed my leg with an antiseptic.

"Ow!"

"Oh, don't be such a baby." She slapped an adhesive bandage on the worst of the scrape and smirked when I jumped.

"Hey! You know, that bedside manner of yours could use a little work. That freakin' hurts!"

She stood and planted a quick kiss on my lips. "You'll be fine."

"Thank you, Florence Freaking Nightingale."

Limping slightly as I walked back to the bike, I pulled it upright and checked for damage. It appeared the soft grass on the shoulder had saved both the motorbike and my hide from any serious damage. I was lucky the shoulder hadn't been gravel. Now that I had time to think about it, the whole situation could have been much more serious.

What if the driver hadn't regained control before he hit the van? What if I had been about ten feet closer to the curve that had so unexpectedly produced the speeding automobile?

Paranoia again. But who could blame me? In the last six hours, I had witnessed a mass exodus from the city of Houston as her citizens, myself included, abandoned ship. I had seen that most of those refugees were armed with deadly weapons. Worst of all, I had seen my father die and had been forced to abandon my own mother, not knowing where she was, or if she was even safe. *And don't forget,* I added mentally, *that you just got to see your life flash before your eyes when some asshole barely missed turning you into a hood ornament.* I figured I was entitled to a little paranoia.

"Debra, I think maybe we should be a little more careful."

"No kidding."

"No, I'm serious."

Waiting to hear me out, she arched an eyebrow. I felt a little silly, but I was already committed. "You and the kids need to stay further behind me. That way, if another idiot comes around the corner like that last one, you'll have plenty of space to maneuver. And I'll slow down before I top any hills or round any corners in the road. All the trees and brush out here muffle most of the sound, so I can't count on hearing oncoming traffic before it's right up on me. Especially through my helmet."

I paused. This next one sounded crazy even to me. I could imagine how it would sound to my wife. Nevertheless, I added, "I also think we need a few hand signals. You know: stop, slow down, hurry, hide."

"Hide?"

Again, I paused. "What if that guy had come flying around the corner ready to blast anything in his way?"

"Oh, come on! Don't you think you're getting a little carried away?" She laughed nervously.

"Not with everything that's at stake here. What if he'd wrecked into the van and hurt the kids?"

She was silent, thinking. I could see the conflict on her face. Pacifism was her chosen point of view, but threaten her children at your own risk. She would use any and all means possible to defend them. We'd had enough "what if" conversations in the past for me to know this about her, much like I had gone through with Megan. "What if someone kidnapped Zachary, raped Megan, hurt or killed any of us?" I knew from her answers that her point of view took the form of shades, not blinders.

She finally acquiesced. "Okay, but we'll also need a signal to ready the rifle."

We settled on six basic hand signals: stop, forward, slow down, hurry, hide, and danger. Megan already knew those signals. They were the same ones we used when she and I played paintball once a month.

Upon seeing the "danger" signal, Megan would ready the rifle, and Debra would pull over, perpendicular to the road and ready to turn around if necessary. Zachary was to stay down and under no circumstances let himself be seen.

We went over the signals a few times, making sure Debra knew them as well as Megan and I did, then continued on our way. According to the map, we had just over an hour's drive.

As we traveled, the van about a hundred yards behind me, I began to feel a little better about our situation. We'd had a frightening brush with disaster but, other than my scrapes and bruises, no one was hurt. And it had served to make us a little more careful. Besides, the odds of another accident occurring on roads as deserted as these had to be astronomical.

Fifteen minutes later, I topped a hill in the road and stopped. In the little valley below, it looked like someone had beaten the odds.

* * June 13 / 4:56 * *

The road down the other side of the hill was long and steep, one of those lengthy slopes that thrill children. It dropped nearly two hundred feet before rising again. At the bottom, two vans, a pickup, and a station wagon were scattered all about the roadbed. They were accompanied by six bodies. The whole area looked burnt, as if the vehicles had caught fire after the wreck.

Shocked, I barely had the presence of mind to signal for the van to stop before removing my helmet and scanning the carnage below. There was enough room on the right side of the road for the van to pass, but I didn't want the kids to see the bodies if it could be helped. I finally turned the Suzuki around and headed back to where my family waited in the van. Pulling up to Debra's window, I suggested we stop for a break.

"What's wrong?"

"There's a pretty bad wreck over the hill there. Six-car pile-up. I need to see if I can find a way to get the van through."

"Let's just take the van down and push them out of the way."

I shook my head. "Too much glass," I lied. "Megan, would you and Zach make us some sandwiches, please? I'm starving. Your mom and I are going up the hill." Without giving them time to object, I hustled Debra out of the van and up the hill. "Come on, I'll show you why you can't use the van to push."

As soon as we were out of range of the kids' hearing, she asked, "What's wrong?"

"I didn't want to mention it in front of the kids, but there are some bodies down there. I need some time to move them out of sight."

She was silent for a few seconds. "How bad is it?"

"Judge for yourself."

We topped the rise and looked down. She reached out and took my hand. "I don't suppose any of them are still alive."

"Doubtful." There wasn't much more to say. We were turning to go back to the van when she stopped and, with a puzzled expression, went back up to the crest. She studied the wreckage intently for a minute or more. "What do you suppose happened?"

"What do you mean?"

"What exactly do you think caused the wreck?"

I shrugged. "It looks to me as if the second van down there got rear-ended, and the gas tank blew."

The van I pointed out lay on its side on the shoulder. One of the back doors rested on the grass, about thirty feet away. The other door was missing completely, along with most of the rear end of the van. It must have been one hell of an explosion.

"I guess the gas sprayed on the other cars, and the drivers panicked and wrecked into each other." Even as I said it, though, something felt wrong. I was missing something.

Debra pointed it out. "If they were rear-ended hard enough to cause an explosion like that, shouldn't the station wagon's front end be smashed up, too? It was next in line. And what caused the truck in front to wreck?"

I didn't like where this was leading. I didn't like it at all.

Debra caught it, too. "Someone ambushed them."

Quickly, we backed down the hill until we could no longer be seen from the other side. Both of us thought about the implications of the situation. Debra finally asked the question that was on both our minds. "So, now what?"

I thought for a second longer. "Well, we can't very well turn back, and it would be another eighty miles to go around. We're half an hour away from being home free, and we don't know how long we have before things get really rough."

She crossed her arms as if she were cold. "Looks like they already are."

"You know what I mean." We were both all too aware of the nuclear war in the offing.

"Yeah."

I looked over at her. "We've got to go through."

She stared back at me as if I'd lost my mind. "And I suppose whoever blew the hell out of those people down there is just going to smile and wave as we drive past? Get serious, Lee."

"No," I agreed. "It won't be that easy. I'll have to go down first and scout the area. Find out if it's safe."

"And if it isn't?"

"Then I'll come back very quietly and let you know." I grinned in what I hoped was a reassuring manner. "I'm not about to take any chances, babe. First sign of trouble and I'm out of there."

She jerked a thumb over her shoulder, indicating the other side of the hill. "Fine. But what if they have other ideas?"

I could see that her mood was rapidly deteriorating, and I was beginning to get a little exasperated myself. "Look, Debra, we don't even know if there is anyone. I doubt there is, honestly."

That wasn't exactly true. I certainly *hoped* that whoever had massacred that convoy had had the good sense to move on immediately afterward. But they might just as easily have been lying in wait down there, hoping the wreckage would attract more victims as they came to help. I wasn't about to mention this to my wife, however.

"Well, if you don't think there's anyone down there, let's just take our chances and drive on through. We could probably make it through on the right shoulder without any problems."

Uh, oh. "I just said I *doubt* that there's anyone there. I can't be sure until I go down and check it out."

She mulled it over for a moment. "But you really don't think there's anyone there?"

Good. She was giving in. "No, I really don't."

Her smile was very nearly vicious. "Okay then, which side do you want?"

I gaped stupidly as the implications sank into my skull. "What do you mean?"

"Well, if there's no danger, and this is just a precaution, then two of us should get it done twice as fast. And you did mention that time is of the essence." Her smug grin was infuriating.

"Now wait a minute!" I nearly exploded. "I just said I didn't *think* that there was anyone there. There's no guarantee that I'm right. And if you think I'm going to let you risk yourself just because you happen to have a stubborn streak, you're sadly mistaken."

Well, that did it. Her grin disappeared, and genuine anger laced her voice. "And if you think I'm about to go sit in the van and twiddle my thumbs while you go play GI Joe, then *you* are sadly mistaken!"

Our voices had risen as we argued, and the kids looked up the hill. Struggling to stay calm, I asked in a low whisper, "What if I'm wrong, Debra? What if there's trouble?"

"'Then I'll come back very quietly and let you know.' I think that was exactly how you put it, wasn't it?"

"Oh, come on! Listen, I know how you feel, but be reasonable, for Christ's sake!"

Major mistake. Her voice was suddenly icy cold. "Be reasonable?" she hissed. "I *am* being reasonable. You're the one that thinks that just because you're a man, you're more qualified to walk in the woods. Well, you listen to me for a second, mister. I'm smaller than you, lighter than you, and can outrun you. And unless I miss my guess, your precious martial arts training doesn't teach diddly about woodland stalking, so I'm just as well-trained at that as you are. So what do you have to say to that, Mr. Haiya-mama kung fu super shit?"

To say she was pissed off would be like comparing Krakatoa to a Roman candle. The thing that bothered me was that, when I really stopped to consider, she was correct on all counts. I was acting like a stereotypical insecure, macho male. I knew that on an intellectual level. But this was my family, damn it! I didn't want to chance any of them getting hurt if I could possibly help it.

Logic and emotion battled. Logic presented a way out. "All right, what do you suggest?"

Surprise quickly replaced the anger in her eyes. "What?"

I shrugged. "You're right. I'm being an idiot. So what do you suggest we do?"

Quickly recovering her composure, she replied, "Just what I said a minute ago. You take one side, and I'll take the other. We'll get done twice as fast and be on our way as quickly as possible."

"All right." I nodded amiably. "But what about the kids?"

She paused, appearing less certain. "They'll stay in the van. You showed Megan how to use the rifle, so they should be just fine."

"Fine. But what if something does happen to us? Not that anything will, but what if? Say that there *is* someone down there, and they kill us," I said bluntly. "Or even if they just capture us and try to ransom us for the supplies in the van. Do you think Megan could handle a situation like that on her own?"

Debra was quiet, thinking. Finally, she shrugged. "Okay, you're right. One of us needs to stay with the kids. But I still think that I should do the scouting. I'm smaller and quieter, so I have a better chance of getting in and out without being seen."

"But if there's trouble, I'm the one who's trained to handle it," I countered.

I pulled a quarter out of my pocket. "Flip you for it."

CHAPTER 4

Le bras pendant à la iambe liee,
Visage pasle, au sein poignard caché,
Trois qui seront iurez de la meslee
Au grand de Genues sera le fer laschee.

His arm hung and leg bound,
Face pale, dagger hidden in his bosom,
Three who will be sworn in the fray
Against the great one of Genoa will the steel be unleashed.
　　　　　Nostradamus – *Century 5, Quatrain 28*

Watching the van as it passed around a curve and out of sight, I slipped the two-headed quarter back into my pocket. They would wait at a roadside park we had passed a mile back until six forty. No more, no less. That gave me just over half an hour.

If I hadn't made it back by then, Debra had agreed to backtrack and detour around the area, taking the longer alternate route. I had assured her I would follow as soon as possible. It would mean driving an additional eighty miles, but that was better than ending up as part of the litter problem on the other side of the hill.

I pushed the Suzuki into the woods and slipped among the trees to head over the hill. I made my way about halfway down the hill, then stopped to scan for any signs of life. Nothing.

I moved on down, slipping from tree to tree as quietly as possible, alert for any indication that I'd been seen. Finally, I drew alongside the rearmost vehicle.

The station wagon, about twenty years old, with what had once been imitation wood grain trim, was about twenty feet from the tree I hid behind, so I had an excellent view. In the scorched mass of melted plastic and charred paint, I saw that the windshield had shattered, and wispy tendrils of melted plastic trailed from the chromed border. The hood was blackened, and black streaks trailed down the fender. Even the front tires were melted.

Astonishingly, the rear of the vehicle was nearly untouched except for the windows, which were all networked with the millions of breaks characteristic of overstressed safety glass. I figured the heat had probably done that, since I spotted no apparent points of impact.

The idea of impact brought another thought to mind, and I quickly reexamined the wagon. I sighed in relief at the lack of bullet holes, at least not on the side I could see. Checking the other side would mean leaving the cover of the trees, and I wasn't willing to risk that yet, not until I was reasonably sure there wasn't a sentry, or ax murderer, or whatever hiding somewhere in the trees on my side of the road.

I glanced at my watch. Only five minutes had passed since I'd come over the hill.

Yeah, I thought, *time sure flies when you're having fun.*

It took another ten minutes of sneaking around to convince myself that no one lurked in the trees on my side of the road. Unfortunately, I also confirmed that there had been an ambush. Both vans and all of the bodies were riddled with holes, and I saw enough broken glass to tell me how the attack had probably gone.

An initial barrage of Molotov cocktails inundated the convoy, panicking the drivers and their passengers. They abandoned their vehicles, only to be cut down by snipers in the trees. The end result lay before me. Six bodies and four gutted vehicles.

I checked my watch. Nearly half of my time had passed, and I still had to search the other side. If it proved safe, I needed to drag the bodies out of sight. I hesitated for a moment more.

I finally prodded myself into action. I sprinted from the trees to the side of the overturned pickup. Then I waited, listening for a response.

Nothing. So far, so good. I ran for the trees on the far side of the road and crouched next to a large pine. The trees were quiet, and the only sound I heard was the pounding of my heart. Still, I couldn't shake the feeling that something was wrong.

I began the search, picking my way as quietly as possible through the trees, uphill to the motorcycle. I had nearly finished my inspection, keeping close track of the time, when I heard a faint buzzing coming from the thick underbrush about twenty yards ahead. Not quite a buzz, though, different somehow, but familiar.

I listened intently, willing my heart and breath to silence so that I might identify the tantalizing sound. I finally realized that, while I sat there frozen in place by a noise in the brush, my time was steadily ticking away. I couldn't afford to wait around for the source of the disturbance ahead to jump up and identify itself. So I stepped out from behind the tree to investigate. As I did so, two things happened simultaneously.

The first thing was relatively insignificant. Something in my head clicked, and I finally recognized the buzzing as the faint sound of a carrier wave over an open radio channel. As soon as I realized that, I froze. That sound indicated that someone was watching the road, which in turn indicated that the road was unsafe for travel.

Even as this ran through my head, and I prepared to carefully work my way around and up to the motorcycle, something much more critical occurred. I heard the sharp "snick-chak" of a semi-automatic handgun being cocked behind me.

"All right, buddy, you've got two choices here," the voice behind me gloated. "You can either raise your hands and come with me real quiet-like, or you can make a run for it. Who knows? You might even make it." He paused. "Well, what's it gonna be?"

I could tell he was too far away for me to try for his gun and, even if he were closer, I didn't know whether it was at the level of my head or back. Since I wasn't feeling particularly suicidal, I surrendered. I raised my hands, glancing at my watch as I did so. Six twenty-nine, just over ten minutes left.

"Smart move," the voice said. "Now, why don't you do us both a favor and unsling that machete."

Chancing a glance behind me to see where he was exactly, I did as he told me.

"Face front!" he yelled. "Did I tell you to turn around? Huh? You do what I tell you, only what I tell you, and only when I tell you to do it. Got it?"

When I failed to reply, he practically screamed, "Got it?"

"Yeah, I got it."

"You can call me 'sir,' asshole."

I toyed with the idea of doing just that, but restrained myself. He might overreact if I called him "Sir Asshole," and I really didn't need a hole in my back. "Yes, sir."

"Good boy!" he sneered. "Now, why don't you pull that pig sticker out of your belt and drop it, too. And move real slow... I wouldn't want you to get hurt."

I slowly removed the Bowie and tossed it on the ground next to the machete.

"Okay, now stay real still." I heard him shuffling toward me. He picked up my knife and machete then edged around, keeping about ten feet between us until he reached the bushes in front of me. The first thing I noticed was his clothing: hunter's camouflage coveralls. He was about thirty-five, hard years, from the look of the lines on his face. Most importantly, he pointed a large-caliber handgun at my chest.

I had a sudden, intense desire to urinate, but managed to suppress it.

He reached into the bushes and pulled out a walkie-talkie. "Larry? It's Frank."

I heard a slight British accent in the reply, "Yes Frank, what is it?"

"Larry, I found someone sneaking around in the woods down here."

"So what's the problem?" The voice sounded bored. "Kill him and get it over with."

The need to urinate returned instantly, more powerful than before. It took a conscious effort to hold back.

"Naw, listen, Larry. He was snoopin' around. Kept looking at his watch. I think he's working with someone else."

Wonderful. How long had Frank been watching me?

Pause. Then, "All right, bring him in."

"On my way." Frank sneered. "Okay, prick, hands on your head."

When I had done so, he continued, "Now, we're going on up the hill a little ways," he pointed east, "and if I see your hands leave your head just once, I'm gonna put a hole in ya. Got it?"

"Yes… sir."

"Good, you remembered! I'm impressed. Now move."

We moved out onto the road and about two-thirds of the way up the hill. There, we turned onto a small dirt road hidden from the highway by some recently planted saplings. It wound through the woods for about half a mile, ending in a small clearing dominated by a little country cabin. In front, a group of four men stood waiting, all but the largest armed with both rifles and sidearms. The exception was a huge Asian—Bruce Lee on steroids.

Frank stopped me about ten yards away. "Wait here. And if you know what's good for you, you'll stay real still."

He walked over to one of the armed men and held a whispered conference for a few minutes. Then the one Frank had been speaking to stepped forward. Incredibly, he actually stuck out his hand. "Good evening. My name is Larry Troutman."

Real smooth customer. "I'd be happy to shake hands, Larry, but your man Frank has informed me that lowering my hands could be detrimental to my health."

He clucked his tongue in apparent dismay. "Frank, don't be so antisocial. Of course you can lower your hands, Mr….?"

"Dawcett."

"Mr. Dawcett. Fine. I can see that you're going to be most cooperative, aren't you?"

I guessed his smile was supposed to be reassuring. Unfortunately, it only brought to mind the "Inverse Law of Enemies," the one that said the more civilly an enemy treated you initially, the nastier his ultimate plans.

I could already tell I was in for an extremely rough time. Nevertheless, I shook his hand. "I'll cooperate as much as I can, of course." I could play games, too.

His smile broadened. "Fine, fine. Now, would you be so kind as to hand me your wallet. Frank, what is that you're carrying?"

Frank handed Larry my machete and Bowie as I pulled out my wallet. Larry tossed the machete aside, but examined the knife intently, turning it over and over. "Very nice. Custom made. This must have cost you quite a bit—" He stopped mid-sentence, noticing the maker's logo on the blade.

"You made this?"

I shrugged.

"Quite impressive. A man of talent. I presume you have a sheath for it." I unclipped it from my belt and handed it to him.

"Thank you, Mr. Dawcett." He stuck the sheathed blade through his belt and opened my wallet to my driver's license.

"Mr. Dawcett... may I call you Leeland?" He went on before I could respond. "I see you're from Houston, Leeland. That seems a long way to travel on foot." He looked at me pointedly. "Where is your car?"

I'd learned as a kid that the best way to lie was to tell the truth, withholding as little as possible. "I was riding a motorcycle, but some jerk in a Rabbit ran me off the road about ten miles back. I've been on foot ever since."

"In a Rabbit, you say? Was it green, by any chance?"

I nodded. "You know him?"

Almost wistfully, he sighed. "We recently offered him our hospitality, but he declined our invitation. Frank, how long ago did he leave us?"

"'Bout an hour ago."

Larry was sharp. He caught my blunder before I even realized I had made one. "You traveled ten miles in an hour on foot? Somehow, I find that difficult to believe."

Motioning to the other three men, he sighed. "I believe Mr. Dawcett is being less than honest with us. Michael, Edgar, please restrain him."

As they grabbed my arms, the one on my left that I assumed was Michael, yelped. "Hey! He's packin' somethin' up his sleeve."

Larry whipped out his pistol and aimed it directly at my right eye. "Why, Leeland, I'm very disappointed. And we were getting along so well. Carrying concealed weapons into a friend's home is very bad manners. It indicates a certain amount of distrust, and that's certainly no way to start a relationship."

He shook his head, clicking his tongue in apparent disappointment. "I'm afraid I'm going to have to ask you to remove your jacket, Mr. Dawcett."

When I hesitated, he thumbed back the hammer of his revolver. "Please."

"Well, since you ask so nicely." Two minutes later, they had me stripped to my underwear, my clothes in one pile, my toys in another. Larry uncocked his revolver as he knelt and examined them.

"Quite an interesting arsenal you have here. Karate?"

I shrugged. I wasn't going to try to explain the differences in various martial arts just now.

"Frank, come here. Have you ever seen anything like this before?"

Frank went over and squatted next to Larry. "Like what?"

"Like this!" Larry backhanded Frank with the barrel of his pistol. Frank dropped to the ground, stunned and bleeding. "What the hell were you thinking? First, you let that runt in the Volkswagen get away, and now this? Don't you have any brains at all? God knows, I don't expect genius-level brain work from you, but an occasional glimmering of intelligence would truly be appreciated.

"Let me spell it out for you, Frank. Bringing someone in here—in front of me! —bringing someone into my home without searching him first is stupid! He could have had an Uzi under that jacket for all you knew."

Magically, the barrel of Larry's revolver rested against Frank's temple. "Perhaps there's just no hope for you. I don't think you will ever learn. Perhaps I should put an end to your miserable little existence."

He cocked back the hammer again. "What do you say, Frank?"

Frank's eyes widened until I thought they were in danger of rolling out of their sockets. "S-sorry... I'm sorry, Larry! I screwed up, I know. It won't happen again, I swear!... Oh God, oh God, oh God! Please, please, Larry!"

He was getting hysterical. Larry drew the moment out for a few more seconds, then stood and holstered his pistol. "See that it doesn't. Now stop your sniveling and go get cleaned up."

Frank scrambled to his feet and sprinted for the cabin. Larry turned his attention back to me, once again the urbane sophisticate. "Now, Mr.

Dawcett, I would like some answers. What were you doing sneaking around in the woods here?"

I hesitated a moment. How should I go about this? He would undoubtedly kill me without a qualm as soon as my answers displeased him. And, I didn't think he would be terribly pleased to learn I had lied. But I couldn't tell him about Debra and the kids until I was fairly certain they were safely out of his reach. I had to draw him out and string him along. Then, just maybe, they'd get careless enough for me to risk attempting escape. "Okay, but it's sort of a long story."

"I've got time," he replied. "Han," naming the last, and by far the largest, man of the group. "Please get my camp stool and some rope."

Han trotted back to the cabin. "Interesting fellow, Han. A true warrior monk—or so he says. My family sponsored his sister when she immigrated, and now he seems to think he's indebted to me. Quite handy to have around. Never questions orders, so long as they don't go against his beliefs."

Han reappeared with the requested items. Larry seated himself on the little folding stool and watched as Han stepped up to me holding a short length of nylon rope.

"That really won't be necessary." Once my hands were tied, my chances of escape would be minimal.

"Possibly, Leeland. Possibly. But you've already proven yourself to be less than honest and," he indicated the pile of weapons they had confiscated, "there is considerable evidence that you could be dangerous at close quarters. You'll understand if we tend to be a bit cautious with you."

Resigned, I held my hands out toward Han.

"No, no, you misunderstand." Larry shook his head. "Behind your back, please."

"But, Larry," I quipped, "I thought we were going to be pals."

For the first time, Larry frowned. "I'm afraid I have my doubts. Please, Mr. Dawcett, I dislike having to repeat myself. Turn around!"

Han didn't give me another chance to hesitate, but spun me quickly around and secured my hands as Michael and Edgar stood by to make sure I didn't resist. He wheeled me back to face Larry once again. Michael and Edgar resumed their grips on my arms as Larry stood and walked up to me, still playing the country gentleman. "Now, Leeland, I believe you were about to tell us a story."

"Sure." I paused. "By the way, do you happen to have the correct time?"

Larry's smile vanished, then inverted. "Frank mentioned you were keeping close track of the time. Somehow, I don't think I'm going to like this little story of yours." He glared a moment longer before finally glancing down at his watch. "Six fifty-five."

I grinned. Debra and the kids were gone by now, even if she'd waited longer than the six forty deadline, and I imagined she would have, hoping that I was just running a little late. Fifteen minutes was long enough, though, that she would know something had happened. She wouldn't like it, but she had agreed to take the kids to safety. Now I could concentrate on getting myself free.

Larry, watching my face intently, knew he'd lost a round. Though he didn't know what the stakes had been, he was obviously not a man used to losing. I could tell my expression infuriated him. Perversely, that made me grin even more.

"Han, make him talk," Larry ordered. "Now!"

Eerily quiet, Han stepped toward me. I barely had time to think "Oh, shit!" before he went to work. About my height, Han was gifted with a Herculean physique, not someone I would ordinarily go out of my way to antagonize. He hammered away at my gut for the next ten or fifteen seconds, though it seemed considerably longer. When he finished, I hung limp in Michael's and Edgar's grips.

A martial artist who couldn't take a few punches to the abdomen wasn't much of a martial artist. It was a simple matter of keeping your abs in good condition and knowing when to tense and when to relax. Learning to ignore or rechannel surface pain helped, also. Though Han tested my abilities, I wasn't in nearly as much pain as I pretended.

Any savvy street fighter knew you could often snatch victory from the jaws of defeat if you could just gain the element of surprise. So I hung there, arms tied behind me, gasping for air I didn't really need and pretending to gag, waiting for fate to intervene on my behalf.

"Now, Leeland." Larry reverted to his original cocky attitude. "Do you understand the predicament that you're in? I ask a question, and you answer it. It's actually quite simple." He went back to his campstool and sat, looking up at me. "You know, I already know quite a bit about you. I can see that you are a man of some intelligence. No, I'm not trying to flatter you."

He nodded toward my weapons. "You obviously understand the world is in the midst of a major upheaval, and the old rules of society no longer apply. You have prepared accordingly. You evidently have some skill in the martial arts, since many of the weapons you carry require considerable training and practice to use properly, especially the *manriki gusari*."

My surprise must have shown. Not many people, other than martial artists, could identify the Japanese fighting chain by name. For that matter, not many martial artists could, either.

He smiled at my expression. "Oh, yes, I have some small knowledge of the arts, myself. Among other things, Han is my Sifu. We have a symbiotic relationship, each helping the other." Larry waved his hand at the pile of my weapons. "I must admit, though, most of these items are beyond my modest skills." He patted my Bowie knife stuck through his belt. "However, I do appreciate a well-made blade.

"So let us speculate here for a moment. You are an intelligent man who recognized the mortal wounds our society has received for what they are, and you have prepared yourself with weapons that were, by the old rules of that society, quite illegal to carry, especially concealed.

"Yet you carry no food. No water. No tools or medical supplies. Not even the most basic camping gear. Why is that? You don't strike me as the type of person who would prepare so thoroughly for a fight that might or might not occur, and yet not prepare at all for the nuclear devastation that has already begun.

"So answer a question for me, Leeland. Who were you scouting for back there? And I do emphasize the word *scouting*."

Again, I told the truth, in a manner of speaking. I changed only my destination and the existence of my family. "I was riding my motorcycle from Houston to my parents' place in Louisiana. I had it made until that idiot in the Rabbit ran me off the road. And don't start beating the crap out of me again! I'm not lying. I may have been off on the distance or the time, but I'm not used to traveling long distances on foot. And as far as my *scouting* goes, what would you do if you were walking down the road and topped a hill overlooking a mess like the one you've got back there? You'd stick to the trees and try to sneak by as quickly and as quietly as possible."

He appeared to think it over for a moment. I'd covered all the angles I could think of. Now all I could do was sweat it out and hope it was good enough.

He looked up at me again. "Very well, Leeland. Assuming this is true, it still doesn't explain your lack of provisions."

"My folks have got all the supplies we'll need. They have a twenty acre spread with a freshwater spring."

"What about the time? Frank said you were keeping close track of the time."

"I wanted to get to the next town before dark. Like you said, I don't even have basic camping supplies. Before the wreck, I could probably have made it all the way to my folks' house. After the wreck, I figured I'd be lucky to make it to the next town."

Larry stood and began to pace back and forth in front of me. He considered my story for a moment, probably weighing what I had told him against what he already knew about me.

"Well, Leeland, perhaps I was wrong about you. Let's see now, you were riding your motorcycle from Houston to Louisiana. Where, exactly, in Louisiana?"

What a time for a geography quiz. Wasn't Shreveport nearby? I didn't have time to think about it, or he'd get suspicious again. I gambled. "Shreveport."

He never batted an eye. "Very well, then, Shreveport. You wrecked the motorcycle and were forced to continue afoot from there. Then you came across our little hollow and decided that you would rather be safe than sorry, so you took to the woods in an attempt to quietly sneak by and reach Shreveport as quickly as possible. Is that correct?"

"Exactly."

Larry whirled and backhanded me across the face hard enough to bring tears to my eyes. He had a serious flair for melodrama, probably from watching too many war movies.

"Now what?" I yelled.

He reached down and grabbed my beard, jerking my head up viciously. When I saw his malicious sneer, I knew I was in trouble. "Why were you heading *west* when Frank discovered you? Shreveport is *east*!"

Oops. I was busted. The only chance I had now was to infuriate him enough to where he might make a mistake. "You know, a good mouthwash would clear that liver and onion smell right up, Larry."

His eyes glinted coldly. "I thought you were smarter than this." He let go of my beard and turned away. "Han! Don't hold back this time."

Han stepped forward. His fist flew, and it felt like I'd been hit with a sledge hammer. I wasn't going to be able to take very much of this new assault. The second blow exploded in my belly, and I screamed—partly in pain, partly to help tighten my abs… mostly in pain.

I glimpsed the next punch as it flew toward my nose and tilted my head forward. Han's knuckles collided with my skull instead, making my vision swim. I had a sudden, piercing headache, but also the satisfaction of hearing Han yelp in pain. When my sight cleared, I saw that he had split his knuckles on my skull. Mom always said I was hardheaded. I just hoped that my skull was in better shape than his knuckles.

"Stop!" Larry yelled. He walked over and examined Han's hand, then pulled a tube from a small kit on his belt. "Put some ointment on that, Sifu. I'll finish this."

Han nodded once and stepped back as Larry turned to me. "Well, Leeland? Last chance. Will you cooperate, or do I finish what Han began?" Han stood silently rubbing the white cream onto his knuckles.

"Not… going to let… him… finish… his own… work?" I gasped.

Larry shook his head. "For all his fine skills, my teacher has some simplistic beliefs. He would never willingly take a life, except in self defense or honorable combat." He pulled my knife from its sheath. "I, on the other hand, have no such qualms."

I sighed. A lot of options went through my mind at that point. I could continue to comment on his breath, or even spit in his face. For that matter, he was close enough for me to break his knee, since they hadn't seen fit to tie my legs. But all of those grand gestures would undoubtedly result in my immediate demise, or worse, my slow execution. And I had an intense desire to live as long as possible.

So I spilled my guts. I told him everything that had occurred since I had seen the fireball. It didn't matter; my wife and kids were safe. The only lie that I clung to was our true destination. If I didn't make it and, at that point it didn't look good, I didn't want Larry going after them.

When I finished my tale, he shook his head. "So you've deceived me all along. You lied about being alone. You stalled for time so your family could get away. And worst of all, you deprived me of the supplies they were carrying in your van." He sighed. "That was stupid. Very stupid. I could have ransomed you back to them for those supplies. I might even have dealt in good faith and let you all live."

Larry gestured with my Bowie, waving it before me. "But now, I can't trust you. I can't ransom you. And you know, of course, I can't afford to feed you or have you go to others with what you know about me. Actually, Mr. Dawcett, it appears that your usefulness is at an end." He raised the blade to my throat.

It's now or never, I thought, and kicked as fast and as hard as I could, connecting with his knee, hearing it pop, and at the same time trying to pull my neck as far away from that blade as possible.

Larry's eyes bugged out, and he shrieked as, to my amazement, a wet, red-streaked shaft erupted from his left shoulder and buried itself in Edgar's throat. Edgar released my right arm and dropped to the ground clawing at the crossbow bolt protruding from his throat. Michael shoved me away, and I fell on my face.

I heard the crack of a rifle. Michael screamed and fell, twitching briefly beside me. His lifeless hand gripped a pistol, and I saw with horror that the barrel pointed directly at my chest.

Han froze, looking at the carnage of the last two seconds, then slowly raised his hands. I struggled to my feet. Larry lay screaming, thrashing about on the ground. Michael and Edgar were both apparently dead.

Debra's voice rang out from the edge of the tree line. "Don't move, big guy, or I'll kill you, too!"

Han's eyebrows rose slightly, probably at the sound of a woman's voice, but he didn't move. I smiled shamelessly. The cavalry had arrived.

CHAPTER 5

* * JUNE 13 / 7:02 P.M. * *

Lors que Saturne & Mars esgaux combust,
L'air fort seiché longue traiection:
Par feux secrets, d'ardeur grand lieu adust,
Peu pluye, vent chaut, guerres, incursions.

The year that Saturn and Mars are equal fiery,
The air very dry parched long meteor:
Through secret fires a great place blazing from burning heat,
Little rain, warm wind, wars, incursions.
    Nostradamus – *Century 4, Quatrain 67*

Debra cautiously approached from the trees with her rifle pointed conspicuously at Han's chest. "Lee?" Her eyes never left her target as she spoke, "Are you all right?"

It was a ludicrous question, considering the circumstances, but I couldn't bring myself to laugh. Besides, I didn't think she would find it very funny. "Fine," I croaked "You want to untie me?"

She pulled a little utility knife out of a belt sheath. One good thing about being a knife maker, everyone in the family had a sharp blade.

As soon as she cut me free, I went over to Michael's body and relieved it of the pistol he had been reaching for so desperately. Then I went over to my clothes and began to dress. As I pulled my boots back on, I noticed that Larry had stopped struggling and sat up. His left arm dangled uselessly, and his left leg bent awkwardly at the knee. I could see he was in a lot of pain, but his eyes held more hatred than anything else. I stood and pointed the pistol at him. "Okay, Larry, it's my turn now. Toss me your pistol… slowly."

He continued to glare as he complied.

"Thanks, Larry. Now I'd like to have my knife back."

He tossed it without a word, bare of its sheath. He had still been clenching the blade as he thrashed about on the ground. It was a lucky thing that he hadn't hurt himself severely, or maybe not so lucky. The world would probably have been a much better place without him.

"Toss me the sheath, too."

When I'd gotten that, I walked over to him and searched his clothing for concealed weapons. Then I gave Han the same treatment.

Debra startled me, speaking from directly behind me. "Are you really all right?"

"Yeah, just a little bruised up."

As I turned back to her, her eyes widened. "Oh, my God, doesn't that hurt?" She reached out to touch my neck, pulling back bloody fingers. It's funny how a wound you don't know about doesn't hurt… until it's pointed out to you. As soon as I saw those bloody fingers, my neck began to sting as if I had been branded. I wasn't as fast as I'd counted on; I hadn't totally evaded the knife, after all.

"Didn't even know it was there until just now." I reached up to feel the shallow slice on the side of my throat, wincing as I touched the length of it. "Now it hurts like hell, though."

Debra yelled back toward the trees, "Zachary! Bring the first aid kit. Hurry!" My wife, being who she was, had prepared for this eventuality. I would have been surprised if she hadn't.

47

Zachary came into the clearing at a dead run clutching the kit to his chest. I noticed he steered around the bodies, but couldn't seem to keep from looking down at them. I knew there was no help for it, but I wished he didn't have to be exposed to that, despite what I had said about his having to grow up in a hurry. His eyes widening as his mother's had at the sight of my neck, he handed her the kit. My wound must have looked pretty bad. Once cleaned, however, it proved to be no more than a scratch, one that bled profusely and burned like fire, but a scratch nonetheless. I covered Han and Larry with my pistol while Debra cleaned me up. It was eerily silent as she worked on me. No one said a word. Like truculent children, we refused to acknowledge each other. After a minute of that I turned my attention to Debra. "What are you guys doing here? Not that I'm not grateful, but I thought you'd be long gone by now." I hissed as she wiped hydrogen peroxide on the cut.

She kept her voice low as she told me what had happened. "When you didn't make it back in time, I was afraid you'd gotten yourself into trouble." She finished washing my neck and reached for a tube of ointment. "Good guess there, huh? Anyway, we waited another five minutes to make sure you weren't just running a little behind, then we came back. We found a hidden road just a little ways down the hill and followed it here." Squeezing the ointment on my neck, Debra pulled a cotton swab from the kit and proceeded to smear the gooey mess along the cut. "We got to the edge of the clearing here in time to see that guy," she glanced up at Larry, "pistol whip the other one. When he sent him into the cabin, Megan said she could sneak up on him and get a shot at the others from inside. I was going to wait on her to make the first shot, but then that one came at you with the knife." She nodded at Larry again, and her voice got lower as she whispered, "I thought they were going to kill you."

Debra opened an adhesive bandage and gently covered the cut on my neck. I saw tears in her eyes, but she blinked them back. She sniffed and took a deep breath, then jerked her chin to indicate Larry again. "I figured I couldn't wait any longer and was just about to shoot him when you kicked him, and he screamed and fell. Megan shot the guy holding one of your arms, and the other one pulled a pistol, so I shot him." She shrugged. "We got lucky."

I nodded agreement. Though the timing had been accidental, it had nevertheless been perfect. Megan stepped out of the cabin at that point, interrupting what promised to degenerate into another bout of silence. "Mom? Dad? Take a look at this." There was no mistaking the paramilitary design of the assault rifle.

"Bring it here, Megan." I turned to Larry. "What kind is it?"

He just glared. I pointed the pistol at him. "I am *not* in the mood for this, Larry. Now, what kind is it?"

"AR-15," he growled.

"Full or semi?"

"Converted. Fully automatic."

Megan handed it to me and unholstered a pistol she'd acquired to cover Larry. I recognized the pistol as Frank's—hers now, the spoils of her first and, hopefully, her last combat. I examined the machine gun. Not knowing much about them, it took me a minute to find the *select fire* mechanism and make sure it was set on *safety*. Slinging the rifle over my shoulder, I went about replacing my arsenal. As I strapped the various weapons to my person, I asked Megan, "Were there any more inside?"

She shook her head. "I didn't see any. But there were some boxes full of ammunition and dynamite. And lots of food and supplies like we have, only more." She frowned as if what she was saying was distasteful. "I think these guys are survivalists, too."

"No." My voice was sterner than I had intended, but she had struck a nerve. "These guys are thieves and murderers, not survivalists. They're the kind of people that newscasters like to call survivalists because it's a catchy term and attracts attention, but they're no more than common criminals."

"I beg to differ." Larry finally broke his silence, speaking from where he sat in his own pooling blood. "Our methods may differ from yours, but we are, indeed, survivalists. Truth be told, we are probably a purer breed of survivalist than you. We have seen and understood the same signs of the end that you have seen. We have prepared for it, just as you have. Better than you have, from what I can see. The world is about to enter an era wherein the strong shall rule over the weak. I plan to be one of the strong. I plan to rule, Leeland, and I am honest enough to admit it."

I shook my head in amazement. He sounded like a demented television evangelist. "Do you really believe that crap, or do you just use it to recruit these mental midgets you've gotten to work for you? 'Survival of the fittest' doesn't mean that anyone you kill is less fit than you. It's a form of natural selection, and you don't look like Mother Nature to me."

Seething, I continued, "Tell me something, Larry. If you're so damn sure that you're going to be a ruler in this 'New Era,' then why are you the one sitting there with a hole in your shoulder? Eh? You've been beaten. My wife and daughter defeated you. Does that mean you're going to serve them as your new masters?"

"I was surprised," he snarled. "Ambushed."

From the look on his face, he realized his mistake, but the words were already out. I pounced. "Like those people on the road out there? Does that mean that you should be killed, too?"

He laughed. "You wouldn't do that. You're incapable of such an act. That is your weakness."

"Tell it to Edgar and Michael," I snapped.

"You didn't kill them, Leeland. Your wife and daughter did, and then only to save your life. Only in self defense, as it were. All of you are incapable of killing in cold blood, even when you're convinced it's for the best. Am I not right? Aren't all of you convinced that I am a murderer? And as such, don't I deserve death? Don't I?" He smiled. "You see? You're incapable of making the hard decisions.

"I had to have supplies. I set up an ambush and, when opportunity presented me with the appropriate caravan, I took it. 'Veni, vidi, vici.' You couldn't have done that, Leeland. You're too weak."

I mulled over his words. "You're right, Larry. Things have changed, and somebody has to make the 'hard decisions' now."

I raised the pistol and aimed at his head. His eyes widened as I walked over to him. Then, he regained his composure. "You won't do it. You can't."

"You believe in God, Larry? You've got three seconds to get things right with Him before I pull the trigger."

"You're bluffing."

"One."

"You don't have the balls!"

"Two." I cocked the hammer.

"B-bullshit. You can't do it!" Terror in his voice, Larry clenched his eyes tightly closed, apparently finally convinced that I could. He abruptly began sobbing.

I couldn't resist. "Three!" I aimed at the ground and pulled the trigger. Larry screamed at the top of his lungs and jerked his body rigid, cracking his head on the ground. He must have shrieked for a full five seconds before realizing he still lived.

I wasn't sure what would have happened if he had remained defiant. Maybe I would have done it. I knew I truly intended to. But when he broke down, despite what he had done, I just couldn't. I knelt next to him after he had quieted. "If I ever see you again, Larry, one of us won't walk away from that meeting."

"You can count on it," he replied shakily. The hatred returned, worse for his humiliation. "And I'll be looking forward to it."

I turned back to Megan. She looked pretty shaken up. "You said you tied Frank up in there?" She nodded.

"Was there any more rope?"

She kept her pistol trained on Larry. "By the front door."

Inside, I found much more than rope. Boxes were stacked all over the interior. Some were marked as dried or dehydrated food, some as camping gear and, more interestingly, four crates were marked "Ammunition," one "Dynamite," and a smaller one labeled "Fuse Caps."

"Real nice place," I muttered.

As I grabbed the spool of nylon rope, I noticed Frank, gagged and bound, lying in the doorway of the bathroom. He was still out cold. The porcelain sink lay in three pieces, the largest piece bloody from almost stopping his head from impacting with the floor. Lying next to him was the roll of duct tape that Megan had used to tape his mouth shut. I took the tape and walked back outside.

"Okay, Han, hands behind your back."

He didn't argue, and I soon had his wrists tightly bound. I took the added precaution of taping the fingers of each hand together. I didn't want him to have any chance of untying the rope. That done, I had him sit while I tied his ankles and knees. When I finished, I told Debra, "All right, babe, you can relax a little." She lowered the rifle. "Keep an eye on him, but I don't think he'll be going anywhere just yet."

I turned to Larry. "Your turn, 'Your Majesty.'" God, how I despised him!

He smiled weakly. "You don't mind if I remain seated, do you?" Despite his nonchalance, I noticed he was extremely pale.

"Suit yourself." I bound his good arm to his ankles, again taping the fingers together. I left his wounded arm untied. Much as I disliked him, I didn't see any reason to cause him any unnecessary pain. He wouldn't be able to use it much, anyway. Against my better judgment, I patched up the hole in his shoulder. I debated on whether I should try to set his leg, but eventually decided it wasn't immediately life threatening. Besides, a limp might make him just a little less dangerous to others in the future.

"Megan, watch these two while your mom and I go get Frank."

Debra and I went back into the cabin and dragged out Frank's unconscious body, laying him with Han and Larry. Leaving them under Megan's watchful eye, we went back to look through the cabin's supply dump.

"Do we have room for any of this?" I asked.

She looked a little startled. "You want to take their supplies?"

I turned one of the crates around, exposing a charred corner. "You heard his speech. Larry and company weren't the original owners. The real owners are lying in the road back there, well beyond needing supplies."

"Okay… yes, we can carry some of it."

Examining the crates, she got to business. "You'll want the ammunition. What about the dynamite?"

I remembered the rear end of the van on the highway. I was willing to bet that there were originally two of those little crates. It might be a little risky hauling dynamite, but there would be considerably less risk involved without someone throwing Molotov cocktails at us. And dynamite could come in very handy. Besides, I wasn't about to leave it for Larry.

"Definitely."

"Okay, what else?"

Half an hour later, we were reloaded and on our way, leaving Larry, Han, and Frank where they lay.

* * *

We arrived at Amber's forty-five minutes later. Amber, my mother-in-law, must have heard us pull up, because she came out to greet us. "I had a feeling I might be seeing y'all. Come on in. Anybody hungry?"

Thankful, we headed for the sanctuary of her open door.

"What the hell happened to you?" Amber asked, as I came in behind the others.

"Tell you later." I grinned wearily, happy to have finally reached our goal. The aroma of home cooking wafted in through the air. "What smells so good?"

"Forget the smell. You don't get zip until you let me see that neck." Amber was a retired nurse turned small-time chicken and goat farmer and took health risks very seriously. She wasn't satisfied until she had removed the gauze from my neck and treated the wound herself.

She got the story from Debra and the kids as she did so. When the story reached the point of all the shooting, though, the kids went silent, and Debra continued a bit shakily, "I killed a man, Mom. I know it had to be done... I... but, I just don't know how to deal with it right now."

Amber kept quiet. Nothing she could say would change anything, and she was wise enough to know that. But it obviously pained her to see her daughter in such anguish. She opened her arms, and Debra curled into them, tears sliding down her cheeks, comforted in her mother's arms. The tie was ancient and instinctive.

Everyone had been facing me as Debra spoke: Amber treating my neck, and Debra, Zachary, and Megan watching her. When Debra broke down, Amber and Zach were busy comforting her. So when Megan slipped away, I was the only one to notice.

I patted Amber on the arm and pointed toward the kitchen to let her know I was leaving for a moment, then went to follow Megan. I found her in the back yard sitting in the shadows. She didn't move as I sat next to her, and we sat together in silence for a time before she spoke.

"This isn't what it's going to be like from now on, is it? This is just the first day, Dad, and we've already had to kill people."

I started to reply, but she continued, "I know you told me just this morning that it could happen, but I didn't really expect anything like that. Did you?"

"No, I didn't."

But she wasn't listening to me. "Now Mom is crying because she had to do exactly what you told me I might have to do. So should I be crying, too? Is there something wrong with me?" She turned to me, her face completely devoid of tears, but no less anguished than her mother's. "I'm not sorry I killed him; I know he would have killed us if he could have. So is there something wrong with me?"

I reached to pull her close, draping my arm around her shoulders as I groped for an answer. "No, babe, there's nothing wrong with you. Different people just react differently to stress."

Megan nodded. "I know, but she didn't have any choice. She knows that, doesn't she?"

"Yeah, she knows. She knows it intellectually. But knowing something in your head isn't the same as knowing it in your heart. I've taught you for the past six years that there may come a time when you'll have to fight, and that you might even have to kill. You've had time to deal with the idea.

"But your mother has always tried to live a peaceful life. She's always thought people are basically good, deep down. Now she can't think that way. She can't afford to. Those guys would have killed me. They would have killed all of us to get our supplies, and your mom knows it. To her, it's like life just reached out and slapped her in the face. That's why she's so mixed up right now. Give her a little time to put her head and her heart in sync."

Megan said nothing, and after a time she laid her head on my shoulder, and we watched the clear night sky that could only be seen far away from cities.

CHAPTER 6

La grande cité sera bien desolee,
Des habitans vn seul n'y demeurera
Mur, sexe, temple & vierge violee,
Par fer, feu, peste canon peuple mourra.

The great city will be thoroughly desolated,
Of the inhabitants not a single one will remain there:
Wall, sex, temple and virgin violated,
Through sword, fire, plague, cannon people will die.
     Nostradamus – *Century 3, Quatrain 84*

Frank led me at gunpoint to the clearing, where Larry and the others stood laughing at my ineffective struggles against the rope that bound my hands behind my back.

"Han! Don't hold back this time," Larry screamed, still laughing.

Then came the beating I was powerless to prevent, but somehow it didn't really hurt. Each time Han hit me, I jerked, expecting the terrible pain, and each time I felt nothing. It was amazing. I began to laugh with Larry and the others. Wasn't this a grand joke? I was being beaten and couldn't feel a thing.

Larry quit laughing and screamed, as blood began to pour from his shoulder. He pulled my knife from its sheath on his belt. "Actually, Leeland, it appears that your usefulness is at an end."

Frantically struggling, I looked to my right and saw Edgar holding my arm with one hand. He used his free hand to rip a bloody shaft from his throat. To my left, Michael held my other arm while he bled profusely from a gaping hole in his chest. He gave me an eerie grin.

Larry slowly hobbled up to me on one broken leg and brought the knife toward my neck. Sunlight reflected blindingly off of the knife's brightly polished surface. It came closer, getting brighter by the second, and I knew no one would save me this time. I struggled as the knife came closer, brighter, deadlier, until I slowly... finally... felt excruciating pain as it bit into my neck. I put my last breath into a desperate scream.

My scream awakened me, as well as nearly everyone else in the house. But concern over my nightmare immediately vanished as we all saw the intense light streaming in through the curtained southern windows—a glaring light, brighter than the sunniest summer day. I squinted at my watch—almost midnight.

"Everybody get away from the windows!" I ran through the house. "No one look outside! It'll blind you! Don't look!"

As I ran into the kids' room, the light, which had been fading, seemed to pulse brighter. I realized that a second explosion had occurred. I burst into the room with two things on my mind. *Don't let them look out, and get them away from the windows in case the blasts were close enough for the pressure change to fling the glass into the room.*

Megan was already stirring, sitting up in the bed. Zach still slept soundly. I snatched him up, and yelled at Megan, "Come on! Out of here. Get in the bathroom!"

The bathroom was the only room I could think of that was fairly well-protected and had no windows. Not that it would make much difference if the explosions were nearby, but we would know that within a couple of minutes, possibly seconds. And if they were that close, being in the bathroom would hardly be protection against the house coming down around us. If they were further away, however, and I was pretty sure they were, since the whole reason that we'd come to Rejas was because there wasn't a viable target within a hundred miles, the most we had to worry about for the time being was flying glass and minor structural damage.

"Everybody into the bathroom!"

They all rushed in ahead of me, even as the light pulsed again. I handed Zachary to Debra and slammed the door behind me. Plenty of light streamed in from under the door, more than enough for me to check my watch. Eleven fifty-nine. We counted seventeen more pulses during the next two minutes. Then, the light under the door began to dissipate. The last thing I saw in the fading light was the toilet, and I couldn't help thinking that rather appropriate.

* * *

I checked my watch. The phosphorescent hands had received enough light to glow brightly in the dark bathroom. Exactly midnight. "Okay, the explosions started a couple of minutes ago, so we should know within a few minutes if any were close enough to cause us any immediate problems."

"How many is a few?" Amber asked from the darkness to my left.

I tried to calculate in my head, but my thoughts were too jumbled… all right, panicked. "I'm not really sure, but five minutes from the time of the first explosion should be plenty. That's about two minutes from now."

It was the longest two minutes I had ever waited, all of us crammed into that tiny, dark cubicle. I must have checked my watch at least thirty times, always amazed that so little time had passed. Finally, I saw the numbers I had been waiting for. 12:02.

"Okay, I'm going to go check out the house. I'll be back in a minute." I slipped through the door and closed it behind me before anyone could protest.

I immediately noticed that the house wasn't as dark as it should have been. Turning to the southern window, my throat tightened as I saw why. Across the clearing to the southwest, the sky above the trees glowed orange, a sign that, two hundred miles away, much of the area around Houston was now a raging fire storm. Swallowing the lump in my throat, I stumbled blindly to the kitchen, where I knew Amber kept one of those magnetically attachable flashlights on the refrigerator.

Quickly retrieving it, I checked the windows and walls for damage, but it appeared we had made it through unscathed. Apparently, the explosions had been quite far from Rejas. Houston had probably been the closest, and it was nearly two hundred miles away. Good news for us, bad news for anyone still around Houston.

As I headed back to the bathroom, I felt a faint rumbling, as the house began to vibrate. Distant thunder.

I checked my watch. Twelve-oh-three. We had gone into the bathroom at approximately eleven fifty-seven. That meant between six and seven minutes had passed between the initial explosion and the arrival of the sound wave. I would have to check later on the specifics, but I was fairly certain that indicated a pretty fair distance.

I opened the bathroom door and shined the flashlight inside. "Okay, the coast is clear." I stopped them as they started to exit. "Hang on a minute. There are a couple of things everyone needs to know. First, if you see any more bright lights, don't look at them and get away from any windows! Immediately!"

Everyone nodded agreement, and I backed out of the way. "Next, we have to get started on a shelter... right now."

I anticipated protests, but they just waited for me to continue. "It took just over six minutes for the shockwave from the closest explosions to get here. I don't know offhand just how far away that means they were, but I'm pretty sure they were a fair distance. Judging from the view outside, I'd be willing to bet Houston was the target."

That silenced everyone, everyone but Zachary. "They blew up Houston?"

"Not all of it, I'm sure. Just parts of it." It sounded inane put like that, but we didn't have time for drawn-out explanations. "Don't worry about it right now. Okay?"

We didn't have time for much of anything, including building the shelter we were soon going to need so desperately. I cursed myself for sleeping when we still had so much to do, but I'd been so tired after the day's events. We all had. Unloading the van had taken half an hour. After that, everyone had been exhausted. Besides, I had figured a few hours of sleep really wouldn't matter. Surely, nothing would happen that soon.

But it did, and I couldn't afford to waste more time kicking myself now. Digging a good shelter with picks and shovels would take all of us working hard, nonstop, for at least twenty hours. If those explosions had been the death knell of Houston, we could only hope the wind blew from another direction. If not, we'd be lucky to have three or four hours before the fallout began to drift down upon us.

"Amber, what direction has the wind been blowing lately?"

She thought for a minute, then shook her head. "I'm sorry. I don't usually pay attention to things like that. You worried about radiation?"

"Yeah, prevailing winds in this part of the country are from the west." That was one of the things that made Rejas a good choice for a survival retreat. But just because the prevailing winds were from the west, didn't mean they *always* blew from the west. "If they've shifted to the north, we could be in for some major trouble."

My mind raced as I tried to find some solution to our predicament.

"How long do we have?" Debra asked.

"That's what I'm trying to tell you. It depends on the direction of the wind, dammit!" I was immediately ashamed. "Sorry, but if the wind is blowing fallout this direction, then we just don't have enough time to dig in before it gets here."

"How long do we need?"

"With the tools we have… at least a day."

"What if we had a backhoe?" Amber grinned in the light of the flashlight.

* * June 14 / 12:24 p.m. * *

It turned out that her neighbor ran a construction company. Luckily, this neighbor lived a mere half-mile away. I left Debra and the kids to get things organized at the house, packed Amber in the van, and drove rapidly out to meet Kenneth Simms.

We pulled into his drive to find a middle-aged black couple sitting in their nightclothes on a front porch swing. As we got out of the van, the man rose and came to greet us. "Hello, Amber. I see we weren't the only ones the light show woke up. You think this is it?"

"Depends on what you mean by *it*, Ken." Amber turned to the woman on the porch. "Morning, Cindy. I want you two to meet my son-in-law, Leeland. He's the best one to tell you all the details. Sort of an expert on this stuff."

Kenneth's attention shifted to me. "Hello, Leeland. Pleasure to meet you, though I'm sure the circumstances could be better."

"That they could, Mr. Simms." His handshake was firm, his grip carved from a life of hard work.

"Ken," he corrected. "So, what can we do for you two at this hour? I imagine it has something to do with all the fireworks."

"Yes, sir, it does. I'm pretty sure those lights were Houston being rearranged."

"Interesting way of putting it." He licked his lips nervously. "So, this is really it? Nuclear war?"

"I'm afraid so. Listen, Mr. Simms—sorry, Ken—we're going to need some help from you. And I think we can help you, too."

Ken listened as I explained, and he was at once all business. "The equipment is in the back. Shall we get started? Amber can go back and get your family and provisions."

I shook my head. "We need to do it at Amber's. She has a spring on her land we'll need for uncontaminated water... afterward."

He agreed immediately. "All right, then I'll need more details on this fallout shelter of yours."

"Ken, there just isn't time. We need to get on it right away. Even minutes could make a difference."

"And that's why I need more detail now. If we plan properly to begin with, we'll end up saving time in the long run." He could see I wasn't totally convinced. "Look, I've been in this business for a long time. How much time would we be saving if I had to come back and get another piece of equipment?"

He was right. "Okay." I squatted down, drawing sketches in the dirt while Ken held the flashlight. "Basically, it's like this. We'll need a trench at least six, preferably eight feet deep, by about four feet wide. My books say we should have at least three feet of length per person. Again, if we can get more, great. We'll need supports for the walls, covers for the roof, piping for ventilation, and a way to bury the whole mess under at least three feet of dirt."

He studied the sketches for a minute and nodded. "How much time do we have?"

"I don't know for sure. Two hours at least." His eyes widened. "Or it could be two days," I added. "We won't know until the fallout starts dropping on us. All we can do is keep track of the direction of the wind and watch for fallout."

"Watch for fallout? How do you watch for something you can't see? Especially when it's not even daylight." I reached under my shirt and handed him the necklace I had put on as soon as we had unloaded the van. Debra, Amber, and the kids each wore one as well.

"What's this?"

"PRD. Personal radiation detector. When the white disk in the middle starts to glow green, it's time to find cover. The brighter the glow, the heavier the fallout." I hesitated a moment, then told him, "Keep it. I've got a few dozen of them. Besides, if you're going to help out with the shelter, you're going to be staying with us. And as long as you do, we'll all have to treat each other as if our lives depend on one another. Like a family."

I thought again of my Dad back at the shop, and my mother... some friends who were as close as family. I had left behind a lot of people whose fates I didn't know, and probably never would, a lot of people I would probably never hear from again. "Family is going to be a lot more important from now on, Ken. I intend to do whatever it takes to help keep mine safe."

He held my gaze for a moment, then shook his head. "I can't. I appreciate the gesture, but that thing is like gold right now, even if you have dozens of 'em." He started to hand it back.

"No, I'm serious. I want you to keep it. I know it's valuable. I'm *counting* on it being valuable. But I really do have plenty of them!" I chuckled. "And they're worth a lot more now than when I bought them. I figured they might be a good barter item after this is all over. Think about it. People will be worrying about radiation for a long, long time. In their food, water, soil, rains, strong winds... a long time."

I hung it back around his neck and continued talking, never giving him a chance to protest. "These things are waterproof, and they have an indefinite shelf life. I bought them ten years ago for fifteen bucks each, so don't sweat the cost. Just don't lose it. It has a chemical base, so it won't wear out like a dosimeter will, and EMP won't affect it."

"EMP?"

"Electromagnetic pulse. It's a vicious surge of electricity that's released by the explosion of a nuclear warhead. It's the reason that your power has been out all day, and your car won't run if it has an electronic ignition." A thought struck me that caused my heart to pound. "Your backhoe doesn't have an electronic ignition, does it?"

Ken smiled. "Not to worry. All diesel engines."

My surge of panic subsided, and we spent a couple of minutes altering the sketches on Ken's advice. When we were finished, he asked, "Do you think you can drive a backhoe? I don't mean operate it. Just drive it to Amber's."

"I can drive a forklift. If it's anything remotely like it, I can do it."

"Close enough. It looks like we're going to need a backhoe and a bulldozer. It'll be faster if we just drive them straight down to Amber's, rather than load them on a trailer and tow them. We can leave the women here to load the food and supplies in your van. You drive the backhoe, and I'll drive the 'dozer, and we'll get started on this shelter of yours as soon as I get dressed."

"Good!" I clapped him on the shoulder and rose. "Let's tell the ladies, and we'll get things rolling."

"Hey, Leeland," he said softly, as we walked to the house. I turned, and he raised the detector up from his chest. "I appreciate it. Thanks."

* * *

Twenty minutes later, Ken had the beginnings of a good-sized trench started about fifty yards behind Amber's house. The rest of us grabbed flashlights and started working on some of the other projects that would be needed for the shelter.

Megan and Zachary pulled the gutter spouts off of the house for use as ventilation pipes, while Debra and I began construction of an accurate fallout meter. The little PRDs were fine for actual detection of fallout, but they weren't calibrated to accurately measure the amount of exposure. I had precise plans for the making of a calibrated fallout meter out of a soup can, aluminum foil, wire, cellophane, and various other household items.

An hour and a half later, we had finished the main trench. It was better than I had dared hope for, at twenty-five feet long, ten feet deep, and four feet wide at the bottom, with a slight taper up to about a five-foot width at the top. Ken had started a dogleg addition, as well. Once he finished the trench, the rest of us dropped the other projects we had been busy with and got busy covering the sides with plastic sheeting to help waterproof what would likely be our home for at least the next few weeks. We also worked on shoring up the walls with some of the lumber Ken had brought.

I quickly saw that the small quantity of wood we had would never be enough to shore the walls and cover the top of the entire trench. It wouldn't even come close. But even as I started to worry, inspiration struck.

I remembered seeing plans for a fallout shelter that had a roof covered with doors taken out of a house. That would solve our problem, if there were enough doors in Amber's house. I quickly grabbed a flashlight, ran inside, and started counting. Closets, pantries, bedrooms, bathrooms, and the actual entry doors in front, back, and garage amounted to eighteen doors, each one almost three feet wide by six and three quarter feet long.

Obviously, they would have to be laid lengthwise across the top in order to span the top of the shelter. Eighteen doors times their three-foot width meant fifty-four feet of roof. More than enough!

I ran back outside. "Debra! Where's the toolbox?"

"I put it in the garage."

I left before she could ask what I was doing. Armed with a screwdriver and hammer, I removed the pins in the door hinges with as much speed as I could muster. I pulled down only the interior doors for the moment. Fifteen doors were still forty-five feet of covering. Twenty-five feet for the main trench left us with twenty extra feet of covering. Heading out to tell Ken how much leeway he had, my heart began to pound as I saw light filtering through the trees, then slowed again almost immediately as I realized that it was nothing more than the sun rising, oblivious to the destruction mankind had wrought upon himself.

I looked at my watch. Twelve minutes after six. I had been working on the doors for half an hour. We had all been on the go since the blasts just before midnight, even after a grueling day relieved by less than four hours of sleep. Fear was a truly remarkable incentive.

* * *

Two hours later, we were nearly finished with the shelter. The doors, covered with layers of dirt, plastic sheeting for waterproofing, and more dirt, sealed the trenches. The only way in or out of the shelter was through one of two entrances at either end, which we would cover with improvised blast doors, one of which we had already made. Megan, Amber, and Cindy had also constructed and installed a ventilation system, complete with a simple air filtration system, following plans in an old survival article I had dug out. Ken and I assembled the second blast door. Debra had finished the fallout meter with Zachary's help, and they began work on a makeshift electrical system out of the car batteries, wiring, and twelve-volt lights.

As Ken and I finished up, he suddenly stopped and stared at me, stared at my chest rather.

"What's wrong?"

For an answer, he reached under his shirt and pulled out his PRD. My spit dried in my mouth when I saw the faint green glow. I lifted the detector dangling from my neck.

"Debra! Get that fallout meter." I scrambled to my feet. "Zach, Megan… Everybody! Get in the shelter. Now!"

No one wasted time asking questions, immediately hustling inside. Ken and I dragged the partially completed second door to the opening at the other end of the shelter.

"How long do we have?" Ken kept his voice controlled, but fear was in his eyes.

I tried to reassure him. "The indicators are barely glowing, and there isn't much wind. I'd say we've probably got at least a few hours. We'll know more once we get a reading on the KFM."

"KFM?"

"Kearny fallout meter. It's a homemade fallout meter made out of a soup can and strips of aluminum foil."

"You're shitting me!"

I couldn't help it. I laughed. "As crazy as it sounds, it's real."

As if on cue, Debra popped her head out of the opening. "Here's the meter."

"Got the tape?"

She silently handed me a roll of scotch tape and held up the stopwatch we had brought with us, all the while, her expression telling me what a stupid question I had asked. After all, she was the woman who never forgot.

"Tape?" Ken asked.

"Just watch."

I set the KFM on the ground and quickly unrolled about a foot of the tape two inches in front of the charging wire. "Ever noticed how scotch tape creates a static charge when it's unwound?" Ken nodded. "Well, we're just taking that charge and putting it to good use." I moved the freshly unwound tape about a quarter of an inch away from the charging wire and slowly passed the full length in front of it. The wire accepted the charge, and the aluminum foil leaves on the inside of the soup can instantly separated.

"Time," I called, and Debra started the stopwatch. I quickly measured the distance between the bottom of the two leaves. "Seventeen millimeters. Give me four minutes."

"Got it." Exactly four minutes later, she called, "Time."

I took another reading. "Thirteen millimeters."

We checked the chart together. "A difference of four millimeters in four minutes. That gives us a reading of..." I ran my finger down the reference chart on the side of the can, "point eight rems per hour."

I looked at the second chart on the other side of the can. "According to this, we could stay out here for more than five days, if the radiation level stays the same. Unfortunately, there's not much chance of that happening. It's bound to go up."

"But for now..." I stood and patted Ken on the shoulder. "We can count on having at least another hour before things get critical. So let's wind all this up and get in the shelter as quickly as possible."

"I'll go along with that."

"Debra, you think you know how to read this thing?" I pointed to the KFM.

She pursed her lips and frowned. "I guess it looks easy enough. When should I take the next reading?"

The chart displayed five columns, one each for fifteen-second, one-minute, four-minute, fifteen-minute, and one-hour readings. "Take a four-minute reading every fifteen minutes. If the results start climbing, use the second column on the chart with a one-minute reading every five minutes. If you reach the point to where you lose the complete charge during your one minute timing period, yell out. Then take a fifteen-second reading using the first column on the chart." I grabbed Ken. "Come on, let's get everything inside and cover up this hole."

We herded as many goats and chickens as we could find into the house and covered all of the windows and attic vents with plastic sheeting to hopefully protect the livestock from fallout and ensure that we would have a source of food when we came out. It wasn't a lot of protection for them, and it was sure to create a major cleanup problem, but it was better than leaving them outside. The chickens, at least, were supposed to be fairly resistant to radiation; I couldn't find any statistics on goats. Now all we could do was hope.

Just over an hour later, we scrambled for any last minute items we could think of, then sealed ourselves into the shelter. During that time, the fallout had risen to six-point-two rems per hour.

After we finished latching down the blast door, Ken turned to me. "Now what?"

"Now we pray."

* * *

"Dad, Megan hit me!"

"You farted in my face! What did you expect me to do, you little sh—"

"Megan!" My tone shut them both up. "Don't hit your brother."

Zachary smirked at his older sister. "And, Zach? You do that again, and I'll fix that little butt of yours where farting in someone's face is the last thing you'll want to do."

His smirk evaporated and he trudged back to his hammock. "Don' know why it matters anyhow. This place stinks like farts all th' time."

Debra raised an eyebrow at me, and I shrugged. We were both too tired to worry about another spat between the kids. It had only been a week, but we all felt the pressure of living in a darkened, confined space. And, Zach was right. The place did always smell like farts—or worse. There were seven of us living in less than three hundred square feet of dimly lit tunnel, and around the corner at one end of that tunnel was what passed for our bathroom. There was no way the place *couldn't* stink, but usually I managed to block it from my mind.

The first few days had been pretty bad. Everyone was scared, uncertain about what kind of world we would emerge into—uncertain about when we would be able to emerge, or if we could *ever* emerge without certain death being the outcome. On top of that, I'd been putting off a particular conversation.

I'd waited at first to try and find the right time to tell Deb and the kids about Dad, but I finally realized that there just wasn't ever going to be a "right time." So, on the third day in the shelter, I sat them down and told them what had happened. After the inevitable tears from everyone, the conversation took a turn I hadn't anticipated.

"Dad, do you think Grandma..." Megan hesitated. "Do you think she's still alive?"

Evidently, that hadn't yet occurred to her younger brother. "Whaddya mean? Gramma's all right!" He turned to me for reassurance. "She's okay, right, Dad?"

I sighed and shrugged helplessly. "I don't know, Zach. There's no way for us to tell."

"But you said you left her a note, an' you told her to come here when she got home, right?"

Megan interjected before I could figure out what to say. "She didn't have time to get away from Houston, Zach."

"She did too!" Zachary turned back and forth between his sister and me, his quivering voice practically begged for reassurance. "Dad?"

"No she didn't." Megan's voice took on a bitter tone. "No one who was still there got away. Everyone we knew is gone." She looked at me, tears streaming freely down her cheeks. "Aren't they?"

I couldn't help it. My own eyes began to fill at the thought of my father, and the likelihood of my mother also being dead. *No! Time enough for that later.* Trying to be discrete, I coughed and wiped my eyes on my sleeve. I swallowed the lump in my throat and took a deep breath. "I don't know." Pulling Zach onto my knee, I wrapped my arms around him. "We'll probably never know. All we can do is hope."

Debra leaned over and put an arm around Megan, who buried her face in her mother's shoulder. "Josh is dead, isn't he?"

I felt two feet tall. I'd completely forgotten her boyfriend, and things had moved so quickly that I'd never thought to talk to her about him. Debra answered, "I don't know. It's like your dad just said, we might never know."

Zach turned his face up to me, suddenly realizing the further implications of what we were saying. "What about Jeremy. Or Kenny?"

Ken spoke from his hammock. "I have a brother in California. He lives in the mountains, in Sierra City. I wonder what happened there."

Zachary turned his attention to Ken as Ken sat up and smiled kindly at him. "I like to think he's over there on the other side of the country in a nice cabin in the mountains. I'm sad that I won't ever get to talk to him again, but I think he's probably okay."

"Why won't you get to talk to him again?"

Ken came over and sat on the dirt floor next to us. "You remember how the electricity went out before you came here to see your nanna?" Zach nodded. "Well, if what your daddy says is true, I think the electricity probably went out all over the country, even in California. And without the electricity, a lot of things won't work, things like the telephones, and radios, and a lot of cars and gas stations. There's just a whole lot of stuff that got broken and, without that stuff, I don't have a way to talk to him anymore."

"But you think he's okay?"

Ken nodded. "I'll bet he is. I bet he's up in the mountains wondering if I'm okay, and sorry he won't get a chance to tell me."

Zachary got up from my lap and hugged Ken. "We'll find a way to talk to him again."

I caught Ken's eye over my son's shoulder, and mouthed, "Thank you." Ken just nodded.

Things were pretty reserved for the rest of the day but, after another day of moping, the kids had adapted as well as could be expected. We all knew we had to keep ourselves occupied to keep from dwelling on our losses, so we found different ways to entertain ourselves. We took turns reading our favorite authors aloud by the light of twelve-volt bulbs hooked to the car batteries. It turned out that Cindy was an avid reader of Nostradamus's prophesies and had searched his works for portents of things yet to come. By her estimation, things didn't look too good.

"Here's another one," she proclaimed one evening. "Quatrain number ninety-one in the second book of *Centuries* translates like this:

At sunrise one will see a great fire,
Noise and light extending towards Aquilon
Within the circle, death, and one will hear cries,
Through steel, fire, famine, death awaiting them."

Her voice rose in pitch as she tried to convey the importance she placed upon this prophesy.

Ken groaned. "And I suppose the 'great fire, noise, and light' is a nuke?" He and Cindy had evidently had similar conversations in the past. I could understand his jaded outlook. I had only had to listen to *The Centuries* for a couple of nights. He had probably been forced to listen to them for years.

"Well, doesn't it sound like it to you?" She turned to me for moral support. "Leeland?"

"Oh no, you don't." I laughed. "You're not dragging me into a family argument."

"It sorta sounds like it to me." Megan volunteered from her hammock. When the rest of us turned to her, she seemed to regret having spoken, as if she feared being ridiculed. "Well, you gotta admit that the other morning looked like a lot of 'steel, fire, famine, and death'!"

None of us had a rebuttal to that.

"So then, where is Aquilon?" Ken's mocking tone was aimed at his wife. "No town around here with that name."

"That's because he was from France, so most of his stuff related to France. Aquilon was an ancient city there, but with everything that's going on, who's to say what's happening?"

We played various games. Ken played the guitar, and Cindy, who had the best voice, was a pleasure to listen to when she sang.

We took vitamins, drank Gatorade, ate lousy food cooked over Sterno cans, and did our business in a covered bucket around the corner. We made a man-powered recharging device for our car batteries by attaching a hand crank to an antique automobile generator that Ken had owned.

We all took potassium iodide tablets to prevent our bodies from taking in radioactive iodine, all of us except for Debra, who had a severe allergy to iodine. In general, we tried to remain optimistic. Usually it worked, but not always. There were bad days, dark, dismal, dreary, and depressing days full of anxious and paranoid musings about the type of world to which we would emerge.

Once a day at noon, whichever adult had accumulated the smallest dose would bundle up in rain gear, rubber gloves, boots, and gas mask, all sealed with duct tape, and go outside to dump the waste buckets and take a reading with the fallout meter. Fallout readings had reached their worst on the day after we went underground, reading twenty-four rems per hour. Cindy had gotten the job of taking that first reading. I had gone over all of the charts with everyone; she knew that anything over ten rems was too dangerous, so she came back in immediately after taking the reading. The next day at noon, Debra reported twenty-three rems, and the day after that I got twelve rems. The next day was Thursday, and Ken reported a reading of seven rems. Readings decreased rapidly after that.

Actually, we got off pretty easy. The fallout wasn't nearly as intense as it could have been, and nowhere near fatal in such small doses. If anyone had been unsheltered through all of it, though, they would probably be dead within a month.

A long and excruciatingly painful month.

* * *

After nine days, our PDRs no longer glowed when we went outside. On the twelfth day, it took an hour to get a recognizable reading on the KFM, and even then, it was less than one rem per hour. Simple calculations showed we could stay outside for over seven weeks before things even got close to being dangerous. The next day, the reading was point-oh-three rems per hour... five months of "safe time."

It was time to see what was left of the world outside.

CHAPTER 7

* * JUNE 26 * *

Le deffaillant en habit de bourgeois,
Viendra le Roy tenter de son offense:
Quinze soldats la pluspart Vstagois,
Vie derniere & chef de sa cheuance.

The transgressor in bourgeois garb,
He will come to try the King with his offense:
Fifteen soldiers for the most part bandits,
Last of life and chief of his fortune.
                    Nostradamus – *Century 4, Quatrain 64*

We already knew most of the chickens had made it through all right. Each day at noon when we had emerged to read the fallout meter, we had taken the five minutes necessary to scatter feed for them to ensure our long-term food supply. Several of the hens had even nested in the house, though none had laid eggs. They did seem to have a natural resistance to the radiation.

The goats didn't fair quite as well. There had been forty-five head before we went into the shelter. We had managed to round up twenty-nine of them and force them into the house. Out of those twenty-nine, two were dead, and six were near death and had to be put out of their misery. We buried them all. Though fallout was no longer a major consideration, disease was.

We slaughtered one of the healthiest-looking males, discarded the organ meat and the meat closest to the bone, and cooked *cabrito* for dinner. It was the best meal we'd had in two weeks.

Now that we were out, a multitude of things needed to be done. The first order of business was locating the dead goats, not those from the house, but the unfortunate ones that hadn't been found in time or had been too stubborn to go inside—sixteen goat carcasses hidden somewhere in twenty acres of brush. We couldn't allow that.

I was certain any hospitals in the area were already deluged with more cases of radiation sickness than they could handle. Besides which, everyone was going to be low on food, clean water, and all of the modern little conveniences that kept us all healthy. That meant our immune systems would not be at peak performance, which in turn meant we had to be very careful about health risks, like those involving bloated animal carcasses.

We spread out in a straight line, with about thirty feet separating each of us, a grim search party to find the remaining goats. Within the first thirty minutes, we had found eleven of the sixteen. I also found I was beginning to get sunburned. Only then did I recall some of the speculated effects of nuclear weapons on the ozone layer.

"Hey, Amber!" I shouted. "You have any sunscreen?"

"Back at the house. You getting burned, too?"

"Yeah."

"Me too," Debra chimed in from further down the line.

Everyone else admitted to light burns, as well, everyone but Ken and Cindy, whose darker pigmentations had protected them... so far.

Mentally, I kicked myself. I was supposed to be the expert, and I had forgotten one of the most controversial issues concerning the after-effects of nuclear war. Many scientists claimed that nuclear explosions would deplete the earth's ozone layer, allowing excess ultraviolet radiation to filter through the atmosphere. They claimed that even if you survived a nuclear war, the damage to the atmosphere would be so severe that the resultant UV increase would likely destroy the earth's delicate ecological balance. Vegetation would shrivel and die. Animals dependent on that vegetation for sustenance would starve. The food chain would be interrupted, causing widespread starvation and disease. Large areas on all of the continents, deprived of their bonding vegetation, would erode and turn into giant deserts. In short, claimed these scientists, life on the earth would become a living hell.

Then, there was the other side, the scientists who claimed the others were basing their projections upon faulty computer models. Though they conceded the existence of slight evidence that there could be some damage to the ozone layer, they claimed the extent of the damage would not be nearly as severe as the others feared. According to them, the measurements taken from early nuclear testing indicated less ozone depletion than resulted from industrial pollution, and that the ozone would quickly replenish itself. As for the delicate ecology, they replied that the earth wasn't nearly as delicate as the opposition claimed. The niche occupied by humanity may be delicate, but Nature had repeatedly demonstrated its resiliency. In short, though mankind might destroy itself, Mother Nature could easily carry on without us.

Plenty of facts and figures backed up both arguments. I just hoped I had picked the right side.

"All right," I yelled to get everyone's attention. "Everybody back to the house!"

As we trudged back, I explained, "The ozone layer's evidently been shot to hell by the bombs, and we're taking on too much ultraviolet. We're going to have to go back to the house and take a few precautions. We'll need to wear long pants, long-sleeve shirts, hats, and sunglasses. Anywhere our skin is exposed, we'll need sunscreen. I don't know how long this will last, but we might have to live with it for a long time."

We all retreated to the house and geared up before returning to finish our search. By sundown, all of the goats had been found and buried with the help of Ken's back hoe, and though everyone complained about having to wear so much clothing in the humid southern heat, it wasn't a major problem.

* * June 29 * *

Three days after we emerged from our shelter, Amber, Ken, and I decided to head into town to see how it was holding together. I also wanted to report our encounter with Larry and company to the local authorities, assuming any authorities were left.

At the edge of town, we were stopped at a roadblock—two diesel pickup trucks manned by two rather tired-looking Rejas police officers. One came around the blockade to talk to us. I noticed the other kept his rifle pointed in our direction. Not a good sign.

The first officer never gave us a chance to open our mouths. "Sorry, folks, but Rejas can't take in any more refugees. You'll have to turn around."

"But we're not refugees, Officer—" Amber began.

The policeman cut her off. "I'm sure you aren't, ma'am." His tone said otherwise. It said he'd heard all the excuses and was tired of hearing them. "Whatever you call yourselves, you'll have to turn around right now. Otherwise, my orders are real specific."

Ken shifted in his seat and reached for his back pocket. "Listen officer, we—"

"HOLD IT!"

Ken looked up to see the business end of a 9mm Glock aimed at his head. Eyes wide, he froze and swallowed, "I'm just going for my driver's license, Officer. No need to be alarmed." Then slowly, very slowly, he pulled out his wallet and shakily withdrew the driver's license. "But you see, we live in Rejas."

The cop read the address on the license, then holstered his pistol. "Sorry 'bout that." He didn't sound very sincere. "We really do have a problem with refugees. I guess I should have given y'all a chance to explain, but we got so many people trying to talk their way through here that you just get tired of hearing all the excuses. Can I see the rest of y'all's licenses?"

We handed them over. He examined Amber's and handed it back. Then, he looked at mine.

"You don't live here." Either he was bored silly from this guard duty, or he was just having a really bad day, because the look he directed at me virtually oozed malice. I thought there was going to be trouble, but Amber piped up.

"He's family… my son-in-law. My daughter and grandchildren are back at the house. If it wasn't for Leeland, we would all be dying a slow death right now."

"How's that?"

"He's a survivalist. Knows how to build shelters, filters, everything we needed to make it through the last couple of weeks."

He eyed me for a moment longer, then turned back to Amber. "Long as you vouch for him, I'll let him through." Clearly he didn't like the idea of letting an "outsider" into his town. Nevertheless, he returned my license.

Since he was the first representative of the local police department I had seen, I figured he would be the one to ask about the problem we'd had on the way out here. "Who do I need to see to report an attempted hijacking?"

"What?" He appeared startled.

"My family and I were attacked on the way out here."

"When did that happen?"

"D-day." It was what we had all taken to calling June thirteenth while in the shelter. It was shorter than saying, "The day all the bombs started falling."

He knew immediately what I meant and obviously didn't give a damn that my family and I had been attacked. "Ain't nothin' nobody can do about that now. Hell, that was a couple of weeks ago." He barked out a laugh. "What the hell do you expect us to do now?"

"Well, you might start by sending someone to bury the bodies," I said facetiously. It gave me great satisfaction to see him sober so quickly.

"Bodies? You mean y'all killed 'em?"

"Only two of them," I replied innocently. I saw an opportunity to pay him back for some of the crap he had just dished out.

He finally appeared to be taking me seriously. "How many of 'em was there?"

"Five."

"So there's still three of 'em on the loose?"

"Unless some of the others died from their wounds."

"Wounds?"

This was getting fun. "Yeah. One had a broken knee and a hole in his left shoulder. Another one had a pretty nasty bump and cut on the front of his head."

"How 'bout the last one?" He took the bait.

"Oh, he gave up before we hurt him." I smiled innocently.

"How many of you was there?"

"Me, my wife, my sixteen-year-old daughter, and my nine-year-old son." I saw the disbelief in his eyes. "Look, Officer, it's a long story, and I don't feel like telling it twice. So if you could just tell me who I need to report to, I'll be on my way."

But he wasn't about to be put off after my last comment. "You expect me to believe that you, your wife, daughter, and son killed two bandits, wounded two more, and another one just gave up so you wouldn't hurt him? That sounds like bullshit to me, boy!"

"Call it whatever you want," I replied calmly. "Just tell me who to see in town, and I'll take myself and my bullshit story out of here."

He paused, evidently trying to decide whether the importance of my story outweighed the importance of his teaching me a lesson in manners. "You best get a grip on that attitude of yours, boy, or I'll have to adjust it for you."

I was tired, scared, and didn't know when to leave well enough alone. "I don't think you could adjust your ass with both hands, you stupid—"

Amber grabbed my arm. "That's enough, Leeland!" She turned to the cop. "I'm sorry, Officer. He was hurt in the fight with the hijackers." She indicated the scabbed-over slice on my throat. It still looked worse than it felt, but for once I was glad of it.

"Shee-it," he drawled. "Hunh. Maybe it wasn't all bullshit, after all." He decided to ignore me completely and addressed Amber. "Okay, first thing y'all need to do is go to City Hall. The police station's in the same building. You can make your report to the deputy on duty. Next, go to the titles and notary department and register your vehicle. They'll give you a sticker to put on your windshield. You'll also have to fill out a questionnaire. It'll have a lot of questions about where you're stayin' and how many of you there are. What kind of skills you have. Stuff like that."

He pointed at me. "You make sure you list that survivalist shit. They might want to pick your brain a little. They're still trying to figure out how many of us there are and what we've got to work with. So far, we're pretty much cut off from anyone else. Phones are down, and radios don't work any farther than a mile or two. Hell, if it wasn't for all of these damned refugees tryin' to get past us, I'd think we were the only ones left."

He signaled his partner, who climbed into one of the trucks and pulled it back far enough for us to get past. "Now, y'all remember what I told you. Go straight to City Hall. Otherwise, you'll be in a heap o' shit for drivin' without a sticker. Probably lose your van." He waved us through.

"Sounds like things are pretty serious," I said as we drove past.

Ken cocked an eyebrow at my understatement. "No shit! I just had a gun pointed at my head. I'd say that's pretty damn serious!"

"Yeah," I responded. "Real nice town you got here." I grinned at the lonely finger he showed me.

We pulled onto Main Street and headed for City Hall. Along the way, we passed the only building in sight that showed signs of life, a Church of Jesus Christ of Latter-day Saints. Its parking lot was filled to capacity with vehicles bearing markings from all over the state, as well as quite a few from Utah and Louisiana. I noticed as we passed that many of the vehicles were packed stem to stern with all kinds of supplies. I was willing to bet at that point that most of the refugees of which the officer had spoken were inside that church.

Other than that, however, the streets were pretty deserted. We saw fewer than a dozen people along the two-mile stretch, and only one moving vehicle, diesel, of course. There was definitely no sign of any crowd of refugees. I commented on this to the others.

"They probably started turning people back as soon as they realized what had happened," Ken conjectured.

"Why would they do that?" Amber asked.

He shrugged. "To conserve resources? Someone must have realized early on that we may have to make do with what we have on hand and what we can manufacture or grow for a long time."

"What about the Mormons back there?"

I answered, "Mormons have always believed in being prepared for any emergency situation. They were probably in town before the roadblocks had even been thought of.

"I don't know whether or not it's true, but I've heard a good Mormon keeps enough food on hand at all times to feed his entire family for a minimum of one year."

Further conversation halted as we pulled into the City Hall parking lot. Four other cars were parked there, three of them covered with a thick layer of pine pollen, obviously undriven for several days. The fourth was a shiny, diesel Mercedes.

The plate glass doors were propped open, and as we entered, I was immediately reminded what kind of world we now lived in. In place of the fluorescent lights I subconsciously expected, lanterns lit the building.

We stopped at the door marked *Police* and spoke to the lady behind the desk. In a twangy Southern drawl, she told us that she was only the clerk, but that she would be happy to take my statement and file the report. After hearing my story, however, she asked if I would return on the following Wednesday to speak with the chief. She explained that Chief Davis had called in sick with some kind of stomach bug. We left without comment.

We then went to the *Titles and Notary* door.

"Can I help you?" the lady behind the desk queried.

"Yes ma'am, we were told we needed to register our van and get a sticker for the windshield." Trying to fit in, I played up the country accent. I didn't like being considered an outsider. If the cop at the roadblock was any indication, outsiders weren't very welcome.

"Are you the owner?"

"Yes, ma'am."

She handed me a standard vehicle registration form and a pencil. "Fill out the first two sections and sign at the bottom."

As I did so, she asked, "Have any of you filled out an Assimilation Form?"

"A what?"

She pushed three of the forms at us. I noticed that rather than the fine laser-quality print typical for this day and age, these were mimeographed, something I hadn't seen since I'd been a kid in elementary school. "Please answer all questions completely and legibly." She handed Ken and Amber each a pencil and smiled apologetically. "You can sit over there by the window. The electricity is still out." As if she expected it to be restored at any moment.

Sitting at a desk that had been moved into the sunlight, I stared at the Assimilation Form. *Name, age, address...* All of the standard questions. Then it got interesting.

Previous profession, not just profession... *previous profession.*

Do you have any hobbies or skills that might be of any value in reconstruction? "Reconstruction," a nice, neat, noncommittal term. All of the terminology seemed geared to building an optimistic picture of what had happened. I shook my head. How could they think to sugarcoat a nuclear war?

What provisions do you have stored?

What shelter do you have prepared?

Alarms started going off in my head as I read those two. About a half-dozen more questions of a similar nature followed. I looked up and found my alarm reflected in Ken's furrowed brow. He looked as wary as I felt. His eyes questioned me as his pencil rested on the first of those troublesome questions. I turned to find the same question reflected in Amber's eyes. They were both waiting for my lead.

What provisions do you have stored?

I thought for a moment, then firmly printed *None.* In my mind, it was clear. We had prepared so we could be assured of a fairly decent existence after all hell broke loose. We had not prepared a shelter and gathered food and provisions only to turn it all over to people that hadn't. Call me coldhearted, or call me pragmatic. Either way, I wasn't about to jeopardize my family by drawing attention to the minimal supplies we had.

I glanced up and saw that neither Ken nor Amber had hesitated in following my lead. We finished the forms with a series of *no's* and *none's*, stood together, and returned the forms.

The clerk took the forms and looked them over. "You don't have any provisions? No food or anything?"

"No, ma'am," I responded for all of us.

"How do you intend to live? I mean..." She sounded genuinely concerned. "Things have changed. Y'all understand that, don't you?"

"Yes, ma'am. But we can hunt and, as you can see on my form, I'm a pretty fair herbalist. I can identify most of the edible plants that grow around here."

She shook her head. "There's been radioactive fallout in the area. You can't eat any of the plants or animals."

I shook my head. "No, ma'am, that isn't quite true. You can eat most of the animals around here as long as you stick to the healthy ones and eat only the muscle tissue. And all you have to do with the plants is wash them. 'Course you have to make sure that you wash them real well." She looked at me, dumbfounded.

Still smiling, I explained, "If you check my form, you'll find I'm also a survivalist. Now, could I please get that sticker for my van?"

"Yes, sir, Mister..." She underlined the name on my questionnaire. "Dawcett."

So much for not drawing attention to myself. She passed across a metallic-gold, bird-shaped sticker. The words "Rejas Fighting Eagles" were boldly emblazoned across it in black. "Just put it inside your windshield. At the top center in plain sight."

I thanked her and left without another word, with Ken and Amber right behind me.

We remained quiet until we got into the van. Then Amber positively exploded. "What food do you have? What shelter? What gardening implements? What medical supplies? What *right* do they have to even ask those questions?"

I remained silent as I attached the Rejas sticker to the windshield.

Undaunted, she continued her tirade. "Do they actually think we're so stupid that we don't know what they would do with that information? They want our supplies!" She glared at me, then at Ken. "Tell me I'm wrong," she challenged. "Go ahead! Tell me."

There was nothing for me to say. As we pulled out of the parking lot, I thought about what she said. She was right. Unquestionably. The only possible reason I could see for the town government to be pinpointing supplies would be to create a communal stockpile, a noble gesture perhaps, but futile. There couldn't possibly be enough to go around. Besides, by my estimations, anyone who hadn't had adequate shelter over the last week and a half had a ninety-five percent chance of being fertilizer within another month. Personally, I doubted Chief Davis would be returning to work next Wednesday, or any day.

The town government evidently had good intentions, but we all knew where that road led.

I tried to calm her down as we drove back. "They're just trying to help as many people as they can. You can't blame them for trying."

"But we're barely going to have enough for ourselves."

"And that's still more than they'll be able to say in Rejas in about a month. Think about that."

The rest of the ride was grimly silent.

* * June 30 * *

I found it truly amazing that chickens and goats could so totally wreck a home. Even more surprising were some of the strange things that goats would eat. I had always heard stories of them eating such odd items as tin cans or some such, but I'd never truly believed them.

No more. After seeing what those animals did to the inside of Amber's house, I believed. They actually ate the carpet! Large patches of it anyway. And bits of wood paneling, cabinet doors, even sheet rock! Truly amazing.

The amount of animal crap was pretty impressive as well. Chicken droppings all over the furniture. Goat droppings all over the floors. All in all, the house was pretty well trashed.

After the time in the shelter, we had asked Ken and Cindy to stay on with us, at least until things stabilized. It took all of us several days of hard work to get the house back into serviceable condition. Even then, the kids elected to sleep outside in sleeping bags for four more nights to "get away from all the stinky smells."

We had to scavenge sheetrock and cabinetry from abandoned homes in the area for our repairs. Plumbing was out for the time being, so we built an old-fashioned outhouse in back until we could figure out something else. Ken, with his contracting background, was a huge help in the repairs. He even spoke of rigging up a hydraulic ram system that would use the current from the stream out back to pump water into a raised water tank and feed enough water back into the pipes to give us at least a little water pressure again. I didn't understand it, but he seemed confident.

"The ram will be enough to get us started, and we can add a water wheel to it later." He snapped his fingers excitedly. "We can even tie a generator into the water wheel and get some current for lights, maybe more. Cindy's a fair electrician. Maybe she can rig something up to get us more juice." Lost in his thoughts, Ken turned away, apparently forgetting I was there. "Cindy!"

I shook my head and went back to the more mundane work of patching sheetrock.

On a darker note, the first of the inevitable profusion of deaths had begun to occur in town, with hundreds of people taking sick and dying. Messengers went out to anyone with any medical training, beseeching them to help out in the overburdened hospital. Since Amber had admitted to being a retired nurse on her "Assimilation Form," she was one of the first sought out.

CHAPTER 8

* * JULY 03 * *

Nouueaux venus lieu basty sans defence,
Occuper la place par lors inhabitable:
Prez, maisons, champs, villes, prêdre à plaisance,
Faim peste, guerre, arpen long labourage.

Newcomers, place built without defense,
Place occupied then uninhabitable:
Meadows, houses, fields, towns to take at pleasure,
Famine, plague, war, extensive land arable.
Nostradamus – *Century 2, Quatrain 19*

Almost three weeks after D-day, a pickup pulled into the drive. The same
police officer that had manned the roadblock five days earlier stepped out.
I had been working with Ken, pulling the remains of the soiled and smelly

carpet out of the den when I heard the vehicle and saw him outside the window. I quickly stepped outside. I wasn't trying to be polite. I just remembered that questionnaire and didn't want him to see any of the food and supplies we had stacked in the kitchen.

"Good morning, Officer." I wiped my hand on my jeans before extending it. "What can we do for you?"

"This where Amber Peddy lives?" he drawled, ignoring my hand. "I need to speak to her, if you don't mind."

I dropped my hand and my smile. In the most formal voice I could muster, I asked, "Could I tell her what this is about?" What I really meant was, "Do you mind telling me where the hell you get off swaggering up here like you own the place and demanding to see my mother-in-law?"

He caught it, but my businesslike tone left him no opening to call offense. He looked me over disdainfully, as if trying to determine whether or not I deserved a real answer. Evidently, I didn't. "Sorry, Mr. Dawcett, but that really ain't no concern of yours." He started to step past me.

I moved in front of him, less worried about manners than about keeping him outside. "I'm sure it isn't. But the house is a wreck right now, so if you'll just wait right here, I'd be happy to run and get her for you." Those questions kept running through my mind. *What provisions do you have stored? What medical supplies?* I simply couldn't let him into the house.

He reached down and pointedly put his hand on his holster. The meaning was clear. "Mr. Dawcett, would you please step aside?"

I wasn't about to, and it looked like it was going to come down to a more physical confrontation. I was close enough that I knew that he would never get the pistol out of its holster if he tried, and I had seen the way he carried himself. I was certain that I could take him without any difficulty. The problem was, with or without that attitude, he still represented law and order. Could I afford to make such an enemy?

Ken stepped out of the front door at that point, looked warily at our standoff in the front yard, and saved me from having to make such a decision. "Problem, Leeland?"

"Yeah. Officer… " I glanced quickly down at his badge. "Kelland seems to be very eager to speak to Amber. Would you mind getting her?"

"Sure thing." Ken left quickly.

Kelland stared at me through his shades. He must have seen he wasn't going to be able to bully his way past me, but now he was sure I was trying to hide something. So he tried a different approach. "There some reason you don't want me to come in? Hot as it is, seems like that'd be the hospitable thing to do."

"Officer Kelland, I don't know what I've done to piss you off so much, but ever since the first time you saw me, you seem to have had it in for me. You were rude at the roadblock, and you were rude when you stepped out of your truck just now. Now I realize, as far as you're concerned, I'm city folk, and I've got no business in your town. I also realize that ever since those bombs fell, everyone has been under a lot of stress. But I've got news for you, Amber is family, and technically, I'm her guest. So she's the only one around here I have to please. And she's the only one that can tell me to leave. Until that happens, my family and I are here to stay. That means that this is now my home.

"Now, I'll grant you that things have changed a lot, but not so much that you can come up here flashing a badge and a gun and forcing your way into people's homes." I stopped for a second to catch my breath and let him absorb the implications of what I had said.

"I'm not city folk any more, Kelland. I live here. I'm Rejas folk. And you might need to get to know me a little before you start playing your little mind games." I glanced at his right hand, still resting on his holster. "So if you think for one freaking minute that I'm going to invite you into this house with your sorry attitude, you can just jump up my ass and fight for air."

I turned my back on him and walked to the house. I wasn't sure if he would get the message, but where I grew up, to turn your back on someone like that was one of the worst insults imaginable. It showed nothing but contempt for anything they could do.

Of course, I also watched his reflection in the front window as I left. I saw the curtains in that window move slightly as I stepped up to the front porch, so I knew that someone was watching us from inside. Sure enough, Amber met me at the front door as I came in with Ken beside her holding the deer rifle.

"What's going on?" she asked. "What's he doing here?"

"Wish I knew." I shrugged. "He wasn't real inclined to tell me much, and I didn't exactly help matters any."

"How's that?"

"I think I insulted him a little."

"Gee, thanks. So now that you've buttered him up, I'm supposed to go talk to him?"

"You want me to go out there with you?"

She peeked out the window again at the fuming Officer Kelland. "No thanks," she said dryly, "It looks like you've helped enough."

"Would you rather I invited him in?"

She sighed. "No, I guess not. But I'm not looking forward to this." Taking another deep breath, she opened the front door. "Well, I guess I'd better find out what's going on."

"We'll keep an eye on you." Ken raised the rifle as she left.

I smiled. "What's the matter, Ken? You act like you don't trust the nice officer."

He didn't even bother turning back to face me. "That's the sumbitch that stuck a gun in my face. See if it doesn't change your attitude about a person."

I tried to hear what they said, but Amber and Kelland spoke too softly. At any rate, the discussion lasted only a few minutes before Kelland turned, got back in his truck, and left.

We both pounced on Amber when she came back inside. "Well, what did he want?"

"They need me at the hospital," she replied solemnly. "I wrote on my form that I was a retired nurse, and now it seems they're swamped with people suffering from radiation poisoning. They need any experienced medical personnel they can get. Fifty-seven deaths and over three hundred hospitalized."

It was grim news, but we had known it was coming. We also knew it was going to get worse. Rejas was a pretty small town of less than ten thousand people. It also happened to be the site of two hospitals, each with about two hundred beds. Evidently, they were already doubling up.

She looked me in the eyes. "One of the deaths was the chief of police. That means the officer you were oh, so charming to is now the head authority figure around here." I groaned.

"You picked the wrong man to mess with this time, Leeland."

She reached up and ran her finger across the scarring line at my throat. "I would have thought you'd know better by now." She sighed. "Well, no use crying about it now that it's done. I need to get to the hospital. Would you mind if I took the van? There's no telling when I'll get away, and it's not like I can call you when I'm ready to go."

"No problem. When are you planning to leave?"

"There's no reason I can't go now," she said. "There's nothing here someone else can't do. I'd be more useful at the hospital."

I couldn't argue with her logic. She was useful at home, but medicine had been her chosen field for many years, and I couldn't expect her to ignore its call.

I turned to get the keys from where they hung on the wall in the kitchen. Debra handed them to me before I had completely turned around. She, Cindy, and the kids had all come in the back way to see what the commotion was about. Walking in on the end of my conversation with Amber, Debra had known with that special sixth sense of hers what would be needed.

I passed the keys to my mother-in–law. "Take care," I told her. "We're going to need you back here." Not very eloquent, but for the life of me, I couldn't think of anything else to say. It was the first time any one of us had been separated from the others. It seemed like one of those occasions that should be remembered as significant. But in reality, it was simply Amber going to work. Everyone else gathered around for hugs and goodbyes.

Five minutes later, she was gone.

* * July 4 * *

The next day, trouble visited our neck of the woods. It wasn't subtle, like the dangers we had begun to accept as a part of every day life. We didn't need our PRDs to detect it, or to take extra precautions with our garbage to prevent it. It was loud, and we knew it immediately for the threat that it was.

A short volley of gunfire, followed by several seconds of silence. It sounded like four or five guns being fired at random. Nearly fifteen seconds passed, then more gunfire. Sporadic, this time. Five or six shots, then silence. Then, nearly a dozen shots. And again, silence. It went on like that for nearly two minutes before the short echoes of the last shot were absorbed by the forest.

We were all working on a homemade waterwheel we planned to erect over the small creek that ran down from the spring. If it worked, we would soon have fresh running water and electricity. As soon as we heard those gunshots, however, our priorities shifted radically.

Actually, that wasn't quite true. When we first heard them, none of us wanted to believe what we were hearing. It wasn't until the second volley that Megan asked what the rest of us had been too afraid to. "Are those gunshots?"

Ken got to his feet first. "Let's get everyone inside." None of us argued as we scrambled for the house.

"Megan, get the rifles out of the closet," I ordered. "Extra magazines for each." She nodded and ran ahead. "Ken, are you any good with a rifle?"

"Six years in the Marines and several years of hunting. Good enough?"

I was surprised. He'd never given any indication. "Yeah, how about you, Cindy?"

She shrugged. "It's been a long time, but Ken got me interested when we first got married. He thought he could get me to go hunting with him, but I couldn't see shooting defenseless animals and—"

Ken interrupted, "Cindy, we don't have time for your life history, baby. Just a yes or no."

"Sorry," she said. "Yes, I can shoot."

We entered the house to find Megan laying various firearms out on the floor of the den—dad's old .30-06 deer rifle, a twelve-gauge pump-action shotgun Amber kept around for "shootin' varmints," and a .300 Winchester Magnum, a rifle with more kick than a mule.

In addition, we had the spoils of our encounter with Larry and company: a Winchester .22, the AR 15, two Uzi 9mm carbine semi-autos, and the grand prize, a old 9mm carbine with a helical coil magazine that held one hundred rounds. It had been Larry's personal weapon. Mine now.

Four pistols also lay on the couch, as well as the one Megan now wore on her belt. All in all, not a bad little arsenal.

There was no question as to whether or not we would investigate. We couldn't afford to wait and see what happened. After all, that had been a lot of gunfire, and we were in no position to call the police.

"Okay," I said. "Who goes, and who stays?"

Zachary piped up. "I wanna go!" Quick in the way of an eight-year-old boy, he turned toward the pistols on the couch.

Debra caught his shoulder. "The kids and I will stay here and watch things while you're gone." She knelt in front of Zachary. "Zach, I need you to stay here with me. I'm too scared to stay here alone."

Zachary frowned, probably sensing he was being manipulated. "But I need to go with Dad."

Debra turned to me, her eyes asking for help.

"Zach, come here." I said it conspiratorially, appealing to the part of every child that wanted to be an adult. "Your mom won't admit it, but she's afraid of guns. She's probably going to need some help loading them. Can you do me a favor and look after her?"

Still appearing unsure, but willing to be talked into it, he finally agreed. "Well, okay."

"I'll stay with them," Cindy added.

"I'm going." Megan sounded as if she expected an argument. In truth, I had mixed feelings. On one hand, she was my daughter, just sixteen years old, and I couldn't help feeling that I shouldn't allow her to go into a potentially dangerous situation. On the other hand, however, I would be happy to have her help. After all, I had trained her myself, and she had held up under the pressure of a tight situation to save my bacon once already.

"Fine. Ken?"

"I'm going," he said. "You'll need me to show you the back trails through the woods."

I nodded and picked up the carbine. "Everybody, take your pick." I headed back to the bedroom that Debra and I shared. I reached under the bed and pulled out two canvas sport bags, then quickly stripped down to my underwear. One was my trusty bag of tricks, which I immediately dug into and began strapping my hidden arsenal into place.

When finished, I reached into the other bag and pulled out several pairs of camouflage pants, shirts, jackets, and gloves. That bag contained all of mine and Megan's old paintball gear. Still in the bag were a couple of protective face masks, several safety goggles, a dozen smoke bombs, web belts with plenty of pouches, two paintball guns, and other paintball paraphernalia.

I slipped on camouflage pants, a t-shirt, and a jacket over most of my toys, until I was dressed much as I had been on the drive out from

Houston, except camouflaged from head to toe. I also grabbed half of the smoke bombs and stuffed them into a pouch on my web belt. Each one would put out a huge cloud of thick white smoke when you pulled the ring on the side. They had been a lot of fun when playing paintball and worked well in thick brush.

I left the room in a hurry. "Megan," I called, "your cammies are on the bed in our room. Make it fast!" She grabbed one of the Uzis and headed for the bedroom.

I turned to Ken. "There are some more cammies in the bedroom. When she comes out, why don't you see if any of them will fit you?"

Ken waved and went back to coordinating the defense of the house with Cindy and Debra. With the rest of us leaving, it would be up to the women to defend the homestead if anything happened. It quickly became obvious that Ken knew more about firearms than I ever would.

He had never mentioned his hitch in the military during our two week incarceration in the shelter. They were evidently memories he preferred to forget, but he hadn't forgotten the knowledge of weapons he'd acquired. He went from Debra to Cindy, recommending weapons and positions for defense of the house. I just watched, listened, and learned.

Debra had a problem with depth perception, so she got the .30-06 with the telescopic sight for long range where she could take her time in aiming. If any action began to get close, she would have to switch to the twelve-gauge so the spread could help compensate for her vision.

Cindy got the Uzi that Megan hadn't taken. They had enough ammunition to take on a small army, and Ken showed Zachary how to load rounds into the empty magazines for the various firearms. Everyone was taking it very seriously. Maybe it would turn out to be nothing, but it sure hadn't sounded like it.

Megan emerged dressed in her camouflage. In addition, she wore one of our old team patches on her shoulder and had slung the crossbow across her back. She had already proven herself with it, and we might need a good, long-range, silent weapon. Her philosophy and mine were much the same; better to have it and not need it, than to need it and not have it.

While Ken hurried into the bedroom to change, Megan and I took the opportunity to help each other stretch our legs and arms for maximum flexibility and blood circulation. It occurred to me that this was the first time since we had gotten here that we had so much as thought about our martial arts training, and I vowed it would become part of our daily routine.

Ken returned wearing cammies. He had helped himself to one of my sheath knives, as well. Everyone was ready, or as ready as we were likely to get. We told the women we would be back before dark and set up recognition signals, so they wouldn't shoot us if we came back in a hurry.

I turned to Megan. "Just one more thing. This isn't paintball."

Her face was set, silent and intense. She tended to get that way when concentrating on something important. I had seen her like that many times before sparring in class or tournaments.

I continued, "There are two big differences. First, the range on these guns is much farther than paintball guns. Always remember that." She nodded.

"And second—"

"I know," she interrupted. "If you get hit, you don't come back in for the next game."

"You got it." I pushed back an urge to force her to stay behind. Instead, I turned to Ken. "Ready to go?"

Ken hefted the AR-15. "Waiting on you."

I took a deep breath to calm my nerves, then slung my machete over my shoulder. "Let's find out what all the ruckus is about."

* * *

Megan and I quickly taught Ken our hand signals, and we trudged through the brush in silence. For me, the feeling of déjà vu was intense. The last time I had gone sneaking through the woods like this had very nearly been fatal. Actually, it *had* been fatal, to Edgar and Michael.

The shots had come from south of Amber's spread, past Ken and Cindy's place. That was all we had to go by, so Ken led us through the brush on barely seen game trails. He whispered that he and some of his neighbors used many of these trails when they were hunting, so a multitude of crisscrossed tracks led to and from most of the homes in the area.

After several minutes, Ken signaled for us to slow down and come forward cautiously. When we moved next to him, he whispered, "This is the back of old man Kindley's place."

I pointed out that the house looked vacant.

"Yeah," he agreed. "Do you want to check it out?"

I remembered what Amber had said about all of the deaths and radiation sickness in the area. "Not really…" Visions of grisly, mummified carcasses filled my head. "But I guess we should."

First, we skirted all around the house making sure no unfriendlies hung about. Then, we quickly ran up to the back door.

"What do we do now?" I asked. "Kick it in?"

Ken turned the knob, and the door swung inward. "The trouble with living in the city is that you can't trust anyone." He grinned. "You wouldn't even dream of leaving your house unlocked, would you?"

I shook my head, and Megan and I followed him in. A quick search of the dark and musty interior revealed it to be mercifully empty. We noted a pantry full of canned goods that we could come back for at a later date, but there were no bodies.

The next house was two miles further, and turned out to be much the same as Kindley's. As we trekked down the trail, Megan snapped her fingers to get our attention. She pointed to her nose and mimed sniffing the air.

I sniffed and, sure enough, I faintly smelled burning wood. Ken nodded as well. We were getting close to something.

He led more cautiously, stopping frequently to peer intently ahead before leading us into any especially thick brush. As we proceeded, the smell got stronger. And every so often, we could hear the faint sound of voices, several voices.

Finally, Ken signaled for us to stop and wait. The sound of voices had grown steadily stronger until we could nearly distinguish the words of the conversations. It sounded like someone was throwing a party, and we were nearly on top of them. Ken inched his way around a curve in the trail ahead. He returned only a few moments later, jaw clenched in barely controlled fury. "Just around the next bend is John and Pat Robertson's place," he whispered. "There's a group of eight men dressed in camouflage and armed to the teeth having a party on the back porch."

Obviously, there was more, so I just waited for him to drop the other shoe.

He took a deep breath before he continued, "It looks like they killed John. They just dragged his body out into the backyard and left it."

Now I thought I understood. Ken felt the need to avenge his friend. But he also knew we couldn't afford to do anything to attract attention to ourselves unless we had no choice. John Robertson was beyond help, and revealing ourselves this soon wouldn't change that. But perhaps his wife was still alive.

"Mrs. Robertson?" I asked.

He answered slowly, watching for my reaction. It occurred to me that he seemed more unsure of me than I was of him. "She's the party. They're taking turns..." He glanced at Megan. "They're gang-raping her."

I knew it wasn't logical the way my gut twisted at those words. After all, they had murdered a man. But hearing that they were raping the man's wife put them into an even lower category. They were lower than animals—diseased.

I looked Ken directly in the eyes. "If we do this, we shoot to kill. No one gets away. We can't risk any of them following us home."

He didn't bat an eye. "Suits me fine."

I turned to Megan. "Do you think you can find your way back?"

"No way," she slung the crossbow and hefted the Uzi she'd brought. "I'm staying. I don't have any problems with this." I recognized the stubborn set to her jaw, the same one her mother displayed when her mind was made up about something. "It's not like murder, Dad. It's justice. Besides, what do you think would happen if we didn't kill them? They would find us on down the road tomorrow or the next day, and they would come after us next. Or maybe they'd find someone else. We have to stop them now."

She was right, of course, but I was surprised to find that she saw the same implications in the situation that I did. As far as she was concerned, the discussion was over. I couldn't force her to go back, and she knew it. She would simply follow as soon as I turned my back.

"I know what the stakes are, Dad."

"All right, then," I conceded. "Just don't forget what you learned in paintball. Don't stay in one place too long. Shoot and move. Don't get pinned down."

She nodded, and we planned our attack.

First, watching for any guards, we skirted around the tree line to the right. We found only one. He was poorly hidden in the trees and obviously more intent on watching the abuse of Pat Robertson than doing his job. We got within twenty feet of him, where Megan felt sure of her shot. A single bolt from behind into the base of the skull ensured his silence.

I searched her face for a reaction. I saw her pain at having killed again, but there was also determination.

Ken and I left Megan there, where she would wait for a gunshot from one of us. At that point, the element of surprise would be gone anyway, so we would all simply try to take out as many as possible, as quickly as possible. The tricky part would be doing so without hitting Mrs. Robertson.

Ken led me back to our original location, directly opposite the back porch, and then skirted alone around to the left side of the house. When he got into position, he would signal by beginning the melee, and Megan and I would join in after his first shot.

From where I knelt, I had a clear view of the proceedings in the backyard. One rough-looking man sat in a chair smoking a cigarette, apparently in deep contemplation of the universe. Four more were having a great time as they sat on the tailgate of an old four-wheel-drive pickup passing a bottle of bourbon. I could hear them joking and congratulating themselves on the ease with which they had "wasted that old geezer."

Pat Robertson was tied to a picnic table where two men with no pants waited their turn behind the one currently violating her. Mercifully, she appeared to be unconscious. I carefully took aim at the head of the man hovering over her. When Ken fired that first shot, the rapist would never hear the second one. I waited for ages.

A quick barrage of machine gun fire came from the trees to my left, and the tailgate party dissolved into blood and screams. Ken had taken all four of them out of the fight before they even knew they were in one.

I had expected a single shot. I had, in fact, forgotten that the AR-15 had been converted, so the burst of half a dozen shots in one second startled me. I reflexively squeezed the trigger just as the scum on Pat Robertson turned his head. A nickel-sized hole appeared where his nose had been, and the back of his skull splattered the far wall.

I fought the bile back down my throat and aimed at the next pantless man, but he fell screaming and clutching his chest as Megan's Uzi echoed from my right. I shifted aim and fired at the next rapist. There were now seven men dead or dying in the yard. The cigarette smoker had been either fast or lucky and had managed to get into the house. If we gave him time to dig in, he'd be able to hold us off forever.

Ken must have realized the same thing because we both rushed toward the back porch as one. "Megan!" I yelled. "Cover us!"

She immediately began firing round after round into the house at random locations. The 9mm slugs plowed through the walls and windows, ricocheting around the interior. Ken and I were halfway across the yard when two men came rushing out of the back door and dove for cover behind a large planter. Another smashed out a window to aim at Ken as he quickly backpedaled to the trees. I fired wildly at the window, more to make the guy duck than out of any hope of hitting him. Ken fired a stream of bullets at the planter to keep the other two down, and we retreated back to the cover of the trees.

I cursed myself for not anticipating more of them in the house—another stupid mistake that could have gotten us killed. For that matter, it still could. I heard shouting and return fire around the corner of the house and, as I peeked through the brush, I saw a line of several men run into the trees across the yard. Megan was in trouble.

I grabbed Ken by the shoulder. "Come on!" I hissed, and retreated deeper into the woods so we couldn't be seen from the house. We ran full throttle toward where we had left Megan. A moment later, the gunfire stopped.

I figured there was no reason for us to be quiet. They knew we were out here, and I didn't relish the idea of being shot by my own daughter. "Megan! We're coming in from behind!"

No answer. No gunfire.

A second later, Ken grabbed my shoulder and yanked me down to kneel beside him. "We have to slow down and get off of the trails, or we're gonna run into an ambush." It ate at my gut, but he was right.

It slowed us down considerably as we eased ahead silently, scanning every clump of brush thoroughly before we moved close to it. As we neared the area where we had left Megan, I thought I heard whispers, though it was difficult to be certain with my own heartbeat pounding in my ears. I grabbed Ken's arm to get his attention, pointing first at my ear, then to the woods ahead of us. He nodded, understanding. We eased back slowly to circle around, all the while fear for my daughter gnawing viciously at me.

We snuck around to come at the area from the side. Time seemed to crawl slower than we did, but finally we peered through the brush and saw the backs of four men waiting to ambush us as we barreled down the trail. Four shots later, they joined their buddies in Hell.

We moved back into the brush before the echoes had faded. Almost immediately, we heard shouts from our right.

"Jimmy! Rick! Did you get 'em?"

When Jimmy and Rick didn't answer, the voices began a worried muttering amongst themselves. We slowly eased around to come in behind their location until Ken abruptly signaled a stop. He gestured me to come even with him and pointed. Up ahead and barely visible through the scrub huddled a group of more than a dozen men… and Megan. A dozen of them! How could we possibly take them all?

They all faced away from us, to where we had left Jimmy and Rick facedown in the trees. One of them held Megan as a shield. Every few seconds, one of them would nervously scan the trees, occasionally peering into the clump that hid Ken and me. We couldn't get closer without risking exposure, yet we weren't close enough to get them without endangering Megan. I was in a quandary.

The men finally provided the answer. The one holding Megan pulled out a sheath knife and put the blade to her throat. "All right, you bastards! You get out here where we can see you, or I'll waste the girl."

There was my chance to get closer, and seeing the way the man held the knife to Megan's throat gave me an idea. He had unknowingly put Megan in a situation she had been in hundreds of times. It was a classic self-defense situation in our advanced classes— Knife Defense Technique Number Twelve. I hurriedly whispered to Ken and sketched a hasty drawing in the dirt at our feet. He gave me a quick thumbs up, and I quickly began to back away. Soon, I was far enough out and began to run back in the direction from which we had originally come. I wanted to come in from the trail where they expected us, so as not to give away Ken's location.

The poor fool holding Megan shouted, "You've got ten seconds to show yourselves. Then I'm gonna slit her throat!"

"One!"

He had no idea that from the moment he had put the knife to her throat, he was at her mercy. Even if every other man in that group survived, he didn't stand a chance. I knew exactly what she would do. I only hoped she would wait a few more seconds.

"Two!"

I leaned the carbine against a tree to the right of the trail.

"Three!"

I pulled out one of the smoke bombs, latched the snap of the pouch through the pull ring, then twisted the pouch around to the right side of my web belt where the dangling incendiary wouldn't be as noticeable.

"Four!"

I began moving quickly down the trail, making more noise as I moved.

"I hear you out there!" he screamed. "Now come out with your hands over your head, or I swear I'll kill her, man! Five!"

"Okay, I'm coming out!" I raised my hands and stepped around the last bend in the trail. Instantly, all guns pointed at me. They all peered down the trail behind me waiting for more of us to appear.

"Where's the rest of you?" the knifeman demanded.

"All around you. They all have their guns pointed at you." I put on my best poker face, scanning the group. There were fourteen of them. "If anything happens to either me or the girl, you're all dead men."

They looked even more nervous, rapidly scanning the trees around them.

"Tell them to drop their guns and come out, now!" he shouted frantically.

"If I did that, you'd kill us. That wouldn't be very smart on my part."

"What's to stop me from killing you now?"

"Think about it, you idiot," I sneered. "Twenty guns pointed at you, and you have to ask a stupid question like that?"

I looked at Megan. Her right eye puffed shut, and the cheek beneath was swollen, but her attitude remained defiant. She'd had worse from tournaments. "Down and out." I said in a conversational tone.

She furrowed her brow in puzzlement.

"Twelve, down and out," I said just as calmly. The position of her feet and hands told me she was already prepared to execute the knife defense. What I was trying to tell her was that she needed to drop down immediately after she had done so. She needed to get down and out.

"What the hell does that mean?" the man asked. Megan's expression asked the same question.

Well, why not? "It means she needs to drop down and get over here after she executes a number twelve."

Comprehension dawned on Megan's face, and she set her weight. All she needed was a distraction. I smiled at the guy. "Don't worry about it, just hurry up and kill her."

Now he was really confused. "Wha—?"

It was the last thing he ever said. One of the main things I drilled into my students was that the human brain has about a half-second reaction time. In other words, if the brain was busy doing something else, it took that long to react to new stimulus. As soon as he opened his mouth to speak, Megan knew he was concentrating on something other than her. With the distraction she needed, she shifted her weight and twisted her head, swiftly bringing her left hand to grasp the thumb of his knife hand, pulling it over her left shoulder as her right hand slapped behind his elbow and drove the knife into his own throat.

His throat fountained scarlet, and he instinctively threw himself backward as Megan dove for the ground, but it was too late for him. One of the men closest made a grab at her, but missed. For a heart stopping moment, I saw every gun in the group shift toward us. Then Ken opened up with the machine gun, and I saw five of them die as they turned to face the new threat. The others dropped to the ground as I dove and yanked the smoke bomb off of my belt, leaving the retaining ring dangling from the pouch snap. As smoke began to billow out, I tossed it into the crowd. The smoke washed over them as they shot blindly into the brush from which Ken had fired. Megan and I belly-crawled away as quickly as possible, hidden now by the advertised "fifty thousand cubic feet of thick white smoke." The minute we hit the trees, we scrambled to our feet and started running.

It would only take a few seconds for them to realize that Ken was no longer shooting at them. The plan had been for him to fire a quick burst, doing as much damage as possible, and then to leave the area before they could get a fix on his location. After that, he would follow my earlier route and meet us back on the trail.

Megan and I tore down the trail and rounded the first curve. I saw the carbine leaning against the tree where I had left it and grabbed it on the run. As we rounded the next curve, I grabbed Megan's shoulder and pulled her off of the trail to the right, where we ran only a few yards through the brush before kneeling in some scrub to hide and pant for breath.

Handing her the pistol from my holster, I fumbled my belt pouch open to grab another smoke bomb. Then I swung my carbine up to cover the trail. "Ken should be along at any time," I gasped. "Don't shoot him."

She didn't waste her breath on an answer, just nodded. Sure enough, ten seconds later, Ken came trotting through the trees. He slipped quickly and silently through the trees and, as I watched him, I realized my newfound friend had some hidden facets. If I hadn't known approximately where to watch, I probably would have missed him altogether. I whistled lightly to get his attention as he crossed the trail, and he veered over to squat next to us.

"Good to see you back with the good guys." Ken reached out and gingerly touched her swollen cheek. "Looks like they popped you pretty good, though."

She winced a little at his touch. "It's all right," she said. "He won't pop anyone ever again."

Ken nodded and turned to me. "Okay, now what?"

"You still think we can get all of them?" I was honestly beginning to doubt it.

"I don't know," he admitted. "But we can't lead them back home."

I worried about the same thing. We couldn't lead them home. We couldn't take them head on. Our only chance was to ambush them, and finding a way to do that now would be tough. They would be watching for us.

Megan complicated the situation with an observation. "What about Mrs. Robertson? We still have to get her out of there."

Ken and I glanced at one another. In the heat of the battle, we had both forgotten Pat Robertson, still tied to a table in her backyard. "Let's get them out here," I said.

Ken shook his head. "We can't take them on like this. There are at least eight of them left, and they're all looking for us right now."

"All I said was to get them out here." I grinned. "I didn't say we were going to wait on them. We fire a few shots to get their attention, get them moving down the trail, then circle back the way we came. Back to the house. You know the trails; they don't."

He thought for a moment. "Well, let's get them out here."

I smiled wearily. "Is there an echo around here?" I raised the carbine. "Everyone ready?"

When they nodded, I fired four or five shots into the air. Less than a minute later, we heard the sounds of a pack of inept woodsmen crackling through the brush. As soon as I saw movement, I tossed out two more of the smoke bombs and fired. I was out of effective range, but I wanted them to know exactly where we were before we were within range of their weapons. Some of them returned fire; others dove for cover. Within moments, smoke obscured everything. We turned and ran down the trail making enough noise for a blind man to follow. I stopped once to fire back into the smoke, and yelled, "Back to the house! Back to the house! Hurry!" We all turned abruptly to the right, ran about fifty yards, and dropped into the thickest briar patch we could find.

The smoke bombs burned for two more minutes before the cloud slowly began fading. It was difficult to see through the brush of our hiding place but, after a minute or two, we could hear the marauders cautiously moving past. For a second, I entertained the wild idea that it would be the perfect time to impetuously spring to our feet spewing bullets in all directions in a glorious attempt to take out the last of them at a single stroke. Unfortunately, I could tell from the sounds of their passage that they were much too spread out. They were all around us, whispering orders designed to "herd them back to their house."

We would never be able to get them all. Though the wait was maddening, I sat silently in the briars with Megan and Ken, ignoring the multitude of scratches, bruises, and abrasions our nasty little game of hide and seek produced.

A few minutes later, when we were finally sure that they were past us, we raced back to the Robertson's home. Ken reached the house first and rushed straight for the back porch.

"Damn! Damn them all!"

I rounded the corner of the house to find Ken kneeling next to the table to which Pat Robertson was tied. As I neared, I could see the bruised and bloody condition she was in. He looked up as Megan and I came toward him. "She's dead." Anguish lined his features as he spoke. Pain for the woman and her husband… for his neighbors, his friends. "The filthy animals beat her to death," he sobbed.

I hesitated a moment, then walked over and laid a hand on his shoulder. "Ken? Ken, I'm sorry. I'm sorry, man. But we have to go."

He was unresponsive, his grief overwhelming.

"Ken! I understand, but the others are still on that trail. We don't have time for this."

"What the hell do you mean, no time?" He slung my hand violently from his shoulder and stood. "Pat's dead. John's dead. We didn't save anyone. All this," his arm swept out to indicate the bodies littering the area, "was for nothing!" He stepped over to the nearest of the bodies and kicked it. I heard the distinct cracking sound of breaking ribs. He kicked it again and again, caving in an entire side of the corpse. The whole time we could hear him sobbing and saying, "All for nothing!"

The violence of Ken's reaction startled me. I really didn't know what to say to get through to him. I was about to try to reason with him when Megan stepped in.

"Where did the rest of them go, Ken?" She asked it quietly, simply, and somehow it got through to him. He stopped the destruction of the corpse and turned to face her, uncertainty on his face.

"Isn't that trail they're on the same trail we took from the house?" she prodded. "Where will they end up if they follow it all the way out? Back at the house, right? Back to your wife and my mom and brother."

The change was immediate. He wiped his eyes. "Okay." He sniffed, and I could see the difference in his eyes. He was back with us. For now. "Yeah, let's finish this. How long ago did they pass us on the trail?"

"Nearly five minutes," I estimated.

"Do you think we can catch them in time?" Megan asked. Five minutes on those trails could translate to more than a mile, and the distance grew as we spoke.

"We can do better than that." I jerked my thumb at their truck. "If we can find the keys."

When the interior of the truck failed to yield anything but broken glass, the windshield having been one of the casualties of the fire fight, we had no choice but to search the bodies, something none of us were thrilled about. Feeling sympathy for Megan, I gave her a choice. She could go retrieve the crossbow and Uzi she had lost earlier, along with as many other weapons as she could find lying around, or she could help search the bodies. She took one look at the men in the back of the truck and left to find her weapons.

Meanwhile, Ken and I readied ourselves for the grisly work ahead. "Which one do you want?" he asked.

I noticed that one of the four in the truck bed had a sunburn on his left arm, as if he'd had that arm exposed to the intense sunlight. The right arm was fine. "This one." I was pretty sure I had found the driver.

Sure enough, his right pants pocket clinked when I patted it. Digging the keys out still proved to be a nasty business, though. The man had evidently been drinking for quite some time before Ken shot him, if the amount of urine staining his pants was any indication. We got the keys, and I started to drag the bodies out of the truck.

"Leave 'em in the truck." Ken's voice was gruff. "I have an idea."

I gave him a quizzical look but, after his earlier outburst, I wasn't about to argue. Together, we rolled the bodies further into the bed of the truck and closed the tailgate. Megan returned with several rifles slung over her shoulders and, within minutes, we were flying down the road at eighty miles an hour.

I had never been a conservative driver, but the way Ken slid and whipped around blind turns scared the hell out of me. "Think we'll make it?" I shouted to be heard above the combined roars of the engine and the wind screaming through the broken windshield.

Ken nodded. "No problem!"

"Think we'll make it in one piece?"

He grinned maliciously and eased the speed all the way down to seventy-five. "Better?"

Before I could reply, he slowed abruptly and swerved right at a mailbox marked "Kindley." The sudden turn slammed Megan into me and me into Ken. I was just getting ready to shout a commentary on his driving skills when he slammed on the brake, throwing us into the dash. The entire trip had lasted less than four minutes.

"End of the line, folks. Megan hurry and open the garage door. We don't want them to recognize the truck."

She jumped out and hastened to comply. I scrambled out after her and ran to the front door, which was of course, unlocked. As Ken pulled the truck into the garage, I rushed to the fireplace and opened the flue. Our hastily constructed plan called for us to attract the attention of the approaching bandits. As far as they knew, we were just ahead of them. Hopefully, they still thought they were driving us back to our home. We needed them to think this was it.

We started a fire and pulled the four bodies out of the back of the truck, dragging them inside through the garage door. We propped them up at various windows behind their own rifles. By the time we finished, from the outside of the house, it looked as if someone was standing guard, waiting for trouble.

"This is what you wanted them for?"

"Yeah."

I shuddered. "What exactly did you do in the Marines?"

"Whatever needed to be done." He turned away without further comment.

Ken and I took positions in the brush around the house. Megan climbed a massive oak and hid in its huge branches above a small fork in the trail. From there, she would have a perfect sniper's view of the two possible routes to the house. I ducked into some bushes on the side of the trail nearest the edge of the clearing. Ken handed me one end of a roll of kite string he had found in the Kindley's house and ran further down the trail unwinding it behind him.

We would wait until the bandits were busy watching the house, then Megan would start things rolling with some strategically placed shots. Ken and I had opted to depend upon our knives and surprise rather than firearms since our positioning would put us in each other's line of fire.

So we waited. And waited. It reminded me of the night of the bombs. Each time I checked my watch, I expected to find that ten minutes had slipped by. Instead, only two had passed. My imagination kicked into overdrive. They must have slipped around us. Maybe they realized that we'd circled back to the Robertson's, and they had turned back after us. I knew a thousand things could have gone wrong, and I convinced myself that at least one of them had.

Then I heard them. Five miles of hiking through the woods had obviously not improved their stalking skills at all. If anything, they sounded louder than ever. Many of them dragged their feet through the leaves and pine needles, stumbling over roots and branches as they walked, while others whispered complaints to their companions. A group of four of them came within five yards of where I squatted in the bushes between two trees. They peered out of the trees at the Kindley house, saying something about smoke, but I couldn't tell if they were worried about my smoke bombs, or if they were talking about the smoke from the fireplace. I didn't care, as long as they kept their attention focused on the house.

Trying not to move any more than absolutely necessary, I quietly scanned the area for the others. I knew there were still at least four more in the band, but where were they? A hint of movement to my right revealed that two more had just passed beneath Megan's hiding place.

That left two. I looked back down the trail and saw them trudging along, completely ignorant of the slight movement in the pile of pine needles between two trees. A moment after they passed it, I tugged on the kite string and the needles rose and dispersed, leaving Ken's dark form in their place as he stood and began to sneak up behind the pair, a knife in each hand, eyes hard. From my vantage, I could see their deaths in Ken's eyes and felt a moment of compassion. Then I remembered Pat Robinson. I turned to my group, machete in my right hand, Bowie in my left.

Careful to keep a tree between myself and Ken's quarry, I stood slowly, catching Megan's eye. I nodded, and she rose to her knees in the crook of two of those enormous branches, raised the Uzi, sighted in on the two below her, and opened fire.

As soon as she did, the four in front of me spun to face her. I waded in from behind with the machete, and things moved in a blur from there. I decapitated the first of them before the others even knew I was on them. At almost the same time, I drove the Bowie knife high into the back of another and felt it lodge in his spine. With no time to work it loose, I left it, spinning to confront the other two. Both of them tried to bring their rifles to bear, but the quarters were too close. I slashed one across his left shoulder as he turned, then reversed direction and jabbed the point upward through his throat. He died instantly, wrenching the machete from my grip as he fell.

The last man succeeded in getting his barrel up, but I was practically on top of him. I slid right, parried the rifle barrel, and slipped up alongside him. A head butt and a hard uppercut broke his nose and cracked ribs, loosening his grip on the rifle. I yanked it out of his grasp and slammed the butt into his diaphragm as hard as I could. He went to his knees with a wheezing exhalation, gagging until I silenced him with the rifle stock on the base of his skull.

I whirled to see how Ken was doing just in time to see the last of his two drop to the ground, bleeding profusely from the neck. Looking back toward the oak tree, I saw Megan jumping down from the lowest branch.

It was over.

Less than ten seconds had passed since Megan's first shot. Megan's two were unequivocally dead, as were both of Ken's. Of my group, two were dead, and one was dying with a knife in his back. The last one was unconscious with a bloody nose, broken ribs, and a nasty bump on the back of his skull.

With no minor trepidation, I yanked the knife from the spine of the dying freebooter, knowing as I did so that it would likely kill him. It did, leaving us with a lone survivor and an ethical question that none of us wanted to deal with.

Should we kill him, finishing what we had started, or rather, what *they* had started? Or should we let him live? To be, or not to be? This perverted version of Hamlet's dilemma now faced us squarely in the guise of this helpless young man.

"Kill him," Ken said bluntly. He looked at me with the pained expression of a person caught between two equally distasteful choices. "You're the one who said we would have to kill them all."

He pointed to the unconscious form on the ground. "Kill him, and it's over."

He was right but, still, I hesitated, my emotions clashing with my logic. "How will you feel about it when we do kill him?"

I intentionally used the plural pronoun so that he couldn't distance himself from the event. "He's beaten and helpless. Hell, Ken, he may die anyway! But do you really want to live with the idea that we killed him in cold blood?"

"Don't try that judge, jury, and executioner philosophical crap on me! This guy is a murderer and a rapist! He and his buddies killed John and Pat. How many others have they killed? For that matter, how many more would they have killed if we hadn't gotten them today?"

"I don't know." I shook my head wearily. I was exhausted, tired of the whole situation, both mentally and physically. Still shaking my head, I handed Ken the crimson coated knife that I had just pulled from the other man. "If you're that determined, if you are that sure you're right, then go ahead. Because I honestly don't know what's right and what's wrong at this point. All I know is, I don't want anything to do with it." I took the coward's way out and headed for the house.

Megan followed behind me, and we left Ken staring at the bloody knife in his hand.

A couple of minutes after Megan and I walked into the house, I heard the back door slam behind us. Turning, I saw Ken standing in the kitchen with the would-be bandit slung over his shoulders. "We need to get him to the hospital."

CHAPTER 9

* * JULY 4 / EVENING * *

Le ciel (de Plencus la cité) nous presage,
Par clers insignes & par estoilles fixes,
Que de son change subit s'approche l'aage,
Ne pour son bien, ne pour ses malefices.

The sky (of Plancus' city) forebodes to us
Through clear signs and fixed stars,
That the time of its sudden change is approaching,
Neither for its good, nor for its evils.

Nostradamus – *Century 3, Quatrain 46*

The next few hours were difficult for all of us. At first the police,
led by the intrepid Chief James Kelland, confiscated our weapons

107

and threw Ken and me in jail. Of course, the weapons we had when we walked into the hospital were not the same weapons we had used against the freebooters. We had dropped them and Megan off at the house with instructions for the women to hide them, as well as all of our other firearms. Then Ken and I told Kelland a story wherein we had disarmed a few of the bandits and turned their own weapons against them.

He wasn't having any of it. It was a stupid idea on our part anyway. We hadn't taken into consideration a major flaw in our reasoning. It was soon brought to our attention when the kid we had lugged into the hospital recovered enough to talk almost immediately. He told a story about a group of men who had attacked him and his innocent friends as they partied. He claimed several men and a young girl had attacked his friends for no apparent reason. He stated that the young girl had killed two men with a rifle, two with a crossbow, and one with her bare hands.

The questioning began in earnest, and I began to have second thoughts on the wisdom of having spared the kid's life.

In light of his story, I figured it was time for us to tell the truth, starting with the gunshots we'd heard earlier that afternoon. The only thing we held back was the existence of our supply stash. I was still unwilling to give that up, and I guessed by Ken's silence on the subject that he agreed.

Our only problem was that since we had already lied once, Kelland was trying very hard to try to rip our story to shreds. And he loved every minute of it. The first thing he did was separate us so they could question us individually and hopefully get conflicting stories. We each went into interrogation rooms just like in the movies, only they always appeared larger in the movies. I didn't think this was terribly smart of him. After all, he'd already allowed us to stay together earlier while I told him what had happened.

After we were separated, Kelland sent an officer to question Ken. He evidently wanted the pleasure of making me squirm all to himself. Most of the questioning was pretty predictable.

"Y'all heard gunshots?"

"Yeah, we already told you that."

"How far away were they?"

"We couldn't tell."

"So you decided to find out?"

"Yes."

"Y'all dressed up like GI Joe, went trompin' off through the woods huntin' for a few gunshots?"

"It wasn't just a few gunshots; it sounded more like a war."

"And y'all went lookin' for a war? Sounds pretty stupid to me."

"We had to find out what was going on. With the phones out, we couldn't very well call the police."

"You gettin' smart with me? I don't like it when folks smart off to me."

"I'm not smarting off. Just stating facts. We couldn't call the police. Amber had the van, so we couldn't send someone to get the police. The only option we had left was to investigate for ourselves."

"So you ran through the forest, found your war, jumped into the middle of it, and whooped up on twenty to twenty-five men? That's seven to one odds, boy! You expect us to believe that you, your nigger friend, and a scrawny little girl could each take on six grown men?"

I held my anger in check. "We took them by surprise, in small groups. That way we only had to take a few at a time."

"So you admit you jumped them without provocation!"

"They killed John Robinson!"

"You saw 'em do it?"

"No. But we saw them raping Pat Robinson!"

"Was she protestin'?"

"She was tied to a table!"

"Maybe she liked it that way."

"With her husband's dead body lying in the yard a few yards away?"

"How did you know he was dead? Could be havin' her husband play dead while she got it on with a bunch of men was just some kinky sex thing with them."

It went on like that for nearly an hour. It seemed his main goal was to try to implicate me, or rather us, in the murder of several innocent individuals. I knew he didn't like me, but I hadn't thought it was anywhere near that bad.

Or maybe he just wanted to see me squirm.

At any rate, he had questioned me for nearly an hour when another officer stuck his head in and called him outside. Kelland returned a few minutes later with a manila folder and a rather strange expression when he looked up at me.

He kept doing that, glancing up at me with that look, then reading some more. What the hell was he reading, anyway? It was as if he didn't quite know what to make of me. He stood inside the door reading through the folder for a minute more before he spoke again.

"When I heard that kid's story in the hospital, I guessed the 'young girl' he talked about must either be your wife or your daughter. Especially since, according to your 'killer hijackers' report," he waved a sheet of paper from the folder at me, "both of them have already killed people."

A chill ran up my spine at the way he said that. As if I wasn't already worried enough, now he was after my wife and daughter.

"So I sent a couple of officers over to pick them up."

Oh, Lord.

"By the way, they're here now, along with Mrs. Simms and your boy."

He smiled a little at the anguish in my expression before he went on. "I also sent some men over to the Kindley's and the Robinson's."

Finally! Concern for my family was somewhat alleviated by the thought that we were finally getting somewhere. "And they confirmed exactly what I told you, didn't they?"

"They confirmed that there were a lot of bodies layin' around. That don't mean nothin' 'cept somebody killed a bunch of people out there." And again, that look.

But I thought that I possibly understood it now. Kelland was the kind of man who respected strength, or what he understood of strength anyway. He still didn't like me, but to his way of thinking, anyone who could take on odds like the ones he had mentioned earlier must be a strong individual. It didn't matter that we had at no time faced anywhere near that many opponents at once. The way he saw it was simply that we had faced impossible odds and won.

He respected that; ergo, he respected me, maybe even feared me a little.

He moved to the table and sat down across from me again. Scooting his chair back, he propped his feet on the table and began a new tactic. "You know, when Chief Davis died, and I took over, one of the first things

I did was to read the statement you filed on your run-in with those hijackers." He waved the report at me again. "Then I sent two men out to the site."

I wondered where this was heading.

"They pretty much confirmed what you said about the ambushed convoy. All the wreckage and the bodies matched your report. And they found the hidden little road where you said it was and the cabin in the clearing." He peered intently into my eyes. "And they found three bodies in that clearing."

"Three?" We had killed two, Edgar and Michael. Who was the third?

"One was a man whose throat had been punctured," *Edgar*, I counted. "Another man had been shot in the back." *Michael*. "And the third man had a hole in his shoulder and a broken knee." *Larry*.

He must not have recovered. I remembered leaving him tied up, but we'd left his left hand untied, his wounded arm. It would have been painful, but I felt sure he would be able to get his right hand untied from his ankles with a little work, unless he had reopened the wound in his shoulder and bled to death in the process. Why hadn't I thought of that at the time?

"He must have bled to death," I said lamely.

Kelland nodded. "That's what the officers guessed."

"So what does this mean?"

"It means that you killed three men on the way out here, and then reported it to the authorities as soon as you could." He sat back in his chair having found something in my reaction that satisfied him that I wasn't hiding anything. "That tells me you're either honest, or sneaky. When I mentioned three bodies, it surprised you. You didn't expect three of them to be dead. That leads me to believe you're honest. And it tells me you didn't intend to kill the third guy, even though according to your report, he was gonna kill you."

He remained silent for a moment, tapping his pencil on the table between us before he continued, "I took over when Davis died because my men and the mayor thought I was the best man for the job. So do I. I'm good at it. It may not seem like much to you, bein' from a big city and all, but right now, right here, I'm the best there is. And I learned a long time ago that in this job, you've got to learn to trust your gut.

"The facts that we have, Mr. Dawcett, say that you are either a magnet for bad luck, or you're a homicidal maniac. Either way, I'm not wild about having you in my jurisdiction." He surprised me then by smiling. "But I think we had that conversation yesterday.

"A homicidal maniac wouldn't be surprised to find one of his victims was dead. He wouldn't give details on where the bodies were and how he took them by surprise, and he sure as hell wouldn't drag one of them back to the hospital. All of your bodies are right where you said they'd be.

"I don't think you're lying." He swung his legs off of the table and leaned toward me. "'Course, I don't think you're tellin' me the whole truth, either. There's the matter of a cabin full of supplies my boys found in that clearing by those bodies."

Leaning on the table, he queried, "Why would a person as much into survival as you say you are leave all of those supplies when you could've just loaded them in your van and taken them with you?" There was obviously a lot more to Chief Kelland than first met the eye. "Maybe 'cause your van was already full?"

Ouch! And he was just getting started. "And what happened to the weapons those hijackers had?"

Uncomfortable, I tried to answer that one. "The two survivors must have taken them."

He shrugged. "Could be. But I don't think so. You'd have been stupid to leave them there," he drawled. "I think you got 'em. I think you got all their weapons. And I bet if we search y'all's place real good, we'll find that you folks have been hoardin' enough food and supplies to last you a long, long time."

No, *uncomfortable* wasn't a strong enough word. *Scared.* That was the word. In this post-holocaust version of Rejas, Texas, just how serious an offense had hoarding become? Through a very dry mouth, I asked, "Why would you think that?"

"Because most of the boxes y'all left in that cabin were marked as food. You left the food and a good selection of tools and supplies. That tells me you already had a van full of that kind of stuff. By the way, the food in that cabin went into our community food supply."

Was that what he was after? Our food and supplies? "You'd need a warrant to search the place."

"Says who?" He smiled. "What are you gonna do? Call the police?"

He had me with my own words. Kelland leaned back and raised his hands in a placating gesture. "Don't worry, Mr. Dawcett. I ain't sendin' my boys out there. Hoarding ain't a crime out here. Not yet, anyway. I just want you to know you ain't hidin' near as much as you thought you were.

"See, I'd rather have you workin' with me than against me. Especially seein' how the last bunch that went up against you ended up."

"I didn't do it by myself."

"Yup." He pulled another sheet of paper out of the file on the table. "Kenneth Simms spent six years as a scout in the U.S. Marines. I got nothin' but respect for a man who served in the Gulf."

"Is that why you called him a nigger?" I couldn't let that slide.

It didn't seem to faze him. "Nope, I did that just to piss you off. I figured you shared a shelter with the man, broke bread with him, and spilled blood with him. You wouldn't go through all that with someone you didn't trust and care about. I figured if I made you mad, maybe you'd slip up, give something away."

The man was a lot smarter than I had ever given him credit for. But he had all but told me that he no longer thought I was a cold-blooded killer. "Look, Kelland, what exactly is it you want from me?"

He stopped for a second as if considering the question. "Well, at first I wanted your ass in jail. More than that, I wanted you hangin' from a rope." He gave me that infuriating grin again before he continued. "I thought I had me a killer on my hands, the likes of which we ain't seen since the Reverend Jim Jones. Now, though, I think you just have a talent for bein' in the wrong place at the wrong time. I guess you really did me a favor out there at the Kindley's place, gettin' them boys like you did. No tellin' how many others they'd 've killed if y'all hadn't stopped 'em."

He paused only a second before surprising me again by standing smoothly and extending his hand for me to shake. "So I want to thank you. And I want to apologize for the way I treated you. I had no call for it. And most of all, I want you to think about somethin' you told me yesterday. You told me you weren't city folk anymore, that you're Rejas folk now. Well, Rejas needs help, all the help it can get. Think about that." Somewhat dumbfounded, I shook his proffered hand.

"I trust my gut, Mr. Dawcett. I don't like you much; you're too selfish for my taste. But you're no cold blooded killer, either." He waved at the door. "You're free to go."

A very sobered individual, I walked to the door. During the course of the last few minutes, I had grown to respect the man that I had before despised. He had given me a new perspective on things. I reached for the knob, then stopped. Staring intently at the doorframe, I spoke again. "Something I didn't put on that questionnaire."

Turning to face him, I took a deep breath. "I'm a self-defense instructor. Or I was. Anyway, I'd be happy to train any of your men that are interested." I grinned weakly. "No charge."

"Looks like you probably know what you're doing in that area, too." He returned the grin. "I'll pass the word to my men. It's a start, Mr. Dawcett, it's a start."

* * July 5 * *

The next day Ken, Megan, and I found ourselves answering questions for Mr. Fred Morgan, the top reporter for *The Rejas Chronicle*. He was also the editor and owner. Truth be told, he *was The Rejas Chronicle. The Chronicle*, it turned out, was a small mimeographed newspaper, not much more than a few sheets of paper stapled together, mostly consisting of announcements and official notices of the goings on of what was left of the town government and where they needed work. Ours was just the type of story *The Chronicle* needed, Morgan told us, to break the monotony. Readers were tired of reading nothing other than where volunteers were needed and who had died in the night.

"'Justice Triumphs over Evil,'" he exclaimed enthusiastically, his hands tracing imaginary headlines. "It's just what the doctor ordered!"

We were surprised to find that news of our battle had spread so rapidly, even more surprised to find that we were considered heroes by half of the town. As I showed him to the door, I asked how he had found out about everything.

He chuckled. "You kidding? I'll bet y'all hadn't been out of the jailhouse five minutes 'fore Kelland had a runner over to see me and give me most of the details. Said it might give folks a little bit of sunshine in the middle of all the gloom that's been goin' 'round."

Kelland had again surprised me. I shook Mr. Morgan's hand before he left.

The next day, we all got a kick out of reading about our incredible victory over a veritable army of marauders. Then I sobered as I read the notice beneath the story.

VOLUNTEERS NEEDED FOR BURIAL DETAIL
Death toll nears 1,000. Rejas City Council to begin using emergency mass graves. Volunteers please report to Jake Olson, Rejas Sanitation Dept.

Ken and I volunteered our backs and Ken's digging equipment for the excavation, and so the next couple of weeks were filled with a hectic, morbid activity. Amber only made it home sporadically, as the hospital was unbelievably overburdened, and she was often simply too exhausted at the end of the day to make the drive home. After the fifth day, on her second trip home since she had left, she said there were rumors circulating that they would soon have to implement a triage program and offer a euthanasia alternative to those victims with little or no hope for recovery. Two days later, the rumors proved to be true. The death toll had risen to more than nine hundred fifty and showed no signs of slowing down.

Burial detail was a gruesome but necessary duty if we wanted to minimize the spread of disease. Everyone knew it. Everyone hated it. Everyone did it.

We worked in staggered teams of ten, one day on burial duty, two days on search detail, two days on pickup duty, and two days off. Standard operating procedure for search detail was to knock on the door and hope someone would answer. If someone were home, we would introduce ourselves, explain what we were doing and why, and ask if they had any pertinent information on any of their neighbors. Then, we would mark their mailbox with a white X.

If no one answered, we would have to break into the house and search it, hoping it would be empty. If empty, the mailbox got a green X. If we found a body, a red X went on the mailbox and the door, and we made note of the address.

The following day's pickup detail would take the "red list" of addresses, don their gas masks, and pick up the bodies. When finished, they would mark over the red Xs with yellow circles. The circles indicated the house was empty, but still a potential health hazard. Then they would deliver those bodies, along with any picked up from the hospital, to the current burial site. It was a hell of a way to meet people, but I found myself gaining many close friends as we worked side-by-side loading and unloading our gruesome cargoes.

This went on for two more weeks. Finally, all of the homes in the area had been searched and cleared, and the number of fallout deaths tapered off at the hospital. The total death count for the first month after D-day tallied two thousand, nine hundred eighty-nine, nearly a third of the town's population.

There would have an even greater number of deaths had it not been for a swift education campaign mounted by the Church of Jesus Christ of Latter-day Saints. As soon as the first explosions occurred, giant flashbulb brilliance in that clear June morning sky, the Rejas Mormon Church had begun passing out flyers describing the effects of nuclear weapons and their aftermath. People were told what to expect for those next few weeks and warned to stay indoors and seal up their windows and doors as airtight as possible. The flyers described various methods for sealing the home against fallout, inspecting, cleaning, and preserving foods, symptoms of radiation sickness, and other items of interest for the times ahead.

The ward bishop personally went to the mayor to volunteer the services of his entire congregation. It was unfortunate that more people hadn't paid attention to him. Many, if not most, of the deaths might possibly have been avoided.

The mayor himself was one of those deaths, though whether or not his could have been avoided was debatable. He had been seventy-nine years old and in poor health to begin with. The combination of age, radiation, and the strain of the current situation proved to be too much for him, and we laid him to rest in the last of the communal graves on August seventh. On August eighth, the search teams reported that the last of the homes in the area had been searched and marked, and the ninth marked the end of the flood of deaths from the hospital.

We closed the last of those huge graves on August tenth amidst a confusing blend of emotions. Sorrow and grief for the dead mixed with relief, anxiety, and hope for the living. The townsfolk seemed drawn to the gravesite, coming in a steady stream to pay their last respects. When we finally finished covering that final, massive interment, an impromptu crowd of hundreds of mourners gathered. As Ken shut down the last dozer, the still, unnatural silence was deafening. No motors, no voices murmuring, no traffic noise in the background or power lines humming—only the sound of the wind through the trees broke the quiescence of the moment.

Then someone began to sing.

It was a hymn, of course. Anguished and mournful, and yet expressing a hope and a faith so poignant and beautiful as to be painful. Tears formed in my eyes as I looked around, searching for the source of that fine baritone. I was an avowed agnostic and had been for years, but at that moment, I envied that soul his faith in what was to come. I looked at the sea of faces gathered there at the burial mound as more and more people joined in until it seemed the very sound of their voices could wash the pain and fear from my soul. I wept openly, as did most of the others present.

I don't know how long I stayed there listening as they sang hymn after hymn. Individuals came and went, but the crowd itself had become a living entity possessed of an angelic voice that would not be silenced for many hours.

* * INTERLUDE * *

During the next several weeks, the town of Rejas went through many changes. Weather patterns settled down, so we weren't constantly worried about hot winds or rain. We no longer sunburned as easily, either. The ozone layer had evidently begun to replenish itself.

We discussed the subject around the barbeque grill on several occasions. Having no television or radio meant that we usually spent much of each night in deep discussion of recent events and, since the stove no longer worked, the grill out back had become our regular gathering place in the evenings. The general consensus was that it had probably been a pretty simple process for Mother Nature to manufacture the O_3 once she no longer had to compete with industrial pollutants. Of course, none of us really knew for sure. It was yet another thing we would probably never know.

Of Rejas's seventeen Ham radio operators, all but two had lost their radios to EMP. Those huge antennae had collected much more than they were designed for, passing the pulse on to the delicate circuits of the radios. The two surviving radios had been disconnected and disassembled for repairs on D-day. They were connected to a couple of generators that had survived, and so far, they could talk to one another, but hadn't picked up any outside transmissions. The operators said they couldn't tell if that was because there simply wasn't anyone left with a transmitter, or if there was some kind of atmospheric interference left over from D-day that prevented it.

Chief Kelland relaxed the roadblocks around the town to allow "qualified" refugees to settle into some of the newly emptied homes, and the survivors in many of the smaller surrounding towns trickled in to take advantage. Small towns soon became ghost towns, and scouts reported more and more of the neighboring municipalities were nothing more than empty buildings. Some of the inhabitants joined us in Rejas, and some moved elsewhere to try and find friends or family in other parts of the country. But no one seemed to want to stay in a small town anymore.

Those who came to Rejas were allowed one day to fill out the good old "Assimilation Form" and three days to settle in. Five days after they passed through the roadblock, they were to report to the community labor pool, located in the parking lot across from City Hall. Failure to comply resulted in Kelland and his "boys" visiting the offending party. If they had no reasonable excuse, they were unceremoniously railroaded out of town. Rejas had no time for freeloaders.

Assuming they did follow the rules given when they passed the roadblocks, then during their settling-in period, their forms were examined to see if they had any critically needed skills or supplies. If they did, they or their supplies were sent where needed. It was considered the price of admission.

If they had no skills or supplies, they paid for their new homes with menial labor until someone in a more skilled field needed a trainee. Not many wanted to spend the rest of their days as a grunt, so trainee positions were highly sought after. Commerce was all done in barter, and if you didn't have goods to trade, you had to have a needed skill.

Trainees were selected primarily by prior experience, and secondly by the amount of time they had served in the labor pool. But exceptions were made if necessary. For instance, to help construct and run a forge, I needed someone with a strong back and arms.

The man I selected had obviously been a body builder before D-day and had the physique I felt would be necessary, but he had only been in town for a week. His name was Mark Roesch, a pre-D criminal trial lawyer. There wasn't much demand for lawyers anymore, so he went into the pool. When I picked him for my trainee, it raised protests from Brad Stephenson, an older man who had been in for two months. Two months was longer than anyone else, so he would normally have gotten the next shot at an apprenticeship based on this seniority.

Stephenson was in pretty fair shape himself, as anyone would be after two months at hard labor, but he was still not in the same league as Mark. I tried to explain that the job required a lot of strenuous activity. I didn't want to come right out and say it but, with his age, I was afraid he might not be able to handle the work.

"Take us both, then," Brad pleaded. "I'm sixty-two years old, and I'm not getting any younger. I need to learn a trade that'll help keep me alive, and there isn't much call for accountants nowadays."

Seeing my hesitation, he pressed his case. "I might not be able to swing a hammer all day, but I can pump the bellows as well as the next man, and I guarantee you I'll work till I drop if you just give me a chance."

I ended up taking both of them with the understanding that the one who performed best would keep the job, and the other would go back to the pool. I had no doubts as to which one of them would stay on, but I wanted to give Stephenson a fair chance. Both of them worked their tails off, and I fully expected them to develop a competitive animosity but, to my surprise, they quickly formed a tight friendship.

They further surprised me one morning a week later when I came back from teaching my self-defense classes and found that they had begun construction on a second forge. Brad explained their logic. "This way, if you get loaded down with work, between the three of us we can have both forges running and get twice the work out in nearly the same amount of time. Mark can run you and me both into the ground, but you and I can take shifts on the second forge and keep up with him that way."

I thought for a second and nodded. "Whose idea was this?"

Mark gestured to Brad. One thing I had noticed about Mark, he didn't talk unnecessarily. I got the impression that something had happened to him on the road to Rejas, but I hadn't asked, and he hadn't offered.

Everyone had a pre-D story. Most of them dealt with the deaths of friends and loved ones.

I had also learned that everyone dealt with their losses in their own way. Mark had turned to reticence and was comfortable with things the way they were for the time being.

I turned to Brad, who grinned affirmation. "Guess you figured I couldn't afford to send you back to the labor pool this way, right?"

His grin lost some of its confidence. "Well, the thought did cross my mind. But I figured it was a good idea any way you look at it." Then he got serious. "Look, Leeland, I know you said you only have time to teach one of us, and that you were only going to keep the best worker. And I know that I'm an old man who's never going to be able to keep up with you two on those forges. I agreed to those conditions, and I'll stick to that agreement. But I would like to stay and learn the trade. Just because I'm older doesn't mean I can't help you out." He laughed. "Hell, just cut my salary to whatever you think I'm worth."

I chuckled. Money was a thing of the past, and we all knew it. A person's value now hinged on what he could do, not how much money he made. "Mark, he'll cut into your learning time. How do you feel about it?"

Mark never hesitated. "I'd like him to stay. We work pretty well together. He thinks like I do. Always knows what I'm trying to do or say nearly as soon as I do." He paused to gather his thoughts before he went on. "You're the boss. You have to make the decision. But if I get a vote, I vote to let him stay."

Until then, I didn't think I had ever heard Mark string so many words together at one time. I figured he must feel pretty strongly about keeping Brad.

I turned back to Brad. "Building a second forge was a good idea, and I like anyone who can think for themselves that way." I offered my hand to seal the deal. "You stay as long as you want. I can afford a little more time when I know it'll pay off in the long run."

And so I acquired two apprentices for a skill I barely knew myself. It was a hell of a world we lived in.

* * *

After the mayor died, the town coasted along as if on autopilot for a while, but it soon became apparent that some sort of leadership would be necessary. On September twentieth, nominations were taken at a town meeting held in the Rejas Eagles Football Stadium, and on September twenty-seventh, Chief of Police James Kelland was elected mayor.

I sheepishly recalled the day he had come to ask Amber to work at the hospital. Wanting the excuse to humiliate him, I had waited almost eagerly for him to attempt to draw his revolver. My feelings had changed since that day, and I was a little ashamed. The man had just been doing his job.

That was what made Kelland such a good choice for mayor. He did whatever was necessary to get the job done. He didn't care if he hurt somebody's feelings, angered a mob, or stepped on somebody's toes in the process. He got the job done.

And if he didn't know how to do it, he would find someone that did. The man knew his limitations and had learned to draw on the talents and knowledge of those around him, allocating jobs as necessary.

One of the first things he did was appoint several committees to study the state of affairs locally and abroad. "I can't get nothin' done 'til I find out what needs doin'," he'd proclaimed.

The mayor coerced Ken into accepting a position as a "special advisor" to the new Chief of Police, Chris Henny, to help coordinate the town's defenses. Ken's experience in military tactics and weaponry made him a natural, and his popularity after the attack of the marauders didn't hurt any. Everyone knew him, and everyone was more than willing to cooperate with him.

I ended up as an aide to a couple of the mayor's committees. Sort of a jack-of-all-trades, master of none, I could often help pinpoint problems and leave others to work out the solutions. Debra volunteered to help organize reports from the committees to the new mayor, and as soon as her organizational abilities were recognized, Kelland snatched her up as his personal aide.

I directed the Resources Committee's attention to the fact that we needed to scrape the top few inches of soil off of as much of the farmland as was possible. If we waited much longer, the autumn rains would mix the fallout-contaminated topsoil with the deeper, cleaner soil too well to separate the two. Ken and his construction crew worked at the chore with bulldozers, dump trucks, and gas masks.

I also convinced them to supplement the present food stockpile, to which the Dawcett clan had finally donated a van full of provisions we had gotten from the pantries of many of the surrounding abandoned homes, with a hunting team. There was considerable opposition to that idea at first since the fear of fallout was still paramount in everyone's mind. Everyone knew the dangers of ingesting fallout, and most knew that local wildlife would have had to have eaten contaminated flora at some point since D-day in order to survive. So, they were understandably hesitant to risk eating "contaminated" meat. With the help of one of the doctors from the hospital and several books from my personal library, I finally convinced them it was safe as long as proper precautions were taken.

The chosen hunters were instructed to pick only the healthiest-looking animals. They would field strip the animals as soon as they made the kill and leave behind any organ meat, as well as the muscle closest to the bone. Organ tissue and bone marrow were where any fallout the animal had inhaled or consumed would be concentrated. That would provide Rejas with safe meat and leave some of the hardier scavengers with some extra food as well.

The bishop of the Mormon Church and several hundred of his followers searched every abandoned home in the area, gathering any supplies that might have been left behind, and locating several small gardens that still had some usable fruits and vegetables. They added everything they found to the stockpile, canning the fruits and veggies in mason jars.

The LDS group grew by leaps and bounds as the locals saw that they weren't some outlandish cult, but just good God-fearing people whose beliefs, though quite different in some respects, did happen to include preparing for whatever tests God might fling at them. The LDS congregation before the bombs had numbered about two hundred strong in Rejas. The day after, Rejas found that caravans of Mormon refugees had arrived in the night to swell their ranks to nearly eight hundred. Others had trickled in over the last few weeks, and there had been a rash of conversions, as well, swelling their ranks to more than fifteen hundred members.

Though Rejas had begun rationing immediately after D-day, fuel was another immediate concern, and all of the stations were quickly down to critical levels. In reality, this was actually a threefold problem.

First, we had to find enough fuel to keep Rejas functional over the next few years. That should be enough time to determine whether the country was ever going to get back on its feet, or if the U.S.A. was gone for good. If the former, we could probably count on some kind of assistance eventually. If the latter, we were on our own and would have to search for long-term solutions.

Next, after we found enough fuel to keep us going for a while, we would have to find a way to preserve it. That problem was more difficult. Fossil fuel would store only for a matter of months before autoxidation set in, the decomposition process which would break the fuel down into a variety of lacquers and gums, rendering it unsuitable for use. I had read about it years ago and purchased two sixteen-ounce bottles of a fuel preservative that might prove to be the answer. Each bottle was guaranteed to prevent autoxidation for up to five years. Unfortunately, thirty-two ounces would only treat a hundred gallons, hardly enough to supply a whole town.

Enter Wayne Kelley, Rejas High School chemistry teacher. Wayne was able to analyze and duplicate enough of the preservative to treat millions of gallons. He claimed it was actually a simple compound to copy, made of alcohols and other fairly common substances, and he soon had a small production facility set up in an abandoned warehouse.

The third part of the problem was transportation. None of that fuel would do us a bit of good in surrounding towns. We had to get it back to Rejas. So Kelland sent out an appeal through the *Chronicle* for volunteers.

First, we needed scouts to check neighboring towns and locate fuel, as well as any other usable items. They would take with them enough fuel preservative to treat any fuel tanks found.

Next, truck drivers were called for, anyone with experience in driving eighteen-wheelers.

Volunteers began pouring in immediately. Hundreds volunteered for the scouting runs, and fifty-eight truck drivers came forward, including three that had previous experience hauling gasoline. From those fifty-eight, Kelland selected the forty-eight that were in the best physical condition and divided them into two teams of twenty-four for our sixteen trucks. The remainder would serve as standby drivers.

Each team would take half of the trucks, three men per vehicle: one driver, one sleeping, and one riding shotgun— literally. Each truck had one person awake at all times, besides the driver, with a loaded firearm to discourage hijackers.

Within a month, the scouts had located and preserved enough gasoline and diesel to last Rejas for at least six years with a minimum of rationing.

So every few weeks one of two groups of twenty-four men armed with rifles, fuel pumps, radiation detectors and gas masks, went to nearby towns and returned with enough gasoline to fill the empty tanks at any of the twelve gas stations around town.

As expected, they did occasionally run into minor trouble. One of the first teams ventured too close to the suburbs of Houston during a bad storm and was scared silly when the winds blowing across the remains caused their PRDs to glow. Discretion being the better part of valor, they immediately donned their masks and turned tail.

On another occasion, a team ran into a small band of armed marauders that tried to hijack the convoy. Unfortunately for the would-be hijackers, the truck ran into *them*, and the team never looked back.

It began to look as if we might actually make it. Just like a mythical Phoenix rising from the ashes of its destruction, Rejas too began to gather its strength.

CHAPTER 10

* * APRIL / YEAR 3 * *

Le changement sera fort difficile,
Cité, prouince au change gain fera:
Coeur haut, prudent mis, chassé luy habile,
Mer, terre, peuple son estat changera.

The change will be very difficult:
City and province will gain by the change:
Heart high, prudent established, chased out one cunning,
Sea, land, people will change their state.
     Nostradamus – *Century 4, Quatrain 21*

Two years later, life had settled into a kind of routine. Amber, Ken, Cindy, Debra, Megan, Zach, and I had turned Amber's little goat ranch into more of a fortress by hiding caches of supplies and weapons in various places around the property. We were actually beginning to adapt to our new lifestyle, and I sometimes wondered how I had ever coped with the frantic pace of pre-D life.

"Debra? We're heading into town. Anything in particular I should look for?"

She came out of the kitchen wiping her hands on a shabby dishtowel before draping it over her shoulder. "See if you can find a hydrometer. Cindy says she thinks a couple of the car batteries are going bad." She paused, thinking a second. "Oh, and see if Sarah has any more cans of that condensed milk that she found. Maybe we can make some ice cream and get a little relief from this heat."

I gaped for a moment. "Is the freezer working?"

"Yep. Cindy hooked the invertor into the circuit so we'd have enough power to run a couple of appliances. I thought we could celebrate with some ice cream."

"Sounds amazing. I think I'm drooling a little." I tried to remember what else we needed for homemade ice cream. "What about rock salt?"

"I'll break up a piece of the salt lick."

"All right. The kids'll be tickled. Hell, *I'm* tickled." I kissed her and started to pull away, but she grabbed my shirt and extended the kiss for several seconds longer.

"Come on, Dad!" Zach shouted impatiently from outside. "Let's go already!"

I scowled as Debra giggled at me.

"How about we pick this back up later?" She waggled her eyebrows suggestively.

I grinned. "Sounds like a date."

"Daaaaddd!"

"How old are you, Zachary?" I yelled.

He hesitated. "Ten."

"If you ever want to make it to eleven, you'd better quit yelling at your dad when he's trying to smooch your mom!"

"Ewww!"

"Go on." Debra pushed me back and turned me toward the open door. "I'll see you when you get back." As I stepped away, she popped me with the damp dishtowel.

"Hey!" I jumped and grabbed my hindquarters, rubbing briskly to take the sting out.

I turned to find her already turning away. "Hurry back," she shot over her shoulder, "and I'll be happy to take a look at that injury for you."

I smiled at the implied promise and walked out the door.

Five minutes later, I had the cart hitched to the back of the motorcycle. I tossed a few bundles of trade goods in it, and Zach clambered aboard to sit in on top of them. Megan climbed on the motorcycle seat behind me and, as we pulled slowly down the street, she yelled in my ear, "You think she knows what we're up to?"

I twitched my shoulder in a lazy shrug. "She probably knows something's up, but there's no way she could know exactly what."

"Um, have you *met* Mom?"

"Yeah," I conceded. "You've got a point." But there was nothing I could do about what she might or might not know, so I didn't worry too much about it.

Twenty minutes later, we were winding our way through the foot traffic at the edge of the market square. I parked the motorbike in front of an abandoned convenience store and killed the engine. Slinging one of the trade bundles over my shoulder, I tossed the second to Megan, took Zachary's hand, and the three of us waded into the crowd.

The market had started as a simple enough thing. With little to no electricity to run internal lighting or air conditioning, shopkeepers had taken to setting tables outside their doors. The practice had grown, spawning more tables and stalls, quickly spilling out into the streets until the town council simply barricaded off a four-block area of town and allowed it to grow into what everyone now referred to as *the market*.

We wandered through the makeshift stalls, looking at some items, avoiding others, winding our way through the buzzing and shouting of the ever-present dickering. At the outskirts, we saw the normal handcrafted items: candles, soaps, woodcarvings, pottery. As we burrowed deeper into the crowd, we also came across plenty of scavenged goods such as canned foods, car parts, and some small electronics like CD players or flashlights still in the original plastic. We had found that many of the less complex, basic electronics that hadn't been plugged in or connected to batteries on D-day still worked, and those still in the original packaging were almost guaranteed to work. The more intricate items that depended on delicate circuitry had a lesser chance of working. And of course, all of them still required some sort of power source.

But here in the market, that too was available. Generator kits were prevalent, based on everything from bicycle generators, to automobile parts and current inverters. They were fairly common at the moment, but I feared the day would soon come when we would no longer be able to find the parts necessary to make them. Windmill and waterwheel kits to turn the generators were also a valued commodity and, when I heard some of the haggling being done for them, I was thankful we already had ours.

I saw my goal ahead and shouldered my way through the crowd to Wayne Kelley's booth. Wayne had been Rejas High School's chemistry teacher, and had put his education to good use. He had everything from fuel preservatives to perfumes available at his booth. If you wanted something that required a knowledge of practical chemistry, Wayne was your man.

"Hey Wayne, how's business?"

"Leeland!" He smiled. "Business is good. You here to make it better?"

"I hope so." I gestured. "Hand Mr. Kelley that bundle, would you, Megan?"

She hefted the bundle off her shoulder and slung it to an empty spot on his table. Wayne untied the knot and unrolled half a dozen uncured goatskins. He thumbed through them, checking the thickness and quality of the skin. "Still no kids?"

"Nope. We still don't have enough stock to warrant slaughtering any of the kids. We need to let them breed another year or so. Maybe then."

Wayne sighed. "Well, Connie will be happy to get these. Same arrangement?"

I nodded. "You process them and keep half."

Wayne stuck out his hand. "Deal. You want the skins from the last batch?"

"If they're ready."

"Just give me a second." Wayne stepped back into his shop.

A moment later, his wife came out to greet us. "Hi, Leeland, Megan." She turned a special smile to Zachary. "My goodness, Zachary, you get bigger every time I see you. What are you doing in town?"

Zach loved the attention. "We're shoppin' for Mom's birthday."

Connie turned to me. "It's Deb's birthday?"

"Day after tomorrow. But there's no need waiting to the last minute."

"Two days before her birthday isn't last minute?"

I raised my hands. "This one's just a matter of timing."

Wayne came out and saved me from further explanation as he handed a smaller bundle back to Megan. "Here you go. Four skins of the eight you brought in last month. Want to examine them?"

"No need." I leaned in close. "I know where you live."

He and his wife both chuckled.

"Thanks Wayne, Connie. See you in class tomorrow?"

"We'll be there."

As we headed toward our next stop, Megan tugged my sleeve. "Dad, you mind if I stop by the library?"

"I don't see why not. What are you after?"

"Nothing really. I just kinda wanted to look around." Her voice trailed off as she looked away evasively.

"She wants ta go see An-drew!" Zach squealed. Megan flipped a quick kick at the seat of his pants. "Ow! Dad, Megan kicked—"

"I don't want to hear it."

"But she—"

I pointed a finger in his face. "Not a word, do you understand?"

"Yes, sir."

"Don't pick fights, and you won't get hurt." I took the bundle from Megan and handed it to Zachary, while pretending not to notice the glare he shot at his older sister. "All right, Megan, meet us at Sarah's shop in an hour."

She bounced up on her tiptoes and kissed my cheek. "Thanks Dad." And she threaded her way into the crowd.

I watched her fade into the mass of market-goers for a moment before taking my son by the hand. "Okay Zach, now tell me about this Andrew kid."

Zachary grinned conspiratorially. "He's not a kid, Dad. He's the same age as Megan."

I smiled. "That old, huh?"

"Uh huh. He's Mr. Eric's son."

"Eric Petry? From the morning classes?"

"Yes, sir. I think that's where they met." He leaned close to me. "I caught 'em kissin' in the woods last week."

I was definitely surprised. Megan had never let on that she had a boyfriend. But I knew Eric and recalled meeting his son a few times. He had seemed a likeable enough young man. And Eric was a good friend. He was one of the town's police officers, and a third-degree black belt in Shotokan karate. We had met him through the self-defense classes I had volunteered to Jim Kelland.

Most mornings, we taught a growing number of Bruce Lee wannabes in the clearing behind Amber's house at sunrise. Lessons usually lasted two to three hours, depending on the number of people who attended and how difficult the day's activities were.

When we had first begun the classes after the last of the burials, it had been just Megan and me teaching. Four of Kelland's men had come by for training. We taught them exercises to stretch the tendons and ligaments in their arms and legs, and showed them the proper way to do some basic *katas*, or forms, to strengthen their legs and improve their balance.

Then, we showed them some of what they really wanted to learn: the actual self-defense aspect of the arts—the innumerable joint locks of small circle jujitsu, basic grappling techniques, and the first twelve variations of Kali's angles of attack. They had been impressed enough to convince others to join.

Word of the Kindley Massacre—their name, not mine—had spread quickly after the article in the *Chronicle* and, as other attacks occurred, people began trickling in by twos and threes. Eric had shown up the second week to volunteer his skills, and we were soon teaching anywhere from fifteen to fifty people each day.

While I considered the local police officers to be the core of the classes, there were also housewives, grocers, shop owners, and mechanics—to use a common cliché, people from all walks of life. I wished my school in Houston had been so full.

And sometime during all that, Andrew had evidently gone from being one of the students to being my daughter's boyfriend. It had happened under my very nose, and I'd been completely oblivious.

I sighed and rubbed Zach's head affectionately. "Well, your sister's growing up. You'll be better off staying out of her business."

He furrowed his brows and turned to look up at me. "Is she gonna get married and move away?"

"I'm sure she will, eventually. But probably not for a while yet."

He grinned. "When she does, can I have her room?"

I laughed aloud. "We'll see about that later."

"When?"

"Later."

"Later when?"

"When she moves out. For now, though, we have more shopping to do."

We shouldered through the crowd and eventually made our way to a darkened shop with an open front door. Walking in, I heard the methodical sharp tinging of metal on metal from the back room, and I shouted, "Travis, you here?" The tinging stopped, and a shuffling took its place. Seconds later, a white-haired, bespectacled head peered around the doorframe.

"That you, Leeland?"

"Yep."

"Gimme a sec, an' I'll get your order."

I heard more shuffling, and Travis came limping out of the back carrying several items. He casually tossed me a pair of hand-tooled goatskin boots. They were loosely cut, and gusseted to adapt for wear under or over pants. I looked at the bottom and laughed aloud. "Tire treads? Really?"

Travis nodded. "Plenty of it around, and it's made to last with two tons of metal ridin' on it. Figured it'd last with yer ornery ass walkin' on it for a while."

I held one boot to the bottom of my foot to check the size. "Looks perfect."

"Well, that ain't no way to check it. Put th' damn thangs on. I wanna see how they fit, too."

I wasted no time skinning off my worn out tennis shoes. I was embarrassed by the condition of my socks, but didn't let it stop me as I slid my legs into the calf-high leather boots. I wove the leather thong through the grommets on either side of the folded gusset and tied it over my pant legs. Standing tentatively, I took a few steps.

"Well? How do they fit?"

After walking around the room, I finally turned back to him. "They're a little stiff, but they'll wear in soon enough. I think they'll do, Travis."

He harrumphed at me. "'Course they'll do. I don't make crap. That's why you come to me."

"That's true enough. You have the rest of it?"

He pointed to the bench, and I walked my new boots over to see the other items. Travis glanced over at Zachary. "Yer daddy made you a knife yet, son?"

Zachary mumbled something.

"Sorry, son, but ah couldn't hear ya."

"Yes sir, but I lost it." He hung his head as he said it.

Travis looked at me, and I nodded.

"Well, mebbe this'll help ya keep track better." He tossed something to Zachary. The boy caught it and yelped in delight when he realized what he held. I had made him a pair of throwing knives that Travis had fitted with arm sheaths.

"Whoa!" He immediately began strapping the left sheath on his forearm.

"Zach, what do you say?"

The boy never even paused. "Thanks, Mr. Travis. This is wicked cool!"

Travis smiled. "Yer welcome. 'Course it was yer daddy what made them knives fer ya."

Zach grinned at me. "Thanks, Dad."

"You're welcome. But I need you to listen to me a second." He stopped and turned his attention to me. "You leave those blades in their sheaths while we're at market. You only take them out when you're completely alone and practicing, or if Megan or I are teaching you. You understand me?"

"Yes, sir!"

"All right. And you know what happens if you disobey?"

"You'll spank me?"

"*And* you'll lose the knives. Those aren't kid's toys. You can't treat them like it."

"I won't, I promise."

I held his eye for a minute to make sure he understood how serious I was, then turned back to Travis and winked. He stifled a smile. "I'll wrap Megan's set in with the rest of the stuff."

"Thanks. So, you want to see what I brought you?" I pushed the bundle of tanned goatskins across the counter, then started rummaging through the leather goods Travis had made. There were three leather aprons with various pouches and loops, designed for working the forges, and another pair of throwing knives in arm sheaths for Megan.

Travis ran his hands over the cured goat skins. "Kelley tanned 'em?"

"He did."

Travis harrumphed. "Man does good work."

"Yep. *He* doesn't make crap, either." I unrolled a sewn cloth bundle on the counter. "And here are the tools you wanted." I laid out several punches of various sizes, a half-moon shaped blade, and two small curved knives made to his specifications for working leather. He turned to me grinning from ear to ear.

"Lordy, lordy. These look like they'll fit th' bill jus' fine." At that moment, I was struck by how much the leatherworker's expression resembled Zachary's from just a few minutes earlier. "You ain't got no idea how much easier you jus' made my work."

"Glad to hear it. So we're square?"

"Ah believe so." He stuck out his hand, and we closed the transaction with a handshake.

"Good. Then we'll see you next time we're in town. I know Ken will probably want a pair of boots like these when he sees mine."

"Well, send 'im on over, an' I'll give 'im a good deal."

"I'll do that." I saw Zachary trying to strap the right-hand sheath on his arm. "Here, Zach." I helped him lock it in place. "Now, let's go. There's more to do."

The next few stops were pretty straightforward. At the first, I traded a pair of razor-sharp eight-inch combat knives with staghorn handles for four automobile leaf springs and made arrangements to pick them up on my way out. Each spring was nearly four feet long, and they would be too heavy to lug around the market. At the second stop, a meat cleaver got me two solid walnut table legs. I figured each leg would yield enough wood to make at least five or six knife handles, maybe more if I could split them straight enough. Without a power saw, that was never guaranteed.

Finally, we got to Sarah's shop. She greeted me as we walked in. "Heya, Sensei, what can I do for you?"

Sarah was another one of my students. A tiny slip of a girl, she moved like a tiger on amphetamines in a fight. She was also head of the scavenging committee and, as such, was often able to find items that others couldn't.

"Debra wanted me to see if you have any more of that condensed milk."

"Yessiree. I have three cans left. Four, if you don't mind going past the expiration date."

"How far past?"

She pulled the fourth can out and checked the label. "What is this, March?"

"April."

She thought for a second. "Looks like four months over then. You feeling lucky?"

"What do you want for them?"

"What do you have?"

"Need any nails?"

She shook her head. "Sorry, no use for them."

"Goat jerky?"

"No thanks."

I opened my backpack and dug through it, looking for something she might have use for.

"What about that?" I looked up to find her pointing at the PRD dangling from my neck.

"The radiation detector?"

"Yeah. I could use something like that."

"I don't know, Sarah. I only have a few left." That was true enough. Between the ones I'd given Ken, Cindy, Amber, and the trucking crews, plus the ones I'd already bartered away, I only had six left. Those last six were still in the wrappers, though, and they weren't doing anyone any good there. "All right, but you're going to have to sweeten the deal for one of these."

I got the four cans of condensed milk, as well as two bags of macaroni, a can of aerosol cheese, three cans of corn, a jar of local honey, and a hydrometer. Megan wandered in while we were dickering and helped me load the items in my backpack.

"Dad? This one's swollen."

Sure enough, the top of the can bulged outward with the pressure of growing bacteria. Obviously embarrassed, Sarah grabbed the corn from Megan. "Shit. Sorry about that. I try to check them all before I bring them in. That one must've gotten by me." She grabbed another one from the shelf. "Here you go."

"No harm done." I handed her my PRD. "Wear it in good health."

Slipping it over her head, the girl nodded. "That's the idea." She stuck out her hand. "Pleasure doin' business with you."

I handed the backpack to Megan, and she "whuffed" as she slid it over her shoulder. I slung the other bundles over one shoulder and hefted the table legs. "All right, guys, one more stop and we can head back."

Zachary and Megan both grinned. We were all looking forward to the next stop. We tromped back down the street, making our way to a quiet little side alley, then knocked on the door of a house on the outskirts of the market.

Our knocking set off the dog alarm, and loud barking underscored our arrival. From further back in the house came a sharp command, "Blackie, Cricket–quiet!" Several seconds later, the front door opened, and an elderly woman squinted out at us. She smiled in recognition. "Hello, Leeland. Hi, Megan, Zachary. Ain't you two growin' up!"

The kids returned the smile and replied in unison. "Hi, Miss Phillips."

By this time, the dogs had also recognized us, and the barking gave way to wagging tails and whining. Judith Phillips pushed open the screen door and stepped back in invitation. "Well, don't just stand out there in the heat. Come on in and sit a spell."

We slipped past her and into the darker confines of her home. All the windows were open, but the temperature inside was only a little cooler than out.

"Sorry, Judith, but we can't stay. I have some goods I need to pick up on the way out and, if we don't get back pretty soon, Debra's gonna wonder what we're up to."

When I saw the disappointment written briefly on her face, I felt more than a small twinge of guilt. But she covered it gracefully with a smile and ruffled Zachary's hair. "Well, then, let's head out back and look at some puppies."

Both of the kids scrambled for the back door. Seconds after the door opened, I heard excited barking, the yipping of puppies, and the giggles of a happy ten-year-old. I smiled and offered my arm to Judith. "Shall we?"

She took my arm, and I paced myself to her gait as we walked through her den to follow the kids. Judith was a sweet old lady, a bit too frail to walk very far, and always seemed so lonely. She was in her late seventies, and her health was questionable at best. I had met her three months ago when I'd been asking around for some kind of dog to help manage the goats. Word of mouth led me to her door, and her Catahoulas.

Catahoula leopard dogs were reputed to be ideal herding and hunting dogs. They were supposed to be very smart, and fiercely loyal to their packmates. The trick, I was told, was to make sure they recognized their two-legged packmates as dominant. They sounded like exactly what I wanted. Better yet, Judith had let me know that one of her bitches had puppies on the way. Now two months old, those pups were weaned and ready to leave their mother. We had visited more than a few times in the last several weeks so the dogs would get used to us, and we were ready to take one home.

When I opened the back screen, Judith and I found Zachary sitting on the ground giggling, while six puppies crawled all over him, tails wagging so hard their entire bodies swayed with the activity. Each one whined with pleasure as they tried to climb his body, licking any exposed skin in a frantic competition for his attention.

Megan stood to the side, cooing over another pup she cuddled to her cheek. "All right, guys. We need to pick one and get home."

Zachary latched on to a particularly energetic black and white speckled puppy. He and Megan replied at the same time, "This one!" And each of them had a different dog.

"Sorry, guys. Pick one or the other."

Judith patted my arm and shushed me. "Take them both. You'll be doing me a favor. I can't afford to feed all these little mouths, and the kids will take good care of them." She turned to the two of them. "Won't you?"

"Yes, ma'am!"

Four pairs of puppy dog eyes looked my direction, and only two pairs actually belonged to the puppies. I knew when I was beaten. "All right. Let's get home."

***

August, Year 3

"Leeland, the dogs are in the garden again!"

At the sound of Cindy's complaint, Mark and Brad looked at me and grinned. "Go on," Brad told me. "We'll finish up here."

"You sure you got it?"

"Go! You don't want to get Cindy mad at you."

"Thanks." I stripped off the leather apron and hung it on a peg beside the forge, then trotted to the garden. Sure enough, two gangly, six-month-old speckled pups were chasing each other around the well-tended rows of garden vegetables, scattering cucumbers and winter squash as they ran. Cindy chased them around, trying to shoo them out of the garden, but it appeared they thought it was all part of the game, and they chased around her as well.

Cindy saw me and threw up her hands. "They're going to ruin the garden!"

"Ginger! Oreo! No!" The pair immediately stopped and looked at me. "Sit." They hadn't learned too many commands yet, but they knew *no* and *sit* well enough, and my tone told them they were in trouble. They plopped their tails in the dirt immediately and, as I advanced, they cowered, half-rolling into a submissive pose. I approached the gate and opened it, giving them the only other command they had learned well–"Out!"

Tail tucked between her legs, the black and white Oreo came through first, obviously fearful of my tone, but more afraid of disobeying. The red and white Ginger was less afraid, but seemed eager to please. Both of them came directly to my side and sat panting. "Good girls." I didn't think they would understand if I fussed at them for the damage their rampage through the garden had caused, and I didn't want to confuse them by scolding them after they had followed my commands so well. Cindy didn't see it that way, though.

"They are *not* good girls. Just look at what they did!" She indicated the damage to the vegetables.

"I'm sorry, Cindy. How'd they get in?"

"They jumped the fence again."

I sighed. Ken and I had originally built a four-foot-high chain-link fence around the garden to keep out the goats. The dogs had learned to jump that a month ago, so we'd replaced it with a six-footer. We had assumed that would be tall enough to keep them out. So much for assumptions.

"I'm really sorry, Cindy." I entered the gate to help her salvage what we could from the damage.

"No." She stopped me as I approached. "I'll take care of this; just get those dogs away from here!"

I'd never seen Cindy so angry. "All right. I'm really sorry—"

She cut me off with a raised hand. "Just go."

I hurried away. Some days, I regretted bringing the puppies home. Ostensibly, they had been Debra's birthday present, and she had loved them. But we soon found that two gangly, four-legged furry balls of youthful energy were sometimes more than we'd bargained for. "Ginger. Oreo. Come." I took them back to the house to look for Zachary.

I found him in the barn, milking the nanny goats. "Zach, are you about done there?"

"Yes, sir, this is the last one."

Grabbing a length of rope from a hook on the wall, I tied the makeshift leash to their collars and watched as he moved the pail and released the nanny from the milking stanchion. When he stood up, I stuck out my hand for the bucket of goat's milk. "Here, then, let me take that." I traded him the bucket for the dogs. "Would you please take the girls out to the woods and wear them out? They got in the garden, and I think Cindy's about ready to fix Catahoula stew for dinner."

His eyes lit up as he handed me the bucket. "Sure, Dad."

"I know how much you hate playing in the woods."

Mouth upturned, he shrugged. "Yeah, but if you're gonna insist."

"Just make sure you keep them away from Cindy and the garden."

"Yes, sir." And with that, he became a fading blur, running with the pups toward the tree line at the edge of the property. I turned to take the milk to the house and reflected again on how much life had changed for us—how it had slowed down, allowing us time to realize what was really important, things like allowing a young boy to enjoy time with his dogs.

I frowned, remembering other things were important, too. Just a few years ago, we would have been shopping to get him ready for his next year of school. Now, there *was* no school. We were still too busy with day-to-day survival. I mulled that over on my walk to the house and, the more I thought about it, the more dour my mood became.

Debra interrupted my musing as I arrived at the back door. "What's got you looking so down in the dumps?"

"Just thinking about how much everything's changed. I mean, Zach should be in school. Megan should be getting ready for college. I would be back at the shop…" That, of course, made me think of my parents, and though my grief had lessened considerably in the last two years, my chest still tightened with emotion, further darkening my mood.

"Yeah, maybe." Debra took the milk pail from me. "But we're alive." She raised her eyebrows, and I had to concede the point. "And every day above ground's a good day, right?"

"I suppose."

"So yeah, we've lost some things. But it's not *all* gloom and doom. We're regaining a lot of lost ground, and we'll get the school going next fall. It's not like we're going to let civilization completely fall apart. We just need time to regroup."

I took a deep breath and got my emotions back in check. I could always count on Debra to snap me out of it whenever my temperament took a dark turn.

Nodding, I smiled at her. "Thanks for the pep talk, coach."

"Any time, kid. Now, go get back in the game."

I kissed her lightly and headed back to the forge, where I could hear the whoosh of a bellows forcing air across the coals and the steady pounding of Mark's hammer on hot iron as he and Brad continued to work. I rounded the corner of the barn and watched the two of them for a moment. Debra was right. Things weren't all gloom and doom.

Mark, while still a quiet man, was no longer the solemn, taciturn giant who never spoke to anyone. After a year with us, he had finally opened up enough to begin to mingle and had married Jennifer Yarley, a young Mormon girl. They moved into the old Kindley house down the road and had recently announced that Jenny was pregnant. Brad had moved into another nearby home and built himself a smaller forge that he used to pound out more intricate projects in his spare time. I had taught him about making knives, and he showed a particular interest in Damascus steel. Because of my own interest in knife-making, I had always kept several books and articles on the subject as part of my "survival library," and I let him read everything I had. Making Damascus required time and finesse, folding and layering different types of steel into patterns that both strengthened the blade and pleased the eye. It was something I had never had the patience for. He began to experiment on his own and was soon producing blades that were works of art I would never be able to match.

Each morning shortly after sunrise, he and Mark came to stoke the forge, or both forges if we needed them on that particular day, and prepared for the day's projects, while I taught the morning's self-defense classes.

Everyone kept us pretty busy repairing hand tools and pounding out nails. Nails! I got so tired of making nails! Everyone had to have nails by the hundreds. We spent nearly half of each working day with some aspect of making nails, melting scrap iron into billets, roughing out various sizes, driving roughed nails through sizing holes in the homemade anvils, then trimming and tipping them into finished product.

I would be the first to admit that much of the problem stemmed from the fact that I really didn't have the slightest idea what I was doing. I had made the forge with the idea that knives would soon become a much sought after item. I figured that with a little help, I could soon be producing viable barter goods. But I soon found that though a smith was definitely in demand, knives alone wouldn't keep me going.

George Winstedt, the local carpenter, came to me as soon as he heard about my forge and requested five hundred nails. No big deal, I thought. I worked out a method for making nails from scrap metal and had his nails in a few days.

Until that time, I simply hadn't realized how much we needed nails. Anyone making repairs on a house or barn, anyone building… well, anything, soon discovered how much they needed them. It wasn't long before they found out where to get them. Therefore, Mark, Brad, and I stayed very busy making them.

We repaired or reshaped garden tools. We made more nails. I actually learned to shoe a horse, and that wasn't nearly as easy as they made it seem on those old westerns. We made still more nails. We also made meat cleavers, rotisserie skewers, horseshoes, axe heads, and other items for trading at the local market.

And of course, we made more nails.

But it wasn't all like that. Some of the projects were enjoyable. The work I truly enjoyed came gradually. It derived from the attrition of brass cartridges for bullets. As they disappeared, more and more people began inquiring about knives, skinning knives for the hunters, as well as simple utility and butcher knives for the populace in general. Then the real fun began.

My students were the first to begin ordering combat knives and daggers. It was only logical, as the Kali that I taught was a molding of empty-handed, knife, and stick combat techniques, and I constantly surprised them with impromptu demonstrations of what I called *iai* knife techniques. *Iai* was the Japanese art of the sword quick draw. When I cocked my leg back for a side kick and magically had a knife in hand from a hidden sheath on my leg, they were usually quite impressed. I used these tricks to stress some of my personal philosophies.

"Never let yourself be taken by surprise," I told them on one particular occasion. "Just because an opponent appears to be unarmed does not mean he *is* unarmed."

I scanned their faces. "If you go into a situation expecting that the worst will happen, and you prepare yourself beforehand, then you deny your opponent the split-second of surprise he may be counting on. This, in turn, may give you the advantage since, when you don't react the way he expects, he'll have to readjust his actions to the new situation, which takes approximately half a second. Plan your attack with this in mind, and you might walk away from a fight that would ordinarily kill you."

A week after that particular class, a group of bandits attacked one of the outlying homes. They were fought off, but at the cost of one Rejas citizen and nearly three hundred rounds of ammunition.

Seeing the possible end of the ammunition supply in sight, everyone wanted throwing knives and hideaways for backups. Then came the natural progression to swords and machetes. Finally, we were making arrowheads and crossbow bolts, spears, pole arms, and nearly any other hand-held weapon imaginable. My kind of toys.

They were crude at first, but functional. As our skills at the forge got better, so too did the quality of the products we made.

There were several more encounters with wandering bands of raiders in the next few months, and no one downplayed the necessity of self-defense. Firearms hadn't disappeared, but bullets became increasingly valuable as more casings were lost in the field, damaged in accidents, or otherwise rendered unusable. Many people in town had presses and dies for reloading, but they had long since run out of extra casings and required the spent brass to be brought to them.

No one had access to the machinery necessary to manufacture precision parts, such as bullets. Even if we had, we didn't have a reliable power source with which to run said machinery. Until we got the power station up and running, precision machining was a pipedream.

I had mixed feelings on that. As an experienced machinist, I yearned for precision manufacturing to reenter our lives. Automotive parts, gun parts, parts for wells and gas pumps, hundreds of little things that everyone had once taken for granted, all required tighter tolerances than we could presently hold. So I longed for the old conveniences along with everyone else. On the other hand, I was certain that once the call went out for machinists, I would end up drafted into wearing yet another hat, and there weren't nearly enough hours in the day as it was.

Since I'd been clued in by Zachary, I began to notice how much time Megan spent with Eric's son. Apart from occasional smiles and lingering touches in class, she and Andrew kept their romance pretty subdued. I noticed that the two of them often disappeared together after classes, though, and Megan often didn't show up at home for a few hours afterward. I knew it was getting serious when she started referring to Eric as "Pops." Andrew seemed a nice enough young man, and a fair student, but it bothered me that I had barely even noticed him until my ten-year-old son pointed out his relationship to my daughter. Then, one morning, Andrew asked to see me privately.

"Mr. Dawcett?" He seemed nervous as he pulled me aside after class. "Could I speak to you for a minute?"

"Sure, what can I do for you?"

"Well, um, I was wondering if I could... I mean..." He took a deep breath and held it a second before he practically exploded. "Mr. Dawcett, I'd like to ask your permission to court your daughter with the intention of marrying her and the assurance that my intentions are fully honorable, and I'd like you to know I would always treat her right, and I'd never do anything to hurt her, of course, I probably couldn't hurt her even if I wanted to, but I'd never want to, sir, and I'd do my best to make sure she always had whatever she needed as long as it's within my power, and I'd never do anything to disrespect you or her, and I swear I'd treat her right. Did I already say that? Oh, yeah, but it's true, and I'd be truly grateful if you could see your way clear to give me your consent to court her."

By the time Andrew blurted all that out, *I* was out of breath. I didn't know whether to laugh at his nervousness, thank him for respecting me enough to ask my permission, or to try to get him to loosen up a little. For a few seconds, I simply stared at him in surprise.

He licked his lips nervously, shifting from foot to foot, and I finally realized that if I didn't say something soon, the poor boy was likely to implode.

"You want my permission to date, er, court Megan?"

"Yes, sir."

"And if I understood all that, you intend to marry her if she'll have you?"

"Yes, sir."

"What would you do if I said no?"

The poor boy's mouth fell open. "Sir?"

"What if I tell you I don't want you to see my daughter, and I forbid you from ever coming around here again?"

"But... you can't, I mea... you wouldn't, would you? Sir?"

I simply stared at him.

"But we love each other!"

Still, I remained silent.

Finally, Andrew straightened his shoulders. "Mr. Dawcett, Megan and I have spoken about this a few times. We know how we feel about each other, and we both know that we want to continue seeing each other, and we felt you and Mrs. Dawcett deserved to know. But with all due respect, sir, if you were to tell me I couldn't see her anymore," he paused and swallowed nervously, "well, I guess I'd end up sneaking around behind your back. I ain't saying it's right, but I don't think I can just stop seeing her. It's like I said, I love her."

I raised my hand to rub my chin, and nearly laughed aloud when he flinched at my movement. "Well, Andrew, if you're determined to see her no matter what I say, then I guess I'd better not forbid you, huh?" I grinned at his dumbfounded expression.

"Hell, son! You don't think I'm going to try and tell that girl she can't see you, do you? She'd probably hurt the both of us!"

Andrew shook his head as he finally realized he'd been had. "Yes, sir, I guess she probably would."

"Just one thing, Andrew."

"Yes, sir?"

"If you're planning to marry Megan, I think you'd better learn to stand a little stronger for what you believe in."

"Pardon me?"

"If you never planned to stop seeing my daughter, you didn't have to pretend you needed my permission to see her. You're both adults. I appreciate you wanting to let me and Mrs. Dawcett know, and I definitely approve of your motives, but it would have been just as good if you'd simply told me your intentions as a matter of respect, rather than go through all the rigmarole of pretending that anything I had to say would make a bit of difference in the matter."

Embarrassed, the young man nodded. "Yes, sir. I see what you mean."

"And you're really going to have to learn to stand on your own two feet if you plan on marrying a headstrong woman like my daughter. It's one thing to love her; it's another to let her walk all over you. She'll never respect you if you do that."

"Yes, sir. It's just that it's a little different talking to you, sir."

I grinned. "Why don't you drop all the 'sir' stuff?" I stuck out my hand. "Just call me Leeland. If you're planning to marry my daughter, we're going to be seeing a lot more of each other."

CHAPTER 11

* * AUGUST 14 / YEAR 3 * *

Lune obscurcie aux profondex tenebres,
Son frere passe de couleur ferrugine :
Le grand caché long temps soubs les tenebres,
Tiendra fer dans la playe sanguine.

The moon is obscured in deep gloom,
his brother becomes bright red in color.
The great one hidden for a long time in the shadows
will hold the blade in the bloody wound.
    Nostradamus – *Century 1, Quatrain 84*

Rejas was nudged onto the path to war on August fourteenth, though at the time, we were unaware of where we were headed. For me, it began as I lectured a group of my students on knife fighting and personal philosophy.

"So what makes this stuff you teach any different than the old taekwondo I took when I was a kid?" René Herrera had started classes a year ago after her husband had been killed during a skirmish with a band of looters. A fierce, determined woman, her attitude sometimes bordered on belligerence. Her fighting style was aggressive, but effective. In René's particular case, I was less concerned with her fighting techniques than with her mental and emotional self-control. So when she asked a seemingly insolent question, I usually chose to ignore the tone and address the question itself.

In this instance, I had a ready answer since I had often been asked the same thing when I spoke with prospective students back in Houston. "It's a different way of looking at things. Let me ask you something. If a rattlesnake attacks you, what do you do?"

"Get out of the way"

"And if you can't? Say, if your back is to a wall, and there's just no place to run. Then what would you do?"

"I guess I'd try to kill the snake."

"All right. So what if you were back against that same wall, and you were being attacked by a mouse?"

She chuckled. "What?"

I repeated, "You're in the same corner, nowhere to run, but this time it's a mouse coming after you."

"I think I'd probably wet myself laughing!" Many of the others laughed, too. I smiled with them as I paced.

"Why? What's the difference? Why are you more worried about the snake than the mouse?" I turned back to René. "I know it seems silly, but there is a point to this."

The young woman looked at me like I was crazy. "'Cause the snake is poisonous?" Her uncertainty made it seem as if she was asking a question.

"So what if I tell you that the snake isn't poisonous, and the mouse is? Then which one are you more worried about?"

"The mouse, of course."

"So it isn't the snake you're afraid of, it's the bite, right?"

"Okay," René conceded cautiously, apparently wary of being caught in a trap.

"Now, what if you're being attacked by the same rattlesnake, but he hasn't got any fangs? Are you still afraid of him?"

Her answer was firmer this time. "No. If he can't bite me, he's just dinner."

"Exactly! If you take away his fangs, he's no longer a danger. So if you and I are fighting, and everything about us is equally matched—skill, speed, weapons, reach, determination—are you afraid?"

"Not if everything is equal. Sounds like a standoff."

"That's it. But what if I lose my weapon? I'm just like that rattlesnake, right? No fangs. In Kali, we learn to de-fang snakes. The difference in this and what most martial arts teach is simple, but it's important. If a man punches at you, and you've studied a traditional martial art, you'll more than likely block or parry, then counterattack, usually by punching or kicking to the head, legs, or torso.

"If the same man punches you, and you've studied Kali, your block *is* your counterattack, and it's usually aimed at whatever he is attacking you with. If he's punching, you try to injure his hand so he can't punch you again. If he's kicking, you injure his foot. If he's using a weapon, you take away his ability to use it, either by injuring the hand that holds it, or by simply disarming him. No matter what he does, your goal is to take away his fangs. If he's no longer a danger, the fight is over."

It was time to move on to the next part of my lecture. "There are very few things you can count on in life. The pre-D saying was that the only two things you could count on were death and taxes. But I haven't seen the IRS in quite some time."

They laughed obligingly, and I continued, "That seems to indicate the only thing that's inevitable is death. Now you may not be able to avoid Death, but with the right attitude, and proper preparation, you can usually convince Him that there are easier pickings elsewhere."

"Rule number one." I pulled a throwing knife out of my belt. "Always carry at least two knives. Always. If you lose one…" I threw the blade, and they all watched as it stuck in the wooden target. When they turned back to face me, I had drawn two others from hidden arm sheaths. Image and attitude were everything in martial arts, so I continued unperturbed, as if I

only. Leeland and I argued out there for some time about whether or not we should finish you off. Leeland won that argument, and that's the only reason you're standing here right now. I was ready to slit your throat." He glared for a moment, making sure he was getting his point across. "So I'm going to give you the only order I'll ever give you."

He pointed at me. "You do anything Leeland Dawcett tells you to do, when he says to do it, and better than he wants it done, or I'll do what I should have done then."

Then he had stalked out of the room, leaving my slave and I equally dumbfounded.

"Sensei?" Billy jarred me back from my reverie. My eyes were drawn to the large black encircled "7-34" on his forehead representing the month and year he would be eligible for freedom. If his review was not favorable, the date would be tattooed over leaving a solid black circle, and he would spend the rest of his life as a slave.

In the time since Billy's sentence, Rejas had had six more instances of marauder bands attacking some of the outlying homesteads and dozens of individual pilferers. The town had lost seven more people to the gangs, among them René's unfortunate husband. But we had acquired thirty-eight more slaves. Two of them had been shot when they fought against the tattooist. The others had spread the word among themselves, and we hadn't had any further trouble. Since the death of her husband, René hated them all.

"Sorry, Billy. Who is it?"

"Mayor Kelland. He's waiting in the house."

"Thanks." He nodded and turned back to the house. I turned the group over to Eric and went over to where Megan was sparring. "Megan, I'm going inside. Finish up out here."

I watched as she swept one opponent off of his feet and locked his arm over one knee, under the other as she knelt over him, evading a strike from the other opponent. She grabbed the second attacker's arm and twisted her wrist in a way that Mother Nature never intended it to bend, bringing that opponent to the ground with an awkward thud. Then she held both in place for a moment to show that she was in full control of the situation before releasing them.

She stood and turned to me. "No problem, Dad."

I grinned as I headed back to the house.

The mayor looked up as I entered. "Somethin' funny?"

"I was just remembering how frustrating it can be to be beaten so soundly by someone half your size."

He shook his head, obviously having no idea what I was talking about, and just as obviously not caring. He paced the room with a worried look on his face.

That bothered me. As I said before, my feelings for James Kelland had changed a lot since I'd first met him. He had gone from someone I couldn't stand to a man whom I genuinely respected and trusted, liked even. "What's the problem, Jim?"

He stopped his pacing and sat on the sofa. Stress still lined his brow. "The trucking crew got in today—without the trucks."

That got my attention. The tanker trucks were part of the key to this town's long-term survival. They were our only means of transporting the fuel we had staked out across the southern United States. Now Jim was telling me we had just lost half of them.

He continued in a subdued voice, and his tone worried me as much as what he had to say. "They brought a bit o' news back with them."

I took a seat in the easy chair across from him. To say that Jim had a talent for understatement was... well, an understatement. "I'll bet they did. I take it that it wasn't good news."

He shook his head. "You know, I ain't exactly sure." Mayor Kelland was just full of surprises this morning.

"How do you mean?"

"Todd Waitfield was the lead driver."

"I know him," I said. "He's one of our part-time students."

The mayor shrugged. "Who ain't, nowadays?"

That was true. Since we'd had so much trouble with freebooters in the more recent months, I had literally hundreds of students. On top of that, many of the senior students had begun teaching even more people at other locations around town.

"Anyway, he said they came up on a roadblock just this side of San Marcos, a roadblock manned by the U.S. Army. They had a tank sittin' smack dab in the middle of the road! Confiscated the fuel in the name of the *U.S. Reconstruction and Distribution* effort and questioned the hell out o' the drivin' crew. Wanted to know what kind of condition we were in. Waitfield said as far as he knew, all of the men stuck to the drill. The only difference was that they had to tell them where they were heading, since they were depending on them for a ride."

All of the drivers had been coached in what to say if questioned about where they were headed with the fuel if they ever ran across any organized groups. Part of the story was that they were members of a group based in Shreveport, Louisiana. They were to emphasize what a hard time their group was having, and how tough things were for them.

Jim continued, "'Course he couldn't be a hunnerd percent sure, since they were all questioned separately, but he talked to his team afterward, and they all told him they'd played down the town's resources and played up the problems we've all had. He trusts his team completely. Said he was willing to stake his life on their word."

I nodded. "Makes sense, I guess. They've had to trust each other in some rough situations."

"Yeah, but now he's staking *our* lives on their word." Jim took a deep breath before continuing, "Anyway, the army boys took the trucks and sent the crew back in a personnel vehicle. Waitfield said they told him they're gonna be out this way later this week to discuss our contribution to the 'Reconstruction Effort.' You believe that shit?" He laughed wryly. "The hell of it is, I don't know whether or not to be happy about it."

"How so?"

"Well, it looks like the government's startin' to get back on its feet, which to my way of thinkin' is a good thing. But the first thing they do is start confiscatin' our goods." He stood and resumed his pacing. "And that, to my way of thinkin', ain't such a good thing at all."

"Well, what do you expect, Jim? Compared to us, the rest of the country probably hasn't got squat. We've got freshwater springs all over these parts. Crops are in. The closest hot spot is Houston, a hundred and eighty miles away. We haven't had any hot winds in nearly six months. Hell, compared to what the majority of the country's probably going through, we're living in a freaking garden!"

"And we worked damn hard to get here!" he exclaimed bitterly. "So why should we just up and give it away?" He forced himself back to a calmer state, the effort plainly visible. "I got a lot of people depending on me to make decisions right now. The right decisions, Leeland, and I'm not sure what to do." I could see how much the admission hurt him, and I sympathized. I had once been forced to make some similar decisions. Ironically, it had been Jim who had forced them on me.

I remembered the feeling well. He was torn by the necessity of the choices he had to make. He could turn the town's hard-earned supplies over to the Army, or defy them and chance the retaliation of the military.

He sat back down. "I need some advice, or at least someone to discuss this with. The bitch of it is that there aren't very many people I can talk to about this."

"I'm flattered," I replied, "but I don't know if I'm the one you should be talking to."

He raised his eyebrows. "Maybe you don't realize just how many people look up to you nowadays. You're an example to them. You and Ken and Megan."

"That was over two years ago!" I laughed. "There have been a lot of other fights like that since then."

"Not like that one." Jim shook his head. "You forget who the investigating officer was. I know what you three went up against."

He pointed his finger in my face before I could open my mouth. "I know that you never faced them all at once! You've told everyone who'll listen, over and over. But I also know that when a known killer held a knife to Megan's throat, instead of panicking or breaking down, you and Ken worked out a plan to distract the bad guys. And instead of panicking or breaking down, Megan killed the guy with his own knife!"

"Ken did the shooting and drew their fire," I protested, "and Megan killed the guy. All I did was throw a smoke grenade and run. Of the three of us, I was in the least danger of all."

The mayor took a deep breath and slowly exhaled. "Leeland, you're modest. I can admire that. And it ain't false modesty, either. You're good people, and I thank God for sending you and your family to Rejas. But this ain't the time for it, so shut the hell up, and let me tell you a couple of things about yourself!

"First, Ken told me that plan was yours, and I know you're the one that trained Megan. And you forgot to mention that fight at the end. Billy told me you took him and his three buddies before they ever got off a shot. Everyone in town knows about that. I made sure that story got around. It was great for the town's morale.

"Second, that karate shit of yours has spread to where at least two thirds of the folks in town are either training with you or some of your students. You've given them the knowledge, not to mention the courage and confidence to defend themselves against armed bandits. That means you're at least indirectly responsible for saving the lives of a good portion of the population here. Yet you insist on being treated as 'just one of the guys' outside of class.

"Third, you and your forges have helped keep Rejas from sliding back into the Stone Age. I know you get a lot o' help from Brad and Mark, but the idea was yours. You're the closest thing to an expert we have on post-D survival, but you won't head up any of the committees, even though we've asked you over and over. Instead, you insist on being an advisor. You're one of those people that knows a little bit about a lot of things, and that's what we need now."

Though others had told me these things in the past, I still felt embarrassed when a conversation took this turn. So of course, I did what I always did. I tried to lighten the mood with a joke. "So you're saying I'm a know-it-all?"

Jim threw up his hands. "I give up. I try to get some help, and all I get are your lame-ass jokes!" He stood and headed for the front door. "Sorry for wasting your time."

"Wait, Jim!" I jumped up and went after him. "I'm sorry, I just… I get uncomfortable… I mean…" I fumbled for a second. "Look, let's just forget about what a wonderful person I am, okay? You stop telling me about it, and I'll stop denying it. Meanwhile, I'm happy to help any way I can."

Kelland stopped and turned around. Then, he nodded and stuck out his hand. "Deal."

We shook on it.

As we returned to our seats, I asked, "Why me? Modesty aside, what makes you think I can help you with this one?"

"Cheryl suggested you. The first person a man talks to is his wife, least that's how it is with me. But she told me I should come talk to you. That you had a way of makin' folks see things they already knew, but didn't know they knew, or some shit like that. Nowadays, I don't even know what she's talkin' about half of the time. Ever since she started takin' your classes."

He beamed with pride. "Too late to stop her now, though. She'd probably beat the hell out of me if I tried."

He was probably right. Cheryl was one of my better students, one of the few who truly understood that the system I taught was more than a method of self-defense, but also a way of looking at life and attacking its problems. She had shown a lot of faith in me, sending Jim like that. I didn't want to let her down.

I thought for a moment. "Come take a walk with me." I walked to the back door and waited.

Kelland stared at me for a minute, then grinned. "Oh hell, this is gonna be one of those school lessons she was tellin' me about, ain't it? One of those walks where you make me 'see the light.'" He waggled his fingers and rolled his eyes.

"You know, if you would come to the classes ever so often..."

He shook his head. "I got no time. Every time I turn around, somebody wants me to decide how we're gonna do something, or when we're gonna do something, or if we're gonna do something. I barely got time to eat, sleep, and occasionally take a piss."

"I get the picture." He was nothing if not eloquent. "So take a break for a minute and walk with me. I want to show you something."

He stood and smiled. "Lead on, O Great One."

We walked out back, and I led him to the shelter in which we had lived for nearly two weeks. There, I began my "lesson."

"I planned a long time before the bombs ever fell about what I would do when and if it ever happened." I leaned over to open the blast door. "I learned all I could about the effects of radiation, how to build shelters, air filters, water filters, anything related to nuclear warfare. And I learned to prepare for the worst. The way I see it, if you're ready for the worst that can happen, you can handle anything less with no problems."

He looked down at the shelter. "Looks like a lot of work went into this."

"Yeah, it did." I descended to the fourth step and flipped a toggle switch just inside the entrance. Twelve-volt automobile bulbs came to life inside. "Come on in."

Jim descended the rough wooden steps into the shelter, and his eyebrows arched. "This is pretty impressive."

"Like I said, I tried to learn all I could." I led him down the short corridor lined with simple wooden shelves and benches. "When we first built this, the lights ran off three car batteries that we kept charged with a hand-powered generator. Now we've wired in the waterwheel generator, and we've got enough power to run just about anything we want, either in here or in the house."

As if on cue he asked the question I was waiting for. "So, if you're so hot on always being prepared, why are the shelves all empty?"

"Because of you, Jim."

"Me?"

I smiled at having so easily caught him off guard. "Remember when you questioned me on the night of the Kindley mess? You called me a selfish S.O.B. and said you suspected we had a stockpile of provisions that Rejas needed."

"I never said any such thing!"

I stared at him silently until, finally, he amended, "Well, not in so many words."

"If you recall, it was shortly afterward that we brought a van full of supplies to the town stockpile." We reached the end of the tunnel and turned the corner into the tiny little alcove where we had put our five-gallon toilet during our confinement. At the end of the aisle were wooden stairs similar to the ones we had descended at the other entrance. I stopped just before them and continued my talk.

"It occurred to me that if I didn't bring them in, and things got really bad, people would eventually come after them. And if things didn't get bad, and the town prospered without any help from us, we could probably count on being known as 'the bums that sat there nice and cozy while the rest of the town had to struggle.' Also, we figured it wouldn't do much good for us to live through a nuclear war, if we just had to watch everyone else die. You convinced me that it was better to survive as a town than as a family."

He was silent for a moment as he thought my analogy through to its logical conclusion. "So you're tellin' me that I need to give up all we worked so hard for, because it's better to survive as a country than as a town?"

"Not exactly." I reached down, grasped a latch under the bottom stair, and lifted. The stairs rose as a single unit, hinged and counterweighted at the top, to expose a hidden room. Our clan, in which we included Ken and

156

Cindy, had worked long and hard to keep it secret. The mayor's jaw dropped in astonishment when he saw the room lined with fully stocked shelves.

Given a choice between good will and selfishness, I usually tried to compromise. I briefly wondered if his mouth could possibly open any wider. I guessed I could find out if I really wanted by simply telling him about the other two stashes hidden nearby. Nonperishable food items, weapons, ammunition, and tools. "I never said you needed to give up everything," I told him.

It took several minutes for him to stop laughing long enough for us to begin planning.

CHAPTER 12

* * AUGUST-16 / YEAR 3 * *

Dans cité entrer exercit desniee,
Duc entrera par persuasion,
Aux foibles portes clam armee amenee,
Mettront feu, mort, de sang effusion.

The army denied entry to the city,
The Duke will enter through persuasion:
The army led secretly to the weak gates,
They will put it to fire and sword, effusion of blood.
　　　　Nostradamus – *Century 9, Quatrain 96*

We still had eight tankers in town. The USR&D team confiscated half of our sixteen trucks, so the others had been busy for the last two days moving our gasoline and diesel supply back into some of the gas stations in nearby towns. Seventy-five percent of the food stockpile was now hidden in attics, buried in backyards, or otherwise stashed away. Many of our general supplies were cached as well. When our visitors arrived, no one would have any reason to suspect that we had any more than a modest surplus of anything.

So Thursday morning saw most of the people of Rejas lining Main Street as if in anticipation of a parade. I stood with several of the ad hoc committee heads in front of City Hall, all of us decked out in our Sunday best.

Of course, hard work and hard times had reshaped most of us so our Sunday best hung off of us in places where they had once been tight and fit snugly in places where they had previously been loose. The so-called honor guard for the visiting representatives of the reviving U.S. looked more like a group of cleaned-up hobos than official representatives.

The tension poured through the crowd as word radioed in from the roadblock stations. The convoy was headed into town. It was strange, the disparity of emotions I felt at the sight of all of those military vehicles and uniforms. After all the time I'd spent wondering what was going on with the rest of the country, there was a feeling of relief in knowing that at least a fragment of our government had survived and was struggling back to life. Many of the townspeople must have felt it as well, for as those Humvees rolled down Main Street, they cheered and clapped. American flags appeared in the hands of many.

I smiled with the others, but my smile was strained, as were those of many of the committee members. We were the few people in whom the mayor had entrusted the knowledge of how much the government's struggling reemergence was likely to cost us, if they got their way. And from the looks of things, they had enough troops and hardware to make sure they got their way.

As the Humvees pulled up to the steps of City Hall, Mayor Kelland stepped down to make nice to the muckety-mucks unloading from the first vehicle. I had never been good with uniforms. Belt rankings, I understood, but chevrons and pips were foreign to me. So I strained to hear the introductions as "Captain Brady" shook hands with Mayor Kelland. Brady stood a lanky four inches over six feet and, judging from the way his uniform hung on him, he had been through some pretty lean times recently. Looking around, I noted that none of the other uniforms fit any better. I heard a distinct Boston accent when he introduced himself as the personal aide for "the general."

It seemed a tank had broken down on the way into town, and the general had elected to oversee the repairs personally, but would follow at his earliest opportunity.

"Meanwhile," the captain said, "I assume the ladies and gentlemen standing so patiently behind you are persons of some importance, or they would be out with the rest of the crowd." The man was smooth, a born diplomat.

"'Course, Captain, I'd like to introduce you to my emergency committee heads, and chief aides." Jim led the way over to us. I noticed how he exaggerated his country accent, playing the bumpkin. "If it weren't for these people, Rejas would prolly be a town full o' dead n' dyin'."

It was Captain Brady's turn to make nice; he shook hands with each of us. As he introduced us, Kelland had a little comment about the individual contributions we had made. "This here's Leeland Dawcett. We didn't exactly see eye to eye when he first got here, but he's shaped up real good. He's a survivalist and has helped us hang on by the skin of our teeth."

Captain Brady's eyes seemed to bore into mine for a moment, staring intently, as if trying to memorize my features. "Mr. Dawcett. Your name sounds familiar. Ah, yes! One of the truckers last week mentioned you in relation to… town security, was it?"

"No sir," I replied. His question seemed ingenuous enough, but his gaze made me uneasy. Up close, he reminded me less of a diplomat and more of a bureaucrat, a definite step down on Darwin's ladder. "Well, not exactly. I'm an aide to Ken Simms, who is in charge of town security."

His brow furrowed as if he were trying to recall the conversation. Finally, he shrugged apologetically. "That must be it." He looked at me for another second, as if he wanted to say something more, but evidently changed his mind. "Well, it's nice to meet you, Mr. Dawcett." And the mayor moved him on down the line, leaving me to wonder what was going on.

After the final introductions, Jim turned to the captain. "If you like, Cap'n, folks have put together a little spread in your honor. I'm sorry there ain't enough for all o' your boys at the table, but we have got a bunch o' volunteers that'd be proud to feed one or two of the good ol' U.S.A.'s fightin' men."

"That sounds very generous, Mayor. Thank you very much. Just let me return to my vehicle for a moment, and I'll tell my men."

"Sure thing, Cap'n. How many men do I need to make arrangements for?"

"Two thousand, nine hundred, seventy-six, when the general gets here with the rest of the troops."

Jim stood silent for a second, astonished into rigidity. Then he nearly fell down the steps as he rushed to catch Captain Brady. "Twenty-nine hundred? You're bringin' twenty-nine hundred troops into town?"

Brady turned back to the mayor. "Closer to three thousand, actually. Is that a problem? I've got more than fifteen hundred with me now. The rest will be here within a few hours."

Our intrepid mayor stammered as the rest of us tried to decide whether to be shocked at the number of armed troops coming into town, or amused at the stunned look on Kelland's face as he rapidly scanned the large number of Humvees, trucks, and armored personnel carriers he had allowed into Rejas.

Finally, though, Jim managed to regain his composure. "Well, honestly, Cap'n, I hadn't expected that many mouths. I'm a little embarrassed to admit it, but I don't think we've got enough to feed that many."

Captain Brady laughed and clapped Jim on the back. "Not to worry, Mayor. My troops all carry their own rations. All we ask is a roof and some civil company."

The mayor managed to look relieved and nodded. "I think we can manage that much at least."

"Well, then, on behalf of my men and the general, I thank you, Mayor."

Brady went back to his vehicle and got on the radio. A few seconds later, men began pouring out of the vehicles.

* * *

The men were divided into pairs, two soldiers to each of four hundred fifty families, with the remaining troops stuck watching the convoy and supplies. Our dinner proceeded as planned. Brady and his aide joined the "Emergency Committee" heads for a dinner in the City Hall cafeteria—barbecued chicken, egg salad, squash and eggplant casserole, sliced tomatoes and cucumbers, sweet potatoes, and acorn bread with butter.

Captain Brady eyed the food with a smile. "I see you folks are doing well. I haven't seen a spread like this in quite some time."

We had anticipated his reaction, had in fact debated on the idea of fixing such a meal. Many felt we should present a more poverty-stricken appearance, but the majority had argued that it would seem more suspicious if we didn't try to make a good impression to the first sign in two years that the U.S. still existed. Each item on the menu had been carefully planned.

Kelland launched into his explanation of the food. "Yes, sir. We found out that chickens don't seem to get radiation sickness as easy as other animals. 'Course you have ta cook 'em a might, to make sure you kill the salmonella."

Captain Brady blanched a bit at that, but Jim continued as if he hadn't noticed. "An' when you got chickens, you got eggs for egg salad. Different folks around town got a few gardens for veggies, and one of the hunter's wives came up with this acorn bread. Here, try some." Projecting the image of a country bumpkin trying to impress a superior, he pulled a piece off of the end of a loaf and handed it eagerly to the captain.

"Yep," he drawled, "we pulled out all the stops fer y'all's visit." The act was perfect. His apparent pride in the food made it seem that the meal was something extraordinary.

Brady's smile diminished, even more so when he bit into the bread and discovered just how bitter acorn bread tasted. "Delicious," he lied. "Is the rest of the food so good?"

"Well..." The mayor hesitated. "I'll admit it ain't all that good, but then again, some of it's even better!"

I noticed that Brady's smile suddenly seemed more forced than it had been.

The meal went fairly well, with all of us eating dry, stringy chicken slathered with spicy barbecue sauce. "My own recipe," Jim bragged as Brady gasped and downed half a glass of blackberry mint tea. There was overcooked squash and eggplant, mealy tomatoes, and overripe cucumbers. The hard part lay in convincing Captain Brady that this was a special treat—without any of us getting ill in the process.

After sampling a little of the food, Brady soon contented himself with shoving it around with his fork and engaging in small talk. It became apparent that he was attempting to gather information about our resources. Watching the verbal sparring between our mayor and the captain was the best entertainment I'd had in months.

It ended somewhat more abruptly than we expected. Brady and Kelland were discussing the advantages of having so many freshwater springs in the area and ideas for the USR&D group's distribution of the water to other parts, when the sound of an explosion interrupted them. As we all jumped to our feet, Brady's aide calmly drew his pistol and pointed it at Jim. Everyone froze.

Shouting and sporadic gunfire suddenly erupted from various locations in the streets around Rejas. That seemed to surprise Brady more than the explosion, but he quickly recovered his composure. To everyone's further surprise, the captain then drew his own weapon and pointed it at me!

"Well, gentlemen, the dinner was delicious, but the general has arrived with our tanks, and we must get on with the business at hand. Mr. Dawcett," he gestured with his pistol as he spoke, waving me toward the main doors of the dining room. "The general will soon be waiting outside, and during the last few months of my acquaintance with him, he has repeatedly expressed an intense desire to see you again. Please, let's not keep him waiting."

I was thoroughly confused. It was obvious that I was on someone's list, but an Army general? What was going on? Playing for time, I asked, "What does a general want with me? I've never even met any generals!"

"But of course you have." He calmly reached for the radio on his belt as he chuckled. "General Lawrence Troutman."

For the life of me, I honestly didn't recognize the name at first. Then it hit me as he thumbed on the transmitter. Larry was alive. And he was evidently still pretty pissed off at me.

"Brady here, General. I have the Council with me here in City Hall."

Pissed enough to come after me with a tank.

"And I am happy to report that I have a pleasant surprise for you, sir."

My fears were confirmed as the radio squawked a reply. The reception wasn't great, and I hadn't heard that voice in two years, but it still chilled my blood instantly. "Yes, Captain?"

163

I probably wouldn't survive thirty seconds past the trip out the front door with Brady—time to do something unexpected.

I turned to Jim. "You idiot! I thought you told me Larry was dead!" I launched myself at him, all the while hoping Brady wouldn't shoot me in the back as I vaulted the dinner table.

Instant bedlam ensued. Everyone must have thought I'd lost my mind as I scrambled across the tabletop. Poor Jim couldn't have had any idea what was going on when I punched him in the cheek and followed him to the floor. Brady shuffled around trying to stuff the radio back in its pouch with his left hand and keep me in his sights with his right, all the while yelling at everyone else to get out of his way and screaming for me to get up before he shot me.

"You stupid bastard!" I yelled into the mayor's face. Then I slipped the small push-dagger out of my belt buckle and pressed it into his hand. I hissed, "Use it!"

Pulling him to his feet, I shoved him into his guard, knocking them both into the wall. James Kelland may not have been one of the many martial arts students in Rejas, but he was a street cop from way back. As he hit the captain's aide, he grabbed on and spun so that his body blocked Brady's view of the little three-inch blade slamming into the aide's chest.

The soldier spasmed, fingers convulsing on the trigger of his pistol, which blew a hole in the wall next to Jim. At the sound of the gunshot, Brady swung his gun around to cover Jim. I immediately took advantage of his distraction. Dropping the flat throwing knife out of my sleeve, I hurled it at my target. It was the first time I had ever used a throwing knife on a live target, and I made a nearly fatal mistake. I forgot that, unlike my wooden targets, people move.

I'd practiced for years, and never once did a target move when I threw at it. But I neglected to tell Brady that, and so he reacted naturally. He dodged.

I, on the other hand, didn't. I threw my knife and stood there like an idiot, waiting for Brady to oblige me and fall down dead. I realized my mistake during the half-second flight of the knife blade, but by then it was too late.

Brady must have seen me from the corner of his eye because he stepped forward and began to shift his aim back toward me. The knife hit him chest high, pommel first. Luckily, it hit hard enough to spoil his aim, and the table beside me sprouted splinters.

Ken tackled Brady from behind before he could get off a second shot. Three seconds of Brady's skull bouncing on the floor took the last of the fight out of him.

As Ken finished basketball practice, I scooped my knife off the floor and ran to the front window to peek through the closed blinds. I quickly discovered that knowing there was a tank aimed and ready to introduce you to your maker and actually seeing the huge muzzle of the cannon staring back at you were two very different things.

As that first tank rolled down Main Street toward City Hall, I saw the night sky aglow behind it, the fire from the burning high school silhouetting its ominous shape. Larry had obviously chosen to come in with a full demonstration of the power at his command, destroying the school in an attempt to nip any resistance before it occurred, and simultaneously signaling his arrival to his troops. We had obligingly invited his men into the homes of our townspeople, and now they were attempting to force them out of those homes and into the streets. The sound of gunfire was everywhere, as were the screams and shouts of open conflict. Larry had evidently counted on surprising a quiet little town of meek, complacent survivors. I was gratified to see that the people of Rejas no longer fit that description. They fought back. Unfortunately, we were sorely outgunned since Rejas had stockpiled and hidden much of its weaponry.

Brady's radio came to life with Larry Troutman's voice, reminding me of the situation at hand. "Surprise, Captain?"

I realized that less than a minute had passed since Brady's last transmission.

"Everybody out!" Jim held the dead guard's pistol and waved it toward the receiving door in the back of the tiny complex. None of us questioned his order. We ran for our lives through the exit and into the violence of the night.

The chatter of gunfire surrounded us as we rushed down the block, keeping City Hall between ourselves and the tanks rumbling down the street. We rounded the corner and ran into a nearby abandoned storefront.

"Everyone all right?" Ken asked.

I could see the others nodding and panting in the darkness. Jim handed me the tiny push dagger that went in my belt buckle. "Thanks," he said. "Guess I'll have to get you to make me one of those things."

"Once we get out of this." I slapped him on the back. "Anybody see how many tanks he's got?"

"I saw six," Ken replied. "Could be more, but I don't think so."

"Six tanks!" Jim spat. "What the hell can we do against tanks? We got handguns and deer rifles! What good are they?"

"I learned a little about them back when I was in the service. These are Abrams. They're tough, no doubt about it, but I think those are A1s, and I know some of their strengths and weaknesses. We might still have a chance."

The mayor didn't seem convinced, but evidently decided this wasn't the time to discuss it. Instead, he simply ignored Ken and turned to do a quick headcount while we caught our breath. "Okay, looks like everyone made it out all right. So, now what?"

I looked up to find him staring at me, waiting for an answer. "Me? No way, Jim, you're the mayor!"

"That may be, but you seem to be the one at the middle of all this. It's you they want, and if I understood things right, it's you that might have a little previous experience with the head honcho. So I need to hear your take on the situation."

Anything I might have said at that point was forgotten as my heart jumped into my throat at the sound of Larry's voice coming from behind Ken. "Brady, report!"

I went for my knife, desperately searching past Ken's shoulder for my target when Ken grinned and reached behind him for the two-way. He had taken it from Brady and tucked it in his own belt before our flight from City Hall. "Captain Brady, please report your situation."

"I take it that's the guy you told us about, the guy that tried to hijack you on D-day?" Ken asked.

I nodded.

The radio squawked again. "Brady!"

I shoved my fear back into its little corner and motioned to Ken for the radio. He handed it to me without question.

"Brady, get on the radio, now!"

I keyed the transmitter. "Sorry, Larry, Brady's a bit tied up at the moment." Suddenly, a thought came to me. "That's something you should be able to relate to, isn't it, Larry? I seem to recall the last time I saw you, you were tied up, too. As a matter of fact, I was told there was a body out there where I left you, a body with a broken knee and a hole in his shoulder. How'd you manage that one?"

There was a noticeable pause before he replied, "Dawcett? Is that really you?" He laughed. "How wonderful! I've finally found you. Too bad Frank isn't still alive to share in our joyous reunion, but I'm afraid it was his body in the clearing. I'd had quite enough of his incompetence."

"So you killed him and made the wounds match yours. That way anyone I told about you would find the body and report you dead." I shook my head in disbelief. Troutman was unbelievably callous.

"Yes. It took me several months to heal." He paused a moment. "But that's behind us now, Leeland. I've spent quite some time searching for you. You promised me that you would be waiting for me in Shreveport." I could almost hear that frown of his. "You lied to me again, Leeland. This seems to be a recurring flaw in your character. Tsk, tsk."

"'Tsk yourself, Larry. Remember the other promise I made? It had to do with what we agreed would happen if we ever met again. Remember? Just before I scared the piss out of you back at the cabin?"

The pause was longer this time. Finally, anger clipping his speech, he replied, "Yes, Leeland, I remember. I remember quite well. We agreed that one of us wouldn't walk away from that meeting."

Ken arched an eyebrow. I hadn't ever told that to anyone. Larry continued before anyone else could say anything. "And unlike you, Mr. Dawcett, I keep my promises."

I was just about to taunt him again when City Hall unexpectedly exploded behind us in a deafening roar. Flaming debris showered the streets, adding the noise of a lumberyard falling from the sky.

I stared for a moment, realizing that Larry thought we were all still in there. Then my anger flared, and I thumbed the radio back to life. "That's not quite what I meant when I said one of us wouldn't walk away, Larry. I seem to recall there being something about us meeting face to face. What's the matter, *General*? Too frightened to face me?"

"I should have known it wouldn't be that easy, Leeland. You do seem to have the devil's own luck, don't you?"

"Yes, I do. Unfortunately, your Captain Brady doesn't. He was still inside that building. He and his driver."

"How unfortunate for them."

"I take it that doesn't bother you too much?"

"You should know better than that, Leeland."

His cold-heartedness never ceased to amaze me. As it occurred to me that Larry was probably straddling the fence between genius and insanity, the shouts and sounds of the battle for Rejas intruded. "Sorry, Larry, I don't have time for another debate. It seems my friends here are in the middle of a fight. You'll just have to wait."

"Leeland!" He practically screamed in to the radio. "So help me—"

I clicked off the power in mid-threat. "Okay, Jim, you wanted my advice?" I turned to face him. "The guy's a nutcase. You can't reason with him, so don't bother trying. I say we split up and gather as many of our people as we can. We'll meet at our place as quickly as possible. Larry's bound to find out where it is sooner or later, but by then we should be long gone."

"Why your place?" he asked. "I can think of a dozen places a lot closer."

"You remember that stash I showed you?" He nodded. "That wasn't the only one."

"What?"

I grinned. "Better to have it and not need it—"

"Yeah, yeah," he interrupted. "I've heard it before. Save it." He turned to the others. "Everyone know where Amber Peddy's place is?" Everybody nodded.

"All right, get as many people together as you can find and meet there in…" He turned back to me. "How long?"

I gave it my best guesstimation, "Three hours should give us enough time to gather people, spread the word, and get through the woods to Amber's."

"Okay. Eleven o'clock, no later than midnight. Let's go!"

We scattered, each of us rushing to get to as many Rejans as we could. With an ulterior motive, I ran south, down a fire-lit Main Street. I knew Megan was eating with the Petry's tonight, and that they had planned to volunteer to feed some of the visiting "soldiers." That was my first destination.

I stuck to the flickering shadows, running in darkened doorways and alleys. It got easier as I got further from the twin conflagrations that had been, mere minutes before, Rejas High School and the City Hall. Turning left on Madison, I soon found that those weren't the only fires in Rejas, only the most obvious. As I headed into the residential area of town, I found several homes ablaze. In front of one, I saw two of Troutman's men using an abandoned car for cover as they pinned a family inside the burning building with gunfire. I drew my knives and took them from behind before they ever knew I was there. Yelling to the people in the house that it was safe, I grabbed the soldiers' weapons.

As the family emerged, I recognized the man, though I couldn't recall his name. Tossing him one of the soldiers' rifles, I told them about the proposed meeting at Amber's. They headed north, and I continued further south. Two blocks down, I turned right onto Dowling, the Petry's street, and spotted bodies lying in several of the yards. This was one of the nicer sections of town, and many of the townspeople had moved into the suddenly abundant empty homes after D-day, making it one of the most densely populated neighborhoods in Rejas. Tonight it looked like a war zone.

Three houses on the street were aflame, illuminating the macabre scene, and while I saw no signs of life, there must have been thirty bodies visible by the flickering light. I was relieved to see that the vast majority of them wore uniforms—Larry's men. I also noted with approval that none of the corpses still had their weapons. That meant several armed citizens were in the streets nearby. All I had to do was find them without getting myself shot by friendly fire.

An abrupt volley of gunfire punctuated the night, and I instinctively ducked behind a tree before I realized the sounds had come from several blocks north. Checking for any signs of life, I scanned the other houses. Nothing. No movement anywhere. Were they hiding nearby, waiting to shoot the first thing that moved? Or had they moved on to another location? The Petry home was three doors down on the right, but I hesitated at the thought of making myself visible. Instead, I went to the back of the nearest home and began scaling fences until I reached the backyard. Inching my way up to the kitchen window, I peeked inside.

"No!!" I screamed, and threw myself to the ground just as the window exploded above me, and the relative quiet was shattered by the sound of a shotgun blast. Glass shards rained down on me as I tried to identify myself.

"Wait! Eric, it's Leeland!!" I rolled to the side of the window in case Eric Petry hadn't heard me before correcting his aim. During that panicked moment, I heard the elder Petry pump the shotgun once more before my words must have registered.

While I was trying to do a belly-crawl through the broken glass at the speed of a desert jackrabbit, I heard his hesitant call. "Leeland? Lee, is that you?"

"Unless you fire that next round, it is! Jesus H., Eric. You nearly blew my head off!" Panting, I rolled onto my back and stared up at the beautiful trail of the Milky Way above. As my heart tried to burst through my rib cage, it occurred to me just how close I had come to never seeing those stars again.

"Lee?" Eric's voice was above me, concerned, perhaps a little frightened. I looked up and saw his face, upside down from my perspective, as I lay there in the grass… and the glass. "Lee, did I hurt…? Aw, hell, did I shoot you? Are you shot?"

"No," I gasped. "But not for lack of trying. Oh God, Eric!" I nearly laughed, I was so giddy with relief. Then the pain hit me. "Jeez, I think my arms are cut up from crawling through what's left of your window." Raising my arms, I saw that the cuts were all superficial—painful, but far from dangerous.

Megan's future father-in-law reached down through the empty window frame and offered me a hand. "Better get in here before the shot attracts attention."

"Yeah." I groaned as he helped me through the window. "Everyone all right?"

"No." He turned and walked back into the kitchen. As I followed him in, I saw the blood. God, there was blood everywhere! On the walls, the floor, Eric, and splattered on the food at the table. Smeared, bloody footprints were all over the place. A uniformed man sat in a pool of blood in the far corner, staring down through sightless eyes at the steak knife protruding from his chest. It had been done right, shoved in and twisted, maximizing the damage beyond what the little knife would normally do. The man had probably gone into shock immediately.

"Megan got him." Petry explained. "She was faster than the rest of us." He shook his head. "Me and Andrew just sat and stared when they went for their guns. But not Megan."

My heart jumped into my throat. "Where is she?"

"We realized what was going on then, and we jumped after the other guy." He nodded to another body, fallen behind the dinner table. "But he had his pistol out by that time. Andrew got to 'im first, and then me, and by God, Leeland, Megan was right there with us. She was so freakin' fast!" He began to sob. "She just wasn't quite fast enough. None of us were."

I was frantic. "Eric, where is she?"

Eyes filled with tears, he pointed upstairs. "I don't even remember hearing the pistol go off. She tried, Leeland. God in Heaven, I *never* saw nobody *try* so hard!" His emotions finally got the better of him, and he sobbed out the rest. "She just wasn't quite fast enough."

I tore up the stairs, following a trail of blood so solid it looked as if someone had painted it on the carpet—a trail that led to Megan. She was sitting on the floor of a bedroom with her eyes closed, leaning back against the wall. Her shirt was nearly solid red, covered with blood, her face and hands coated as well. I wanted to scream, but my voice caught, trapped behind the constricting of my throat. My daughter... my baby!

Then she opened her eyes, and I *did* scream as I stumbled back against the doorframe. "Dad?" she sobbed. "Daddy?" She staggered to her feet, and I barely caught her as she fell against me. It took a moment for me to comprehend what she was saying as she sobbed against my chest. At the sight of Andrew's body lying on the bed, I finally understood.

"They killed him. They killed him." She kept repeating it, her personal mantra, her litany of anguish.

"She wouldn't leave him." Eric's voice behind me gave me a start. "How could I do less? The others in the neighborhood left a few minutes ago, but Megan wouldn't go until we got him up here and laid him out proper. She wanted a few minutes alone with him, so I went downstairs. When I heard you comin' over the fence... well, you know the rest."

I suddenly felt self-conscious, holding my daughter in front of Eric, while just a few feet away, his son lay dead. I knew how he must be feeling since I had just run that gamut of emotions myself. But mainly I was just grateful that it wasn't Megan lying on that bed.

He didn't seem to notice, though. He stared sightlessly at Andrew's body.

"Where were the others going, Eric?"

"Big Cypress Creek." His voice was as distant as his sight. "Said they'd wait there for a little while 'til they could figure out what to do next."

"How many of them?"

He finally pulled his eyes away from Andrew's body and turned to me. "'Bout fifty, I guess. But a few of 'em were hurt pretty bad, so there might be some that didn't make it."

"Can you show me the way? I'm supposed to help gather folks up and get them to Amber Peddy's place as soon as I can."

Eric nodded. "Go on downstairs. Give me a minute with Andrew."

Megan sobbed as I half-carried her out of the room and down the stairs. We waited by the front door until Eric came and led us out without a word. As we left the street, I looked back to see the house aflame, burning from the upstairs bedroom down. Turning to Eric, I saw tears and anguish, but mostly I saw hatred—raw, burning hatred for those who had taken his son. I never once saw him look back.

* * *

We made it to the creek with no trouble and found the impromptu meeting place where Eric's neighbors, along with others, had gathered. More than a hundred people were assembled trying to cope with the fact that their lives had just been irrevocably altered in the last hours as much as they had been on D-day.

I sat Megan at the edge of the water and began to clean the blood off of her while listening to the frightened whispers of the crowd. Megan was in shock, unresisting, but not helping either, so it took me a few minutes. As I finished, I scanned the faces around us.

It was immediately evident that these people had absolutely no idea of what to do next, so it took little coaxing to convince them to accompany me to the rendezvous at Amber's. We broke into three groups, and each took a different route to gather as many people as possible along the way.

A ragtag parade of Rejas refugees, our group skirted the town, gathering others before making it to my home just before the appointed time. When I got there, I had to push my way through a crowd to make it to the house. People milled about, crowded together like the proverbial sardines in a can.

Finally reaching the back door, Megan and I entered to find the inside even more chaotic than the yard. Debra, Cindy, and Zachary, as well as several others I didn't know, were busy tending the more seriously wounded. Debra saw us as we came in and ran to help as I led Megan inside.

"What happened?" Her voice shook, and she was obviously fighting to keep control. "Oh, my God! Is this blood on her? Her whole shirt is…" she trailed off and frantically began to unbutton Megan's shirt. I closed the door behind me to preserve my daughter's modesty.

"She's not hurt, Deb." Debra didn't stop until she had confirmed it for herself. Then she turned frightened eyes to me.

I hesitated, not wanting to mention what had happened in front of Megan. But then I thought that any reaction was better than the stupor she'd been in since I took her out of the Petry's house. "They got Andrew."

"Oh, God…" She put her arms around her daughter.

"Zachary," I jerked his attention away from the blood on his sister. "Go get Megan another shirt from her closet." He ran.

I turned back to Debra. "It all happened right in front of her." I studied Megan's face as I spoke, hoping to see some reaction, but she just stared at the floor.

"Where's Amber?" I wanted her to have a look at Megan to make sure there wasn't anything wrong with her beyond the emotional shock of losing her fiancé.

"I think she's still at the hospital." Her voice quavered a bit as she continued, "I haven't heard from her since she left this morning, anyway."

It made sense. Amber wouldn't leave with people still under her care. Zach returned with one of his sister's shirts and handed it to Debra.

"Is Ken back yet?" I asked.

Cindy had come over by then, and she answered, "He's out at the number three stash."

That was about a half-mile into the woods to the south of the house. "Okay, I've got to talk to him and find out where we stand. If anything happens while I'm out—" I stopped, realizing that I had no idea what to do if we were attacked here and now. "I guess we play that one by ear," I finished lamely, and ducked out the door to find Ken and Jim.

It was a fight to shove my way through the massive crowd in the back yard. People milling, moaning, sitting, standing, staring… but nowhere did I see anyone who appeared to know what they were doing. Most had a bewildered look in their eyes. It was a look I could relate to, for though all of us had become accustomed to the idea that violence was more prevalent now than it had ever been before D-day, only Ken and a few other veterans had ever seen the kind of destruction we had just witnessed.

Rejas was at war. Only now could I really begin to understand what that meant.

* * *

I found Ken and Jim, as well as most of the other committee heads, coming back toward the house through the woods. Ken squeezed my shoulder and smiled wearily. "Good to see you made it."

I simply nodded. Maybe I was still a little shocked at everything I had seen, but I just didn't know what to say.

"I'll second that." Jim clapped me on the back hard enough to stagger me for a second. "I still need to pick your brain about this *General Troutman* o' yours."

Turning to walk back with them, I rubbed my aching neck. My mind struggled for a moment, trying to come up with something to say. "Did you get all the supplies passed out?"

"Yeah. It took less than twenty minutes to empty all three caches."

I blinked. "But there were hundreds of guns. There was food, and tools, and…"

"I know," Ken interrupted, "but have you looked at how many people there are out there?"

We stopped as we re-entered the clearing at the back of the house.

"Take a look for a minute," Jim advised, waiting beside Ken as I scanned the area. Amber's was a huge backyard by the standards that I had been used to in the Houston suburbs. Nearly three acres of cleared land. I tried counting the number of people in an area roughly equivalent to a tenth of the yard—just over two hundred. Multiplied by ten, that gave us more than two thousand people.

"Good Lord! So many people—" I stopped when I saw Jim shaking his head. "What?"

"Rejas had nearly seven thousand people this mornin'." His words put the crowd in proper perspective. "This ain't near crowded enough for my likin'."

Undoubtedly, hundreds, possibly even thousands, were still scattered throughout the woods, unaware of our grouping at the homestead. But as much as I might wish otherwise, I couldn't believe that more than four thousand of our people were wandering around out there. Our dead must number in the hundreds, at least. The rest had to still be in town, either fighting, or captured if Larry's army had been instructed to take prisoners.

"Oh, my God." I turned to Ken. "We've got to go back. There are too many still back there."

The faint sounds of gunfire from the direction of town punctuated my words, but Ken shook his head. "With what? We've got a couple of thousand people. Some are wounded; some are kids. Altogether, I'd guess we have about seventeen hundred, at the most. Seventeen hundred civilians with whatever guns and ammunition we could give them. A few had time to bring their own or take weapons off of the soldiers they killed. But still, I estimate that less than half of us have any kind of firearm."

I looked again and saw that he was right. We had concentrated on hiding most of our weapons and supplies before Larry's troops got into town. "We've still got to do something! Send back small armed groups to help gather more of our people."

Bowing to his experience as a vet, Jim turned to Ken. "Would that work?"

Ken shrugged. "It's a gamble. We could just as easily end up losing whoever goes back, and their equipment, and still not get anyone out of town."

"What if we send out some groups to help get people out, and others to get to some of the stashes where we hid guns and supplies? At least some of them are bound to get through! And we'd be bringing back enough supplies to make it worth the risk." I was nearly pleading.

Jim turned from me to Ken, and back again. "I don't know. I don't like leavin' folks in town any more than you do, Leeland. But I got a bunch of 'em here an' now that I'm responsible for, too."

Afraid he was going to waffle, I made a stand. "I'm going back. If I have to do it alone, I will, but I'm going back. There are too many people back there."

The mayor opened his mouth to protest, but stopped when he realized there really wasn't anything he could do to stop me.

Ken made it worse. "I guess you'll need someone to show you the back trails again." He looked at Jim. "I'm going with him."

Mayor Kelland's brows tried to reach his hairline. "But I thought you were the one that was against all this!"

"I just said it was a gamble." He paused as if to gather his thoughts. "I figure our people's lives are worth the risk."

Jim blew out a deep breath. "Okay. Ya'll gather up as many as you think you'll need. I'm gonna get the rest of these folks deeper into the woods." He turned back to me. "Nice as this place may be, it's just too close to town. Sooner or later that bunch'll find it, an' I'd rather not be here when they do."

"Where are you headed?"

He turned to Ken. "You know the old Vogler fertilizer plant?"

"Yeah. That's a bit of a walk, isn't it?"

"Yep. But it's also on the other side of Cypress Creek and the reservoir. I'd like to see 'em try to get a tank in there if we rig the bridge with some of that dynamite ya'll had stashed out back." He grabbed my arm. "I ain't gonna complain about you not sharin' that before now, since it all works out in our favor this time around. But you ain't got nothin' else like that hidden around here, do ya?"

"Sorry," I told him, "you got it all this time."

"Well, it was worth askin'." He looked disappointed. "Don't guess it matters that much, I understand that you can do some real nasty things with fertilizer, if you know how to mix the ingredients right."

I snapped my fingers as an idea formed. "Did Wayne Kelley make it out?"

Ken nodded. "I think so. I'm pretty sure I saw him helping with the wounded."

The mayor chuckled. "Yeah, I guess a chemistry teacher might come in handy, huh?"

"Especially with some of the recipes I have in my library. Give me a couple of minutes to get the right books, and he ought to be able to mix up enough mayhem to... well, enough to stop a tank!"

"By damn, that's the best news I heard all night!" Jim headed to the house at a brisk pace. "C'mon, fellas, we got things to do."

176

CHAPTER 13

* * AUGUST 17 / MIDNIGHT * *

Grande cité à soldats abandonnee,
On n'y eu mortel tumult si proche:
O qu'elle hideuse mortalité s'approche,
Fors vne offence n'y sera pardonnee.

Great city abandoned to the soldiers,
Never was mortal tumult so close to it:
Oh, what a hideous calamity draws near,
Except one offense nothing will be spared it.
Nostradamus – *Century 6, Quatrain 96*

Déjà vu.

Once again, I watched my family drive away, though this time they had a considerable entourage. The van was loaded with wounded, as was the Simms' pickup, which Cindy drove. In addition, Ken had hooked an old flatbed trailer to his backhoe, and it, too, was filled with wounded. Jim drove the backhoe at the front of the convoy, guiding his people like Moses headed for the Promised Land. All others walked.

Though I had never been to the Vogler plant, the others told me it was about fifteen miles north of Rejas. More than three hours at a brisk walk, and not many seemed to be walking all that briskly on this night. I guessed it would probably take closer to four or five, barring unforeseen problems. I didn't care to speculate on what those problems might be.

Ken and I turned back to our group—twenty men and eleven women, all armed and dressed in dark or camouflaged clothing. Our firearms ranged from deer rifles to Ken's AR-15 and, while the ammunition supply wasn't exactly critical, if things got intense, none of us could afford to get trigger-happy. Once more, I wore my old paintball gear, complete with the trusty smoke grenades that had stood me in such great stead before. The faces around me were those of some of my finest students. Seven of them had been part of the Rejas police force.

I looked closely at those faces—Ken, the man who had gone from stranger to brother during the last couple of years; Mark, the quiet, gentle giant who helped me on the forges each morning; Eric Petry, Andrew's father, who had obvious reasons for being with us; Sarah Graham, René, Jenna, James. I wanted to remember each one because odds were, some of us wouldn't make it through the night.

Ken broke the silence. "I guess this falls into the security category." He got a couple of half-hearted smiles, but most of us appeared to be too nervous to appreciate his humor. If they felt anything at all like I did, they were rapidly discovering that it was one thing to say you were ready to jump back into the fray, but it was quite another to face the idea after having had time to think about it.

"Security is my department," he continued, "and that's why I'm here. If any of you have any second thoughts, leave now and no one will think any less of you. I know it sounds a little clichéd, but it's true. We can use you to help protect the convoy."

He waited a moment. "All right, then. Line up in single file. I'm point. Leeland, you take the rear. When we get to the edge of town, we split into groups of five. Odd man goes with me."

Ken continued talking as we shuffled into position. "Our targets are the abandoned fabric store on Bellmont, the concession booth at the football stadium, the storage room at Felix's Video Rental, the back room at Computer Outlet, and the B & S Furniture Warehouse. All of those places are major stashes of food, tools, and weapons that we need to get to the fertilizer plant. We also need to find as many of our people as we can and get them out, if possible. Just don't take any fights that you can't win. You can't help anyone if you're dead." He stopped, then opened his mouth as if he wanted to say more. Closing it again, he took a deep breath and shook his head. "Everyone count off. One through five, I'm one."

Sarah Graham was next in line. "Two!"

"Three!" "Four!" "Five!" "One!"

I finished the count with, "One!" I wondered if Ken had intentionally put me in a position to be in his group.

"Group One will take the fabric store on Bellmont. Group Two takes the football stadium. Group Three takes Felix's Video Rental. Group Four, the Computer Outlet, and Group Five takes B & S Furniture. Everybody know where your targets are?"

We nodded. Once again, Ken looked as if he wanted to say something. Finally, with his lips held in a tight line, he gave another curt nod. He seemed to be reassuring himself that he was doing the right thing. "Okay, people, let's go get 'em."

Ken led us at a dogtrot back toward town. I took one last look back at the other, larger group leaving the house for the plant before I turned and followed Ken.

* * *

As we began the trek back toward Rejas, we could still hear occasional sounds of fighting, but they were becoming more and more infrequent, as if one side was being worn down. It frightened me to think that it was probably our people on the losing side.

As we jogged through the woods, there were several occasions when I thought I could hear the crackling of twigs breaking in the brush nearby. My imagination played games with me, gifting me with images of people following us. Once, I could have sworn I caught a flash of movement off to our left, deeper in the thicket. Convinced we were being followed, I dropped to one knee and sighted the carbine—dead center on an armadillo.

"Damn!" Sweating with nervousness as much as the warmth of the night, I cursed my panicked reactions and silently thanked Ken for putting me at the end of the line. No one else had seen my momentary agitation. Taking a deep breath, I hurried to catch up to the others while trying to ignore the myriad woodland noises.

We reached the edge of town, and Ken signaled a halt, gathering us together for a final talk. He paused, examining each and every face, much as I had done back at the house, memorizing, knowing better than any of the rest of us just how risky this was. "I can't stress enough to you people just how important it is that you avoid the fights you can't win. We estimate that there are probably close to four thousand of our people still in Rejas."

Some shocked gasps and mutters erupted at the proclamation. Most hadn't realized how many of us were still in there.

Sarah Graham asked what most were thinking at that point. "You don't expect us to leave them in there, do you?"

"Yes!" Ken responded vehemently. "Some of them have probably made it out to the forest, and others are already dead." I could see that his bluntness didn't set well. "I would guess most of the others have been captured or are hiding. There's no use getting yourselves captured or killed in a hopeless situation. We have to wait and plan how to get our people out the right way. Otherwise, we'll just make things worse than they already are."

Seeing he hadn't convinced many of them, I offered an observation. "Listen." When they turned toward me, I shook my head. "Not to me. Just listen. Listen to the town. Do you hear any gunfire? Any more yelling? Anything to indicate that anyone's still fighting in there?"

It was true. The sounds of battle were gone. Rejas was uncannily silent, considering the sounds of just half an hour ago.

I pointed toward the outskirts of town. "It's over in there. But, we have more than two thousand people that are safe, for the moment. I don't like it any more than you do, but they have to be our first priority tonight. They're depending on us."

Ken shifted his weight, as if still uncertain of himself. "It's our job to make sure they stay safe. Our job is to find some way of getting some of the supplies stashed in town out to the fertilizer plant, where they'll do some good. Then, and only then, can we think about getting out anyone we find in Rejas." He looked around, pleading with his eyes for everyone to understand. "I'm not saying we leave everyone no matter what. If the circumstances are right, and you can get some of them out without risking the rest of your group, then do it." That seemed to appease some of them.

"In the meantime, keep your eyes open. If we know what they've done with our people, we can plan to get them out later on. Does everyone understand?"

I saw heads nodding as they reluctantly accepted the harshness of our situation.

Ken relaxed visibly. "Good." He looked away from the group for a moment, staring into the town. Rejas was eerily silhouetted by a few burning buildings. "Leeland, you still have that radio?"

I couldn't believe I'd forgotten about it. "Got it right here." I pulled the little transceiver off of my belt and started to hand it to him, but he stopped me with a shake of his head.

"Just turn it on and see if we can tell what's going on in there."

As I flipped the switch, an unfamiliar voice was speaking over the static. "... in. We should... ny more trouble..."

"All ri... if you mess th... I'll hav... for it!" Troutman's voice was barely recognizable over the static, but he sounded as if he'd had better days.

"... don't, we can... ill... st 'em... tanks."

Ken shook his head. "Too far away. This dinky radio isn't much better than a kid's walkie-talkie. Might as well save the batteries 'til we get closer."

I clicked it off. The tiny bits of conversation had been more tantalizing than informative.

"All right, people. Divide into your groups and hit your targets. This has priority. Get as many of those supplies to the plant as quickly as you can."

All hell broke loose.

* * *

The sudden sounds of gunfire had me scrambling frantically for cover. I dove for the shelter of the nearby tree line and saw most of the others scattering in all directions. Behind me, someone stood in the open like an idiot, shooting in the direction of the enemy fire. I couldn't tell who it was, but he didn't last long. A line of bloody holes stitched themselves across his chest within a matter of seconds, and he fell to the ground thrashing horribly. From my spot behind a huge Texas pine, I saw that two more had been caught in the attack. Dead. How had they found us?

Many of our group began to return fire, aiming in the general direction of our attackers. I looked, but couldn't see a thing. The sounds of machine guns firing at us told me about where they were, but I wasn't confident enough about their location to risk wasting bullets. I put my back to the tree and tried to calm down enough to think.

My heart hammering with instinctive fear, I assessed the situation. Hiding behind a tree at the edge of the forest a half-mile out of Rejas, enemy firing from somewhere between myself and the town, three of my companions down, presumably dead, and the rest of the group scattered, disorganized, wasting bullets on an opponent they couldn't see—not a very reassuring predicament. Then I caught a glimpse of furtive movement in the trees off to my left. Ken.

Just as I recognized him, he began speeding through the forest, skirting the edge of the tree line; I realized he was attempting to flank our attackers.

It was time to piss or get off the pot, as Jim was fond of saying. "Oh, hell," I muttered. "I sure hope you know what you're doing, Ken." I took off after him, bullets singing their terrifying song through the trees, accompanied by the distinctive scent of cordite wafting through the air.

Running through the trees, leaping over scrub that appeared out of nowhere in the darkness, I wrestled with my fear. I was probably more frightened at that moment than I had ever been in my life, and it took a major effort to get a grip on my emotions. Finally, I convinced my pounding heart that, though the trepidation was natural, I had no time for it. So I continued the insane race through the trees, chasing the elusive ghost that was Ken, and concentrated on clamping down on the cold knot of fear deep within my abdomen. Ultimately, I managed to fan it into a cold, resolute anger. By the time I left the trees, I was furious.

Ken was just ahead, thirty, maybe forty feet at most. With his black BDUs, I could barely make him out by the light of the crescent moon as he ran through waist-high grass, jumping over small scrub bushes, plowing through others, and then, abruptly, he was gone. He just wasn't there. A moment later, the ground gave way beneath my feet, and I flailed wildly, involuntarily beginning a yell that was choked off as I hit the icy black surface of one of Rejas's many springs.

"Damn, Leeland!" Ken hissed from the bank. "Shut up and quit all the splashing. You want to get us killed?" He reached forward. "Here, take my hand."

"What happened?" I asked stupidly, as he helped me out of the water. We were in the bottom of a small ravine that had been carved out over the years by the flow of water from a nearby spring. "How'd they find us?"

"They must have night-scopes or starlight goggles." He pulled me out of the water, through the slippery mud of the streambed, and over to hug the embankment as he listened to the sounds of the battle raging to our right. "I didn't think of that, or I would have kept us back in the trees until we were ready to move out." He cursed under his breath. "I'm the one that's supposed to know this kind of thing. How many did they get?"

"Three that I saw. I think all the rest of us made it to the trees."

Ken's head sagged. "I only saw one before I hit the ground." Sounds of the ongoing firefight punctuated the night as he sighed. "Jenna... she took one in the neck." I saw his fist curl in the faint moonlight. "All because I didn't think of a simple thing like night goggles." He closed his eyes, leaning his head back to rest against the muddy drop-off. "I might as well have killed them myself."

I grabbed his arm and shook it to get his attention. "It's not your fault, Ken. We all made the same choice tonight."

He didn't reply, just sat there with his head leaned back against the dirt, eyes and ears closed to the battle above.

"Ken?" No answer. "Ken? Don't you zone out on me!" I hissed. "I need you here. We all do!"

His eyes opened and locked with mine; for the first time, I could see the age in them. I saw the tired and haunted look of a man who had lived through this, and worse, and had managed to put it behind him to get on with his life. Now war had come calling on him again, and he was forced to answer. He nodded wearily, accepting the responsibility. "Yeah, I hear you."

Ken turned away for a moment, and I was afraid that I had lost his attention again. Then he jerked his chin downstream. "This bank stays pretty high, and the gully curves around behind the clearing out there, about five hundred yards or more to the south. It ought to hide us well enough to let us get behind whoever is doing all the shooting up there."

"Sounds good. Any idea how many of them there are?"

"I only hear eight or nine. That doesn't mean there aren't more, but there are only a few guns firing right now."

"Just eight?" The gunfire had sounded like a small army to me. From our protected position in the streambed, though, I could tell that Ken was right. I could hear our people in the trees to the west firing like crazy, but the return fire from downstream was relatively small.

"You got an idea?" I asked "or were you just planning to run up and try to take them from behind?"

"Actually, I'm open to suggestions," Ken said with a sheepish look. "'Cause that's pretty much what I had in mind. What are you thinking of?"

I shook my head. "I was hoping that you had some brilliant plan in mind."

He frowned. "Well, sometimes the best plans are the simplest ones." He took one last deep breath. "Let's go."

Ken's words didn't inspire much confidence, but we began our run, splashing and sliding through the mud and water, slowly curving around and drawing constantly nearer to the sound of enemy gunfire. A few minutes later, Ken slowed and held up one hand, signaling me to a stop.

He pointed to his eyes, then to top of the bank. I nodded. He was going to peek over the edge. Picking his footing carefully, straining to keep from sliding, Ken climbed the dozen feet to the top. Slowly, ever so slowly, he raised his head over the grassy crest of the eroded stream embankment. Standing motionless, hanging precariously onto the top, he waved me up next to him. I tried to move as carefully as he had, fearing a misstep might send me sliding back down into the water and possibly give away our position.

When I finally peered over the top, I was stunned. By the dim light of the crescent moon I saw that our group, nearly thirty people strong, were being pinned by fewer than a dozen of Larry's thugs. They were hidden behind three of the many Humvees that had paraded into Rejas. *Was that really just a few hours ago?* They were a little over fifty feet away, and I started to bring up the carbine, but Ken grabbed my arm to get my attention. He shook his head and drew me back down to the streambed.

"Wait 'til I can move a little further downstream," Ken whispered. "The stream curves a little, and I'll get another angle on them from around the bend."

I nodded, and he continued, "When I start firing, I should be able to get a few of them before they change position to take cover from me. If things go the way I hope, that will put their backs to you. Then you can open up on them from behind. Between you, me, and the others shooting from the trees, these guys won't have any place to hide."

I nodded understanding once more. He was setting up a three-way crossfire. "I'll wait for you." He squeezed my arm once and quickly slipped away into the humid Texas night.

It must have taken only a few minutes for him to find his place, for the sounds from above changed abruptly. There was more of the automatic gunfire than there had been, accompanied by a cacophony of screams of agony and outrage. That was my cue. Scrambling to the top of the embankment, I planted my feet and fired at the first target I could see. Ken had gotten two with his first burst, and he had called their response exactly. They had all shifted to take cover from his attack, completely ignoring their backs.

The sound of my carbine was almost totally masked by the clamor of the hundreds of rounds fired by the others. That suited me just fine as I let off one shot after another, getting three of them from behind before they even knew I was there.

One of the guys saw the man next to him go down with my bullet in his back. Realizing what was happening, he spun to face me. It was an eerie sight. His face appeared insectile, eyes covered by an outlandish contraption extending into a monocular three inches past his nose. I realized that those night vision goggles made me so visible that it might as well have been broad daylight, while I could barely make out that he was looking at me. Luckily, I was the one that already had my weapon on target, and he died without getting off a shot.

They were down to four, but they were desperate animals with their backs to the wall. Another of them realized that someone was shooting at them from behind and dove to the other side of a Humvee, only to be cut down by our people in the trees. Three left.

The last three saw number four jump over the hood and turned to find me gunning at them. As one, they spun to fire at me; one raised up to one knee to steady his aim. Just before I dropped below the ridge, I saw the top of his head removed by a quick burst from Ken's direction.

The last two disintegrated the crest of the bank above me as I slid back to the bottom. If I had stayed there… well, I didn't care to dwell on that thought. As it was, dirt, rocks, and chunks of grass rained down on me from above. Time to move.

Fearing that the small amount of dirt at the top wouldn't be enough to stop the bullets, I scrambled along on hands and knees, ignoring the gouging rocks, until I reached my new position about twenty yards back upstream. From the new location, I risked another climb to the top for a quick peek and got off one shot. Missed. Once more, I was forced to drop for cover as the stream bank showered me with debris.

I headed downstream again. I popped up about halfway back to my original position, just in time to see Ken fire a burst from his new site. He missed, too. They were too well protected from his direction and were simply waiting for me to pop my head up again. When I did, they were expecting it, swinging to fire as soon as they saw where I was. Kicking back with my feet, I let gravity drop me down the eroded embankment.

I continued to pop up from various places along the bank four more times, never in the same place, always in about fifteen to twenty second intervals, establishing a pattern. Then on the fifth time, I dug my feet into the ledge before I popped up. They swung their guns toward me and I dropped again as I had before. This time though, I maintained my footing on the crumbling embankment, and as soon as the return fire had stopped I jumped back up in the same place.

The one on the left appeared confused for a moment, aiming first at me, then shifting further upstream, as if he couldn't believe I was really in the same place. It was a fatal mistake, as he momentarily crossed into his buddy's line of fire. The other soldier, rather than shoot his only remaining ally, raised his rifle for the second that it took me to take advantage of the confusion. I got off several shots, hitting the confused thug in the chest and head and clipping the other in the shoulder. I dropped again before the wounded man could recover and return fire.

Further upstream, further from Ken than I had yet shifted, I once more jumped up to try for the last soldier, but found only scattered bodies. I couldn't very well hope the fight had gone out of him and just let him lay there, but neither could I afford to go over the top and search the bodies.

That would expose me to those damned night vision goggles. Sticking my head and rifle back up where I could scan the slaughter, I examined the bodies carefully. The gunfire died out as our people slowly realized that they were the only ones doing any shooting, and the smoke from the enemy guns began to thin in the light breeze. There was no sign of movement.

Keeping my eyes and gunsight on the still bodies, I yelled, "Ken? You okay?"

"Yeah, you?" His voice came from exactly where I had expected it. He was still positioned to catch any movement from that side of the bend.

"So far, but there's one left..."

I could hear movement from downstream in his direction, then more movement from upstream, the rapid clattering of light-soled shoes running through water, gravel, and mud. The noise came toward me quickly and was accompanied by a shouted, "Noooo!" I spun to face the scream, losing my footing as I did so. It was only about five feet back down to the streambed, but I was completely out of control as I slid directly toward this new attacker and landed in a sprawl, the carbine six feet away. Fearing that it was in vain, I struggled to my feet, hoping there might be a chance that I could reach my rifle in time. Looking up, I faced my attacker and knew it was too late. A man dressed in black, face smeared with mud and dirt, ran screaming toward me, pistol already drawn and aimed.

There was no way I would be able to get to my weapon before he got off a shot. In that slow-motion moment before he fired, I scanned wildly for someplace to go, to get out of the way. But there was only the dirt ledge of the bank on one side, and the slick footing of the muddy streambed on the other. I had inadvertently trapped myself. I dropped back to the ground, intent upon getting out of the path of the bullet that had to be coming.

Finally, he fired. Three shots, deafening at such intimate range, and for the next second or two, I waited to feel the agony of a bullet ripping through me. When it didn't happen, I realized he had somehow missed, and I gathered my legs beneath me and launched myself at him. Diving to the ground in front of him, I tucked and rolled, lashing out with my feet as I spiraled out of it. One foot behind his ankle, the other on his knee, and he dropped to the ground in a heap. I rolled to my feet, relinquishing the hold, and stood on his knee for a second as I leapt for the pistol that had gone flying from his grip. I expected to have to fight him for the gun; the leg-lock I'd used might hurt a bit, but it was far from debilitating. Surprisingly, I got the handgun and spun to face him again without resistance. He just lay there with his hands above his head as I pointed the pistol.

"It's me, Sensei!" a familiar voice screamed, terrified. "Don't shoot!"

"Leeland!" Ken's voice came from behind me.

It was all happening too quickly, and I stood confused for a moment, panting and trying to sort everything out. Eyes wide and frightened, Billy lay on the ground before me. I was stunned, disbelieving. But as I looked closer, there was no doubt. By the faint moonlight, I could just make out his features, even the mud-coated tattoo on his forehead.

"He was going to shoot you," Billy babbled. "I didn't have time to warn you! I'm sorry, but I followed you, and… I had to show you I wasn't like them. I had to show you! I just wanted to help!"

"Leeland!!" Splashing, running footsteps came up from behind as my mind began to comprehend what the boy was telling me; I whirled around to look. The last soldier lay dead in the mud. It hadn't been Ken I'd heard coming from downstream. Ken was just now rounding the last bend, rifle at the ready, trying to make sense of the scene before him.

"Lee? What's going on?"

I dropped my aim wearily. "It's okay." They were the right words for both Ken and Billy. "Everything's okay."

* * *

Ken went back up the ravine to regroup our people, while Billy explained how he had followed us to the tree line—I recalled the noises in the trees on the way out—and had seen Ken and me running to the ravine. It had taken him some time, but he'd finally made it to the gully to follow us. The sounds of our battle had kept him cautious, and he repeatedly poked his head above the top, much as Ken and I had, to keep track of what was happening. By the time he got close enough, only two soldiers remained. One of them spotted Billy and started to shoot, but I cut him down before he could fire. Billy had watched as I ducked, and the last soldier scuttled to the edge of the ravine and dropped into it downstream from my position. He realized the danger that Ken and I were in and raced desperately to help, arriving barely in time.

Billy and I searched the soldiers and had an interesting assortment of equipment piled up when Ken returned with the rest of our people.

Automatic weapons, ammunition, radios, and several of the strange-looking night goggles. Ken immediately began issuing orders. "Doug, weren't you a mechanic?"

The man turned. "Yeah."

"Check out those Humvees. See if any of them are still drivable." As Doug jogged over to the jeeps, Ken addressed the rest of us. "I want two people per body. Search them for anything we can use. Take two minutes only. We don't know whether or not they got word to anyone else, so assume the worst."

When they appeared to hesitate, Ken yelled, "Go!"

Ken didn't know that Billy and I had already searched the bodies, so I got his attention and waved him over. We showed him the small pile of gear we had gotten, and he examined the night goggles with interest.

"Generation threes," he declared. "These weren't around when I was in the service, but I've read about them." He slipped them on, feeling along the right side and muttering, "Should be a switch. There!" He turned and looked around. "Whoa!" Reaching up, he tripped the switch again. "Very nice! Both lowlight amplification and infrared."

He flipped the switch and removed the goggles. "How many did we get?"

"Looks like ten," I told him. "We lost a couple to head shots." My stomach threatened to rebel again at the thought of one particular body, the head above the eyebrows missing as he lay facedown in the brush. That particular sight had caused me to heave the contents of my stomach into the bushes nearby. "We also got three more of the walkie-talkies."

Ken handed the goggles back to me. "Good, two goggles per group. Pass out the radios, too." He checked to see what frequency they were set on. "Change the radio settings. Set them all on thirty-seven. That gives us four radios. My group will do without a radio, the rest of you take one per group. Keep each other informed of your progress. If you run into trouble, pull back and yell for help. We can't afford to lose any more people."

Everyone nodded. The latest skirmish and the resulting deaths had brought home just how vulnerable we were.

Doug the Mechanic trotted over to Ken. "Two of the Humvees are shot up from hell to breakfast, too damaged to use. The last one has two flat tires and a lot of holes in the chassis, but the engine turns over and seems to run all right with no fluid leaks I can see. I got some people getting tires from the others, and it'll be ready to go in a minute."

"Okay." Ken turned to the rest of the group. His expression somber, he addressed us. We were his to command. We knew it and, finally, he seemed to know it as well. "All right, folks. We lost some people… some good people. But we got some good equipment, transportation," he paused as he glanced at Billy. "And it looks like we gained us a good man, too."

Billy looked surprised at the compliment and grinned shyly.

"Let's get into town and get our supplies," Ken finished.

* * *

As luck would have it, all three of our casualties were from group two, so Ken assigned Billy and me to them in order to help balance the numbers. Then he and his group took the Humvee and headed for the fabric store. They would be the first into town, and I figured that could go either way. It might be that they would be able to get in and out before any of Larry's boys knew anything was up. If they were spotted, though, they would be the first to be attacked. They would also be far enough ahead of the rest of us that our chances of helping them would be remote, at best.

My new target was the Rejas High School football stadium. I glanced at the faces of my new companions. Sarah Graham, René Herrera, Billy Worecski, and a man who had the unlikely name of Gene McQueen. Gene was the only one I didn't already know.

"Who knows the quickest way to the stadium?" I asked.

"Denley Avenue to the warehouse district," Sarah piped up, "skip east three blocks to Stadium Drive. That'll put us right in front of the gate."

I handed her one of our group's two sets of PVS-7s, showed her how they worked, and waved her to the point position. "Lead us in."

She slipped on the goggles, fiddled with the adjustments for a minute, and headed out at a trot. I put on the other pair and took the rear.

* * *

We made it to the stadium without further incident, but there, our plan fell apart. "I guess we know where the rest of our people are now," Sarah whispered dryly. Just as she had promised, we had come out of an alley directly across from the Eagle Stadium. We hid in the dark confines of a large warehouse, staring out at what had been transformed into a makeshift concentration camp. The trashcan fires out front had forced Sarah and me to turn the light amplification on our goggles down to minimum.

"Lord," I whispered, comparing this crowd to the density of people I had seen back at Amber's home. A rough estimate placed the majority of Rejas's citizens in the stadium, either on the football field or in the bleachers. They were well-guarded with a number of Larry's boys, armed to the teeth, placed around the perimeter.

"Now what?" René's voice came from behind me. I turned and saw her form illuminated in the ghostly green of low light amplification. I reached up and turned off my goggles.

"Hell if I know." I blinked for a moment against the darkness. "Anyone have any bright ideas?"

"Check with the other groups," Billy suggested.

I nodded. "Sounds like a plan. Maybe someone else will have a suggestion."

I pulled out the radio and keyed the transceiver. "Dawcett here… anyone listening?"

A second later, Eric answered, "I'm here, Lee."

Mark chimed in. "What've you got?"

"I'm just across from the stadium," I responded. "Looks like they're keeping all our people here. They're turning the place into a concentration camp. There's no way we can get to the supplies without creating a stir."

Ken's voice surprised me. "Can you get any of our people out without any major risk?"

Just hearing his voice made me feel a little better. I had expected to have to make this decision on my own. "Man, am I glad to hear from you. I thought you didn't have a radio."

"I didn't. We ran across a couple of Larry's men that won't be needing theirs any more."

"Understood."

"So, can you get anyone out?"

"We could probably get most of them out, if we could get everyone to work together, all at the same time. But we would probably lose a lot of people doing it. There's about thirty guards scattered around."

Sarah cursed and whipped off her goggles. She dropped rapidly to a sitting position beneath the window sill and rubbed her eyes. "Better take a look down the street to the west. And turn off your goggles if you don't

191

want to be blinded." She looked directly at me, so I could tell she hadn't suffered any serious eye damage.

"Hang on, Ken. Something's happening."

I slipped up to her window and peeked out.

"Um, Ken?"

"What is it, Lee?"

"Things just got a little more complicated." I watched one of Larry's M1's, a single spotlight mounted on front, trundling up the street toward the stadium.

"Where exactly are the supplies?" Sarah whispered excitedly. I could tell that she had thought of something, but I also knew we were about out of time.

I shook my head. "They're in the storage room behind the concession stand. We'd never make it without being seen."

I turned my attention back to the radio. "Ken, one of the tanks is on its way here."

"Damn!" It was silent for a moment. Then he came back on, sounding resigned. "Okay, Leeland, get out of there."

I hesitated. I knew there was no way for us to get in without a fight and, with that tank coming toward us, there was no way we could win that fight. Still, I racked my brain, trying to think of an alternative.

"We need those supplies, Ken!" But it wasn't the supplies I was worried about, and we both knew it. I was pleading with him. *Come up with something,* I thought fiercely at him. *Pull that rabbit out of the hat again!*

"Not now, Lee. We'll have to find a way in later."

"C'mon, Ken, we can't just leave these people here. There must be something we can do."

But I knew better. So did Ken. "Leeland, you've got to get out of there. You can't win against that Abrams." I turned to the four faces around me.

"I know it's hard," Ken continued, "but we all knew it could happen."

They would follow my lead. I could see that.

"You have to leave." Ken's voice again.

I didn't answer right away, thinking through my options.

"Leeland? You hear me?"

If I decided to fight it out, they would stick by me, no questions asked.

"Leeland?"

Ironically, it was that realization that decided me.

"Leeland, you have to abort!"

I couldn't lead them into a no-win situation.

"Leeland, abort your mission! You made me take command of this thing, now you'd better take my goddamned orders! You hear me?"

I stared at the radio as if it were something foreign.

"Leeland!"

I slowly raised it back up to my mouth and keyed the mike once more. "I hear you, Ken," I said quietly. "You're right."

None of the others questioned me. They knew what was at stake. "We're aborting." I felt numb as I released the transmitter.

I noticed my hands shaking and took a deep breath to help steady them, then looked at the rest of the group. "Let's go home." One by one, we slipped out of the warehouse.

Sarah, once more taking the point position, was first out the door. Gene followed, then René and Billy. I took up the rear again. It wasn't until we were five blocks away that Gene noticed Sarah had disappeared. He passed the word back down the line, and I got a sudden sinking feeling in my gut, remembering the excitement in her voice when she had asked where the supplies were. I feared I might know what was going through her head.

Flagging the others down, I gathered them around me. "I have to go back and stop Sarah before she does something stupid. The rest of you get out to the fertilizer plant. Try to link up with the other groups if you can."

I handed Billy the radio. "Wait until you're out of town and in the trees. Then call for everyone's status. Find out where the closest group is and try to get to them. Wait a bit, though." I sighed. "Ken'll know something's up when he hears your voice instead of mine, and I don't want to give him a stroke just yet."

"You want me to come with you?"

I shook my head. "We started out with five in this group. It's bad enough that I'm just sending three of you back. I can just imagine what Ken will say when you tell him what's going on with me and Sarah."

Billy frowned. "Just when I'd gotten him to think of me as a person."

I squeezed his shoulder. "That won't change." I grinned a little. "What he'll think of me is another thing altogether."

Billy smiled a bit.

"Go on, kid."

He nodded and joined René and Gene. Together, the three of them disappeared into the darkness.

CHAPTER 14

* * AUGUST 17 / 2:18 A.M. * *

Par grand dangiers le captif eschapé,
Peu de temps grand a fortune changee:
Dans le palais le peuple est attrapé,
Par bon augure la cité assiegee.

Through great dangers the captive escaped:
In a short time great his fortune changed.
In the palace the people are trapped,
Through good omen the city besieged.
Nostradamus – *Century 2, Quatrain 66*

"Here we go again," I thought, once more slipping through the shadows of Rejas. It took only a few minutes to retrace the route we had taken from the warehouse. Slipping inside, I looked around for Sarah. "Sarah?" I whispered. No response. I hadn't really expected any.

I peered through the window again. The tank sat just outside the main entrance to the stadium. The hatches were open, and the spotlight shone on the street before the armored monster. Someone had rewired an old CD player and hooked it into the tank. An unknown rap group proclaimed their philosophy in barely intelligible English to a deafening thunder of bass.

"Beat yo' woman 'til she scream, 'cause you know the bitch, she live fo' it."

Dozens of uniformed men thrashed and gyrated in the circle of light before the tank. Someone had found some booze, and most of them had a bottle of their preferred poison in hand. Several of the guards were milling around, joking with the tank's crew and smoking. I wondered where they had found cigarettes, and just how desperate you had to be to smoke two-year-old tobacco. The scent of marijuana reached me about the time that I noticed the cigarettes were all hand rolled. Tobacco was a thing of the past around here, as the local climate wasn't conducive to its growth. Cannabis was apparently not as selective in its climate.

I scanned the area for some sign of Sarah. Nothing.

I slipped the goggles on my head and turned the switch to infrared. The world of infrared disoriented me at first. Tiny dots danced around, flaring briefly before glowing red faces as the men toked, smoked, and joked. As I got used to it, I quit trying to focus on details, instead watching the larger picture. The men around the tank I could ignore for the time being. If they had seen Sarah, they surely wouldn't be standing around partying.

I looked for other heat sources. The light on the tank, the trash can fires that were illuminating the area, the glowing red blob writhing inside the stadium that was the crowded mass of prisoners. Several guards still glowed where they patrolled outside the chain link fence that surrounded the football field.

"Come on, Sarah," I muttered, "where the hell are you?"

My jaw dropped when I finally spotted her. It never would have worked with seasoned military troops. Hell, it never would have worked with any disciplined group, but these clowns were hardly disciplined. And they were obviously not observant enough to spot a single hidden hitchhiker lying flat on the pavement underneath the very tank they were partying around.

Truthfully though, if she hadn't shown up as a heat source, I probably wouldn't have seen her, either. The spotlight that brightened their impromptu dance floor left the night outside their oasis of light a solid, opaque black. Someone would have had to shine a light directly under the tank to spot her. From what I could see, there was no way for her to get any closer to the stadium without crossing in front of the perimeter guards.

Her dilemma was obvious. She would never make it any further without help, but neither could she retreat without being spotted. Unfortunately, the solution was just as obvious.

"Wonderful," I muttered, "just freakin' wonderful!"

I bolted out of the door and back into the darkness, this time heading away from the stadium for a block before cutting right and jogging down the next block parallel to Stadium Drive. I imagined how I would explain this one to Ken and Jim. "Well, guys, she was already under the tank. What else could I do?"

I seemed to recall that Jim had a distinct dislike for people who "dressed up like GI Joe" and went off "lookin' for a war," but I thought he just might understand this time.

I tried the door at the back of Outland Sales, but the relaxed security that Ken had shown me in the suburbs didn't seem to extend to the business sector of town. I did manage to find an unbolted window though, and slipped inside. The building was empty, and dust rose in my footsteps as I searched for a window with the view I wanted. I found it and looked out onto the same party zone I had just left, only now I was about a block up the street.

I debated for a minute over whether to go for the lights or the tank crew first, then realized I would have a better chance of surviving this fiasco if I could take out the crew. They would be the ones most likely to know how to fire that cannon. After sliding the window open, I took careful aim at the thug sitting closest to the hatch. He was just beginning to lean back when my bullet found him. Before the others had a chance to react, I shot the second closest to the hatch. It became a scramble as the rest of them realized what was happening. I began firing at anyone who seemed to be heading to any of the hatches and got three more before any got in. Even then, one of them had to drag a bloody leg in after him. Once a couple of them made it in, I dropped a smoke bomb, fired a few shots in the general direction of the spotlight on the front of the tank, and ran like hell without bothering to see if I had hit anything.

I made it a block before they gathered themselves enough to attack the building. Bullets ripped through the sheet metal walls by the hundreds. I stopped behind the next building I came to.

Looking up, I found a fire escape leading to a third story roof, and I climbed up to watch the fun. I could see the group of them getting braver and braver as they continued firing and drew no response from the building. Nothing could have lived through the rain of bullets they poured into that warehouse.

Finally, the tank started up. It had evidently taken the poor slobs who had gotten into it this long to figure out how to start it. Slowly, it began to trundle down the street toward Outland Sales. I wondered if they would figure out how to fire the cannon. Then, as the tank left the scattered bodies on the street behind it, I saw one of them rise to its feet and run toward the chain link fence.

Sarah evidently still had her goggles on, because I saw her whirl and fire at one of the perimeter guards, dropping him before he ever raised his rifle. The single shot was lost in the ongoing volley that Larry's men were still firing into the old warehouse.

She took the eight-foot fence in seconds and quickly disappeared into the crowd of prisoners.

"Good luck, girl," I wished her fervently. "You're sure gonna need it."

* * *

"She did *what*?" Ken's initial reaction was every bit as volatile as I had expected.

"Watch the road!" I yelled, as he turned to shout at me and swerved toward the shoulder. Mark's group had managed to steal three more Humvees, and Ken's group had gotten one of the covered personnel trucks from Main Street. That gave us four jeeps and a truck to use for hauling supplies. My group rode with Ken in the lead, me in front, and the others in back.

"She snuck into the stadium," I told him. "There wasn't anything I could do to stop her, Ken. By the time I found her, she was already committed. There was no way she could have made it back."

"She made it in, didn't she? How'd she manage that?"

This was the part I dreaded. "Um, I helped her."

He laughed, though there wasn't a shred of humor in him at the moment. "You helped her," he repeated, as if savoring the taste of these strange words. He shook his head in amazement. "Why doesn't that surprise me?"

There was nothing I could say to that, so we traveled along the road in uneasy silence. I glanced into the back to see the rest of my group sitting reticent, heads hung low, looking for all the world like children trying to avoid an angry parent's attention.

After a few minutes, Ken seemed to calm down. "Tell me exactly what happened." So I did, starting with when we had noticed Sarah was missing and ending with my return to the group.

"Do you have any idea what she had in mind? What we can expect her to do?"

I had thought about that ever since she had turned up missing. "She knows where the supplies are. She knows where our people are. And it just so happens they're all in about the same place. I think it's obvious."

He sighed. "That's what I was afraid of. How long before she'll try it?"

I shrugged. "No way to know for sure. I doubt she'll do anything with that tank out front, and the guards are going to be a *lot* more cautious after tonight's shootout. If the tank stays during the day, she'll definitely wait 'til night. If it's still there come nightfall, she may wait another day. But the longer she waits, the greater the chance that she'll get caught." I thought about what I knew about Sarah. "Sarah isn't one for subtlety. She'll move as soon as she can. I'd bet on tomorrow night, or maybe the next."

Ken nodded. "You're sure no one saw her get in?"

"Pretty sure. There was one, but she got him before she went over the fence. Everyone else I saw was busy shooting at where they thought I was hiding."

He was quiet again, thinking. "We'll have to come back to help her bust them out."

I sighed with relief.

* * *

In half an hour, we reached the bridge to the fertilizer plant, and Ken pulled to the side of the road and turned to the back.

"Billy, we need to send someone in on foot to let our people know that the vehicles coming in are friendly. Wouldn't do to get shot by our own people. You mind?"

Dumbfounded, Billy just stared at Ken for several seconds. I realized this was probably the most that Ken had spoken to him since the day he had been brought to our door. It was perhaps a little gruff, but I think it was Ken's way of apologizing. He was telling Billy that after what had happened tonight, he considered Billy an asset rather than a liability.

Billy nodded, leapt out of the back, and ran down the road.

"Hey, kid!" Ken yelled. Billy stopped and spun so abruptly that he nearly slipped on the pavement.

"Don't get yourself shot. We're going to need you tomorrow."

Billy cracked a shy smile and sprinted across the bridge.

I turned to Ken. "That was damn near human of you, Ken."

"Shut up, Lee."

I shut up, smiling nonetheless.

* * *

When we finally pulled the vehicles into the parking lot of the Vogler Fertilizer Factory, a crowd had gathered to greet us. Word had spread as soon as Billy made it to the gate. Cindy and Debra were in the forefront, but we barely had time for a quick hug and a few reassurances before Jim herded us into his *office*. He had converted the office area of the plant into his personal staging area. Maps and charts from an age long gone decorated the walls. Electric lamps and fans lay piled in the corner, seen by the light of a couple of camping lanterns.

As soon as the door closed behind us, Ken and I collapsed into chairs in front of the desk. He was evidently every bit as exhausted as I was.

Jim took the seat opposite us, and I noticed that his left eye was a bit swollen from the punch I had given him in City Hall. "So what happened? I heard there was trouble."

Ken nodded and began explaining in general what all had happened. At times, Jim or Ken would ask me to fill in some detail, but I tried to keep my mouth shut and let Ken do most of the talking. When he reached the point at which Sarah hopped the fence, I expected Jim to explode, but the mayor just sat there twiddling a pencil with his feet propped on the desk. It reminded me of the time he had questioned me after the Kindley affair. At least this time we were on the same side. The question and answer session went on for nearly an hour, with Jim asking dozens of questions to be sure he had the entire picture. Finally, he seemed satisfied.

"We figure she'll make her move tomorrow night or the next," Ken finished.

Jim sighed. "Well, I guess it's really gonna hit the fan now, ain't it?"

Ken and I were silent. No response seemed necessary.

Jim suddenly became animated. He dropped his feet off of the desk, stood up, and began pacing. "So what do we need to do to get our people out of there with as little risk as possible?"

"Let us send in some more volunteers tomorrow," I jumped in. "Small groups like we did tonight. We can send them in a few at a time and have them set up to help her when she makes her move."

"Ken?" Jim was the mayor, but he deferred to Ken just like the rest of us when it came to battlefield strategy.

Ken didn't look happy with the situation, but had finally accepted the responsibility. "That's about the only thing I can think of, too. But you have to understand something here." He paused. "We're going to lose some people, Jim. There's no way around it."

"How many?"

Ken shrugged wearily. "How many are going to panic under fire? How many are going to shoot when they should duck for cover, or duck for cover when they should shoot? We're not talking about seasoned troops here. We're talking about a bunch of auto mechanics and schoolteachers armed with deer rifles.

"They're going up against guys with military grade hardware who have made killing into a way of life. On top of that, they have a tank sitting where our people will have to go right past it, and at least five others somewhere in town. Our only advantage is Sarah's inside and knows where the supplies are, so we'll have people shooting from inside *and* outside of the stadium. That will hopefully catch Larry's boys with their pants down." His tone left no doubt that he expected the worst.

I couldn't help feeling that Ken was being overly pessimistic, though. Maybe it was because I had finally begun to feel like I fit in over the last year. Rejas was home, its people my friends and neighbors. They were people I had taught, worked with, and had now fought beside. We had been through a lot together, and I felt obligated to defend them against Ken's pessimism. "Wait a sec. Let's not forget that this last year has been pretty rough on everyone. Plenty of these folks have had to face armed outlaws on their own, and hundreds have trained with you, me, and Eric. They may not be soldiers, but they're not your average businessman or housewife anymore, either."

"Okay," he conceded. "Maybe they aren't. But they're hardly up to military training levels."

"Neither are Larry's men!"

That stopped him—for all of two seconds. "What about ammunition?"

Caught off guard, I responded in stellar fashion. "Huh?"

"Ammunition… bullets. Have you forgotten? We were running low before Larry ever got here! We've probably used more ammunition in the last twenty-four hours than we have in the last six months." Actually, I had forgotten, which was pretty stupid of me, since my favorite tasks at the forge were coming into prominence because of that shortage.

Ken must have seen it in my face. "Don't worry about it just now. It's not like we're going to run out tomorrow. But if we end up in a prolonged fight with these guys, say a couple of weeks or so, *then* we may have a problem."

He turned his attention back to the mayor, who had kept quiet during the exchange. "Look, Jim, all I can tell you is that as long as we prepare in advance, we'll get more people out than we'll lose. Don't ask me for any predictions beyond that."

Jim sighed. "Shit."

We were all silent for a moment, each of us trying to think of something to tip the scales in our favor.

Abruptly Jim snapped his fingers. "There is a little good news, anyway. Wayne Kelley told me to tell ya'll that he found enough ingredients in the rail depot out back to make plenty of explosives. He's settin' things up now."

"Good," Ken said. "Maybe he'll come up with something that will make a difference."

The mayor nodded. "Let's hope so. Meanwhile, you boys go get some rest. If you're plannin' to go back into town tomorrow, you'll need all the rest you can get."

Ken and I rose, nearly dead on our feet. "What about you?" I asked.

"I doubt I'll get any sleep tonight," Jim said. "Gotta get some people organized. You go on and don't worry about it. I'll sleep after you're gone."

Too tired to argue, we left without further comment.

* * *

Ken told me he needed to walk a little to clear his head before trying to rest. I was too exhausted to do anything but nod and wish him goodnight. Then I wandered through the complex searching for my family. It was harder than I had anticipated, as we had more than two thousand people trying to find someplace to sleep in a building never intended to hold more than a few hundred. And it was definitely not designed for sleeping. Refugees were scattered all over the place, sleeping on the floor, on storage racks; I even saw one man curled up on top of the protective cage on an old forklift. There was barely room to walk.

After asking around, I finally found where Debra and the kids were bedded down and joined them as quietly as possible. I carefully lay down, trying not to wake Debra, but I should have known better.

"I heard it was pretty bad," she whispered.

"Yeah." An image of Jenna's lifeless form came to mind, the way her head lolled as we loaded her corpse into the truck on the way back, the smell of blood and death, the knowledge that it was no longer a person, just a sack of meat. "It was bad." I shuddered and quickly suppressed the image, but my wife knew me well.

She snuggled up behind me as I lay on my side and slipped an arm over my shoulder to gently stroke my chest. She pressed her head up against my back and briefly kissed the back of my neck. "Would it help to talk about it?"

I shook my head. "Not now. Maybe later, but I can't right now." Fearing she might feel I was shutting her out, I added, "I'm sorry, babe, but I have to figure out how to deal with it on my own. It was a mess, and there's probably going to be worse tomorrow."

Her hand stopped. "What do you mean?"

I sighed. I hadn't meant to get into it, but it wouldn't be fair to keep her wondering now that I had mentioned it. "We found where they've got everyone, and Sarah got inside."

"And?" Her tone told me she knew at least part of the rest.

"And we think she's going to try to bust them out."

"When?"

"Best guess is either tomorrow night or the next."

She was silent for a few seconds. "You have to go back?"

"Yeah. They'll never make it without help."

"And it has to be you?" She started to sound upset. "It can't be someone else, some other group? Haven't you done enough?"

"Not this time. I know where she went in and what the situation is like there."

"So write it down. I heard about some of what happened tonight. I don't like the idea of you going out there again!"

I rolled over to face her and was surprised to see tears in her eyes. She sounded angry, but it was evident that the anger was simply a manifestation of her fear and concern. "I have to, Debra. I'm the only one that can this time."

"Why! Why only you?"

"Because I know exactly where she went in, and I know where Larry's men are positioned in the area. I'm the one that talked Wayne Kelley into risking his life to mix up any explosives I could find a recipe for, and I'm the one who knows how to use them." That was not strictly true, as I had only read military reports and directions, but that was more than anyone else had done.

She gripped my shirt in her fist and tugged. "So what? Tell them what to do and let someone else—"

Pulling her close, I wrapped my arms around her and just held her tight, as she buried her face in my chest and sobbed herself silently to sleep. Minutes later, I followed her into an uneasy slumber.

* * *

"Leeland?"

I awoke instantly, not that I had slept well. Jenna's face had kept popping up in my dreams, her dead eyes accusing, haunting.

"Leeland?" Wayne's voice again. I also noticed the strong smell of... chlorine?

"Jeez, Wayne! What's that smell?" I whispered to keep from waking Debra.

"How can you smell anything over your own stench?" she murmured, obviously no longer asleep. Having slept with her head in the crook of my arm, she was intimately acquainted with my stench.

Wayne's voice answered from the darkness. "Your recipes seem to leave some interesting by-product while they're being mixed."

I perked up. "You did it?"

"It's in one of the jeeps. Ready to go."

I rubbed my eyes and sat up, noticing how little activity there was. "What time is it?"

"It's about five thirty in the morning," he answered. "Jim and Ken are waiting on you in the office."

Debra sat up beside me and sighed. "You're going, aren't you?"

"I have to."

The expression on her face must have told Wayne that this was an awkward moment. He cleared his throat. "Uh, I'd better get back. I'll see you there." He left in an obvious hurry to distance himself from us.

I turned back to Debra and sat up to face her, working through the aches and pains shooting up my spine. "You know I have to."

She lowered her eyes. "I don't have to like it, though."

"Yeah. Well, if it makes you feel any better, I don't exactly look forward to it, either. Truth of the matter is, the idea scares the hell out of me."

"Good! Maybe you'll be careful enough to get back, then."

"I'll be back." I reached out and wistfully touched her cheek. "You think you can get rid of me that easily?"

I was taken aback when she slapped my hand away. "Don't joke!" she hissed angrily. The kids slept a few feet away, oblivious. We both wanted to keep it that way. "You always joke this stuff off, and it isn't funny, damn it! It isn't funny!" She stood and stepped away from me, glaring through tear-filled eyes.

I dropped my hand and swallowed. "I know. It's just me." I didn't know what else to say. "I'm sorry."

She nodded acceptance, but there was no way she would ever be happy about the situation. "Just go."

I didn't want to leave like that, but if Ken and Jim were waiting on me, things must have been about ready for the mission.

Some corner of my mind noted how funny it was that I had started thinking in military terms. Just like Jim said, "A grown man dressed up like GI Joe, playing at war." The rest of my mind was on my wife. She stood just out of my reach, her anger flaring once more. I couldn't leave like this. "Debra?"

She must have seen the question in my eyes, for her expression softened. "Go ahead, Lee. I'll be okay."

I dropped my gaze, understanding that this was all she could give me for now.

As I started to stand, my aches and pains became almost crippling. The simple act of getting to my feet abruptly became a painful process. Besides aching as I did from the previous day's activities, I was stiff from getting too little sleep afterward on a cold concrete floor. Suddenly, I felt Debra at my side holding my arm, helping me stumble to my feet. She took mercy on me and hugged me. Then, she pushed me back. "Just make sure you come back in one piece."

A lump in my throat choked off my answer, so I just nodded, turned, and headed back to Jim's office.

* * *

I walked through the office door to find Wayne asleep on an ancient sofa that someone had dragged in. Ken stood in a corner on the other side of the room. He turned when he saw me, nodded, and went back to what he was doing. A few seconds later, he walked over and handed me a hot cup of something that smelled like coffee. Better yet, it actually tasted like coffee. I sighed contentedly. "Pure, unadulterated heaven!"

I saw how bloodshot his eyes were as he shook his head. "Nope. Just Colombian roast. Jim found some in a cabinet. Thought we might need some to help get us going."

"Going?"

Jim walked in from the back, his own steaming cup in hand. I noticed the area around his left eye was now a deep blue. I winced at the thought that I had done that to him. Jim didn't seem to notice it, though, as he picked up on the conversation. "Yep, you're leavin'. Y'all need to be in position before sunrise, else you're gonna be too easy to spot goin' in."

My shoulders slumped at the thought. "Already? Damn, Jim, I'm so tired I can hardly see straight."

Jim laughed. "Hell, Leeland, at least you got a couple of hours. Me and Wayne have been workin' all night."

"You didn't sleep?"

"Didn't have time. I found Wayne out back, and he looked like he could use some help."

"What did you come up with?"

"Somethin' called Astrobrite, I think…"

"Astrolite?" I perked up. "You made Astrolite?"

"Yeah," he answered, "And let me tell you something. That is some nasty smellin' stuff when you're mixing!"

Jim peered at me over his coffee from behind his desk. "By the looks of that grin on your face, I take it Astrolite is good news?"

"Good news? It's probably the most powerful explosive there is, short of a nuclear reaction."

The mayor suddenly appeared somewhat less than pleased. "Nuclear reaction?"

I laughed. "Don't worry, Jim. That just means it has a high detonation velocity. There's no danger of any more radiation."

"You sure? I mean, if it's that powerful, mebbe we should think a bit more about this."

"Look, I'd be lying if I said I really understood all of it. But from what I've read, the way an explosive does its damage is by the rapid transfer of energy through a chemical or nuclear reaction. Astrolite uses a chemical reaction, not nuclear, so there's no danger of radiation."

"You ain't helpin' me any, Lee. If it can do as much damage as a nuclear explosion without the radiation, why didn't the government use it instead of nukes?"

"I never said it can do as much damage as a nuke. I said that it's the most powerful *non-nuclear* explosive. It does its damage with its speed."

He didn't seem convinced.

I leaned over his desk, snatched a pencil and a notepad, and wrote down an old high school formula, $e=1/2ms^2$. "Okay, 'e' is the amount of energy released. 'm' is the mass, and 's' is the speed. It's the reason why people can break boards and bricks with their hands. It isn't that their hands are harder than the bricks. It's simple physics."

I looked up to see Jim and Ken still appearing confused. "Look at it like this. A man hits a brick with a punch that has an equivalent mass of two hundred pounds." I scribbled hastily. "And a velocity of fifty miles an hour. Plug the numbers in, and the energy released is," more quick math scrawls, "two hundred fifty thousand… uh, joules or dynes, or whatever the measurement is."

"Ergs," Wayne piped up from the couch, "but only after you convert to metric equivalents in your formula."

I over at where he still lay with his eyes closed, apparently half asleep. "Wayne! You explain it to them. You're the chemistry teacher!"

His hand waved me off, as if it had volition of its own. The rest of his body remained motionless until his lips moved. "You're doing fine. I'll chime in if I hear you screw anything up." His eyelids never even twitched.

Scowling, I turned back to my scratch paper. "Okay. Now, let's say he hits twice as hard. Four hundred pounds, still traveling at fifty miles an hour…" I scribbled through the math again, "gives us five hundred thousand ergs."

Wayne's voice corrected once more, "'s not ergs 'til you convert it to metric."

"Whatever," I said. "But see what happens when you double the speed instead of the mass. Back to the original two hundred pounds, but now traveling at one hundred miles an hour gives us…" More scribbling. "One million ergs!"

"Not un—"

"I know! Not until I convert to metric! But I'm no good with metric units. So pretend I already did it, okay? The important thing is that the higher the detonation velocity…"

Jim finished, "The bigger the boom, right?"

"And then some." I sipped some more of the coffee. "So how much did you make?

"About three gallons."

I nearly sprayed my coffee all over him. "Three gallons? Ken, just one gallon of this stuff can bring down a house! What are we gonna do with three?"

Ken appeared to think about that for a second, mulling it over as he finished a sip of coffee. Then, without the slightest hint of humor, he replied, "We're going to kick Larry's ass."

* * *

Ken and Jim had worked out a plan that called for two groups of fifty people to trickle into town over the next few hours. The first team's objective was the stadium. We were to take out the tank, if possible, and get our people out and to the stadium.

The second team was to get to the hospital, where we had learned that some of our people had headed the night before. So far, our attackers had left the hospital alone since the doctors and nurses were treating Larry's wounded along with our own. We couldn't count on that being the case after we busted three thousand hostages out of the stadium, though. We had to plan on springing our people from both locations at the same time.

For once, I didn't have to do anything but ride along, at least until we reached the edge of town, so I leaned my head on an ice chest in back and caught up on some much needed sleep.

I awoke when the vehicle pulled to a stop. Looking around, I found myself back in the yard at Amber's. Ken yelled instructions to everyone.

"Leeland, you and Eric grab that ice chest in the back and bring it with you. Wayne, grab the Astrolite in the back of yours. Come on, people, gather 'round! Let's move! We have to be in place before sunrise." I noticed that each Humvee carried a couple of ice chests.

Within a few minutes, everyone circled around Ken, much as we had the night before. This time, though, we met deeper in the woods, safe from any of Larry's patrols.

Once he saw we were ready, Ken signaled for Eric and me to bring him the ice chest we had carried. The ice chest was quite light, so I waved Eric off, thinking to carry it up to Ken alone.

"Let Eric help you, Lee. We don't want to take any chances with that stuff."

I froze as I suddenly realized what I had been carrying so nonchalantly. I hoped no one noticed as I carefully backed away when Ken opened the chest and withdrew an odd-looking contraption consisting of a liquid-filled test tube topped with a black rubber stopper from which two wires gracelessly dangled—Wayne's homemade blasting caps.

He had shown one of them to me before we left, and explained,. "The Astrolite's completely stable as long as you keep it away from the accelerator. In fact, I could probably drop a beaker of that stuff on the ground, and the only explosion I would need to worry about would be Ken and Jim blowing up at me for ruining several hours of work.

"But these little babies," he held the test tube gingerly, "these are the touchy ones. The stoppers have been partially hollowed out, filled with gunpowder, sealed, and placed on the test tubes filled with HMTD."

"Filled with what?"

"Sorry. I figured you'd know about it, since I found the recipe in one of your books."

"Well, if I knew everything in my books, I wouldn't need the books, would I?"

He shook his head. "Guess not. Well, HMTD is one of the less stable soups in your cookbook. Not as bad as nitroglycerine, but still pretty touchy. I run wires to the gunpowder and run a charge through the wires. This causes a spark, which sets off the gunpowder, which sets off the HMTD..."

"Which sets off the Astrolite." I finished.

He had nodded and gently laid the glass tube down on his makeshift workbench. What I didn't know at the time was that he had also devised a strange-looking contraption in which to carry those test tubes. It consisted of hundreds of strands of rubber bands that acted as a makeshift suspension system, protecting the caps from any sudden shock. A suspension system inside of an old ice chest, the same chest upon which I had rested my head during the trip out here, and from which Ken now gingerly extracted a single test tube.

Ken turned, giving everyone a chance to see exactly what he held. "Okay, people, it's last chance time again. We're splitting up after this. Group One is with me. We hit the stadium and take out the tank that we know is there. Group Two goes with Eric Petry to get our people out of the hospital.

"Do it quietly if you can, Eric. If you wait for us to start the fireworks, that might set up enough of a distraction for you to get in and out without the bad guys ever knowing about it."

Eric nodded, obviously ready to get to it. "Group Two, gather 'round me!"

Ken interrupted. "Wait a second, Eric. I got something else to say here." He paused for a minute, evidently trying to figure out the best way to say all that needed to be said. "Some of you were with us last night. We got caught with our pants down and lost some good people."

I could see that he still blamed himself, but he didn't make any excuses. "I didn't expect it. And this time I'm counting on it being worse. So this is the last chance for you to turn around and go back. No one will think any less of you. I would rather have you leave now if you have any doubts, than to have you hesitate under fire and get yourself or someone else killed." No one budged. Everyone had known from the beginning what they were getting into.

"Okay, I need twelve volunteers for extra hazardous duty. These twelve will have to go in alone. Not with each other. Totally alone."

He had everyone's attention with that one. He held up the hand with the test tube. "I have a dozen explosive charges that need to be carried into town separately. Six go with each group." Voices muttered in protest.

"Wait a minute!" He raised his voice to cut off the objections. "These aren't the main charge. They're just homemade blasting caps."

Just? I thought, recalling Wayne's lecture. *Just blasting caps?*

"They're mostly stable, and it's not very likely that they'll explode from anything less than someone actually dropping them, but there's still the chance. The thing is, we can't afford to have all of them together if one does explode, because then we lose all of them. Separately, if someone drops one, we only lose the one." More murmuring, as people realized exactly what he was saying… or rather, what he *wasn't* saying. He neglected to mention that if someone dropped one, we also lost the person carrying it.

"I'll take one."

Billy stepped forward and held out his hand. Ken pursed his lips and regarded the boy before him. Then he handed the tube to Billy. "You're with Group One, right?"

"Yes, sir."

"You know where the Regency Warehouse is?"

Billy nodded. "Yes, sir."

"All right. Get there as quickly as you can, but don't let anyone else see you." Billy turned and headed out, walking carefully. The crowd parted before him like the Red Sea before Moses.

Ken called after him, "Be careful, boy."

Billy grinned nervously. "I will." With that, he turned his full attention back to the delicate task at hand.

"Who else?" The rest of us raised our hands at once, shamed into volunteering by a boy who was a slave, who couldn't even claim he was fighting for his home.

Ken distributed the packages to twelve individuals. "Get to the warehouse as quickly as you can. Be careful, but be fast."

He turned to the rest of us. "The rest of you divide up into five-man groups. One group leaves every five minutes. Make sure every group has someone in it that knows where their objective is. I don't want anyone getting lost and giving us away. I also don't want anyone seen! Understand?" We all nodded.

"Good. Now, we don't know when, or even *if,* our people are going to make a break for it. We have reason to believe that if they do, it will be either tonight or tomorrow night. That means Group One gets into position, and we wait. We wait all day long. You can sleep if you want, or play pinochle for all I care, but nobody leaves cover once we're set. If nothing happens tonight, we wait until tomorrow night, all day long again. Most of these chests have food and water in them. There should be enough to last two days, easily. After that, if nothing has happened, we'll slip back out of town and try to figure out something else. But our best guess is that we'll be plenty busy before that happens.

"Group Two, you wait 'til you hear from us. You don't make a move until I tell you to. This hit has to be synchronized, or it's all wasted effort. Do *not* let yourselves be seen. Some of these guys have night vision goggles so don't count on hiding in the shadows. Pretend it's broad daylight, and plan every step accordingly." He looked us all over again. "Questions?"

When no one piped up, he turned. "Group One with me. Group Two with Eric. We stay in touch by radio." He looked around one last time. "Okay, folks, let's go."

I was in Group One since I'd had the most recent experience with the setup at the stadium and knew the route we'd taken to avoid contact with Larry's boys. Going in was actually anticlimactic compared to all the excitement I'd had helping Sarah get into the stadium. There was no gunfire, no yelling or screaming. We snuck in like proverbial mice, quiet as....

It took us twice as long to get in, and I felt strange as we passed by the volunteers making their way, step by careful step, into town, but not one of us was spotted, and we all made it without incident.

CHAPTER 15

* * AUGUST 18 / SUNSET * *

Cris, pleurs, larmes viendront auec couteaux,
Semblant fuyr, donront dernier assaut,
L'entour parques planter profonds plateaux,
Vifs repoussez & meurdris de plinsaut.

Cries, weeping, tears will come with knives,
Seeming to flee, they will deliver a final attack,
Parks around to set up high platforms,
The living pushed back and murdered instantly.
              Nostradamus – *Century 10, Quatrain 82*

The Regency Warehouse was two buildings down from where my group
had holed up the night before and turned out to have much nicer
accommodations, considering the fact that there were plenty of chairs,
sofas, and even a few mattresses in stock. We put a half-dozen people on

rotating guard duty, and the rest of us, myself included, slept as much as we could.

I awoke slowly to the familiar feel of someone shaking my shoulder. "Leeland, wake up!"

I saw upon opening my eyes that the sun was beginning to set. Ken stood over me smiling. I had slept the day away. Considering how exhausted the last few days' activities had left me, I wasn't terribly surprised. Even after all the sleep I had just gotten, I still felt a little groggy.

"Good grief," I growled. "Don't you ever sleep?"

"Not when I'm surrounded by bad guys."

That got my attention. "What's going on? Is it starting?" I grabbed my gear, scrambling to strap my weapons in place.

"Calm down, Lee. No need to panic. Just thought you ought to know. Billy spotted Sarah."

"Where?"

"Come on, I'll show you."

We headed to the third floor, where Billy and three others knelt just inside one of three windows to watch the activities around the stadium. Ken and I carefully crept over to join them.

Billy handed Ken a small pair of binoculars. "She's still out there at the front fence."

Ken peered through the window. A moment later he offered the binoculars to me. "Just at the edge of the chain link near the entrance."

Sure enough, there was Sarah at the front of a crowd of people. She had worked her way to the edge of the refugees and now stared out through the fence at a tank that barred her escape. She wore a desperate expression. She had no way of knowing we were there. "Anyone signaled her?"

Ken shook his head. "Thought maybe you should do it. She knows you best."

"Okay, what do I do?"

He handed me a small mirror. "Don't let anyone else see you. Catch her attention, then we hold up this sign."

They had managed to cut a piece of plywood to fit inside one of the windows. Painted on it in black lettering, large enough to be easily seen, was the short message: "10:45 - GO TO VOGLER FERT."

Ken indicated the setting sun. "You have to get her attention before the sun goes down." He took back the binoculars. "Get to it."

Ken turned to watch her through the binoculars while I tried to capture the last rays of the sun in a two-inch square mirror. I played with the angle for a few seconds, shining the reflection on the wall in front of me until I got it right. Then, trying to hold the same angle, I slowly stepped to the opened window and swept the tiny beam of light toward Sarah.

Almost immediately, Ken stopped me. "She sees it. Hold up the sign!" I tucked the mirror in my pocket, while Billy and another man held up the sign.

Abruptly, Ken laughed. "Okay, put down the sign. She got it."

We dropped back behind the wall. "What's so funny?" I asked.

"She's a smart lady." She saw the sign and signaled back. Two full hands of fingers, followed by four on the right and five on the left. She didn't want there to be any doubt she'd gotten the message."

"Good," I responded. "But now we're on a schedule." I looked at my watch by the fading sunlight. "We have just over four hours 'til things get crazy here. So how do we get the Astrolite to that tank?"

"I wish I knew. Only thing I can think of is going in through the sewer system and trying to get over to that gutter near the stadium."

I peeked over the edge again. "That's still a good ten or fifteen feet away from the tank. We've got to get closer than that!"

He sighed. "I know. I'm open for suggestions."

"Sensei?" Billy sounded tentative.

"What is it, Billy?"

"Um, I think I might have an idea."

* * *

Ken briefed us on what to expect from the tank, drawing what knowledge he had of the Abrams from his Gulf War experience. His opening comments were somewhat less than inspiring. "About the only way you're going to do any damage to that monster is to time it so one of the charges goes off underneath it in the rear. That's where the armor is lightest. You can forget about doing any damage to the front. I heard about tests where they fired repeated rounds from a one-oh-five millimeter, one after the other at the exact same spot. It took seven shots, one right inside the other, to pierce the armor in front. We just don't have that kind of

216

firepower. Even if it doesn't pierce the armor, though, it will likely blow the treads and immobilize it. Once you see it's incapacitated, get back to us, and we'll all go home."

Ivory raised his hand. "'S'cuse me?"

"What is it, Ivory?"

"Well, this might sound dumb, but... well, I saw this cop show on TV a long time ago where some loony got hold of a tank and was driving down the street. He was runnin' over cars and streetlights and shit like that."

Ken nodded. "I saw that show. The tank he was in was an older M-60. What about it?"

"Well, when the cops got to the tank, they just climbed up on top and got into it with some bolt cutters. How'd they do that?"

"The tanks are designed where, if the crew is incapacitated, medics have a way to get in. The old M-60 had four hatches. The commander's hatch, the gunner's, and the driver's are all on top." He sketched a rough diagram on the wall with a piece of chalk. "With an escape hatch underneath."

He drew another diagram beside the first. "With the Abrams, they got rid of the bottom hatch. The three top hatches are here, here, and here. This one," he indicated the left-hand top hatch, "is the only one that can't be locked from the inside. Instead, it's made where you can run a lock through the dogging arm and an eyelet. It's the same design carried over from the old M-60."

Ken turned back to Ivory. "On that show you're talking about, the police simply cut that lock and opened the hatch. Unfortunately, our circumstances are different."

"Why's that?"

"Because that tank was manned by only one person. He wasn't able to man the guns and drive at the same time. With a full crew, no one would have ever gotten close to the tank without being shot to pieces." He searched our faces, making sure that he'd made his point. "Any other questions?"

"As far as a pep talk goes, Ken, this one needs some work," I quipped.

That got a few chuckles, but Ken squashed them immediately. "I'm not here to cheer you up. I'm trying to make you see that what you are about to try is gonna make last night seem like a cakewalk, and they kicked our butts last night. I want you *scared*. Because if you go into this scared, maybe, just maybe, you'll stay alive long enough to get back to your families."

There was a controlled fury in his gaze. You could see that he hated sending us out there, and that he hated that it had fallen to him to command this mess. But you could also see that he was determined to do the best he could.

"Leeland, pick your squad."

* * *

Team Mohammed left at 8:00 p.m. Billy, Wayne, and I were one fourth of the group of familiar faces I had chosen. I wanted people I knew with me.

Two carried the ice chest of Astrolite, two more carried a wooden crate that Wayne indicated had tools and other paraphernalia we would need, and yet another pair carried the chest of HMTD. The rest of us scouted ahead.

It was our job to find an appropriate place, plant the Astrolite, and draw the tank into our ambush. The idea was Billy's, but Ken named the team. Since we couldn't go to the mountain, we were bringing the mountain to us.

The trick was to find someplace close enough to get the tank to investigate without calling in for reinforcements while they left their post, yet it had to be far enough away that we could plant the charges without being seen. Our team had two sets of night vision goggles to help us scout the area, and even then it took us more than half an hour to find our spot.

As with most things in life, we had to compromise. We settled on the intersection of Dullas and South 23rd, a few blocks east and one south of Eagle Stadium. There was nothing special about the location except for the number of potholes in the street.

"Madre de Dios," René muttered, looking with distaste at the poorly maintained street. "Okay, now what?"

Wayne took off his night vision goggles and hung them on his belt. I took my cue from him and did the same with mine. He jerked his thumb at the street, and answered simply, "Now we dig." And we did.

The potholes were pretty severe in places, as road repair was not exactly high on the list of priorities for the Rejas City Council. We pulled the asphalt out of some of the deepest holes, working mostly by feel in the darkness. Digging by hand, I laughed to myself as I contemplated the irony of the situation.

"Qué es… What is funny?" René hissed. You could always tell when she was agitated. It was at those times that her Spanish accent was most prevalent.

I shrugged to show that it wasn't important. Then realizing she couldn't see me, I explained, "For years we've bitched and moaned about potholes. But tonight, if we didn't have them, we'd be up a creek."

She grunted and turned back to digging, obviously wishing she hadn't asked. René Herrera had been like that as long as I'd known her. *Gruff* was the way her acquaintances described her. I found that particular adjective to be a bit of an understatement.

We soon broke through to the soil beneath, digging several of the potholes out enough to hold a beaker of Astrolite. After completion of the sixth hole, Wayne called the rest of us into an open door. Inside the darkened building, we held a quick meeting by the light of a couple of subdued flashlights.

"I really think that these six should be plenty to cover the area," Wayne started. "Hell, from what I read in your books, Leeland, six one-quart charges will probably be enough to completely erase the intersection altogether."

"You think we should save the rest, in other words."

"Yeah."

"All right. Let's plant the charges and move to a safe detonation distance." I paused to think. "Uh, just how far do we need to go to be safe?"

Wayne shrugged. "Who knows? Best guess is about a block. Maybe more."

"You don' know for sure, though?" René prodded.

He snapped, "Well, you know, René, it's not like I do this every day!" I guess he realized how he sounded because he immediately shook his head. "Sorry, I didn't mean that. Guess I'm a little nervous."

Surprisingly, she brushed it off. "No problema," she told him. "Ever'body in the same boat here. We all nervous."

I turned to the rest of the group. "Billy, you've already proven that you can handle this stuff. Pull out six beakers and six caps. Wayne, you know exactly what you had in mind with them. Show him how to assemble the charges." Wayne turned Billy and led him back to the ice chests.

"The rest of it goes back to the main group. René, you and Slim take the chest of Astrolite back as soon as Billy and Wayne have unloaded what they need." They nodded and went to help unload.

That left six people and six blasting caps. Unfortunately, I needed more warm bodies with me to lay the ambush. Time for a snap decision. "Okay. Matthew, Alan, Emily, I want each of you to grab two caps and take them back to the main group. Same as earlier today. One at a time, slow and careful." I shone the light on my watch. "It's ten fifteen. You have half an hour to go three blocks. I don't care if it takes the whole time. Just don't get caught, and don't trip!"

They nodded and trotted off to grab their gear and the explosives.

Turning to those remaining, I continued, "The rest of us get to plant the mines and play decoy. It's going be up to us to draw that tank and as many foot soldiers over here as we can. The more of them we can draw into the ambush, the fewer our people in the stadium will have to deal with."

By the dim light of a covered flashlight, I looked at the grim faces around me. "Any questions?" No one answered. "Okay folks, let's get going."

I walked over to where Wayne and Billy worked on assembling the second of our charges. The first sat on the floor next to them. "What can we do to help?"

Wayne answered without turning, concentrating on what he was doing. "There's a car battery, some tools, and coaxial wire in that box over there." He jerked his chin toward the gear. "Leave one roll of the wiring here and splice the rest of it into six continuous lengths leading over to a building about a block away where you can still see the intersection." He appeared to think for a second, then shook his head. "I think I can localize the explosions, but I don't know for sure if it'll work. Still better to keep a block away. Billy and I will bury these charges and wire them up. You just get the rest of the stuff far enough away that we can set them off without killing ourselves."

One thing caught my attention. "You say you can localize the explosions?"

He didn't answer right away, and I knew better than to interrupt his concentration as he carefully replaced the rubber stopper in the beaker with a tube of HMTD. When he finished, the glass beaker was plugged by another rubber stopper with a test tube attached to it, sticking down into the Astrolite. Two wires, each about two feet long protruded from the other end. Using exaggeratedly slow movements, he set the second beaker on the floor next to the first.

When he looked up, my flashlight showed beads of sweat on his forehead. "We use shaped charges," he replied.

Sam asked before I could. "Shaped? How do you shape a liquid?"

"You put it in pre-shaped containers." He held up one of the unprimed beakers. "If we bury these suckers upside down, the main force of the explosion should go straight up, assuming that those books of yours are right, and that I understood them."

I didn't get it, but there was no time for more explanation. "Okay, I'll take your word for it." I turned to get the wiring supplies he had mentioned.

"Leeland!"

"Yeah?"

"Whatever you do, don't connect the wiring to the battery until we get there. I didn't have time to get fancy with the detonator. You just connect the wires, and it all goes boom. I don't want to be wiring one up when that happens."

I chuckled. "Gotcha."

"Edwin, you help Wayne and Billy. Sam, Ivory, help me get the wiring set up."

It took fifteen minutes to complete the wiring, leaving the battery and remainder of the coax behind an old checkout stand inside a long-deserted convenience store. We ran back to see if we could help Wayne and the others.

They were carefully turning the fifth charge upside down and setting it gently in one of the holes. Wayne held it in place, while Billy and Edwin scooped the dirt in around it. I shuddered a bit when I saw Wayne sprinkling a generous pile of nails into the dirt before the rest of us cautiously finished burying it. When complete, all that was left sticking out of the ground was a pair of wires that Wayne rapidly connected to the ends of one length of the coaxial running down the street. I looked up and saw similar wires leading to the other four holes.

I turned away and cupped my hand over my flashlight, letting only enough light through to see my watch.

10:34.

"Almost time!" I hissed.

We all worked together on the final charge. At 10:38, we were carefully laying broken asphalt and gravel on the last spot and scattering debris to cover the wiring.

"Is that good enough to hide the wires?" Billy indicated a few places where wire emerged briefly from small piles of dirt and broken asphalt.

"It'll have to be. We're out of time," I said. "We have smoke bombs that should cover it. Between that and the shooting, we'll just have to hope they're too busy to notice."

I turned away to shine the light on my watch again. "It's time." When we left the plant that morning, I had brought along my last eight smoke bombs. I had given four to Ken, passed three more out to my group, and kept one for myself.

It was selfishness that caused me to split the group as I did, sending Ivory, Sam, and Edwin off in one squad, and keeping Billy and Wayne in my group. I justified it by telling my conscience that I would work better with people I knew well, but there was a niggling in my brain that accused me of wanting to keep my friends close at hand. My response was the same one I repeated so often lately. *No time to worry about it now.*

Moving back down to Dullas, we picked positions just out of sight from the stadium. I saw Sam and Ivory go into a building across the street from us, while Edwin went around behind it, presumably to sight in around the back corner.

Billy stayed outside at the corner of the building into which Wayne and I went. The two of us inside picked windows facing the stadium and waited. I glanced one last time at my watch. 10:44.

Time. I clicked on the radio. "Ken?"

"Ken here. You about to start?"

"Yeah. Make sure everyone knows they have to sit the first few minutes out, or this is all for nothing."

"Already done."

"Good." It seemed that there should be something else for me to say, but nothing came to mind.

"Leeland?"

"Yeah?"

"Good luck, man."

"Thanks, Ken. You too." Some things just couldn't be put into words. "Out."

I turned back to Billy and Wayne. "Ready?" They nodded.

"Pick your targets and make each shot count."

I took a couple of deep breaths to steady my nerves and sighted in on one of the guards. There was no partying going on. They were actually standing guard. Larry must have really reamed them for the mess we made the night before. Unfortunately for them, they had stupidly increased the lighting in the area, showing us the juiciest targets.

I heard Ken's voice in my head telling me as he had a thousand times before, "Steady... take a deep breath, and squeeeeze..."

My shot signaled the rest of the group, and everyone opened fire. Four of Larry's men dropped before anyone knew what was happening. They quickly figured it out, though, and men scrambled for cover as they searched for their attackers. It didn't take but a few seconds for them to figure out our general direction, and only a few seconds more for Wayne and I to figure out that the front of the building we were in consisted of nothing more than facade and sheetrock. Bullets tore through it like so much wet tissue. The only thing that saved us was the simple fact that Larry's men didn't know exactly where we were. Still, bullets ripped through the flimsy sheetrock, zinging around the warehouse and forcing us to scurry for more substantial cover.

Huddled behind a desk, Wayne yelled, "This isn't working quite the way I imagined it!"

I ducked as the bookshelf I hid behind spat bits of paper at me. "Jeez! We've gotta get out of here! Billy! Cover us!"

He didn't answer, but the rate of fire from the doorway increased significantly.

"Go!" I yelled at Wayne, but he was already scrambling through the door. When he got there, he began shooting with Billy.

"Come on, Lee! They're moving this way!"

Things were moving faster than we had expected. Running for the door, I felt a slight tug on my sleeve. A sudden pain across my forearm that told me I'd been grazed. I wriggled my fingers and knew the damage was minor, but that was all I could tell in the darkness.

Billy continued to fire into the guards as rapidly as his finger could pull the trigger, and I saw several men fall as a testament to his aim. Wayne had evidently discovered, as I soon did, that there wasn't nearly enough room for all of us to sit and fire from the same corner; he was already heading back down the street and around the corner to another position. I scrambled to follow him.

Halfway down the street, I heard Billy's rifle go silent. *He's been hit!* I thought, as I turned back to help, but I saw with relief that he was simply changing clips. Then my heart skipped a beat when I heard the unmistakable sound of the Abrams starting up. Billy heard it, too. I could tell by the stance of his kneeling silhouette as he looked up at the behemoth moving towards him.

"Get out of there!" I yelled. "Pull back!"

I saw him raise his rifle for one last shot before he bailed from his position, legs pistoning wildly as he ran.

He was about thirty feet away from me when the corner where he had just been kneeling disintegrated in a deafening blast that knocked me off my feet and set my ears to ringing. Bricks, bits of sidewalk, and burning wood flew in a deadly whirlwind, and Billy was suddenly airborne, flying amidst the maelstrom, until he landed in a tangled heap, unmoving as the debris fell on him.

"Billy!" Sprinting, I reached him just as the front of the building across the street where Sam and the others were hiding exploded in a similar, deafening fashion. I dove to cover Billy's body with my own as the cloud of masonry and fiery lumber pummeled us.

Wayne tugged on my arm and yelled. With my ringing ears, I couldn't tell what he was saying, but he yanked the ring from his smoke bomb and dropped it in the street before helping me pull Billy from the rubble. We dragged him by his arms as we ran down the street to where I had stashed the detonator.

Once inside, I saw Wayne trying to tell me something, but I still couldn't hear a thing through the ringing in my ears. "I can't hear you!"

He looked concerned and turned my head from side to side, examining my ears. I felt him touch the skin beneath my left ear and watched as it came away dark and wet. Before that moment, it had never occurred to me just how black and forbidding blood looked by firelight.

My stomach clinched at the sudden realization that I might be deaf for life, but there wasn't time for the thought to scare me too much. If the next few minutes didn't turn out better than the last few had, my life wouldn't last long enough to worry about it.

Wayne grabbed my shoulders and pointed me at the detonator setup, then turned me back to face him. His mouth moved, and he pantomimed and pointed. It looked like he wanted to get across the street to set up a crossfire.

I nodded. "Okay, I got it. Go!"

He reached into my belt pouch, pulled out the last smoke bomb, clapped me on the back, and poked his head out of the doorway. Then, he sprinted across the street. I saw him duck into a storefront on the opposite side and disappear into the shadows.

Peering back down the street, I saw three of Larry's men emerge from the dissipating smoke. They hugged the shadows and searched through windows, searching for us. It was eerie seeing them creep closer, yell at one another, and occasionally fire into one of the empty buildings, but unable to hear any of it. Out of the corner of my eye, I caught a flicker of movement, and the last smoker landed among them. Wayne.

Some of them must have seen the direction it came from because they dropped to the ground and fired at the building where he had disappeared. I raised my rifle and fired into the group, but I hastily ducked back at the sudden appearance of several bullet holes in the wall beside me. I whirled to find Wayne pointing his rifle at me.

Why was Wayne shooting at me? He saw me looking his way and dropped his rifle to pantomime touching the wires together.

He must have seen the tank. It must be time.

Then I saw him jerk once as a bullet spun him around. Two more found his back, and he dropped from sight just before the front of the building disintegrated in another blinding explosion.

"Wayne!" I could feel the rawness of my throat as I screamed, but my ears were still useless. The only sound I heard was my voice echoing faintly in my skull.

The ground still trembled from the explosion as I dropped my rifle and dove for the detonator. A silhouette in the doorway warned me that I wasn't alone, and the muzzle of a rifle sought me out in the relative darkness of the building.

My movement gave me away, but there wasn't time to let whoever it was distract me. I had to connect those wires. Ours was a macabre, slow motion race—me fumbling to connect wires to battery terminals, and the thug in the doorway struggling to find me and shoot.

It was a close thing, but he won the battle.

I won the war, though, as his shot went wide hitting the wall nearly three feet in front of me just a split second before I made the connection. The world shook, and my attacker flew forward—within reach.

My fear and rage at losing my squad, the people who had trusted and depended on me, now had a target and was unleashed in a moment's insane fury. My next actions involved a gouged eye and crushed esophagus, but everything else was lost in madness.

At some point, I realized that the man was dead, and my throat was raw. *Must have been screaming* was my confused thought, but for the life of me, I couldn't remember doing so.

Stumbling over masonry and dirt, I made my way to the door and peeked around the corner into the street, into carnage, into the aftermath of an explosion powerful enough to blow a hole in the bottom of the tank and mangle the tracks. It had been enough to shred every exposed person within a city block with asphalt and nails.

No one moved on the street as I staggered outside. Dust drifted, and flames danced in small scattered groups, but there wasn't a hint of life. A slight popping in my right ear hinted that at least some of my hearing was returning, but it took a moment for me to realize I was hearing the sounds of gunfire.

I decided that Ken's group must be moving.

Four weary minutes and two long blocks later, I found myself approaching the outskirts of another battle.

* * *

Sarah led a massive wave of people who had made it halfway across Stadium Drive before a few of Larry's men had caught on to what was happening. When those men turned their guns on the emerging crowd, the folks still inside the stadium had no idea what was going on in the darkness ahead, only that freedom waited beyond the gates. They pushed forward, while those in front pulled back, seeking shelter from the deadly crossfire. The great press of escaping Rejans stalled—and died.

By the light of trashcan fires, I saw our people stumbling over their own dead and wounded, surging to and fro like some panicked horde of lemmings, shoving one another into the waiting crossfire of Larry's men. One silhouette stood out from the others, its appearance inhuman in the firelight. It was Sarah, wearing the goggles she had worn into the stadium the previous night. She frantically directed a small knot of people armed with rifles and handguns by pointing and gesticulating to help them pinpoint Larry's guards, but the darkness worked against her. Although the targets were plainly visible through her goggles, Larry's men were nothing more than shadows to those she was directing.

My right ear was working at about half capacity, and I could hear the screams of people over the gunfire. Where was Ken? There should be more support.

Seeing Sarah reminded me that I had my own goggles on my belt, and I slipped them on, praying they still worked. They did.

Scrambling closer, I could see that there were actually only two groups of snipers shooting at the crowd. The first group consisted of two men with their backs to me ducked behind a rusted-out abandoned Dodge. Suddenly, I realized I had left my carbine lying between Billy and the nameless soldier I had killed.

I drew my machete and Bowie and, once more, I attacked from behind and killed before my victims knew I was upon them. So much for honor in combat.

Grabbing one of the dead men's rifles, I looked up to see the muzzle flashes of two rifles from the ground floor window of a building across the street. The angle was wrong, and I couldn't get a clear shot at the owners, but I figured I could at least keep their heads down while some of our people got clear. Glancing down at the unfamiliar weapon, I found a lever over my right thumb. *Select fire.*

Taking aim at the window, I quickly discovered that a fully automatic M-16 was much harder to hold on target than the movies portrayed. Still, the sudden shower of bullets proved enough to cause them to duck for cover, giving two of Sarah's armed partners time to rush the building and get to either side of the window. Working together, they whirled and fired several rounds inside. One of them fell, but the other waved the crowd on. Sarah and the escapees began scattering through the streets.

I stepped out from behind the car and waved to get Sarah's attention. "Sarah!" I winced again at the pain in my throat and hoped she would recognize my voice. With my impaired hearing, I couldn't even tell if my voice carried over the background noises, but I saw her turn toward me and give a thumbs up as I wove my way toward her through the racing crowd.

"Good timing, Sensei. That was getting hairy."

I looked at the bodies on the ground. Friends and neighbors. Ken had warned us that we would lose people, but I had never imagined it being this bad. There must have been thirty bodies and even more wounded.

I shook my head. "Not good enough. Too many of us are dead."

Sarah grabbed my shoulder. "It would've been worse if you hadn't come along when you did. We'd have lost a lot more."

"But you were supposed to have more support! Where's Ken? We had over forty people waiting to help you! Where are they?"

She looked at me incredulously. "Are you kidding? Can't you hear the fighting?"

"What?"

"The tanks. Jeez, Sensei! There were two more tanks. Ken's people went to draw the other tanks off! They sound like they're about a mile away now."

"What?" I shook my head, dumbfounded. "My ears are a little messed up, Sarah. I can't hear too well."

"What happened?" She looked at me with sudden concern.

"That first tank happened," I said bitterly. "There's no way they can last long against two of them!" I reached for the radio at my belt and turned it on. "Ken! It's Leeland! Ken! Can you hear me? Everyone is out of the stadium, pull back! Pull back, Ken!"

No response. I handed the radio to Sarah. "My ears must not be working well enough. Can you hear anything?"

Sarah lifted it and tried the same thing for a few seconds before shaking her head. "Either it's not working, or they just can't hear us."

"Okay, then can you take me to where they're fighting?"

She watched the flood of people scurrying past us into the darkness. "Yeah, I can take you. Everyone here knows where to meet up. Come on."

She led me through the darkened streets to the east side of town. The closer we got, the more I could hear. And the more I could hear, the worse things sounded. By the time we reached the fighting, I could easily hear the chatter of rifles and machine guns firing, the chaos of the battle. With both of us wearing goggles, we were able to avoid scattered groups of Larry's men, and we soon found our way to a group of our own people.

René busily shouted orders to a squad of several men as Sarah and I first approached them in the narrow lane between two buildings. Further up the street, I saw a white flash that nearly blinded me, and I ripped the goggles from my face. The flash was followed a second later by the sound and vibration of an explosion. The tanks were up there somewhere.

I turned to see Sarah watching me through the insectoid goggles. "Try infrared," was her only comment.

I nodded. Knowing René as I did, I wasn't about to get closer until I knew she was expecting me. "René!"

Her rifle whipped around at the sound of my voice. "¿Quién está?"

Spanish? She must be scared to death. "Leeland and Sarah, coming in from the rear!"

Squinting toward me, she finally decided not to shoot. "Vaya con sus manos. Chinga! Come een weeth your hands where we can see them!"

Raising our rifles above our heads, Sarah and I joined René's group. As we walked up, I saw four men trying to staunch the flow of blood from two others. Neither of the wounded looked to be in very good shape. Still more men and women leaned panting against the wall.

Incongruously, for the first time ever, I actually saw René Herrera smile. It was a frightening thing. Completely feral. "Glad to see you made it, Jefe. Where the others?"

"Dead."

She turned away. "Sorry."

"Not your fault." *It's me they trusted. My fault.* "Where's Ken?"

She pointed several blocks up the road to an old Sears store. "In there."

There had dozens of Larry's men hidden behind a barricade of abandoned cars that had been pushed completely across the street to form a solid wall of metal from which they could indiscriminately fill the walls of the department store with holes. With my goggles, I could see about a dozen people firing back from inside the building.

I pulled out the radio. "Ken? Leeland here." After a short pause, I tried again. "Ken?" Still no response. I sighed. "I guess the radio's dead after all. René, do you know how many other groups of our people are around here?

We're going to have to hit those guys from behind and break Ken and the others out of there."

"Three more."

"Are they as big as your group?"

She shook her head. "Not three groups. Three more people. Ken send us out to try to stop the tank. We get out the back just before they surround the building."

I counted the rest of her group. Ten people, two of them wounded, plus Sarah and me, and the three others that she mentioned.

I started to rise. "It might be enough if we hit them from behind. I gotta—"

René grabbed my arm and yanked me back down. "You gotta get you self killed? 'Dat what you gonna say? 'Cause if you planning to move into dis street, dat's what gonna happen!" She indicated several bodies in the middle of the road. "They think they can walk out there, too." She pointed up the street. "Machine gun somewhere ahead. We don' know for sure where it is."

She pointed to two other storefronts. "Banditos there, an' there. Don' know how many." Then she pointed to the top of a four-story office building. "Tha's where the other three from our group are." Finally, she pointed to the deep patch of darkness next to the office building. "But look close, en de side street."

I flipped the goggles back down over my eyes, and my heart skipped a beat. The muzzle of a tank cannon pointed down the street. The rest of the thing remained hidden behind the building, but there was no mistaking the cannon protruding into the street. For the moment, the tank sat motionless, but I had little doubt that eyes watched from within, alert for any sign of movement. Ken had warned us that the tanks were equipped with a full sensor array. There was little chance that anyone would be able to approach an Abrams unseen.

"They just got here a couple seconds before you," she added. "We think they're trying to figure out what happened to the other tank."

I took the goggles back off. "Other tank? There's another one?"

"Sort of." Once more, she treated me to that frightening grin. "The other tank, she don' work so good no more."

"What?"

"Look all de way aroun' de corner. Up on de sidewalk on dis side." I started forward.

"¡Cuidado!" she hissed. "Don' move fast, or they see you!"

Following her directions, I slipped on my goggles, hugged the wall, and eased forward to the corner; I peered cautiously up the street to find the second tank sitting as motionless as the first. The only difference was that the cannon on this one was completely destroyed, looking much like the remains of Elmer Fudd's shotgun after Bugs had plugged the end with his finger.

"What the hell happened?"

She indicated one of the wounded men lying back in the shadows. "Frankie there, he say he know how to stop the tanks. He say *el cannon* must be clean. Very clean. He pour a bucket of concrete inside, and they shoot him with the little machine guns on the top, but the next thing we know, the whole thing explode! She don' move since then. We figure the explosion also get the people in the tank."

I thought back to the flash that Sarah and I had seen just before we spotted René's group. That must have been the explosion of the cannon, which meant that all this happened just a few minutes ago.

"René! This just happened?"

"Sí. A couple minutes ago. Why?"

I looked across the street to the tank peeking out from between the buildings, then to the office building where René had said our people were hidden. Inspiration struck. "I think I might have a way to pull our butts out of the fire if we move fast enough."

* * *

I looked down through my goggles as I descended from the top of the office building. Hanging from a makeshift rope of cut and tied extension cords, I shook my head. "Leeland, what the hell have you gotten yourself into?"

The little voice in my head ignored the question, instead concentrating on trying to make me see just how foolish I was being. "Get someone else to play hero!" the voice screamed. "Go back home to your wife and kids while you still can!"

"If I don't do this," I answered, "there won't be any home to go to, and I might not get the chance to ever see them again."

231

I looked down once more. *Almost there.* In my head, a jumble of prayers and curses swirled—mostly prayers. For an avowed agnostic, I seemed to be praying an awful lot lately. Dropping closer to the tank, I prayed it would stay in place for just a few minutes more, that none of the extension cords would come untied, that none of the enemy noticed a man dropping down the side of the building like a spider clinging to a strand of silk, that none of the millions of things that could go wrong, *would* go wrong. The more I thought about what I was doing, the more foolish it seemed.

Tightening my grip, I yanked hard on the cord twice to signal a stop. Three feet below, the top hatch of the tank waited. Larry's men evidently hadn't seen the show Ivory had mentioned earlier that evening. Or perhaps they simply never expected anyone to get close enough to try the hatch, and so hadn't bothered to put a padlock on it. Why should they worry? They had one-hundred-eighty-degree coverage from the two small M-240 machine guns on front and three-hundred-sixty-degree coverage from the more powerful top mounted fifty caliber. Combine that with the sensor package on the tanks, and a person would have to be crazy to try getting to that hatch.

So there I was. By coming in from above, I hoped to bypass all of that.

I switched the goggles from infrared to night vision and studied the dogging lever on the far left hatch. It seemed straightforward enough. Slide the lever up and pull. Satisfied that I knew how to open it, I took the goggles off and once more hung them on my belt before readying my rifle. I eased my foot out until only the toe was left in the loop.

Taking a deep breath, I pushed off from the side of the building and swung out over to the far side of the tank. And jumped.

The sound of my feet hitting the armored top of the tank sounded incredibly loud to my ears, but I wasted no time worrying about it. I yanked up the hatch, finding it lighter than I had expected, or perhaps it was just well balanced, and stared into the surprised eyes of a man sitting a few feet below. I fired point blank and tried not to gag at the mess I made of his face as I kicked him out of his seat onto the floor. Dropping inside, I slipped in the blood and landed clumsily on my butt. I turned to see another man sitting slightly above and to the right, struggling for his pistol. Panicked, I fired wildly as I struggled to my feet. My shot missed, and the man ducked. I got back to my feet as he unsnapped his holster and slid down toward me. I realized my rifle was a disadvantage in the tight quarters; I was forced to shift back to get another shot off. I hit him in the neck, and he fell forward, trapping my M-16 between us. A third man to my left swung his pistol in my direction. He was only three feet away. It should have been an easy shot, and would have been, if I could have gotten my rifle free.

Instead, heart pounding with fear and adrenaline, I dropped my rifle, clapped my left hand over his and twisted the pistol backward, causing his finger to pull the trigger about the time that he saw the barrel pointing at his own chest. His eyes widened in fear, and then glazed over.

I yanked my rifle out from under the second man and looked around frantically, searching for another opponent.

Over that quickly? My heart pounded with unspent adrenaline, and the little voice was back. Ken had said to expect four men.

As if my thoughts were the trigger, the tank lurched into motion, first forward, then left. The sudden movement threw me off balance, and I fell back into the seat, feeling the warm, sticky blood that coated it soaking into my pants. *What the hell?* I checked the bodies, thinking perhaps one of the men had fallen on the accelerator. I searched closely for anything that might be a means of driving this tin can, but there was nothing I recognized as such. In a panic, I started flipping levers and pushing buttons, hoping to find something by chance.

I did, though it wasn't at all what I expected. There was a stick-on label that read "TURRET" over a console. Next to it was what looked like a kid's video game joystick. I pulled tentatively on the joystick and saw the turret begin to turn, and an opening appeared in front, growing larger by the second. A separate compartment for the driver, I realized, just as a hand with a pistol appeared through that opening.

I flipped the lever on my rifle to *Auto* and fired a half a dozen rounds into the tiny compartment. The driver twitched once and fell forward in his seat with the Abrams still accelerating.

Before dropping into the tank, my hearing had been slowly returning, but the firefight in the enclosed cabin brought back the familiar ringing that had been my constant companion since the blast that had thrown Billy. Touch, sight, and smell kicked into overdrive to compensate for my lost hearing. Suddenly, the scent of gunpowder and blood was overwhelming, the feel of blood seeping through my clothing from the seat nauseating.

Standing in the seat, I prepared to climb out of the tank. It looked like I was going to have to jump, and I wanted to do it before the Abrams built up too much speed. Then I saw where we were headed. Larry's men were dead ahead, cheering and waving at the tank, unaware that it was driving itself and would run over their barricade in less than a minute.

They thought I was one of the crew. It was too good an opportunity to pass up. I looked at the fifty caliber machine gun in front of me and took the grips in hand. It only took a few seconds to find the manual controls, and only a few more to give Larry's thugs the surprise of their lives. The last man went down just seconds before the tank crashed into the barrier of cars; the lurch as the Abrams flattened the automobiles dropped me back into the seat. There were only seconds left before I slammed full speed into the side of the Sears building.

In retrospect, it probably would have been smarter for me to have just closed the hatch and stayed inside the tank than to have jumped, but by the time I realized just how fast I was really going, my choices were rather limited. I was already outside, on top of the tank with the department store rushing at me at about forty miles an hour. It was either jump or take my chances sitting on the outside of the tank as it slammed into the building. Visualizing a wall of bricks falling on top of me, I decided to jump.

The ground rushed up at me, and then there was darkness.

CHAPTER 16

* * AUGUST 19 / MORNING * *

Triremes pleines tout aage captif,
Temps bon à mal, le doux pour amertume:
Proye à Barbares trop tost seront hatifs,
Cupid de voir plaindre au vent la plume.

Triremes full of captives of every age,
Good time for bad, the sweet for the bitter:
Prey to the Barbarians hasty they will be too soon,
Anxious to see the feather wail in the wind.
                    Nostradamus – *Century 10, Quatrain 97*

"Come on, Jefe. Time to wake up!"

Why was it that lately, I always seemed to awaken to the feel of someone shaking me and calling my name? There must be a sign on my forehead that read, "Go ahead and wake him up! He doesn't really need any rest."

I tried to tell whoever it was to stop shaking me and let me die in peace, but all that came out was "Shunnggghhh."

"That's it, Jefe! We almost home."

"Stop shaking me," somehow got lost in translation once more, although "Shtothing ma," was closer than the previous grunting.

"Come on, Sensei. You can do it." Sarah's voice caused me to turn my head, an act which I had immediate cause to regret. Sudden nausea and dizziness accompanied by pain sent excruciating flashes of light to my brain, which for some odd reason, seemed to remind me that my eyes were still closed. I opened them without thinking, causing even more agony.

"Umph!" I explained firmly, clenching my eyelids tightly closed once more. Now, if I could only get them to stop shaking me.

"He acts like the light hurts his eyes," Sarah said.

"Of course it hurt his eyes! Don' it hurt your eyes when you first wake up? Come on, Jefe!"

This time René's voice accompanied a firm slap to my cheek. The pain in my head hurt immeasurably worse than the slap could account for. "Ow!" The single syllable was simple enough to make it through my scrambled neurons exactly as I had intended. For some reason, however, it only seemed to encourage another light slap.

"Good, Jefe! You need to wake up an' stay awake. You hear me?"

When I refused to answer, someone decided to raise my eyelid to see if I was really home. I jerked my head away and immediately suffered another wave of pain and nausea.

"Jefe, you gotta concussion. You gotta stay awake! Fight it, Jefe. Open you eyes!"

I cracked one lid a fraction of an inch and squinted at the two women hovering over me. Both Sarah and René smiled when they saw that I was mostly cognizant.

"Stoshnme," I mumbled, but it only earned a puzzled frown.

"What he say?" René asked. Sarah shrugged.

I took particular care with my pronunciation, forming my lips into the proper shapes and enunciating slowly and deliberately. "Stob. Shakin'. Me!"

René laughed. "Ain' nobody shakin' you, Jefe. You in the back of a Humvee an' we takin' back roads to keep from being spotted. The roads, they jus' a little bumpy."

I braved the light, cracking my eyelids a bit more. Sarah nodded encouragingly. "That's good, Sensei. How do you feel?"

"Like I'm gonna throw up and die. And not necessarily in that order."

"Considering what you've been through, I'm not surprised." She placed a carbine in my hands. "We were able to get some people back to see what you and the others did with that ambush of yours. We found this and the rest of your squad, most of them dead."

"Most of them?"

"We found Billy and that Filipino guy still alive. What was it, Ed, Edward...?"

I laid my head back and smiled. "Billy and Edwin. They're all right?"

"They say Billy's going to be fine. Don't know about Edwin. He looked pretty bad."

"How about Ken?" I feared what I might hear. The last thing I remembered was the tank rushing directly at the building where Ken and the rest of our people were holed up. My imagination supplied countless scenarios involving a runaway Abrams crushing them all to a pulp.

The reassuring answer came from the driver's seat in front. "I'm doing just fine, thanks to you and your asinine stunt with that tank."

"Ken!" Grinning from ear to ear, I struggled to sit up. René and Sarah helped me, and seconds later I was clapping Ken on the shoulder as he tried to drive and look back at me at the same time.

"'Bout time you woke up."

Somewhere on the ride back to the factory, I lost my battle with consciousness and succumbed once more to the exhaustion that permeated my being. At least I had something to smile about when oblivion reclaimed me.

* * *

My next coherent thoughts involved intense feelings of vertigo and the uneasy, not-quite certainty that something was wrong—not threatening, but still wrong. Confused, unsure of where I was, my mind tried to sort through a collage of unfamiliar sensations.

Soft cushions, the smell of mildewed fabric, and the dank, humid atmosphere served to let me know I was no longer in the back of the Humvee. I heard the echoes of voices in solemn conversation beyond the door of my room. I concentrated on the voices. Only a word or two made it through, but I recognized my wife's, and her tone was somewhat less than friendly. My memory was a bit fuzzy, but I recalled flashes of her alternating between laughter, tears, and anger when she saw my condition upon my return from our raid. Then, after examining my head with the experienced eye of a nurse's daughter, she had decided I was in no real danger and prescribed compresses and bed rest, concussion notwithstanding.

Under her direction, René, Ken, Jim, and Sarah had moved me into Jim's office and laid me down on the sofa, where she threatened dire consequences should I dare get up.

She needn't have worried. As badly as I had felt, it wasn't likely I could have gotten up if the building caught fire. I didn't even recall hitting the cushions, so quickly did my exhaustion overcome me.

My body seemed to have recovered somewhat. I swung my feet over the edge of the couch and sat up, barely catching myself in time to keep my face from introducing itself to the floor. Weak and trembling, I raised my hand to touch a makeshift bandage over a huge knot on the front of my skull; I vaguely recalled everyone's worries about a concussion. Memories of a nightmare tank ride reminded me that if a concussion was the worst of my injuries, I had probably gotten off lightly.

The exhaustion that had previously overwhelmed everything else was gone, replaced by aching, stiff muscles that stubbornly resisted my brain's commands to rise. Synaptic impulse slowly won out, and I carefully limped through the door and down the hall toward the sound of the voices.

I couldn't hear much of what was being said through the door, only enough to hear Debra adamantly refuse to allow some person or persons to awaken me.

Woe to the foolish mortal who dared the wrath of Debra. I smiled a bit at the thought and wondered how long I had slept. Snatches of conversation filtered through the door.

"… let him get some rest… already done enough?" I couldn't hear it all, and my head hurt too badly to concentrate much, but it soon became evident exactly who she was arguing with. Ken's voice, firm and calm as always, answered, though I couldn't hear what he said. Jim joined in a few seconds later.

With a little grimace at the ache in my forearm, I turned the doorknob and entered. The previously animated discussion abruptly ceased, and the three occupants of the room turned to face me, suddenly seeming unsure of themselves. I turned from one face to the other, hoping to show them that I was all right. "Am I interrupting?"

Their lack of response was less than reassuring. I had just heard them arguing about me. Now... nothing. "Come on, guys, how would you feel if you walked into a room, and everyone stopped talking all at once?"

Jim grinned a little and waved me to a chair. "Come on in and sit down before you fall over." Ken pulled the old wooden desk chair out, and I sat cautiously at the table across from Jim. Debra, sitting on my right, reached over and squeezed my hand. I tried not to grimace at the pain caused by that simple act.

"You shouldn't be up." It was a gentle admonishment and, though I could tell she meant it, she also seemed relieved to see me.

"I'm fine," I lied.

"Seriously, how're you feelin', Lee?" Jim's smile and light tone were forced, his expression grim. The black eye made it look worse.

"Like I dove off the high dive into an empty pool." The smile relaxed a little, as did his expression. "So what's all the arguing about?"

The mayor hesitated, apparently loathe to renew the debate.

"Come on, Jim. You look like you just swallowed something that's trying to claw its way back up. What's going on?"

I searched the faces of the three people I trusted above all others. If there was something they were keeping from me, it must be pretty bad. I sighed and looked up at the sunlight filtering in through the office window. From the angle, I estimated the time to be about an hour or two before noon. *I'm too tired for this!*

Turning back to the three around the table, I saw that Ken had on his best poker face. I'd seen it before and knew I wouldn't get anything there that he didn't want to show me. Jim was just the opposite with his face a tortured roadmap of emotion. Above all else, I saw the worry of a man responsible for the fate of an entire town resting on his shoulders. Though the two men's expressions were as opposite as east and west, the results were the same. I could tell nothing about the situation at hand.

I concentrated my gaze on Debra. We had been married for almost twenty years and knew each other better than we knew anyone else. It was hard for us to hide anything from one another. So when I saw the tightness of her lips, I knew she was fighting back her anger. She seldom raised her voice unless she was really riled, so that wasn't unexpected, but her eyes bothered me—just a little wider than usual, a little brighter with moisture. I had seen the expression all too often during our internment in the shelter—fear.

"What is it that's got you three at each other's throats?" I prodded. None of them would meet my eyes, their gazes darting to one another like school children caught at some clandestine activity, none wanting to be the first to confess. "Jim?"

James Kelland, Mayor of Rejas City, the man most looked up to by all of its citizenry, shifted nervously in his seat and studiously avoided my gaze. He turned to Ken as though he wanted the other man to start.

I followed Jim's cue. "Ken?" But Ken also seemed reluctant to take the reins.

I sighed wearily, too tired to properly express my frustration. "Look, guys, I've known you two for a couple of years now, and I've never known either of you to mince words, so I can imagine just how bad this probably is. Right now, though, I'm tired, my head is killing me, my whole body aches, and the only thing you two are doing by passing the buck back and forth is making me even more nervous. I can't take too much of this crap right now, so could you please just spit it out?"

It was the mayor that finally started. "Larry's outside."

Those two simple words froze the blood in my veins.

"Outside where?"

"Out front. He's got two of his tanks on the road outside the factory. One of 'em's on the bridge with its cannon pointin' right at us. The other one's back behind the tree line."

Oh, Lord. "Okay, I don't hear any shooting. What's he doing?"

"He's got hostages." Debra's voice dropped to nearly a whisper, and she wouldn't meet my gaze, choosing instead to examine the grain of the tabletop as if it were the only thing she could bear to look at. As I watched, a tear fell from her cheek to dampen the wood. Here then was the heart of the matter.

I looked back at Ken. "I thought we got them all out. What happened?"

"Eric's group didn't do as well as ours. They ran into some complications with the hospital extraction." Extraction? Was that what it had been? Such a fine, sterile word for such a bloody operation. My thoughts were understandably bitter. "Some of the hospital patients were injured too badly to move, and some of the doctors and nurses refused to leave them. They got as many out as they could, but ended up leaving nearly a hundred behind."

"A hundred hostages?" I groaned.

Ken shook his head. "There's more. Or I should say, there's less."

I shook my head irritably. "No more games! What else?"

He pursed his lips. "When he showed up here yesterday—"

"Whoa!" I interrupted. "Yesterday? He was here when we were in town?"

Ken shook his head. "That was the day before yesterday. You've been out for the last day and a half."

"What?"

Debra nodded confirmation. "You were pretty banged up when they brought you in. When you didn't wake up all day, we figured the best thing for you was to let your body rest and heal itself."

"I slept a whole day?"

Ken nodded, too. "And half of today." He pointed to Debra. "Your lady here threatened anyone who got within fifty feet of you with the violent removal of precious body parts."

I thought back on the bits and pieces I could recall of the ride back in the Humvee. It had been light enough to see René and Sarah—early morning. When I'd seen the light in the window a moment ago, I'd assumed that it was nearly noon of the same day.

I could tell by Ken's expression that he had more to tell me. So I shoved my confusion aside and waited patiently for him to continue.

"When Larry showed up yesterday, he parked his tank just across the bridge and sent out a messenger with a white flag. The messenger claimed Larry was a lawful representative of the United States Army, and that you were wanted for war crimes."

"What!"

Ken held up a finger. "Just wait. It gets better."

"Jim told him you'd been killed in the fighting, and that even if you weren't, in consideration of the damage he'd done the town so far, the good

241

general was going to have to give us more than just his word that he was a legitimate government official before we would even consider turning someone over to him."

I smiled despite the circumstances. "How'd Larry take that?"

"Not well." Jim took over from Ken. "I watched that man take my message back to Larry. As soon as he finished talkin', Larry pulled out a pistol and shot the man where he stood." He shook his head. "I ain't never seen nothin' like it. His own man! Just dropped him 'cause he didn't like what he had to say.

"Then he climbed back in his tank, and him an' the rest of his boys just left like nothin' happened. This mornin', he came back with thirty hostages from the hospital. Turned ten of them loose and sent 'em in with hundreds of leaflets." The mayor slid a piece of mimeographed paper across the table. "Read."

It was the same mimeograph paper as that on which the *Chronicle* was printed. I read silently.

> *Citizens of Rejas. It is my understanding that you have unknowingly harbored a criminal by the name of Leeland Dawcett. He is wanted by the U.S. Government for the ambush and brutal murders of several innocent people on the evening of June 13, 2015, on Highway 189 while en route to your town. Leeland Dawcett is the sole purpose of our expedition, and upon his delivery, my troops and I will withdraw from your town.*
>
> *Today at noon, if he has not been turned over to me, you will then be guilty of harboring a fugitive during a time of martial law, and I will be forced to renew hostilities in order to recover this wartime criminal. Please do not force us to use the full might of the U.S. military against you.*
>
> *Turn this murderer over to us so that we can leave you in peace.*
>
> *Signed,*
> *General Lawrence D. Troutman - USRD*

I had no idea what to say. So many implications were buried in the note that it was overwhelming. "He's claiming I killed those people on D-day?"

Jim nodded.

"The guy's nuts, Jim! I mean, I knew he was a crook, even a murderer. But this?" I wadded the note into a ball and threw it on the table. "He's crazy!"

The mayor shrugged. "No doubt about that, Lee, but he's crazy like a fox. And with his tanks and troops, he has enough clout to make ever'body listen to what he wants to say." He indicated the wad of paper with a wave of his hand. "That note implies that all of the fighting and killing here has been because of you and, if we turn you over to him, he'll leave us alone."

I paused and took a deep breath. "So how many are ready to hand me over?"

"Surprisingly few, actually," Ken interjected. "These aren't the good ol' days when people would blindly believe whatever they saw on the idiot box. These are rough times, and actions speak a lot louder than words. Rejas has seen what you've done for her, and what Troutman has done. What he did to that messenger was just the icing on the cake."

That was reassuring, but it raised a question. "I appreciate the sentiment, but if you weren't arguing about whether or not to turn me over, just what was all the yelling about?"

Jim looked hurt. "You don't really think we considered turnin' you over to that lunatic, do you? It's just that it's almost noon, and we were tryin' to decide whether or not to wake you up. You sorta made that a moot point, though."

"Thanks, Jim, but I wouldn't blame you if you did decide to trade me. You have more people than me to think about."

He pursed his lips. "That may be. But this man has already proven that he can't be trusted. I don't think he'd stick to his word, even if we did give you up. The hostages he released had some other stories to tell when they got back to us.

"Seems Larry was in a hurry to get the hostages here this morning. He was in such a hurry that he couldn't be slowed down with a bunch of sick and wounded."

"Oh God!" I hoped the story wasn't going where I feared.

But my hope proved to be in vain, as Jim continued, "He killed everyone that couldn't keep up and forced the rest to march here overnight. According to Eric's report on his raid, there were over a hundred people left in that hospital. Larry got here this morning with thirty. He didn't leave anyone behind."

I slumped back in my chair. Then something occurred to me. I looked over at my wife, tears flowing silently down her cheeks. "Amber?"

I finally understood Debra's tears. She was in a no-win situation. If I surrendered to Larry, she would lose her husband. If I didn't, she would lose her mother. No matter what happened, she was about to lose one of the people closest to her within the next few hours.

Of course, my first thought was that I would do the *right* thing and turn myself over to Larry. It seemed straightforward enough—my life for twenty others, one of them my mother-in-law.

Then, *"But what if he doesn't keep his word?"* And finally, *"If? Of course he won't keep his word! Remember City Hall? This man will do anything to get what he wants. Anything!"*

I was at a loss. I truly had no earthly idea on what to do. My jaw kept flapping open, then closed, an ugly parody of a fish aground.

"Shut your mouth, Leeland. Nobody's turning you over to that lunatic." Ken's words brought me back to my present surroundings. "Not even you." He held my eye to see that I understood. He had obviously followed my thought process and come to the same conclusion. Larry wasn't trustworthy enough to deal with.

Defeated, I let my fatigue take over and slumped down in my chair. "So what do we do?"

"Well, it's not as bad as you'd think. We have a plan, of sorts. It's just that there are some complications keeping us from acting on it. Twenty of them, to be precise."

CHAPTER 17

* * AUGUST 21 / NOON * *

En cité obsesse aux murs hommes & femmes.
Ennemis hors le chef prest à soy rendre:
Vent sera fort encore les gendarmes.
Chassez seront par chaux, poussiere, & cendre.

In the besieged city men and woman to the walls,
Enemies outside the chief ready to surrender:
The wind will be strongly against the troops,
They will be driven away through lime, dust and ashes.
               Nostradamus – *Century 4, Quatrain 52*

I squeezed Debra's hand and emotionally braced myself to leave her and
Megan with the rest of the crowd that had come out to the meeting with us.

Megan smiled grimly. "Kick his ass, Dad." When they'd brought me back injured, her emotions had made the predictable transformation from grief to barely controlled rage.

I hugged her to me and whispered, "If this doesn't work, it's up to you to watch out for your mom and Zach."

"It'll work."

I appreciated her confidence, but I hadn't told her what I had in mind for this meeting.

Jim and I stepped onto the bridge and away from the grim faces of the people that had come with us to meet Larry. The folks of Rejas brandished a variety of weapons, from machine guns taken off of the bodies of Larry's so-called soldiers to homemade bows and arrows. Each of them had come with whatever they could get their hands on and, though they were outnumbered, outgunned, and quite possibly outmaneuvered, there wasn't the slightest hint of hesitation. Everyone appeared ready to make their stand.

The bridge stretched over the reservoir for about two hundred yards, and I saw two figures approaching us from the other side. As we walked out to meet them, I examined our opposition. Out front, partly on the bridge itself, sat one of Larry's tanks. Just behind it, I could see a few hundred troops. Just past the bridge, the road veered sharply to the right and into the thicket, blocking any further observations, although just at the edge of the bend, I spotted the front of a second tank.

"You call this a plan?" I said through the side of my mouth. We were under the supposed protection of a white flag, but my confidence in Larry's willingness to honor the truce was limited. The whole thing was iffy, at best. Too many things had to go just right.

If Jim had similar thoughts, he kept them well hidden. "Just keep walkin'."

I recognized the two people approaching as Larry and Han. "Larry's leg seems to have healed well. There's no limp at all."

Jim grunted. "Maybe next time."

"One can only hope."

We stopped a few feet away in the middle of the bridge, twenty feet above the murky waters of the reservoir. I was surprised at the hulking leviathan beside Larry. I had forgotten just how huge Han was, or perhaps the rough lifestyle had bulked him up. Whatever the reason, I had to work to keep my jaw from dropping.

"Hello again, Leeland." Larry smirked. "I see your townspeople have determined to do the sensible thing and turn you over to me." He leaned forward and lowered his voice, a wicked gleam in his eye. "Doesn't it frustrate you to find just how little you mean to them? Or that you've wasted your time with a group of people that just don't care much what happens to anyone else, as long as they are left alone to meek out their miserable existences?"

"You haven't changed a bit, Larry. Still a big-headed windbag with delusions of grandeur, eh? You even had to put on a uniform and call yourself a *general* to appease that ego, didn't you?"

His eyes narrowed, and he turned to address Jim. "I'm gratified that you decided to do the right thing, Mayor. I'm truly sorry that we had to use such drastic measures to recapture Mr. Dawcett, but this is a martial law situation. You understand, I'm sure."

"Han, bring him." Han stepped forward.

"Oh no, you don't!" I whipped out the pistols I had hidden under my jacket, planted the first one firmly in Larry's ribs, and jammed the second under his chin. "Tell your dog to stay put, or I'll do what I should have done two years ago."

Larry froze.

Han froze.

Jim froze.

"What are you doing, Lee?" Jim yelled. "This ain't what we agreed on!"

"Change in plans. I'm not about to trust this scum to turn our people loose unless he has to."

I dug the pistol into Larry's side. "This is to make sure he has to."

"What makes you think I'll do it now?" Larry's words were laced with disdain, but I could see the way his Adam's apple bobbed beneath the muzzle of the pistol.

"Because I'll kill you if you don't. It's as simple as that."

"And why should I believe you won't if I release them?"

"Because one of your hostages is my mother-in-law. And if you'll recall, I went through hell and back for my family, even went so far as to take a beating from your pet gorilla to buy them time."

"Leeland, I assure you—"

"Shut up! Your word doesn't mean dick! You'll let those hostages go only as long as I force you to. So get on your radio and send them out. Now!"

I pulled the second pistol from under his chin and tucked it back under my jacket. As I did, I saw Han at the edge of my sight trying to inch closer. Without turning away from Larry, I said, "Go ahead and try it, Han. I'd love an excuse to ruin this pretty uniform your boss is wearing."

He stopped and moved his hands out to the side where they could be easily seen.

"You might be smarter than I gave you credit for. Now pull open your jacket and drop your gun belt. Make it slow. Jim, take his gun and toss it into the water."

Jim jumped, apparently startled. "This ain't right, Leeland. It ain't what we agreed to."

I stole glimpses at the crowds on either side of the bridge. On both sides, people had weapons raised, some aimed at me, some at Larry and Han. Still others aimed at the opposing army. Everywhere though, people appeared uncertain as to what exactly was going on.

"Do it, Mayor!"

He hastened to grab the pistol from the ground, but seemed to hesitate at throwing it into the reservoir. I understood. Firearms and ammunition were valued commodities, rapidly diminishing resources. Nevertheless, it was vital that Larry and Han be unarmed if this was going to work.

"Don't worry, Mayor. I'll still go with them. You'll get to save your precious town. I just want to make sure my family is safe first." I turned back to Larry and frisked him with my free hand. I left the radio on his belt and threw his pistol out to join Han's. The splash told me that it wouldn't be easily recovered.

Jim started to step toward me. "Leeland—"

Whipping my second handgun out again, I pointed it directly at Jim. "Sorry, Mayor, I need you to come over here where I can see you."

Jim looked at me as if he had never seen me before. "What the…?"

"Get over here with these two where I can keep an eye on you."

"Dammit, Leeland!"

"Now!" Jim scrambled to do as I said.

"Now reach into Larry's jacket here and pull out his radio." When he did, I ordered, "Take it, Larry. Tell your troops to release those hostages or, so help me, I'll drop you where you stand, and to hell with what happens after."

He swallowed and keyed the radio. "General Troutman here." He looked up at me and, for a moment, I thought he was going to resist. "Release the prisoners."

I snatched the radio from his hand before he could say anything else. "Now, as soon as I see our people back on this side of the bridge, we can settle things between ourselves."

"What do you mean?"

"I mean, I want to see people moving over here in thirty seconds, or I swear I'm going to ruin your day!" I shoved the barrel of my pistol down the front of his pants. "One. Two. Three—"

Larry snatched the radio back. "Get those prisoners over here! Get them over here now!"

"Seven, eight, nine…" I had reached seventeen when I saw the first of them running across the bridge. Amber was the tenth.

When the last one had filtered through the crowd on our side of the reservoir, I turned back to Larry. Pulling the pistol out of his pants, I shoved it back into his ribs. "We did have an understanding about this meeting, didn't we, Larry? The next time we met?"

"Leeland, no!"

"This is between me and Larry, Mayor. You can go back to the factory now. This will all be over in a few minutes. I'll kill him, his thugs will kill me, and everyone else gets to go home happy."

Jim looked at me with wonder in his expression. "You're just as crazy as he is."

"Maybe so," I acknowledged. "But in a couple of minutes, I don't think that'll matter anymore. Now, get back to the factory, or you're going to get caught here when the bullets start flying."

The mayor lowered his eyes, apparently defeated, and stepped away from Han and Larry. Then, as he drew alongside me, he grabbed my arm and pulled it away from Larry. "This ain't right!"

The two of us struggled for the pistol for a moment before Jim suddenly snatched the second pistol from my jacket and pointed it at my belly. The other was still held aloft, pointing at the sky, where he held my arm locked with his. Turning me to where he could see Larry over my shoulder, he said, "None of this was supposed to happen. We was comin' out here ta negotiate with you. I wasn't gonna let you take Leeland, but I figured I could trade my people for some more of the explosives we used to get your tanks."

He panted a bit from our struggle and looked at me. "You went and ruined it! Damn it, Leeland, none of this had to happen! You've committed us to a war we can't win!"

I looked around. Guns from all sides were trained on the bridge, but everyone hesitated to fire the shot that would no doubt begin a raging battle. "So now what?"

"You two." He jerked his chin at Larry and Han. "Get back to your people and pull back. We'll talk this out later."

"You think they're going to just walk away and let you alone?" I demanded.

"Go!" he yelled, and I heard their footsteps rapidly retreating.

The two of us remained locked together for a moment. I saw Jim's eyes following their progress over my shoulder.

He nodded. "Far enough."

I took a deep breath, then screamed at the top of my lungs, "No, you can't let them go!" I yanked my pistol down from Jim's grip and whirled around, aiming at Larry's back. "Come back here, you son of a bitch!"

Larry turned to see me aiming right at him. Then Jim fired twice. I heard the report and felt the stinging in my back that told me I'd been hit. I turned, "Wha…?"

"I can't let you do that, Lee." He fired twice more at my chest, just as I fired back at him. Screams of disbelief erupted from the townspeople as Jim and I both fell to our knees.

There are so many holes in this plan that it isn't funny…

I dropped my pistol and clutched at the stinging in my chest.

…and if anything goes wrong, I'm dead.

Pulling my hand away, I saw it stained shiny and red. I held it out toward Jim, and there were more screams as people saw the crimson coating. Jim struggled back to his feet just before I fell to my face.

…so many holes..

* * *

I heard the sounds of boots approaching and resisted the urge to move. They stopped beside me, and I felt someone reach down to check my pulse. "You all right?" Ken whispered.

I answered without moving. "Just a little bruised. Forgot how much paintballs hurt at close range."

Ken grunted. "Okay, boys, pick him up and get him back to the factory. Make sure everyone gets a good look at all the red on him when you take him back. Leeland, you're dead. Don't move a muscle." Four sets of hands grabbed my arms and legs, lifting me to shoulder height. I concentrated on being dead as they bore me back toward the factory.

* * *

"The whole thing is iffy, at best," I'd protested. "Too many things have to go just right. I mean, what if they get a good look at the pistols? What if they realize that they don't quite sound the same as regular firearms? What if they don't buy my acting, or Jim's? There are so many holes in this plan that it isn't funny, and if anything goes wrong, I'm dead. We're all dead!"

Ken looked at me, his frustration obvious. "So you got a better idea? Nobody's forcing you into this. Jim and I are fully prepared to do it without you. You can still bow out."

"Bullshit! As bad a plan as it is, it would be even worse without me in it."

"Yes, it is. But it's like Debra said, you've already done more than enough for this town, especially in the last couple of days. Nobody would think any less of you if you passed on this one."

"Except me." I dropped my head and sighed. I looked back up at Ken. "Okay. The trick is going to be trying to keep Larry off balance. He's too smart to fall for it if he has time to think about what's going on."

He nodded, relieved to see I was finally rolling with it. "Suggestions?"

"Piss him off ... scare him. Do whatever we can to keep him reacting instead of thinking. Once the ball is rolling, he can't get a second to gather his wits, or we're all dead."

"And how do we do that?"

"I'm going to remind him of our first meeting. I scared the hell out of him then, and it's got to be eating away at that monster ego of his. I imagine that's why he's so insistent about getting his hands on me now."

Ken nodded. "Makes sense. I take it you have something in mind?"

251

"Not really. Just gonna do like I did in the tank. I'll start pushing buttons and see what happens."

* * *

Less than a dozen people knew I wasn't really dead, and it was all I could do to remain still as they carried me through the stunned crowd to Jim's office. Once behind closed doors, I opened my eyes and saw smiling faces all around me.

"You didn't tell me those things would sting so much," Jim complained. "Still, I guess it's better than the alternative. You look pretty lively for a dead man."

I smiled. "You don't look so bad yourself."

Debra brought over a couple of wet rags and helped me out of my shirt, tsking over the welts on my chest. "I've never understood your fascination with a sport that causes so many bruises." She pulled my head down and kissed me soundly. "But just now, I'm not complaining."

As soon as I could stop grinning, I asked, "Where's Ken?"

"Right behind you." He closed the door behind himself as he joined us. "I've been busy trying to calm everyone down. Had to let one more person in on the act, too."

I turned and found Amber staring at me as if she couldn't decide whether to be relieved or furious to find me still alive. Finally, she decided on the former and came forward to hug me. "You scared the hell out of me!"

"Good. Everybody's reaction had to be natural if we were going to fool Larry."

Ken nodded. "Well, I'd say it worked. From what I could see out there, everyone is convinced you're dead and Jim's dying. Our people are all wondering what hit them."

Jim grinned. "Now, how about we hit back?"

* * *

I felt the explosion more than heard it. The floor and walls shook with a ferocity that threatened to bring the building down around us and, as we ran out of Jim's trailer, we saw that part of the building had, indeed, come down. The far end of the factory was a pile of rubble and swirling dust. People screamed and ran in all directions.

"Oh God." Amber rushed toward the wounded.

"Leeland!" I turned and Ken tossed me my rifle.

"This way!"

I followed as he led us through the mob to one of the front bay doors. People hid behind old, rusted-out steel drums, wooden pallets, anything that presented cover while they fired ineffectually at the tank moving out onto the bridge.

Ken immediately signaled them to follow. We made our way to the forefront, and several folks did a double take when they saw two dead men walking. Smiles and muttered comments passed through the crowd as they realized that we had somehow managed to fool Larry.

A second explosion knocked me off my feet, and I saw several people thrown about like paper dolls in a high wind. Most landed without moving. The few able to move thrashed and screamed in anguish. The sounds of gunfire and screaming were once more all around me as Ken lead us to the fore of the skirmish.

"Hold your fire!" he screamed. "Hold your fire!"

I thought he was crazy at first. Hold your fire? While they bombed the hell out of us? But as more and more folks heeded his instructions, I understood. We were the only ones shooting. Larry's goons lay on the ground on the other side of the bridge letting us waste precious ammunition. He had moved one of his tanks to the middle of the bridge, and the second was fully into the open, among his troops. The tank on the bridge was motionless and appeared to be waiting for something. When the shooting finally stopped, one of the top hatches opened, and a stick emerged waving a white rag.

"They've gotta be kidding!" Ken was clearly enraged. "They expect us to accept a truce after this?" He raised his rifle, but Jim put a hand on his arm to stop him.

"Wait. I need a couple of minutes. Just see what they want." With that, the mayor pushed back through the crowd, leaving Ken and me to figure out what was going on.

"What's that all about?" I asked, but Ken only shrugged.

"I have no idea, but let's give him the time he needs." He turned to the crowd. "You!" He singled out a young man in jeans and a dirty t-shirt. "I need your shirt, son."

Without hesitation, the guy stripped off the sweaty white shirt and tossed it to Ken, who draped it over the end of his rifle and walked away.

At the beginning of the bridge, he stopped and waited for the soldier who had climbed out of the tank to walk the rest of the way to him. I watched with the others as they exchanged a few words, then the man handed Ken something and turned back to the tank.

Ken returned holding another of Larry's radios. "His Majesty is in the second tank." He pointed to the tank in the clearing across the bridge. "Says he wants to talk to whoever's in charge. Wants to talk about our surrender."

I grinned. "Well, hell! This should be fun." I held out my hand, but Ken held back for a moment.

"Don't push him too hard, Lee. You remember how unstable he is?"

I nodded. "I know, I know."

"And that he has tanks?"

Again I nodded, less patiently this time. "Right, don't piss off the crazy man with the tanks. Got it."

Ken hesitated a moment longer before finally handing me the walkie-talkie.

I thought for a second before keying the mic. It was going to be a hell of a tightrope act. I had to keep him talking for a few minutes without enraging him to the point where he fired the cannons again. "Hello?"

"This is General Lawrence Troutman of the United..." He paused. "Leeland?"

"Yeah. It's me, Larry." I figured I would keep it simple and get Jim the time he'd asked for before I started pushing his buttons again. "What do you want now?"

There was about a ten-second pause before he answered, and I could only imagine the fit he was probably having over my survival. When he finally answered though, his voice was maliciously polite. "My, my, Leeland. Allow me to congratulate you on your fine acting skills. That was a wonderful performance you and your mayor put on for us. You truly had me fooled. I don't suppose you would consider coming back to the bridge and doing an encore?"

"Why would I do that? You already let our people go. I got what I wanted."

"But you know there were other people in that hospital. I suppose you don't care about them?"

I shook my head at his audacity. "You lying son of a bitch! You don't have any more hostages. All you have are your troops on that side of the bridge, and your enemies over here."

"But, Leeland, there are more than fifty more of your people back at the hospital. How could you be so selfish?"

"We already heard about the rest of the people at the hospital!" Taking a deep breath to calm myself, I thumbed the transceiver once more. "You think you could kill that many people and none of the others would notice? Or have you just reached the point where you can't tell the truth from your own lies anymore?"

Larry was silent for a few seconds, and I glanced around to see how the others were taking the discussion. I couldn't afford to have any of them believe him. If they did, they might begin to feel that it was wiser to turn me over and take Larry at his word. From the expressions around me, I needn't have worried.

As the radio squawked back to life, I saw a ripple in the crowd that started at the perimeter and snaked its way toward me. I concentrated on my conversation, but watched to see what caused the commotion.

"All right," Larry said. "It was a futile attempt to fool you, I admit. It was worth a try, but I would have been surprised if it had worked. In fact, I think I would have been more than a little disappointed." The ripple turned into a parting in the crowd as Jim returned leading two other men.

"Let's simply return to the original proposition, then. I will agree to let your little town go free if you will agree to turn yourself over to me."

I grinned when I saw the gear the mayor and his men carried. Looking up at Jim, I nodded understanding. I knew how to steer the conversation. "You think I'm about to believe you now? You think anyone here will? Every time you open your mouth, another lie falls out. I might have believed you once, but I know you better now. You can take your proposition and shove it."

"Are you certain, Leeland? Think of all the people you are consigning to death. Shouldn't they have some say in this?"

"Sorry, Larry, I'm tired of your mind games. It's nothing more than some kind of ego-stroking for you—mental masturbation—and I'm not a voyeur."

"This is your last chance. Either you walk out and meet my man on the bridge right now, or I'm afraid you leave me with no other choice than to open fire on your facility."

Jim met my eyes. "Ready."

"I'm tired of talking, Larry, so let me put this in terms you can understand." I pointed, and Jim touched the first pair of wires to the car battery he'd brought up.

I saw the explosion a split second before I heard it. The screams and curses of Larry's men reached us just as the first pieces of debris began hitting the water, and I saw most of Larry's soldiers hit the dirt. Others panicked and bolted for the trees.

"Damn," Jim cursed, "wrong one!" Grabbing the next of what looked like a dozen pairs of wires, he touched them to the terminals, and the bridge almost directly beneath the tank exploded in a cloud of dust and rubble, actually lifting the tank a few feet before tumbling it sideways into the reservoir. Cheers erupted from our side, until people saw the second tank moving into better position.

But the mayor was far from finished. He began touching one set of wires after another to the battery terminals. Explosions like land mines ripped through the enemy, indiscriminately throwing men and vehicles high into the air on the other side of the reservoir.

Trees began to jump into the air and fall among the panic-stricken men. Jim had been busy burying Astrolite charges under some of the surrounding trees. A large pine fell across the front of the tank as it tried to maneuver for a shot, and I thought for a hopeful moment that it was trapped. With my heart in my throat, I watched it back out from under the fallen pine as if it were nothing and realized that I had greatly underestimated the power of the behemoth. Then, I saw its cannon.

"Yeah!" It was curved in nearly a fifteen-degree bend. They would never be able to fire that thing ever again.

The tank began a rapid retreat as Larry's fear for his own safety overcame his obsessive desire for my head. He drove away, unheeding of the men on foot around him, and I saw a few of the slower ones crushed screaming beneath the treads as he fled.

Cheers erupted again, and I joined them unabashedly. Pumping my fist in the air, I whooped and yelled. As I turned about to share the glory of the moment with those around me, I froze. Staggering toward me, tears streaming down her face, Debra came to my arms.

"The second explosion..."

The last several minutes flew through my head as I tried to make sense of what she had said. Larry and Han on the bridge, paintball guns, playing dead, Larry's attack with the tank cannon, Amber rushing to help...

...the second explosion...

I gasped. "Amber?"

Her sobbing was the only answer.

CHAPTER 18

* * AUGUST 21 / AFTER THE BATTLE * *

Deux de poison saisiz nouveau venuz,
Dans la cuisine du grand Prince verser:
Par le soillard tous deux au faicts cogneuz
Prins que cuidoit de mort l'aisné vexer.

Two newly arrived have seized the poison,
to pour it in the kitchen of the great Prince.
By the scullion both are caught in the act,
taken he who thought to trouble the elder with death.
> Nostradamus – *Century 7, Quatrain 42*

The Battle of the Bridge was the beginning of a three-month war that forced us to take to the forest, leaving even the tentative sanctuary of the fertilizer factory behind. Larry had shown us all too well just how fragile its protection was. By day, he held the town and much of the surrounding forest. Using Humvees and the remaining two tanks, his men constantly patrolled the perimeter and kept us in hiding. After dark though, we were able to sneak in and do our damage under night's black cloak.

Night raids became the mainstay of our survival. Though Larry technically held the town, it was patently impossible for his men to guard every alley and side street in Rejas from the people who knew them best. We would sneak in at night using game trails and drainage ditches to scavenge the many stashes of supplies people had hidden in their homes before the USR&D takeover.

While we were in town, it just wouldn't have been polite to leave without dropping off some type of thank you gift for the boys in uniform. Usually it was something simple; a nail-tipped arrow in the tire of a Humvee was a favorite or, when we were able to get close enough, rice in the fuel tanks. Some of the boys got more creative, though.

Mark Roesch got a group together and built a ten-foot slingshot out of surgical tubing. It took seven people to use it properly with two people bracing either end, two pulling back the pouch, and one loader. The giant slingshot could launch a Molotov cocktail into a group of vehicles or buildings from nearly half a mile away.

Not to be outdone, Fred Williams and Mike Tanner, who had built custom irrigation systems before the turn of the century, designed the craziest-looking contraption I had ever seen. About four feet long, it consisted of three pieces of PVC pipe strapped together like a triple-barrel shotgun. On the front, a six-inch metal scale, mounted vertically, served as a gun sight. The back end consisted of an intricate maze of valves, air nozzles, and pressure gauges connected by a hose to what appeared to be an old scuba tank.

When they first brought it out to demonstrate, I was sharing a meal with my family—garden snails boiled in lard, wild onions, and a few other local herbs. The food wasn't appealing at first, but was actually pretty tasty when you got past the thought of what you were eating. Williams and Tanner approached the camp, heading for the mayor's lean-to. A crowd of curious onlookers followed, as if they just couldn't wait to see what the crazy contraption strapped to Williams' back was.

Megan and Zachary raced to join the crowd, leaving Debra and me to catch up. We shouldered our way through the crowd in time to hear Jim put voice to what the rest of us were thinking. "What the hell is that thing?"

"Air cannon." Williams was a man of few words and, rather than verbal elaboration, he simply pointed his chin at a tree across the creek, some hundred yards downstream. "Watch."

He and Tanner conferred for a few seconds while the crowd milled about and speculated on what was about to happen. Debra and I took advantage of everyone's restlessness to shoulder our way over to Jim's side.

Tanner, much more outgoing than his partner, warned, "Better stand back. We've only tested this thing two or three times, and it might just blow." This caused some quick shuffling as folks took him at his word and gave the two men more room.

Tanner pulled three round glass jars filled with water from a satchel and dropped one in each barrel. "Normally, we'll be using Molotov cocktails or open cups of shrapnel instead of water. Right now, though, I don't think we need to set the forest on fire."

Jim appeared to be as much in the dark as the rest of us, but must have felt the need to make some kind of semi-intelligent response. "Um, yeah."

Tanner stepped behind Williams and tapped him once on the head. Williams had already sighted his target and pushed the button mounted by his right hand.

Whoomp!

We all watched as the first jar tumbled through the air to land about twenty feet in front of the indicated target. It shattered on impact and sprayed water in about a ten-foot radius.

Tanner grinned. "Just remember, if that had been a cocktail, everywhere you saw water splash would be burning right now." Then he closed one valve, opened another, sighted over Williams' shoulder, tugged down on the back end of the air cannon, and tapped him on the head once more.

Whoomp!

Again, a scintillating jar tumbled through the air; this time, it landed within three feet of the target, saturating it with water.

Another valve adjusted, another tap, another *whoomp*, and another jar broke within feet of the one before it. The tree was soaking wet from the length of a football field away.

A cheer went up from the crowd, and they began to surge forward before Tanner raised his hand to stop them. "Wait a second! We have one more thing this bucket of bolts can do. Stay back for a minute more." That started a round of muttering.

He reached back into the battered duffel and pulled out three handkerchief-wrapped bundles. Dropping one into each of the barrels, he pointed to a small group of trees just across the creek.

Tap. *Whoomp!*

Tap. *Whoomp!*

Tap. *Whoomp!*

Three handkerchiefs fluttered to the ground amidst mutters from the crowd. From where I stood, I couldn't see that there had been any effect on the trees. Williams, evidently confident of success, had already set the air cannon on the ground and begun walking over to where we stood. Tanner just turned and smiled. "Anyone like to go check them?"

Several people waded across the creek to inspect the trees; the mutters quickly turned to excited exclamations. "They're peppered!" someone yelled. "They're full of nails and glass!"

Tanner just stood there as the people around him began clapping him on the back. Meanwhile, Williams came over to speak quietly with Jim and me.

"Got enough material to make three more. I need six men that have enough snap to know how to read pressure gauges and route high-pressure air systems. Gotta be willing to work hard and take orders, too."

Jim waited for him to continue, but Williams just stood there looking at us. "Anything else?" Jim asked.

"Nope."

Jim turned to the trees that had been filled with shrapnel. "What's the range of those things?"

"Accurate for cocktails at about a hunnerd and twenty yards. Shrapnel at about a third that."

The mayor nodded. "Take anyone you need. Tell 'em it comes from me."

And so we acquired a mortar brigade.

* * *

We put Larry's boys through hell at night. We'd fire cocktails or arrows from the trees at random hours of the night, just to keep them awake, if nothing else. Sometimes we were even able to kill a guard or two if they were careless enough to get within bowshot of the trees.

On some occasions, the opportunity to do some real damage presented itself, like the night one of our raiding parties set an HTMD booby trap in a building the enemy used as a barracks. Watchers reported two dead and nine wounded.

Another time, Ken snuck in and planted a soup can of homemade thermite in the treads of one of the tanks, crippling it. Unfortunately, it was the tank that had already been damaged in the Battle of the Bridge. Larry's final Abrams remained intact.

Other times, things went the other way. We lost three squads before word made it through our camp that if you were on a raid and saw the big Asian guy, the best thing you could do was to run as fast and as far as you could. The lone survivor of the third group to run afoul of Han summed it up simply. "The dude's unstoppable."

Worse though, was an incident a few nights later. An entire foraging group missed its rendezvous. The tracker we sent to find them said he'd found signs of a fight and two heads posted on poles. "They was th' supervisors."

"Just the supervisors?" I'd made it a point to be with Jim when the tracker made his report.

The man nodded at me. "Yup. Looks like they killed th' supervisors an' took th' four slaves toward town. Ah follered their tracks as far as th' treeline an' high-tailed it on back here."

That night, our attack groups came back early. They reported that the slaves who'd been taken had been mutilated and crucified on the outskirts of town.

Mark had led the team that found them. "I ain't ever seen anything like what they did to those poor bastards. Looks like they tortured 'em for a while before they died." He shuddered.

The next night, we ambushed a squad of goons who thought they would teach the locals a lesson. Ammunition was so low at that point, much of our fighting was done with bows, machetes, clubs, and knives, meaning that our attack was silent. We hit them from behind, and most died without even knowing they had been attacked. Two got off a couple of wild shots, but that probably only served to make the incident that much spookier to any observers. We hung their bodies in the trees around town for the rest to see next morning.

Megan began leading a squad with Eric, Andrew's father. Their group became well-known on both sides for their fearlessness. They took pride in sneaking past perimeter guards to zones that the USR&D troops thought were safe, getting into barracks, and slitting the throats of dozens of men before they slipped out again, completely undetected.

Larry had to know we were raiding the buildings on the outskirts of town. He may have even known why. He had no way of knowing where we had our various stashes, however. Still, he began setting random booby traps, so we never knew what to expect when we opened a door or stepped on a floor. Usually, we were able to take someone with us who knew the building and could help spot anything out of the ordinary, but that didn't always help.

After two months, we had lost twenty-three men and women. We made it a point to get particularly nasty with the enemy whenever we lost any of our own, and we did our best to demoralize them while avenging our losses.

Still, we began to wear down. Our lives had become an endless cycle of scavenging for supplies and raiding the enemy. We were constantly on the move, and the pace was exhausting.

Ken and I talked about it one morning as we marched to our new camp. Dew lay heavy on the ground which, combined with the fact that we were wearing makeshift backpacks and threadbare shoes, made the footing, if not treacherous, at least inhospitable. Most of us had learned the trick of feeling with our feet before settling our entire weight into a step, though occasional stumbles and curses marked those who were still in the learning curve.

"We can't keep this up," I told him. "It's draining us. Keep going, and it won't be much longer before we start making stupid mistakes from sheer exhaustion."

Ken was silent until I began to think he wasn't going to answer. "We got no choice. Stop for two days in the same place, and that'll be the day Larry's all over us. We're still outgunned, and he still has that last tank."

"So why can't we stay deep in the woods, where he can't get to us with the tank? We can take a break for a couple of days, recuperate. He'll never know where we are."

Ken shook his head. "Can't do it, Lee. First, we need to keep up the pressure on Larry's troops. We have to make sure they never get a good night's rest. Keep them scared that a cocktail is going to come out of nowhere and set their beds on fire, or that some crazy people with knives are going to slip in and slit their throats while they sleep. We have to keep the pressure on.

"Second, there's the fact that we're too damn big to stop. We're just under six thousand strong. We stay in one place for even a few days, and we'll be sending out so many people in so many directions to gather food that we might as well still be on the move. And each day, they'll have to go farther and farther. By foraging as we go, we help save time on gathering for meals, and we keep hitting fresh territory, which means no food shortage. There's enough area around Rejas for us to keep moving for months without running short on food."

So we were forced to coast along, reacting to events as they were thrown at us.

* * *

After three more weeks of this nomadic lifestyle, the weather began to turn wet and miserable. A deep depression settled in and morale, which had been so high after our initial victory, began to rapidly deteriorate.

Added to that was the pressure of depleted supplies. Food was tight, but with foraging, we would be fine. What hurt us most were other shortages, ammunition, clothing, shoes, and common tools, such as cooking utensils. It was like being part of a tribe of Stone Age hunter-gatherers.

I began to hear people muttering among themselves that they might be better off leaving Rejas to Larry, moving on to another town. Starting over. About the only thing that stopped them was the observation that Larry's men appeared to be in the same boat.

Ken brought up the subject one night as several of us huddled around a small, shielded campfire. "It doesn't look like Larry was any more prepared for a drawn-out fight than we were. I would guess he's used to walking in and taking whatever he needs without any significant resistance."

Jim grinned. "Guess he ain't run into nobody with th' balls o' Rejas."

"Maybe not. But he's still got a definite advantage in hardware and location."

"You really think so?" I asked. "I've been thinking about that. Granted, he has the one tank left, but I don't think I've seen any of his boys using night goggles in the last week. And they hardly ever return fire at night anymore. Looks to me like they're conserving resources, at the least. Might even be completely out of a few things."

"Like maybe the batteries for the goggles?" Ken rubbed his chin, appearing to think about it for a second. "Makes sense, ours didn't last more than a few days. Why should we assume theirs would last any longer? You might be right."

"And as for location," I continued, "well, they might have the town, but all the people who know the best ways in and out are here with us. Seems to me that balances the scales in that department. On top of that, even though we're having a hard time of it getting enough food to keep us going, think about how bad it must be for them. We know the land around town better than they do. We know where the best foraging areas are, and we're using them. What are they doing for food?"

Jim grunted. "Maybe things ain't as bad as we thought."

Ken was still reserved. "Okay, I'll grant you that. But you and I both know they've got some source of food, or they wouldn't have made it this long. Either they brought in supplies in some of their vehicles, or they're sending out foraging teams the same as we are."

"So, why haven't we seen any of them?"

He shrugged. "It's a big forest, and we only cover a tiny bit of it each day. For all we know, they could be sending teams out the south side of town while we work the north. Who knows? The point is, we can't sit here and hope to starve them out."

The talk went on for another hour or so, and the only thing we finally concluded was that we couldn't continue the way things were for much longer. In a war of attrition, the enemy still had the advantage.

* * *

Brad Stephenson was my second on a night raid, but it was ultimately my responsibility. We'd had a fairly useless night, discovering that Larry's boys had already found the supply cache we'd gone after and had left a nest of young copperheads in its place. No one had been bitten, but only because the enemy had left so many booby traps that we had learned to take nothing for granted. At least that trap didn't explode, as some of the others had.

We were slogging back along the bank of a drainage ditch when our point person, René, called for a stop. "Jefe," she whispered, "I think we got some wild garlic here." She pointed out a swath of plants growing near the water. "You want to take some back to camp?"

It was SOP for any raiding party to gather anything they thought might be useful, especially food. Wild onions, garlic, rice, and several other staples could often be found growing near the ditches and reservoirs around Rejas, so everyone had taken to wearing leather sacks on their belts to carry whatever loot they came across. That night, it looked as though it would be nothing more than seasoning for the stew pots, but there was plenty of it, and it was better than nothing.

I sighed. "Might as well. No reason for the night to be a total loss. Everyone fill your sacks."

I had just yanked what seemed like my hundredth plant from the ground when Brad came up beside me. "Leeland?"

"Yeah?" I barely glanced up, concentrating on finding another plant in the darkness.

"I don't think this is garlic."

I found another plant and pulled it from the moist earth. "What is it, some kind of onion?"

I started to lift it to my face to sniff, but Brad grabbed my arm with a sudden force that stopped me cold. "What?"

"I don't think they're onions, either."

I squinted at the plant I'd just pulled out of the earth. It certainly smelled like garlic, but I knew Brad well enough to listen. "You got my attention. Talk to me."

"Look." He held out the plant he had just pulled. The moon had not yet risen, and it was difficult to see what he held—difficult, but not impossible. Attached to the stem, grouped in with a few leaves and tiny berries, was a single, wilted flower, a pale, bell-shaped flower that started alarms in my head.

I had read about those, long ago, while studying in a library for a life I had never thought to lead. My herbal knowledge was sketchy at best, but I still recalled something about white, bell-shaped flowers. "What is it?"

"Lily of the Valley."

I dropped the plant and wiped my hands on my pants. "Everybody stop!" I hissed. "Put the plants back down!"

But I was too late. Behind me, I heard the sounds of someone retching. A young girl about Megan's age knelt on her hands and knees, shaking and vomiting. "Check her, Brad!"

I ran through the squad to make sure that everyone knew what was happening. "This isn't garlic. It's poisonous! Don't rub your eyes. Don't put your fingers in your mouth. Don't get it on any cuts or scratches. This stuff can kill you!" People dropped the plants like they had found another nest of snakes.

"Drop your sacks and wash your hands in the water." It was too dark to see their expressions, but no one wasted time with questions. They dumped everything they had immediately. A young kid of about nineteen dropped to his knees and rinsed his mouth in the creek.

Seeing that, I groaned, knowing that he had probably tasted some of the plant as he picked it. That was common enough while foraging, but this time it could prove fatal. I only hoped he hadn't eaten very much.

"How much would it take to kill someone?" Brad was the one who had realized what we were picking, so I assumed he knew something about the plant.

"Not much, I would guess." The catch in his voice made me turn.

The girl he held was no longer retching or shaking. Nor was she breathing.

"Damn!" I turned to the squad. "Who else tasted this stuff?"

Only one other hand raised, and it belonged to the kid I'd seen rinsing his mouth.

"How do you feel?"

"O-okay."

"You tell me if you start feeling anything, all right?"

"Yes, sir."

I turned to the rest of the squad. "Who knows this girl?"

"I do." René raised her hand. "Se llama…" She took a deep breath. "She… her name is Rosalyn. Rosalyn Johnson." Johnson. I vaguely recalled her as a sometime friend of Megan's who'd occasionally dropped by the house before Megan had begun spending all her free time with Andrew. *Damn.*

"Okay. You four," I indicated four men, "gather up Rosalyn and carry her with us. We're going back to camp as fast as we can. Anyone who feels the least bit sick, sing out!"

Unfortunately, the damage was done. Less than a mile into the forest, the young man I had spoken with began complaining of severe cramps and a headache. He fell, shivering and cramping, and died along the way. Richard Lister complained of his eyes burning and had to be guided by two others. That slowed us down considerably, and it was more than an hour before we made it back to the main camp. We caused quite a commotion coming in at a run, even more so when people found we were carrying two dead and one wounded.

Someone must have told Jim right away, because he was there almost immediately. "What happened, Lee? Booby trap?"

Panting from the long run, I took a minute to catch my breath. "Lily... of the... Valley."

"What? Lily of the Valley?"

"Thought... it was... garlic. Two dead." I hung my head. Two dead. My responsibility. My fault.

Jim must have known what I was thinking and knew better than to try to say anything. He just squeezed my shoulder and handed me an open canteen. I took a quick swig and nearly choked. Now not only was I out of breath, but my eyes were watering as well.

"Jeez! What the hell is that?"

He showed his teeth in a slight smile. "Moonshine. Tastes like mule piss, with the kick thrown in as an afterthought. Don't drink too much."

"No problem there." I handed the canteen back and wiped my eyes. Looking at the tears on the back of my hand, I remembered Richard. I climbed back to my feet and went to see him.

Debra was examining him by the light of the small, shielded fire. As I walked over, I could see how red and puffy the area around his eyes was.

"Can you see my hand?" Debra waved three fingers in front of his face.

He blinked repeatedly and squinted. "Yeah, but my eyes burn like hell!" He blinked several more times, forcing tears from his eyes, and then asked what must have been on everyone's mind. "Am I gonna go blind? Is this stuff gonna blind me?" He kept his tone controlled and matter-of-fact, but his Adam's apple bobbed with apprehension.

Debra was silent for a moment, as if considering her answer. Finally, she answered calmly, "I'm not going to lie to you, Mr. Lister. There's a chance that it will."

Lister's shoulders slumped, and she hastened to continue. "But I don't think so. Your eyes are tearing so much because they're fighting to flush out the sap you got in them. The fact that you can still see after this long, and that your tear ducts are still functioning, seems to indicate that you're going to be just fine. I want you to keep a warm, wet compress on your eyes tonight and try to get some sleep. We'll see how you feel in the morning."

I watched as Richard's wife lead him away before I turned to Debra. "Is he really going to be all right?"

She sighed. "I have no earthly idea. I've never dealt with this before. Mom would have known what to do." She stopped before following too far down that line of thought. "Anyway, I think he'll be okay."

She patted me on the back. "Go get some rest, Lee. I'll tend your men."

I nodded and headed for our lean-to. I was almost there when I realized that one person from my squad was missing. Brad Stephenson, the man who had first recognized the plant, had disappeared.

I thought back to the last time I remembered seeing him and realized that it hadn't been since before our wild run back to camp. Brad was older, granted, but he had gone on raids in the past and never exhibited any tendency to lag behind. The more I thought about it, the more I feared he might have tasted the plant and not mentioned it. That would be just like him.

Now what?

For me, the answer was obvious. The squad leader was responsible for those under his command. I was squad leader and, though I felt I had already made a pretty big mess of things, it was up to me to see it through. If that meant carrying the body of a friend back by myself, then so be it. There was no need to risk anyone else.

Without saying anything to anyone, I slipped back out of camp.

* * *

Finding the right spot on the bank of the drainage ditch wasn't difficult. We had left in a hurry and left plenty of signs that we had been there. But I still found no sign of Brad.

In fact, it wasn't until I crossed the ditch that I picked up his trail. Footprints led out of the ditch and into the town in a direction we hadn't traveled. *Into town? What the hell is he up to?*

I thought through all that had happened, searching my memories for clues. The clue was there, back at the ditch. It was a few moments before it hit me, but once I thought about it, I knew what he was doing.

Breaking into a run, I raced to catch him.

* * *

I was much too late. We had taken an hour to run through the woods to camp. It had taken forty-five minutes for me to get back to the ditch. That was nearly two hours for Stephenson to pull it off.

That I hadn't already run into him coming back meant it had either gone bad, or he had gone back some other way. As much as I hoped for the latter, I couldn't think of any good reason for him to do so.

As I reached the outskirts of USR&D territory, I slowed, taking more care to stick to the shadows. Something was going on, something that had stirred the enemy like a stick in a beehive. Everywhere I went, people were yelling. Some yelled orders, others cursed. Still others screamed in pain and misery. I peered out of the window of an old storefront and witnessed our greatest single victory over Larry's troops.

Dozens of men lay in the streets around their stewpots. Some were retching and moaning; others were silent and still. Those who had been late to the evening meal had been the lucky ones. The first of their companions had probably begun to react to the poison by then and, when enough of them died, it would have become obvious that the food was the culprit.

I pulled back and whispered through the rest of the town. In all, it looked like Brad had gotten to five of the massive stew pots with an end result of well over three hundred dead. Apparently, the sixth pot was where someone had finally gotten suspicious of the old man bringing garlic to add to the meals. There were no dead there, only angry men ranting over having lost their quarry in the woods.

Some of them were colorful in their descriptions of what they would do to Brad when they caught him, but each word sent my hopes higher. He'd escaped! And from what they were saying, he had been forced to take to the trees on the opposite side of town. That was the reason I hadn't seen him on my way in.

Brad Stephenson had managed what none of the rest of us would have dared. He had boldly strode into the enemy camp, sabotaged their cooking pots, disabled hundreds of the enemy, and still managed to escape.

It would never have worked if there hadn't been so many of the enemy, but with nearly three thousand of them in town, there was no way they could all know each other.

"You son of a bitch, Brad." I grinned. "How the hell can you walk with balls that big?"

* * *

It was with considerably higher spirits that I headed back to camp. For two hours, I had slipped through town, barely avoiding the enemy on several occasions, yet never truly worried. I was too excited. Brad had done the impossible! Up to now, we had hardly done more than hold our own against Larry's men. But tonight, Brad had finally done more than simply sting Larry's troops. He had given us a major victory.

My creeping through the town had shown me just how severe a blow had been delivered. It looked like just over three hundred fifty dead, and at least another hundred incapacitated. I could just imagine the celebration that must be going on back at camp, and I couldn't wait to join in. Or perhaps Stephenson didn't know just how successful he had been, having been forced to make a run for it. I couldn't wait. I grinned at the thought of being able to tell him what he had done. I grinned until my jaws ached.

I grinned until I found Brad with an arrow in his side.

* * *

He leaned against a tree to the side of the path with his head back, eyes closed. The arrow moved slightly as the old man breathed.

I knelt beside him and touched his shoulder. "Brad? Oh, my God."

His eyes opened, and his head turned toward me. In the darkness of the woods, it was difficult to make out details, but I could see his chin coated with blood and, when he tried a feeble smile, his teeth were dark as well. I was no doctor, but it looked like the arrow had pierced his lung and, in our present circumstances, that was as good as dead.

"Leeland?" Frothy blood bubbled forth when he spoke. "Hey, boy. I got 'em." The effort of speaking must have been exhausting because he dropped his head back against the tree and closed his eyes again. For a moment I feared I had arrived just in time to hear his last words, but then he spoke again. "I got 'em."

I nodded. "You got 'em good, old man. I counted over three hundred dead. More of them sick."

His grin returned. "That many? Guess it was worth it, then. Least I'm not gonna die for nothing."

There was a lump in my throat, and for an instant I was back in the old machine shop in Houston talking to my father once more. "Hey! Who said anything about dying?"

Brad locked his eyes to mine. Those eyes held so much, and even in the dim light I could see through them to the man's soul. They were tired, and his pain shone through clearly, but mostly they were content. "Don't kid a kidder, youngster. We both know I've had it."

I shook my head. "I could get you back to camp. We could patch you up."

He laid his head back once more. "Never give up, do you? Guess that's why so many folks look up to you." He took a deep, rattling breath. "But this isn't the time for it. I need your help, Lee, if you think you can do it."

Tears ran down my cheeks, and I sniffed. "Anything you want. Name it."

Brad's hand went to his belt, and he hissed with pain as the movement shifted the arrow. Then he relaxed and spoke softly. "There's a knife on my belt. Take it off for me."

I could see that it was a long blade, and the way he sat had shoved the tip into the soft ground beside him, the handle digging into his side. I struggled with his belt buckle for a moment, taking care not to jostle him as I pulled the long sheath free. "Got it."

"Look at it. It's my best one, and I'm real proud of it. Finished it a few days before those bastards hit us."

I drew the blade free and held it out to examine by the light of the moon. It was a dagger, long and sleek. The blade was about a foot long, made of the fine Damascus steel with which Brad had become so proficient. The handle was a finely polished yellow with streaks of brown—*Bois d'Arc*, one of the hardest woods in North America, definitely the hardest that grew within several hundred miles. "It's beautiful."

"Thanks. It's yours. But I need another favor from you first."

I winced as I saw how much blood bubbled out of his mouth and chest. "Whatever you want, Brad."

"I love that knife, Lee. I was an accountant before D-day. I ever tell you that?" I nodded, wondering if his thoughts were beginning to wander.

"All I ever did my whole life was punch keys on a computer. Try to make the right numbers show up for the right people. Not something to give a man much of a feeling of accomplishment."

He coughed, then spasmed as the arrow tore more tissue deep within. "God, that hurts," he gasped. "I gotta finish this. Wasn't until you showed me how to work the forge that I ever actually *made* anything. Later still before I made anything I actually took pride in. You taught me that, Lee. Pride." He nodded toward the knife I held. "That knife's the best I'm ever going to get to make, so I want you to keep it. Think of me every now and then when you use it."

I cleared my throat. "Sure, Brad. I'd be honored." He peered at me strangely.

"What?"

The old man shook his head and laid it back against the tree again. "What?" I asked again.

More blood bubbled from his lips as he gasped in pain. When the spasm passed, I could barely hear him. "It's a lot to ask. More than anyone has a right to ask of another person, so I'll understand if you can't do it." He paused. "I don't want to die this way, bleedin' inside, chokin' on my own blood."

Helpless, I cried in earnest now. "I'm sorry, Brad. I wish I could stop it. I wish I could."

"You can." His eyes were staring into me again. "This hurts like hell, Lee. I want to die clean. Help me. Please?"

I was shocked. I knew what he was asking, but it took his hand on mine to make me accept that I'd understood correctly. I stared down at the knife still clenched in my fist. Brad pulled my unresisting hand to his throat and placed the needle sharp point of the blade beneath his chin. Then he let go. "Please."

I stared unbelievingly, but he turned away and closed his eyes. He began to talk. "I remember about thirty years ago, when Brenda and I went to the Grand Canyon. We drove from Houston through New Mexico, and on to Arizona. We must have stopped at every Indian reservation we came to. Brenda loved Indian jewelry.

"I remember we got caught in a sandstorm in the Painted Desert one day, and I was scared that we'd get lost and drive off the road, so we stopped right where we were and watched the sand blow across the windshield. It would change colors as it went, and Brenda joked about how it looked like Walt Disney had thrown up on our car.

"She died a few months before D-day, sort of a blessing in disguise, because she really wasn't a strong woman. I don't think she would have lasted long after it all fell apart.

"I miss that woman." He sighed, and a tear rolled down his cheek. "I miss you so much, Brenda."

Sobbing uncontrollably, I shoved upward with all my might, hoping I was swift enough that he didn't feel anything.

Hoping he was reunited with Brenda.

* * *

I met Ken and several others on my way back to camp. René had finally realized that Brad was gone and had sent for me. When I turned up missing too, she told Ken. They had put two and two together and gathered another squad to come find us. I was drained by then, both emotionally and physically, and offered no resistance when they took Brad's body from me.

"Lee? What happened, Lee?"

I turned to Ken, barely aware of what was going on at that point. "What happened?" The words rolled about in my mind for a few seconds, looking for some kind of purchase on reality. They finally registered, and I buried my face in Ken's shirt and cried like a baby.

* * *

I eventually managed to tell them what had happened, and Ken sent spotters out to confirm my story. Word spread through the camps like wildfire.

Over three hundred dead! Just by one old man!

Ken and Jim must have immediately seen the effect of the story as they milked it for all it was worth. The people of Rejas acted like they had found a shiny new stone, a gem of determination they had forgotten even existed.

If that wasn't enough, they reminded one another of some of the struggles through which they had all come, the fights that had made them strong.

We went against them to break our people out of the stadium. A hundred men against three thousand! Thirty to one! And they had tanks! Not as many when we got finished with them, of course.

And what happened at the fertilizer plant? Sure, we had to leave, but not until after we kicked their butts again!

Ironically, it was Billy who dragged me back into it, reminding everyone of the day that three of us went up against twenty looters in the early days after D-day, and further reminding them that he was the only living survivor of those looters.

Through it all, Rejas citizens wove their speculative thread into the tales. If so few of us could do this against so many, what would happen if we all quit our whining about how tough things were, and put our minds to beating Larry?

Larry didn't know it yet, but the tide had turned against him. The number of night raids tripled and were no longer simple gathering missions. Status quo wasn't enough. The townspeople had found their courage once more and, though I never mentioned it to anyone, I knew that the Damascus blade I carried at my side was not Brad's finest work. His example had taken the hidden steel of his neighbors' backbones, tempered it with determination, and forged a weapon against which our enemies had no defense.

Brad had given us back our hope.

CHAPTER 19

* * NOVEMBER 15 * *

Le gros mastin de cité dechassé,
Sera fasché de l'estrange alliance,
Apres aux champs auoir le cerf chassé
Le loups & l'Ours se donront defiance.

The large mastiff expelled from the city
Will be vexed by the strange alliance,
After having chased the stag to the fields
The wolf and the Bear will defy each other.
Nostradamus – *Century 5, Quatrain 4*

A week after Brad's death, we managed to deal the coup de grâce. A combination of homemade naphtha, thermite, and a carelessly opened tank hatch had left Larry's biggest remaining advantage a smoldering ruin. It was a fierce skirmish, and we lost five more of our own, as well as the majority of our remaining ammunition, but we managed to hold the enemy at bay while the mortar brigade lobbed dozens of incendiaries into and around the final functioning Abrams.

Two days later, we had a new problem. Larry's men began to desert, and we had to make a quick decision: let them go, kill them as they left, or capture them and add to our slave population?

"If we kill 'em, the rest will have more reason to stay an' fight," Jim pointed out. "Let 'em go and, at the rate they're leaving, Larry's forces'll be down to where we can oust him in a week, at most."

That wasn't good enough for me. "But what happens then? We let them leave, take back the town, and a week later they decide that they had it better inside after all? Then, instead of us surrounding them, they're surrounding us!" I shook my head. "Doesn't sound like much of a solution to me."

Several others argued as well, until a single voice shouted, "Hold it! Hold on a sec! Hey, listen up!"

The arguments faded as we all saw who spoke. Billy stood with his hands raised for silence, looking as nervous as I'd ever seen him. "There's more than just the three options." He pointed to the circled numbers on his forehead. "There's a bunch of us that you folks gave a tattoo. You call us slaves, but most of us figure we got off easy. You could have just as easily killed us, times being what they are. Instead, you gave us a second chance."

"We can't keep that many slaves, Billy. We don't have the food or the means to keep control over that many of them. We just can't do it!"

Billy turned to face me. "Remember what the judge said would happen to me if I didn't pass muster when my sentence was up? The date gets covered over, and I get a solid circle—life sentence. Why not use a different kind of tattoo for these folks?"

Banishment became the sentence. Over the next three days, some seven hundred deserters were marked with a black X and instructed in what would happen if they were ever seen in the area again. Those who balked at the idea of the tattoo were given the choice of death or returning to Larry's tender mercies. One tried to escape, and we were forced to shoot him. Some refused the mark and were escorted back to Larry's territory.

We figured they would spread the word about what we were doing. By the end of the week, it looked like the enemy had lost about half their number.

It was time to take back our homes.

* * *

Thanksgiving morning was blackened by a ferocious Texas thunderstorm—deafening thunder, blinding lightning, howling wind and pounding rain. It was all we could have hoped for and more. We waited through the night as it built, praying that its fury wouldn't fizzle. We needn't have worried.

Under cover of the raging storm, our first group hit from the northeast. Larry's men again exhibited the irresponsible lack of discipline that we were counting on to get us close. They appeared to be more interested in keeping out of the rain than in keeping watch. Still, there was simply no way to completely hide five hundred soaking wet attackers when lightning kept illuminating them like a giant strobe light. They got within fifty yards of the enemy barricade before they were spotted.

Then a bell rang out above the storm, and Larry's men began to pour out of the buildings just behind the street barricades. Yelling and screaming, they actually seemed angrier at being forced into the storm than concerned about the attack.

Hearing the alarm, Team One went to ground, hiding in ditches, behind stumps, taking cover wherever they could. We knew Larry's men were just as short of ammunition as we were, but Ken had planned our attack based on the assumption that they would break out reserves for such a major battle.

He was right. Though we hadn't heard the sound in several days, the sudden eruption of sporadic gunfire was deafening, even over the fury of the storm. Of our first five hundred attackers, only half had any kind of firearm to accompany their bows and arrows. Of those with firearms, most had less than twenty rounds each. Even with half his troops gone, Larry still had a serious advantage in the area of firepower.

The momentum of Team One's charge faltered, then stopped altogether. Larry's thugs laughed aloud when they saw our people apparently trapped. But Ken had planned well.

He personally led the charge of Team Two from the southeast. While the enemy's attention was engaged with trying to pick off hiding targets,

Ken's wing made it within firing range for the air cannons and cut loose with a salvo of Molotov cocktails. The actual physical damage was minimal, but the psychological effect was devastating. Their laughter turned to screams as the naphtha burst among them, blinding against the black of the storm. Plastic and wooden barricades quickly added dense, black smoke to the confusion. Worse yet were the unfortunate souls splashed with the liquid fire. Their screams and stench fed the enemy's fear and sent them into a retreat.

There was no order to their withdrawal, nothing but blind hysteria. And that, finally, was my signal to attack with the final force from the west. Team Three had crawled into town as the fighting began, and lay in wait a few blocks behind. Once they began their retreat, we poured out of the side streets to wash over them in a wave of fury. We lost more than fifty men and women in that charge, for those of us attacking from the west bore nothing but blades and spears against their rifles. But we were relentless. It was our final battle, and we knew it. We waded in, screaming our hatred and terror, and before they had a chance to regroup, we were on them, hacking and slashing, so close that their firearms became more hindrance than help.

I fought once more with a blade in either hand—machete in the right, Brad's dagger in the left. Both acquitted themselves well as I freed my anger and frustration into the fight. The blades came alive, parrying and thrusting of their own accord as I led my team in.

Hoping to find him in the middle of his men, I looked for Larry, scanning the faces of my enemies as they fell, but each time disappointed. My personal nemesis was evidently engaged elsewhere.

To my left, Eric Petry, katana in hand, danced with the enemy, so graceful as he whirled, leaving death in his wake. I saw him slice completely through an upraised rifle to cleave the skull of the man behind it. Amazed, I allowed myself to become distracted and very nearly died as I was smashed in the ribs with the butt of a rifle and knocked off balance. I rolled away but found myself out of range as my assailant reversed his weapon to shoot me.

But Megan stepped in from behind him and, with deadly precision, used her machete to relieve my attacker of his weapon. It took the poor soul less than a second to realize that she had relieved him of his hands as

well. Before he could open his mouth to scream, she further relieved him
of his final burden.

Glancing back to make sure I was all right, she waded deeper into the
fray, counting her deadly coup against those who had killed her fiancé.

In such close quarters, the advantage was decidedly ours. I saw several
of the enemy attempting to block an overhead strike from a stick or
machete, only to open themselves up to an underhand slice to the belly. It
was a basic technique I had drilled into my students, and I was at once
proud and horrified to see how effectively it was being used.

Mercy was neither asked for, nor offered, by anyone, and in less than
twenty minutes, the last of Larry's men in our area lay dead. My blades,
arms, legs, and face were splattered with blood and rain. I looked around,
panting, sickened at the gruesome carnage I had helped to create, yet elated
to be alive.

But it wasn't over, for deeper within the town I could hear the sounds
of machine guns firing. Someone still had an ample supply of ammo, or
had decided to use everything they had in a last-ditch effort to escape. It
didn't take much thought to guess who that someone was.

Determined to put an end to the bloodbath, I sprinted toward the
sound. No matter how many hundreds, or even thousands, of people were
involved in the slaughter, I knew in my gut that it all boiled down to Larry
and me. He was as determined to get me as I was him and, whichever way
the battle went, the war would not end until one of us was dead.

* * *

Ken was already there when I found the fight. It was in the
underground parking garage of the Nation's Bank building, where a pair of
mounted machine guns protected the only entrance. I recognized the sound
of the fifty calibers.

It was a clever idea, getting the huge guns off of the otherwise useless
Abrams tanks. There was no way anyone was going to rush them.

"Any ideas?" Ken shouted to be heard above the storm.

"Me? You're joking, right?"

Ken grinned briefly. "A man's gotta have hope."

"You think he'd surrender if we asked real nice?" I peeked around the
corner. I barely ducked back in time, as the guns chewed up the side of the
building we hid behind.

"Doesn't seem too likely," was Ken's dry reply.

"Can we get behind them?"

Again, he shook his head. "Already tried. The back is natural stonework with a couple of louvered glass windows. Perfect little sniper holes. We lost five people trying. All we got out of it was a report that there are at least twenty people holed up inside, and they're working on something in the garage."

That sounded ominous. My first fear was that if they could rig the fifty calibers from the tanks, maybe they could rig the cannons, too. A moment's thought nixed that idea, though. We had managed to destroy the cannons on all of the tanks, with the exception of the one buried under twenty feet of water at the reservoir bridge. I didn't think it likely that they could salvage that one. So what were they up to?

"What about the air cannons?"

Ken shook his head. "Out of naphtha. I doubt if we could get close enough, anyway. If we had any incendiaries left, I'd try bringing in the slingshots and lobbing in from behind other buildings. Might as well wish for them to surrender."

Several engines sputtered to life, and suddenly we knew what they had been working on. Ten Humvees and a personnel truck skidded out of the garage, each one overburdened with men. All of the vehicles appeared to have been fitted with at least one of the machine guns from the tanks.

I quickly did the math. Six tanks, minus the one in the reservoir, each with one fifty caliber and two of the smaller 7.62mm meant fifteen machine guns.

A few of our people rushed from hiding to fire the last of their precious ammunition at the fleeing enemy and half a dozen soldiers crashed to the pavement. But the machine guns took their deadly payment, and we lost ten more of our own.

Helpless, I could only stare as Larry sped away.

* * *

There was both celebration and mourning as people reunited with loved ones, or found their bodies. We'd had a questionable victory at best, and almost half our number would never know we had won. There were more casualties than we'd had during the entire month after D-day. It was the cost of using sheer numbers to overrun superior firepower, but only after the fighting was over did this really hit home.

According to the signs at the edge of town, Rejas had once been a community of 9,893 "smiling neighbors." We were less than a third of that now, and not a smile in the town.

We knew there were still several supply caches around town that Larry's boys had missed, but only in those areas where they hadn't spent much time. They had demolished just about everything they had occupied. The fighting had ruined even more. We wouldn't know for some time but, from what I had seen, I wouldn't be surprised if we had lost more than half the buildings.

Even worse was the realization that it wasn't that great a loss, because that would still be plenty of room for our reduced numbers. Entire neighborhoods had been destroyed, and still we had room.

Of the survivors, over a hundred were seriously wounded, and many more were in shock. Mostly, everyone was just tired. Tired of running. Tired of hiding. Tired of fighting.

Still, it didn't feel over.

* * *

That night, Jim convened an emergency meeting of what was left of the town council. Eric Petry and I, along with a handful of others, appealed to them to put one last band together to track Larry down.

"You saw them! There's maybe sixty or seventy of them left. We can put together a group to go after them and leave tonight!"

"And then what?" Jim shook his head wearily. "What would you do once you find him? Throw another hundred bodies at them? Two hundred? Three?"

"Yes!" Eric blurted before I could try reason. "Yes, we would! If that's what it takes, then we do it. The man killed hundreds of our neighbors, our wives and children." Tears ran freely down his cheeks. "He killed my son! He destroyed our homes and our families." Eric turned and faced the crowd. "Who the hell here hasn't lost a friend or relative? Did we do anything to him? Did we?

"Troutman started his killing on D-day. The first opportunity he got, he killed a bunch of innocent folks. Tried to kill Leeland. Larry Troutman had four men with him then. Two years later, he had three thousand! From four to three thousand in less than two years! This time, he'll be starting with more than fifty! We can't let him do it again, or next time he'll come in with three times as many people, and there won't be any stopping him."

No matter how much we reasoned or pleaded, it did no good. Then Eric made things worse when he lost his temper, calling them "a bunch of ball-less fucking cowards" before he stormed out.

The vote was unanimous. I couldn't blame them, since I was as weary as anyone else. But neither could I believe that Larry was going to simply leave and let us get on with our lives. His ego wouldn't allow it. He had hunted me for nearly two years for having dared deny him our supplies. The latest defeat would, in his eyes, be infinitely more insulting. It would gnaw at him, festering until he found a way to exact his revenge.

But Jim summed up the town's weariness later when I appealed to him in private. "Let it go, Lee," he told me with a sigh. "We won. It's over."

Our war had simply been too costly, and Rejas's soul had been damaged, perhaps beyond repair.

* * *

Exhausted beyond belief, I walked through streets as dark as my mood. The more I dwelt on the evening, the darker my mood became, working me into a foul depression that made me want to strike out at someone, anyone.

When Eric found me, he was evidently just as angry. "Leeland!"

Swallowing a curse, I scowled back at him. "What do you want, Eric?"

"I want to know why you let them get away with that goddamned ruling. I want to know why you didn't fight with me to get a group together and go after that son of a bitch!" His belligerent tone grated, and it was just what I needed to put me over the edge.

Without thinking, I shoved him. "You've already pissed off what's left of the council, Eric. You don't want to piss me off, too!"

His balance was off for a second, and I think it shocked him that I had actually shoved him. I saw the emotions on his face go from confusion to fury in less than a second. Then, he swung at me.

It wasn't the wild punch of a drunken brawler, telegraphed and uncontrolled. It was a linear missile thrown by a man who had trained his body for striking efficiency for most of his adult life. I barely had time to see it coming before I felt the impact on my left cheek.

I staggered, but managed to stay on my feet as Eric screamed, "He fucking killed my son! You don't know what that's like." His tears flowed freely. "He killed Andrew."

As abruptly as that, his anger was spent, and he raised his hands to cover his face. His sobbing robbed me of my anger as well, and I approached him cautiously. "Eric? I'm sorry, man." I didn't know what else to say and laid an awkward hand on the man's shoulder.

The contact seemed to lend him the strength to push his emotions back. After a few seconds, he sniffed and looked back at me. "Sorry, Lee." Then he pushed my hand away. "You and me, we're the same. D-day changed us all, but you… me… a few others… it's chosen us to be warriors. We've grown into our roles in this world. Not just soldiers, but true warriors. The kind that hasn't existed outside the military in a long time. I've thought of you as a brother because of that bond."

I nodded. "I feel the same way, Eric."

"There are other things that pull us, though. That first night, when they killed Andrew, I knew that it wasn't the poor bastard Megan killed that caused his death. And I knew I would find out who it was, and I would do whatever it took to kill him."

"Look Eric, I know how you feel, but—"

"No, you don't." He shook his head sadly. "I'm sorry, but you still have your kids. You just can't understand. A man would go through hell and back for his kids." His face took on a look of grim resolve. "A man would do anything for his kids."

He turned and walked away, saying, "I'll do whatever it takes."

* * *

There was plenty of work to do over the next several days, and it was eerily familiar. Once more, we gathered bodies and took them to communal graves. Once more, we inspected abandoned homes. This time, however, we were especially careful, looking for any booby traps that Larry's men may have left behind.

I was on one of those salvage crews the next Saturday morning when Ken found me. He'd been running and was out of breath, but the look in his eyes told me there was trouble. "You'd better get home, Lee."

I dropped my shovel. "What's wrong?"

"Zach, it's… Zach…"

I'd been riding the dirt bike around during the days, so I sprinted to where I'd left it and immediately tore cross-country toward home. Debra sat in the front yard when I got there, rocking and holding herself as if holding in a great wound.

"Deb?"

The crowd gathered around her parted as I approached. Someone laid a hand on my shoulder in sympathy, saying things that were probably meant to be consoling.

Jim was there, and he tried to pull me aside, but I wasn't having any of it. I went straight to Debra. Afraid to ask, but more afraid of not knowing, I forced myself to question her. "Zach?"

Still weeping, she handed me a piece of paper. Fearing what it might say, I refused to read it. Instead, I turned to Jim. The expression on his face put a chill through my soul. "Where's Zachary?" *God, don't let him be dead! Not my son, my baby!* I grabbed Jim in panic. "Where's Zachary?"

"We think he's okay, Leeland. Now calm down. You ain't doin' nobody no good like this."

My breath burst forth before I realized that I had been holding it. I took a few deep breaths and nodded. "Okay. Yeah, you're right." *First, do what needs to be done. Time enough for emotions later.* "Okay. What happened?"

"Read the note."

I looked down at the paper I held in my hand. It was one of Larry's old "turn over the war criminal" fliers. Eric's note was scrawled on the back.

> *I'm truly sorry about this, Leeland. I'm taking Zachary to Larry. I made arrangements to meet with him in Bixby. I told him I'd be bringing your son to him to prove to him that I've turned against you. I guess in a way, I have.*
>
> *The way I see it, there are only a few ways this can play out. Either I fool Larry enough to get close to him and kill him, or I don't, he kills me, and you come after him to get Zachary.*
>
> *Either way, I get to kill the motherfucker.*
>
> *If you want Zachary back, you'll have to come take him from Larry.*
>
> *Consider this my veto of the council's vote,*
> *Eric*

I read again before I turned to Jim in disbelief. I couldn't believe what I had read. "Eric? Eric did this?"

"Looks like it."

I'm not sure how long I stood there before I became aware of Ken standing beside me. For the first time in months, I felt truly lost. "He took my boy, Ken. He got Zach."

He nodded, then handed me the bundle he carried. I regarded the bundle dumbly for a moment before recognizing my machetes and knives, the same blades I'd been so eager to put away a few short days before.

Ken's reply was simple. "Let's go get him back."

* * *

There was no discussion about who would go and who would stay. I was going. It was as simple as that. Anyone who wanted could go with me. Anyone who didn't could stay. I didn't care.

I could see Debra felt the same way, and it was with a mixture of sadness and pride that I watched her set personal feelings aside and arm herself. In all the years we'd been together, I had only seen her armed twice, and both of those times since D-day. Even during the long months spent battling Larry's troops, she had elected to stay and help with the management of the exodus, tending the wounded, gathering food.

She was very much in tune with life. I recalled the day she had come to me and told me she was pregnant with Zachary. She had known from the first that she carried a boy, just as she had known with Megan that it would be a girl.

Always calm, never judgmental, she tried her best to walk apart from the conflict that engulfed us, though she never gave any indication she thought any less of those who had fought, or even of those who had killed. It was just that, no matter how much she knew intellectually that the fight had been necessary, her peaceful nature simply wouldn't allow her to contemplate the idea of taking another life.

But now Larry had our son, and she didn't hesitate. That was as extreme as it got for her. I helped her strap on some of my extra blades and gave her the shotgun and shells we had retrieved from one of the hidden caches. All the while, I couldn't help praying she wouldn't have to use them. For though the look in her eye forbore any thought of trying to keep her from coming, I feared she hadn't the skill to last long in a fight.

It took us less than half an hour to gather what we thought we might need and, as we prepared to leave, I looked around Amber's empty house.

Megan walked in the front door without knocking. "I just heard."

I slung the machete over my shoulder. "We're just about to leave."

Megan seemed hesitant, as if something bothered her.

"Megan?"

She shook her head a few times, her mouth working of its own accord, but no words came.

Debra went to her and pulled her close. "It's okay. We'll get him back."

Megan pushed away. "I should have known what he was up to. We had been planning..." She seemed unable to continue.

At first, I thought I'd heard wrong. But I saw her face and knew I hadn't. My chest suddenly tightened. "Planning?" My voice began to rise without my intending it to. "Planning what?"

Megan started to turn away, but I grabbed her arm and spun her around to face me. "You're telling us you *knew* about this? And you didn't say anything?"

"No!" she sobbed. "Taking Zachary wasn't part of it! We never discussed that! We just wanted—"

"What?" It was only with considerable restraint that I was able to lower my voice again. "You just wanted what?"

We were interrupted by a tentative knock at the door. Ken stepped back defensively when I snatched it open. I started to tell him that it was a bad time when I glanced over his shoulder. A small group waited just behind him, Cindy, René, Sarah, Billy, Edwin, and several others, all looking surprised at my apparent ferocity.

"Um, did we come at a bad time?" Ken asked.

"Yeah." I ran my hand through my hair. "Sorry. You might say that. Family business."

He and Cindy started to turn away.

"Ken?" They turned back.

"You two are family." I sighed. "Now would you please get in here before I do something I'll regret later?"

Cindy smiled, and Ken gripped my shoulder as they slipped past me into the house.

I turned back to the rest of the people in the front yard. "Sorry, guys, this shouldn't take too long." I went inside, closing the door behind me.

Ken and Cindy looked a little disconcerted to see Megan sobbing into Debra's shoulder. No doubt they were wondering what they had walked in on.

As soon as I saw Megan, my anger flared again. I couldn't help it. "Megan was just explaining how she had known Eric was up to something. How she had even been making plans with him!"

To Ken's credit, he approached the whole thing a lot calmer than I had. "Megan? What's this all about?"

Cindy went over to Debra and Megan and began stroking Megan's back. "It's okay, baby. Nobody's mad at you."

At first Megan didn't say anything. She just huddled against her mother. Then, so gradually that I couldn't tell where the transition occurred, Megan was laughing. "That right, Dad? Nobody's mad at me?" Her laughter had an eerie edge that bordered on hysteria. "Hey, Ken? Ask Dad if anyone's mad at me, would you?"

I raised my finger, pointing it in her face, and opened my mouth to shout at her, to release some of the pent-up anger from where it wormed around in my gut and let it fly at my daughter. I was past reason for a second or two, and something of that must have shown in my face.

"Leeland, stop it!" Debra never shouted. *Never.* When she got upset or angry, she got quiet—calmly, glacially quiet. Her shout was all it took. As quickly as that, my anger was gone, replaced by embarrassment. Megan was hurting and, no matter what she had done, she deserved better from me than accusations before I heard her out.

"I'm sorry," I mumbled. "It's been kind of a rough day." For lack of anything more constructive to say, I repeated, "I'm sorry."

"Rough?" She pulled away from Cindy and Debra and started toward me. "Try losing the person you're planning to marry!" Debra grabbed her arm, but Megan twisted away and within three steps, stood nose-to-nose with me. "You think you've had a rough day? I've had a rough day for four damned months!" She turned to walk away. Then, apparently deciding otherwise, she spun back to face me. Her slap was slow and deliberate, daring me to stop it.

Maybe I felt I deserved it, or maybe I felt she deserved some act of penance for my apparent insensitivity. Maybe I was just too shocked at the idea that she would actually do it. Somehow though, I sensed that if I stopped my daughter from making this gesture, this token of defiance, it would open an irrevocable rift between us that would be immeasurably difficult, if not impossible, to repair.

She stood there for a second, daring me to respond, daring me to reprimand her, to chide her or somehow treat her like a child. When I didn't, it seemed to infuriate her even more.

"Damn you! Don't you understand? Larry is the one responsible for Andrew's death, and you were all going to sit back and let him get away with it!"

She stepped back and spun to face the rest of us. "We *had* to do something!"

Ken spoke gently, and I heard a touch of admiration in his voice. "You were going after him, weren't you? That's what you and Eric were planning."

Megan nodded. "It was just going to be me and Eric. We weren't going to involve anyone else. We were going to track Larry down, sneak into his camp at night, and kill him."

"You would never have gotten away with it. They would've killed you both." As soon as I said it, I saw that she had accepted that long ago.

"Not until after we'd gotten Larry."

It was a brassy solution. A suicide mission by two of our best fighters with only one thought on their minds—get Larry at all costs. Never mind what it would take, or what might come after, just get Larry. I was numb with the knowledge that, had they succeeded, I would have likely lost my daughter.

"How did you think you were going to get close enough?"

Her shoulders slumped as she turned away. "That was why we hadn't already left. We couldn't figure it out."

Ken spoke softly in the quiet room. "Eric did."

I nodded. "Yeah, I guess he did." My thoughts raced ahead, trying to get a handle on this new information, this new perspective. We were heading toward something that was likely to get very confusing, and there was no time for confusion. "Okay. Megan, there's something here that has to be said, and you're not going to like it." She didn't look at me.

"Look," I started, "I need to know… I mean, Eric's been a friend. He's been a good friend. But this is…"

Debra surprised me then, both by butting in and by what she said when she did. "Eric just found a way to do what you wanted to do, Lee. What *we* wanted to do."

"He took Zachary!" How could she say such a thing? "He took him to Larry!"

"When Jim and the rest of the council decided to let Larry go," she continued, "you and Eric argued loudest against it. You didn't want to leave things alone either, did you?"

"Of course not!" I snapped. "But I didn't kidnap anyone! I didn't say 'Hey, Eric, let's go kidnap someone and take them to Larry so Rejas'll have to come after him!' And I sure as *hell* didn't tell him to take my own son!"

Megan spoke then. "Andrew was Eric's son. Eric couldn't just sit by while everyone let his son's killer walk away!"

Ken stepped in. "So that gives him the right to set your brother up to be killed too?"

Megan looked at him for a second. "What would you have done if Larry had killed Cindy and everyone had let him go?" She turned to me. "I don't even have to ask you. You taught me. I already know your answer. If Larry had killed Mom, you wouldn't have rested until you'd caught him and made him wish he'd never been born." She was right. She knew it, and I knew it.

"Well guess what? Eric loved his son." Tears were running down her cheeks, but her voice was eerily calm. "So did I, and Larry took him away from me.

"I was going to find him. I was going to use every trick I ever learned from any of you, and I was going to make sure he never killed anyone's husband or wife or child ever again!"

She stopped and took a deep breath before turning back to me. "But now you want to know what I'm going to do when we get to Larry? Am I going to help you get Zach, or will I be so caught up with getting Larry that I'll be useless to you? Right?"

"Yeah, basically. This is hard for all of us, Megan. And there's more to it than that. What are you going to do if it turns out that we have to kill Eric?"

Everyone started talking at once. No one else had even considered that.

"I can't believe you even brought that up." Megan shook her head, her expression shifting from disbelief to disappointment, and finally resolving into sudden anger. "I'm sorry I ever told you any of this." She turned away and headed for the door.

"Megan, wait!"

She stopped, but didn't turn back. "I've got nothing more to say to any of you."

"Megan, I understand this is painful for you, but you have to know that if Eric harms Zachary, he's no better than Larry. And to keep that from happening, I'll do whatever I have to."

Her shoulders slumped a bit, but she nodded. "I know. And if it comes to that, so will I. Just don't expect me to like it. And don't ever expect me to like you asking me to choose like this."

"Your Dad isn't the one that's put us in this situation, Megan," Debra said. "Eric's done this on his own. Don't lose sight of that."

Megan stalked out without another word. The echo of the door slamming was the only sound in the house for several seconds. I turned back to the others. "Did I overdo it? Am I wrong?"

No one spoke at first. Finally, Ken shook his head. "That's not a question any of the rest of us can really answer, Lee." He pursed his lips as if considering his next words carefully. "Cindy and I love you guys like family, just like you said a minute ago, but the truth is, as much as we may care for Zachary, he isn't *our* son. So I can't presume to think I know what you're going through. We've never had a child kidnapped."

He looked like he wanted to say more, but wasn't sure how. Finally, he took Cindy's hand, and the two of them started for the front door. As they started to step outside, Cindy stopped and turned around. For the first time since she and Ken had walked in the house, she spoke to me. "Leeland? We may not have ever had a child kidnapped before, but we've never had a child murdered like Eric has, either." She turned, and the two of them left.

Damn, I hated it when they did that.

* * *

The crowd I had seen when I let Ken and Cindy in still milled out front. In fact, when Debra and I stepped out, I saw that it had grown from the dozen or so I had seen earlier to more than twice that number. Sarah Graham stepped forward.

"Heya, Sensei." She turned to indicate the group gathered in the yard. A lump formed in my throat as I regarded the faces gathered there—Billy,

Mark, René, and others that I had grown to know well over the last few months. At the back of the group, Jim waved to me. I returned the gesture as Sarah, who had somehow become the unofficial spokesperson, continued, "We all decided it might be better if we finished things with Larry. We don't feel he really understood how unwelcome he is in these parts."

She asked in all seriousness, "You want to come with us? We could use your help."

For the first time, I understood how much it frustrated people to have to listen to me as I tried to joke off a serious matter. Still, I appreciated what Sarah was trying to do, meet me on my own terms, so to speak. Too choked up to reply immediately, I could only nod. Then, after I swallowed the lump in my throat, I answered as simply as I could. "Yeah, I would. I'd like to come."

Debra stepped forward and hugged Sarah tightly. "Thanks." She turned to the rest of the group. "Thank you all."

As we walked through, our friends parted before us, and I again saw Jim leaning alone against one of the captured Humvees. I walked over to him.

The mayor seemed uncomfortable as he cleared his throat, not wanting to meet my eyes. "I can't go with you, Lee. Too many folks here lookin' to me, now."

"I understand. I didn't expect you to pack up and leave. It's not your responsibility."

The mayor examined his boots for a moment. "Yeah. Still..." He tossed me a set of keys and patted the side of the vehicle he leaned against. "Roads bein' what they are these days, it'll probably take you a day or two to get to Bixby. There's enough supplies in the back to last you for a week. Extra gas in the jerry cans on back. Also, I kinda spread the word around town that anybody that didn't have nothin' better to do might consider takin' a road trip with y'all. 'Course with what these folk have all been through, I don't know if it'll do much good. Still, it might scrounge up a few more hands for you."

"Thanks, Jim. I appreciate it."

Then, James Kelland did something that caught me completely by surprise, something I would never have suspected him capable of doing.

He buried his machismo, leaned forward, and hugged me tight. "You come back to us, you sumbitch. You hear?"

"I hear you. And I promise not to scratch up your fancy new car, either."

"Yeah." He slapped the hood of the banged-up vehicle. "Well, just make sure you don't." He turned and walked away.

Simply as that, it was time for us to go. Our clan climbed into Jim's Humvee, all of us but Megan, who pointedly took a seat elsewhere. The others boarded whatever vehicles they had. I surveyed the pitifully small group and shook my head.

Ken noticed. "Less than thirty people, armed with less than a dozen firearms and an assortment of hand weapons, chasing after three times as many men armed with machine guns and who knows what other hardware."

He inspected the group and shrugged. "Hell. It isn't the first time the odds have been stacked against us, is it?" He was right, of course.

But as we drove through town, our odds grew increasingly better. We picked up additions to our convoy at nearly every other street. By the time we left the Rejas city limits, we had more than tripled our number.

It reminded me of a scaled-down version of the battle we had recently won. Superior numbers, inferior firepower, and though we had won that one, it had cost us tremendously.

CHAPTER 20

* * NOVEMBER 30 * *

De batailler ne sera donné signe,
Du parc seront contraints de sortir hors:
De Gand l'entour sera cogneu l'ensigne,
Qui fera mettre de tous les siens à morts.

The signal to give battle will not be given,
They will be obliged to go out of the park:
The banner around Ghent will be recognized,
Of him who will cause all his followers to be put to death.
      Nostradamus – *Century 10, Quatrain 83*

So began our last great confrontation with Larry's army. It wasn't the short two- or three-day trip I expected. I was off my game—no planning, no strategy, nothing but simple reaction.

We had to stop for the night about halfway to Bixby. As much as I hated to do so, it would have been foolish to try heading into a town where Larry's troops might be camped with our headlights announcing us from miles away.

"I'm gonna see what all we've got in this sorry excuse for an army." Ken climbed out of the Humvee. "Why don't you guys just kick back and take it easy. You've all had a rough day."

"Thanks, Ken," Debra said. "I could use some sleep." She grabbed my hand. "Coming?"

"Sure." I knew I'd never get to sleep. There was just too much going on in my head, but Debra seemed to want the company.

We lay wrapped up in a blanket, my wife tucked in close beside me. Before long, her soft and steady breathing told me she was asleep. I waited a few more minutes, then slipped away to a campfire someone had started nearby.

Ken found me there a bit later and sat beside me as I stared at the fire. "Ninety-three people with twenty-two handguns, nineteen rifles, forty bows, and an assortment of blades. Every one of them here to help you get Zachary back, Leeland." I nodded absently. "So what's the plan?" I shrugged.

Ken slapped me on the shoulder. "Come on. You can tell me. What do you have in mind?"

"What do you mean?" Wasn't it obvious? I was going to get my son. If anyone got in my way, I would do whatever was necessary to get him *out* of my way.

"I mean, how do you plan to get Zachary back? You know you can't just walk in and grab him. So what's the game plan?" He grunted when I hesitated. "That's what I thought. You haven't got a clue, do you?"

"Not really." I admitted. "Before everyone else joined the party, I figured on some kind of sneak attack."

"You mean something like Megan had in mind with Eric?"

I shrugged. "It was all I could come up with on short notice."

"And now?"

"Well, I don't think we're likely to sneak a hundred people to anywhere within a mile of Larry. There's just too many of us."

"Yep." He looked at me. "Want some advice?"

"Oh, yeah."

The relief must have been evident in my voice, because Ken smiled before he began. "Their greatest advantage is their firepower, the fifties and the seven-sixty-twos mounted on their vehicles. So we find a way to take out their vehicles. Larry's gonna expect you to come after him in Bixby." Ken drew an X in the dirt with a stick. "So in the morning, we go to Jennings."

I tried to remember where Jennings was. If I remembered correctly, it was about twenty miles northeast of Bixby. "Why Jennings?"

"So we can get around them and set up our ambush."

"Sounds good. How do you propose we do it?"

"We head north in the morning. Jump up to Highway two seventy-nine and take it east to Jennings. At Jennings, we drop back down to one eighty, on the other side of Bixby. Then we wait for Larry and take out his Humvees."

"All right. And just how do we do that?"

Something thudded into the ground in front of me. A miniature cluster of nails fused together in such a way that no matter how it sat, it always had one point sticking up.

"Caltrops. Mark and I made several dozen this morning." He stared at me like I was crazy when I started to laugh. "Did I miss something?"

"No." I laughed so hard tears flowed. Several seconds later, I got myself under control. "It's just... hell, Ken, I take back every bad thing I ever said about making nails!"

* * *

For as long as man has fought, the idea behind the ambush has been simple. One side attempts to catch the other by surprise and strikes hard and fast enough to compensate for whatever their opponent's advantage might be.

As Ken had pointed out, Larry's advantage was superior firepower. Ours was superior numbers. If everything went as planned, we would turn off the main highway before getting anywhere near Bixby, cut to a parallel road some ten miles north, and drop back south when we got past him.

Everything went as planned.

We weren't foolish enough to think we could take Larry's group head-to-head, not even with the ambush, but the caltrops blew all four tires in the lead vehicle, two in the second, and one in the third. Our snipers took random shots at some of the others before fading into the trees to observe. Larry's boys ripped the surrounding trees and brush to shreds in response, wasting much of their ammunition and hitting nothing but foliage.

After considerable screaming and shouting, Larry finally got them to cease firing. "Leeland!" he screamed to the trees. "Leeland! I know you're out there! I have your son!"

I watched through my binoculars, and my heart leapt into my throat as I saw him reach down and drag Zachary up and lay a pistol to his head. So Eric had already reached him.

Larry yelled into the trees again. "I don't want to hurt him, Leeland. That would complicate things unnecessarily. But I'll do it if I have to! Don't make me kill him!"

Zachary kicked Larry in the shins. "Let go of me you... you, asshole!" I remembered him telling me that I shouldn't use that word—that it was a bad word.

Then Larry cuffed him and lifted him by the collar of his shirt.

As hard as it was, I held my tongue, and Larry eventually must have decided that he'd scared us off. He started yelling orders at his men to get the blown tires off the damaged vehicles and get the convoy moving. Men scrambled to pull spares off of other vehicles and rush them to the front of the line, while others hustled to remove the flat tires.

The binoculars brought the terror on my son's face right up to me. I could see the tears in his eyes, and his ten-year-old determination to keep them in check.

But I thought I also saw something else. Something in the way Han stood beside Larry—a sudden tension in the big man's stance.

> *"For all his fine skills, my teacher has some simplistic beliefs. He would never willingly take the life of another person, except in self defense or honorable combat."*

I sighed with relief as I realized that Zach was safe. My attention was drawn back to the ranting Larry. He screamed at his men about their incompetence, and I had to grin as I saw their problem. Seven flat tires and they only came up with five spares. They were going to have to lose a vehicle.

He finally seemed to calm down enough to accept that fact and was soon yelling orders at his men to get two vehicles going, the machine gun and the two good tires off the final Humvee. I watched closely as two men pulled out simple socket sets and unbolted the makeshift mounting rig from the roof. They carried the big gun with them as they piled in the remaining vehicles and drove away.

Ken slumped down next to me, his relief obvious. "When he pulled Zach up like that, I was afraid he was going to do something stupid for a second there."

"I don't think he can."

"How's that?"

"It's something Larry told me the first time I met him, back on D-day. Something about Han." I explained what Larry had said about his teacher.

"So he can't kill Zach without alienating his teacher?"

I nodded. "His teacher, his bodyguard, and I'll bet Han is also one of the main reasons his men have stuck with him so long. He's a combination mascot and enforcer."

Ken smiled. "So if Han leaves Larry..."

"I'll bet a good portion of his men leave, too."

"Best news I've had all day."

"All right. So, we stopped one Humvee, and two others left with leaking radiators. And I'd guess we used less than a dozen shots."

I put the binoculars back in their case. "And Larry's boys used considerably more than that."

"Yep. And I guarantee you they'll be traveling a lot slower now, too."

"Um, Ken?"

"Yeah?"

"Do *we* have any spares for that Humvee?"

Ken laughed and called Billy over. "Billy, see how many spare tires we have in this group that might fit that Humvee. If you can find four, then we just got another vehicle."

We got another vehicle.

* * *

The tension between Megan and me eased some the next day, and she joined us in the Humvee during our second attempt to get around Larry's troop for an ambush. Ken's driving reminded me of the wild trip in the pickup on the day of the Kindley massacre. Unfortunately, there was something we hadn't counted on this morning.

Again, the idea behind an ambush was simple. One side attempts to catch the other by surprise and strikes hard and fast.

They hit us just before our turn off. Our Humvee was in the lead when a storm of bullets sent us on a sudden swerving, bumping, sliding trip down the steep embankment that took us off the road. Our trip ended abruptly when the Humvee and a pine tree teamed up to prove quantum physics correct—two objects could not occupy the same space at the same time, no matter how much force was put into the attempt.

I sat stunned for a second, but the recurring whine of passing bullets and the sudden cries of the battle brought me quickly back to the moment. In the back seat, Debra stirred and groaned, and I turned to make sure she was all right. Her eyes didn't seem to quite focus properly. *Shock, probably.* But she nodded when I asked if she was okay. Cindy nodded, too.

"Good. Get Megan and get out on her side!"

I turned to Ken and was surprised to find him still in the driver's seat. I had half-expected to find him already out and running toward the fight. Instead, he was turned away from me, bent over and rocking back and forth. I watched with horror as blood began pooling in his seat. "Oh, shit!" I yelled at Debra. "Open Ken's door! He's hit!"

She still seemed dazed, so Cindy pushed past her and yanked it open. I pushed, she pulled, and Ken tumbled to the ground with a yell.

Debra knelt beside him. "He got one in the leg." She took off her belt and tightened it around the limb. "Went all the way through." She and Cindy checked him for other wounds while Megan and I watched for approaching enemies.

Finally, Debra called out that she was satisfied that his leg was the only injury. "It doesn't look like he's hurt too badly. It missed the femoral artery completely. But we have to get him back to Rejas."

Ken had stopped his moaning. "Bullshit," he spat through clenched teeth.

"Damn it, Ken," I said. "This isn't the time for you to play the damned hero. You're going back to the hospital."

Ken shook his head, and I thought he was going to argue. Then he hissed through clenched teeth, "Not bullshit to the hospital, bullshit to me not hurting too badly. This hurts like a son-of-a-bitch!"

Cindy grinned through her tears. "He'll be all right." We all ducked as another burst of gunfire sounded from the trees on the other side of the Humvee. "Assuming we get him out of here, that is."

Our wreck had not only taken us off the main road, but had also separated us from the rest of our convoy. For the moment at least, no one seemed to notice us, and most of the gunfire remained concentrated about fifty yards up the road.

Larry had evidently greatly underestimated the size of our group, and I saw several of our Humvees and four-by-four trucks wheel off-road into the forest to flank his troops.

Fifty calibers notwithstanding, the enemy troops quickly realized just how greatly they were outnumbered and, as our flankers opened fire, they found themselves about to be outmaneuvered, as well. It took less than five minutes to completely rout them. Five frustrating minutes during which I could do nothing but sit and guard Ken.

Debra and Megan looked like they felt the same way. Just a few minutes after the shooting stopped, I saw Debra tense and signal Megan and me.

I slipped up beside her. "What is it?"

"Something moving up on the road." She pointed. I saw a furtive movement on the road where we had slid down the embankment.

"There's another one." Megan raised her rifle.

Then Sarah stepped into the open where we could see her. "Sensei?"

We all sagged with relief. "Down here!" I yelled. "Sarah! Ken's hit. We need to get him back to town."

"We're on our way!" She slid down the embankment to where we sat with Ken.

* * *

All in all, we lost four people and three vehicles. Seven more people, including Ken, were injured badly enough to warrant sending them back to Rejas. That meant that we also had to send people and vehicles back to care for them during the trip. By the time all was said and done, our group was down to eighty-six people and seventeen Humvees, pickups, and station wagons. In order to get our wounded back to safety, we had to send them in three vehicles, cutting our resources even more.

I walked back to the rear window of the lead wagon. Ken lay inside sleeping with his head in Cindy's lap. "Take care of him, Cindy. We've all gotten used to his ugly face."

She smiled. "I will. You just concentrate on getting that boy back."

I walked up to the driver's door where Debra sat behind the wheel. Leaning through the window, I kissed her softly, worried at the thought of being separated from her in dangerous territory, yet relieved that she would be out of the coming fight. She had as much knowledge of first aid as anyone in the group and would be more of a help with the wounded than in a battle. "Bring Zachary back." I nodded. "And you come back, too."

"You got it. "

Once more, she kissed me and cupped my cheek, then she started the engine. Through misty eyes, she ordered, "Go get my son."

"I promise."

* * *

Over the next few nights, we slipped easily back into our guerilla warfare mode. Each morning, we set traps in the road in front of them to slow them down. Each night, we sabotaged their camp or killed one or two of their guards. Finally, we had them down to a single Humvee and the truck.

Those last vehicles had all of the fifty-caliber ammo, but at least we had them pinned down. Or, at least that was what we thought until daybreak three days later.

"Sensei, wake up!"

If I had gained nothing else from the months of fighting, at least I had finally learned to bring my mind into focus the second I awakened. I opened my eyes to see Sarah hissing at me from a short distance away. "Problems."

I sat up and started belting on my gear. "What's wrong?"

"Larry's gone."

"What! How the hell did that happen?"

"They turned the tables on us. Sent scouts out and got our guards. I figure they pushed the vehicles down the road far enough that we couldn't hear when they started up."

"Even with the truck, they couldn't all fit into two vehicles."

"No. Tracks show most of them walking."

"Damn it! Any idea how long ago?"

"Shift change was less than three hours ago. It has to have been since then."

"Wake everyone up!"

We broke camp in record time and, within ten minutes, we were on the road. About half an hour later, we came across a small group of the enemy standing on the side of the road with their hands in the air. Another man lay on the ground at their feet. They must have heard our engines long before we saw them, but they made no attempt to hide.

Sarah and Billy led a small squad to surround the seven men and get their story. The rest of us kept a nervous eye on the surrounding forest, painfully aware that this could be a setup for another ambush.

After only a few minutes of questioning, Sarah trotted over to me. "They say Larry squeezed as many of them as he could in the Humvee and the truck and left the rest to fend for themselves. Most of them took to the woods, but this group wanted to try their hand at trading with us."

"Trade?" I snorted. "What the hell makes them think we'd be interested in trading anything but bullets with them?" As soon as I said it, though, I realized I had missed the obvious question. "What do they have?"

Sarah cocked her head back to the man lying on the ground. "Eric."

Megan and I both scrambled out of the Humvee. She beat me there by half a second. "Pops?" She lifted his head and cradled it in her lap. "Pops? What happened?"

He was in bad shape. Both eyes were swollen shut, and his body was a mass of blood and bruises. His right arm looked like it was broken in at least two places, and his left knee bent at an unnatural angle. Worst of all was the rib protruding through his side.

"-egan?" His speech slurred, and I realized that his jaw was broken, on top of the other punishments he had sustained. Tears began to leak from the corners of his eyes. "-egan? Ith your fadder he'e?"

"Right here, Eric." Up until that moment, I hadn't known how I would react when I finally found him again. Seeing my old friend like that, though, I couldn't maintain my fury. For the moment, at least, all I could feel was pity. "I'm here."

He turned his face to me and tried to open his eyes, but the swelling was too severe. "Thorry, Lee." He swallowed, wincing as if he had swallowed broken glass. "Had ta do thomething ta ge' clothe ta Lawry."

"Yeah. Well, let's not worry about that just now. We'll work it out when we get back."

He shook his head. "Ah not gonna make it back. Fucker meth-h-ed me up too bad. Th' thombitch ith good, Lee. Be cayhful." Megan looked up at me with tears in her eyes as she realized what Eric was saying.

"Who?" I asked. "Who's good? Was it Han?"

Eric swallowed slightly. "Yeah. Methhed me up inthide."

"Why now? What made them do this now?"

"Ah tried ta get Zach out this mornin'. Kicked Larry'th ath, too." Eric grinned for a second, then grimaced as the movement sent pain through his jaw. "Almoth' made it out, bu' Han caugh'd me. Be cayhful, Lee. He don' feel nuttin'. No pain... nuttin'."

"It's all right, Eric. We'll get him."

Eric nodded. "Yeah, jutht don' fight 'im." He reached out his left hand blindly, and I took it in my own. "You get th' chanthe, you thoot th' bathtard."

"You can count on it," I told him.

I held his hand like that for a time while Megan cradled his head, until his hand finally lost its strength. As I lay his hand on his too-still chest, my emotions were so mixed up that I could hardly sort one from the other. In those last few minutes, I was almost surprised to find that I genuinely and completely forgave him. Once more, I found myself weeping over the loss of a friend and, as my daughter's eyes met mine, I think she finally forgave me as well.

No one bothered us for the few minutes that we grieved, though we all knew that time was pressing. Finally though, I felt it was time to go. As hard as it was to leave Eric, there was a more impending matter. "Come on, Megan. Time to go get your brother."

She nodded. "Just give me a minute alone with him?"

"Sure. I'll be in the truck." I walked away with a lump in my throat.

I didn't make it far before a soft voice from behind stopped me. "Sensei?"

I sighed. "What, Sarah?"

"Ahmm, the others?"

"What?" I turned, confused.

She jerked her chin back at the men Larry had abandoned. "They want to know about their trade." The men who had brought Eric to us in this condition.

"Trade?" I spun and growled, "What the hell do you want?" Running up to the nearest one, I grabbed him by the shirt and drew Brad's dagger from my belt. "You march into our town! You kill our friends!" I jabbed the dagger at his throat, letting the tip break the skin. "Our families! Our neighbors! You destroy half the damned town!" I twisted the knife, and a bead of blood welled at the tip. "You steal my son!" His terror showed in the wide eyes that stared in shock at my reaction. "And now you have the balls to ask me for a trade?"

"Sensei!"

Sarah touched my hand, and I flinched away, withdrawing the dagger. I had nearly killed a helpless man. Worse yet, at that particular moment, I didn't really care. I walked a few paces away to try to cool off and heard Sarah come up behind me again.

I closed my eyes and took a couple of deep breaths. When I felt calm enough to be halfway civil, I turned to her. "What do they want?"

"Tattoos."

"What?"

"They heard about the slave tattoos from when Larry captured that foraging group a couple of months back. Seems they've decided they'd be better off as our slaves than fighting in Larry's army."

I thought about it for a while, then walked back to the bedraggled men standing around Eric and Megan. "You're asking for tattoos? You know what that means?"

"Yes, sir," a particularly rough-looking man at the far end of the line spoke up. "Some of the men who were part of the group that..." He hesitated. "That captured and tortured some of your slaves before... before the big fight, they told us about it."

I walked over to stand in front of him. "So what does it mean?"

"It means we're slaves for the town. Means we serve our time and, eventually, we get the chance to work our way out of it."

"It means you would get a chance to live!" I hissed. "So what makes you think I should let you live?"

They looked at one another wildly. It had apparently never occurred to them that we might not allow them to become slaves. "But we brought you—" He stopped as he realized what he had brought us.

"You brought me another friend I had to watch die."

I remembered an argument with Ken. He had wanted to kill a man, the last surviving member of the group who had killed his neighbors. I'd won that argument, and Billy had lived. And he'd gone on to become a fine person, even a friend. But now I knew firsthand what Ken had felt that day, the deep desire to punish someone, and the frustration of knowing it was not to be.

"All right," I told them. "Assuming you don't give us any trouble, and that you survive this trip, you'll get your damned tattoos."

I turned back to Sarah. "Tie them and put them in the back of a truck. If they so much as blink wrong, kill them where they stand."

"Yes, Sensei."

CHAPTER 21

* * DECEMBER 2 - MORNING * *

A L'ennemy, l'ennemy foy promise
Ne se tiendra, les captifs retenus:
Prins preme mort, & le reste en chemise.
Damné le reste pour estre soustenus.

To the enemy, the enemy faith promised
Will not be kept, the captives retained:
One near death captured, and the remainder in their shirts,
The remainder damned for being supported.
Nostradamus – *Century 10, Quatrain 1*

"There. In the brush to the right, just before the road curves. About twenty feet from the edge of the road."

I searched closely where René indicated and saw nothing. "You sure you saw something?"

"Sí. Keep watching."

I had just about decided that the tension had finally gotten to her when the branches of the juniper swayed, and I finally discerned the camouflaged figure behind it. Once I saw what to watch for, I found several others in the area. "I see them. Looks like about a half dozen or so."

"More on the other side," Billy whispered from his perch on the limb above us.

I shifted the binoculars across the road. Sure enough, another group waited there. "Damn." I sat down with my back against the pine I hid behind and rubbed my eyes. I was so tired I couldn't see straight. I was tired of driving, tired of sneaking through the woods, but mostly I was tired of the fighting. And just down the road, it looked like Larry's boys were settling in for one hell of a fight.

Time to review options. "Any ideas?"

René thought for a second, then shook her head. "Sorry, Jefe, I got nada."

I sighed. "Go get Sarah and Megan," I told her. "Tell them what we've got here, and I want all three of you to start thinking of some way around this situation. I want some ideas by the time you get them back here." She slipped off through the woods to get the others. *Damn it, Ken, why'd you have to go and get shot?*

"Billy?"

"Yes, Sensei?"

"Think you can get around those jokers and see what else is down there?"

The young man nodded. "Easier done than said."

"All right. Be back in an hour."

"Yes, sir." Billy started to slip away.

"Hey!"

"Yes, sir?"

"Make sure you don't get your ass shot off."

He grinned nervously. "That's my number one priority."

It was a long hour.

***

I jolted awake to the sound of soft scurrying from the trees behind me. "Sensei?"

I lowered my pistol. "Here," I whispered back to René.

A few seconds later, she slipped up beside me, accompanied by Sarah and Megan. Sarah's head swiveled around curiously. "Where's Billy?"

"Scouting."

I noticed her worried demeanor. *Something going on there?*

She saw me looking at her and immediately lost the expression. "Just curious," she muttered.

I smiled. "He'll be back any minute now."

"Whatever."

I'll be damned.

Before I could comment, Billy stepped out from the trees behind us. "Any minute is right."

I glanced at Sarah and saw definite signs of relief in her face as he sat beside us.

"What'd you find out?" I asked.

"Looks like this is it."

My heart began to beat faster. "What do you mean?"

Billy cleared the pine needles away and grabbed a stick to draw with in the dirt. "Road curves around to the right up here and, about half a mile further up, they got a little camp set up. Looks like their last Humvee gave up the ghost. They got the hood up, and they're goin' apeshit tryin' to do something to it."

"Larry's there?"

Billy nodded. "Down there screamin' at 'em to get the thing runnin' before he shoots them all. The way they're jumpin', seems like they believe him, too."

I was afraid to ask, but I had to know for sure. "What about Zachary?"

"He's there. The big Chinese dude has him."

Megan asked what I should have. "How many of them did you see?"

"Just up ahead, there's about twenty of 'em waiting to ambush us when we hit the turn in the road. They have one of the Humvees just ahead of that. It's blocking the road, with two flat tires and a fifty-caliber aimed right where we would come around the bend.

"About half a mile past there, there's an old highway rest area. That's where Larry's having his screamin' fit. He's got another dozen or so with him. Including Zach. All together, I'd say they have about thirty to thirty-five people."

I clapped Billy on the shoulder. "I'd say you're right then. Looks like this is it."

Sarah grinned. "Half a mile away. We can finish it."

Megan tempered Sarah's enthusiasm with a bitter comment. "About damned time."

"Yeah." I turned back to René. "How many people you think you'll need to ambush the ambush?"

"Why fight them at all? We can just go around them and hit Larry."

I shook my head. "If we do that, we're likely to end up with Larry in front of us, and the ambush jumping in behind us. Our best bet is to use our numbers to hit them on both fronts at the same time. Keep both groups busy and overwhelm them."

She thought it over. "All right. Gimme fifty people, and Sarah to take half of them."

Sarah nodded her confirmation. "No problem, we'll hit 'em from everywhere but where they expect us. Should be over before it starts."

"All right," I agreed. "We head back to camp. You ladies pick your squads. Take anybody you need. Billy, you'll lead the rest of us to where you found Larry. We leave in an hour."

"Uh, Sensei?"

I realized then that Billy had been conspicuously quiet while the rest of us practically gushed. I could see from his bearing that it wasn't going to be good news. I sighed. "What is it, Billy?"

"Well, I think Larry and his group are going to be a little harder to take than you think."

"Why?"

"Well, while three or four of them are working like crazy on the Humvee, he's got the rest of them setting up some pretty good defenses around the restroom in the park. It's all concrete, and they're using the picnic tables and benches as barricades all around it. It's like a freaking fortress."

The walk back to camp was tense as Billy filled in the details. The old rest area was equipped with concrete picnic tables that Larry's remaining troops had dismantled, building a barricade around the public restroom. Reinforced with mounds of dirt, they made excellent small bunkers, which they festooned with hundreds of sharpened stakes. The topper was the fifty-caliber machine gun on the roof.

"But I think I might have an idea on how to get them out," Billy finished. He told us what he had seen on the way back, and Sarah covered her mouth. I couldn't tell if she was going to laugh or gag.

"Geez, Billy," Megan said.

"What? I really think I can pull it off."

"Yeah but, the whole idea, it just…"

"What?"

"It stinks!"

Billy grinned with the rest of us. "I'll need some people to help me."

I slapped him on the back. "Take whoever you need. I think Ben Summers is probably one of the best bow hunters we have with us. And you'll need Mark Roesch, of course."

With a brief glance at Sarah, Billy trotted ahead to find Ben and Mark.

* * *

It took nearly an hour before we were all ready. During that time, I saw Billy leave with his group to get things ready. It took the rest of us another two hours to slip around the ambush and get into position in front of the entrance to Larry's makeshift fortress.

Then we waited for something to happen.

When Billy caught up to us, his arrival was hard to miss. People involuntarily gasped as he slipped past them. And when he settled down next to me, my eyes began to burn.

"Holy crap, Billy!" I took care to breathe through my mouth. "How can you stand that?"

He grimaced. "You think this is bad, just be thankful Ben and the others stayed back. They're the ones that did the dirty work." He pointed back toward the woods, and I saw Ben, Mark, and the other men readying the giant slingshot. "Oh, by the way, we got four, and Ben says you owe him big for this one."

"No doubt of that. So you're all ready?"

"Yes, sir. We took a little time to do some practice shots. Never shot anything this light before. Mark says that the best way is going to be—"

I put my hand up to stop him. "Does he think he can make the shot?"

"No problem."

"That's all I need to know."

Billy looked up and down the line. "So now what?"

"Send a runner to Sarah. Tell her we're ready as soon as she is."

"Already done. I figure it'll take about half an hour for them to start. All we need to do is wait."

"Good. Then, pass the word. No one starts shooting until I do. We want as many of them outside as possible. First objective is to take out the men on that fifty cal. No one is to fire anywhere near my son."

He nodded. "Got it. Anything else?"

"Yeah, don't get dead," Megan told him. "Sarah would be royally pissed off."

He grinned shyly and slipped off to pass on my orders, while Megan and I waited the last few minutes before Sarah and René started their attack.

I unslung my rifle and checked my ammunition. Twenty-seven rounds. I checked to make sure my machetes and knives were ready for use and tried not to worry too much about the next few minutes. Beside me, Megan strung her crossbow and stuck two rows of the handmade thin-iron bolts into the ground within easy reach.

The next few minutes would determine my son's fate. If I screwed it up, he could die. It was a hell of a thought. *So don't screw it up.*

I closed my eyes at that thought and tried to calm my nerves, waiting for my cue. The wait was a short one. One minute, all was calm, the next, the sound of distant gunfire and shouting punctuated the evening.

"It's started." Megan stated the obvious and dropped a bolt into her crossbow.

I held up my fist and signaled up and down the line, making sure everyone knew they were not to open fire. Everyone held firm, and I turned my attention to the enemy ahead.

They were scurrying about, ducking behind their barricades, trying to decide whether or not they were in any immediate danger. We held still. It was an eternity later when I saw Larry come out with Han dragging Zachary by the arm.

"Oh, my God." Megan's words echoed my thoughts. "What the hell have they done to him?"

My heart clenched at the sight of my bedraggled son. He wore a shirt several sizes too large, dirty and torn in several places, and his body slumped with a haunted countenance, as if he had seen too much of the worst of the world to ever hope again.

"He's been through a lot in the last few days," I said. I sent him a mental message, *Don't give up just yet, son. We're here. We're coming for you.*

Larry listened to the sound of the battle for a moment, and my heart leapt into my throat as he turned and studied the trees where we hid. I froze, convinced he could see us, that he could see *me*. I was so convinced that I nearly gave the order to attack. Then, he turned to Han, and they had a quick discussion. The distance was too great for me to tell what was said, but it became obvious when Han tapped half their men on the shoulders and started to lead them away.

"They're gonna try to help their ambush team," Megan whispered.

We had known that was a possibility, and we couldn't let it happen. Sarah and Rene didn't have enough people to withstand an attack from the rear.

I turned and looked back at Mark. He was a hundred yards back and already watching me, waiting for my go ahead. I pumped my fist at him, and he signaled his men.

Seven men popped up wielding Mark's giant slingshot. The pullers backed up to their preset distance where Mark waited with his bloody ammunition.

He loaded four skunk scent glands into the pouch loader, adjusted the aim a little to one side, and splattered the fetid payload against the inside wall of the restroom. Larry wasn't stupid, and I assumed he would know that the sudden, overwhelmingly foul odor was bound to be a ruse to keep him out of the protection of the building. I just hoped the stench would be so strong that he would have no choice but to stay out, in spite of that knowledge.

Immediately, confused and angry shouts were heard as the men scrambled away from the stench. A second later, two more men staggered out of the concrete restroom. Coughing and retching, they kept their backs to the concrete wall.

Han and his men stopped their departure and dropped behind the shelter of the barricades. Larry held Zachary as a shield in front of him as he edged around to the other side of the building.

Our plan appeared to be working, mostly. Larry and the others scrambled along the wall putting as much distance between themselves and the reeking stench of concentrated skunk scent as possible. Zachary cried openly as Larry put a pistol to his head.

Troutman screamed to the trees, "Leeland! I'll kill him!"

It was the hardest thing I had ever done, but I tore my eyes away from my son's plight and took aim at the men manning the fifty-caliber on top of the building. My shot was the first of many as ten others down the line made short work of the poor wretches. Three seconds after I fired that first shot, the two men were lying slumped across the concrete benches they had dragged up for protection. We had finished our first volley.

As soon as the shooting started, Larry had scrambled madly for cover behind a picnic table lying on its side.

"Larry!" I shouted. "You've got fifty men around you!" Megan raised her eyebrows.

"How's he going to know any different?" I whispered.

"And I've got your son!" he shouted back.

"Let him go, and you get to walk away. But if you hurt him the slightest bit, I'll kill you so slowly, you'll beg me to let you die."

Larry was silent. It took me only a minute to realize that *everything* was silent. The sounds of the battle at the ambush were gone.

"You hear that, Larry? Your ambush is finished. Your men are either dead or captured."

"What makes you think it isn't the other way around?"

"Think about it. We obviously knew they were there, or there never would have been a fight. And if we knew they were there, why would we split up our group unless we had the numbers to be sure of success? We sent eighty men against your little group," I lied. "Do you really think your people had a chance?"

He laughed, and the timbre of his voice frightened me. He sounded as if he was completely desperate and trying to conceal it. I knew that now was when he'd be most dangerous.

"You don't exactly give me much reason to keep the boy alive, Leeland."

"How about a compromise?"

There was no response for a moment, and I peeked around the tree to see if he was still there. "Since we seem to be at an impasse," he responded, "I'm curious as to what you have in mind."

"I suggest we simplify things. Take out all the variables."

He was silent again, probably trying to figure out where I was going with that. Suddenly, he laughed. "Leeland? Are you suggesting a shootout? I do believe the sun has baked what little gray matter you have left. Why in the world would I want to enter the dueling floor with you? What possible gain is there for me?"

"No shootout, Larry. No guns." This was where it would get dicey. I had to appeal to his vanity enough to get him to overcome his caution. "You once told me that you were a pretty good martial artist. Let's see how good. Just you and me. You win, and we let you go. No more pursuit, no more running battles."

He shook his head. "I don't believe you. I don't think your people are going to simply pack up and go home if I kill you."

"Think it through, Larry. We're not talking about an after-school brawl, here. This is it. It ends here. The way I see it, there are a limited number of possible outcomes to this fight. I kill you, or you kill me. If I win, we take my son and leave. At that point, I don't think you'll have any further say in the matter." Larry's only acknowledgment was a grunt.

"On the other hand," I continued, "if you win, you won't have any further use for him. You turn him loose, and my people will let you go."

"Why should I believe you? What makes you think that they'll just stand aside and let me leave?"

"They will if you let my son go. He's the whole reason we're all here. You took him to get to me."

"I didn't take him at all. One of your own people brought him to me!"

"All right," I conceded the point. "You kept him to get to me, though. And if you kill me, there won't be any reason to keep him. Let him go, and my people will take him back to Rejas. It'll be over."

"It seems to me that either way this goes, you get what you wanted. Your boy goes home."

"Yes, and either way, you get what you wanted. I won't be chasing you anymore."

Larry thought it through. Finally, he yelled back, "All right, Leeland. You have your duel."

I exhaled my relief. Zach was going to get out of there. That much was certain. Now all I had to worry about was saving my own skin.

"But I stipulate one slight change." *Damn. Now what's he up to?*

"I don't trust your men to honor your agreement, so I'll stay right where I am with your son. You will fight my champion instead."

My mouth suddenly went dry, and I knew then that I had overlooked a flaw in my reasoning.

I was going to have to fight Han.

CHAPTER 22

* * DECEMBER 2 - AFTERNOON * *

Loing de sa terre Roy perdra la bataille,
Prompt eschappé poursuiuy suyuant prins,
Ignare prins soubs la dorée maille.
Soubs faint habit & l'ennemy surprins.

Far from his land a King will lose the battle,
At once escaped pursued then captured,
Ignorant one taken under the golden mail.
Under false garb & the enemy surprised.
   Nostradamus - *Century 6, Quatrain 14*

Han and I faced each other in the clearing between the tree line and Larry's makeshift fortress. Larry's people and mine surrounded the two of us in a loose ring, an uneasy truce holding everyone's weapons at bay pending the outcome of our fight. To one side, Larry held Zachary, pistol resting lightly against his neck. Despite what I had said earlier, it really did remind me of an after-school brawl.

Megan stood beside me, and we watched as Han stepped forward into the makeshift ring.

"You sure you can take him?"

I looked at the behemoth standing across from me. "No."

She nodded, taciturn and solemn for the moment. "Do you trust Larry to let Zachary go?"

I laughed. "I don't trust Larry as far as I could throw him. But when we first ran across Larry's ambush, back on D-day, he commented on Han's strict code of honor. And we've seen how they've argued over the way they treat Zachary. So I'm pretty sure that if I lose, Han will insist that Larry stick to the terms of our agreement. And Han is the only thing holding Larry's people together."

Megan nodded. "So if Han wins and Larry tries to go against his word, Han will leave?"

I shrugged. "I'm betting he won't continue to serve someone that dishonorable."

She smiled grimly. "And if you kill Han, he's still the only thing holding Larry's group together."

"Yeah. Either way, Larry's army is finished." I exhaled slowly, trying to release some of the tension in my shoulders. "You want to wish your old man good luck?"

Megan pursed her lips as if she were trying to figure out what to say. "You know, we've been standing here trying to be clinical about what happens if you kill Han, or what happens if Han kills you." She shook her head. "And I'm trying my best to stay unemotional about it all because I know you don't need any more pressure right now."

She stopped as her voice cracked and knuckled away the single tear that fell down her cheek. Then she nodded at where Larry held Zachary. "But that prick over there is responsible in one way or another for killing three people I loved and dozens of my friends. Now we're standing here talking about what happens if you die, too." She shook her head again and patted her crossbow absentmindedly. "I'm willing to give your way a chance, but if that doesn't work I want you to know something."

She paused a second, then said with complete sincerity, "I'm gonna kill that son of a bitch." As she said it, I saw a touch of the madness that had overtaken her for a time after Andrew had been killed, and it pained me to finally accept the fact that it would always be a part of her.

I pulled her to me and hugged her close. "If my way doesn't work," I whispered, "I won't be in any position to object. All I ask is that you get your brother home safely first."

She nodded, and I stepped away, into the clearing with Han. We approached each other warily and stopped about ten feet apart. He surprised me by bowing as if this were a simple sparring match in a dojo. Not knowing what else to do, I bowed in return. Then, we began to circle one another.

I studied the way he moved, hoping to find some sign of weakness or fault in strategy. The last time I had seen him this close, he had been pounding my abs. Herculean as ever, he had led a hard life since then, which had only served to enhance his already formidable physique. Lightning fast, he shot a fist toward my face, and the crowd around us erupted into shouts. I parried, only to find it was a ruse. I barely skipped aside in time to save my knee from a crippling kick. Before his foot touched the ground again, Han leapt and spun backward in the air with a speed that belied his size. The heel of his boot grazed my cheek as I scrambled away.

If that kick had connected, it would have been the end of the fight. From the intensity of the shouting, everyone around us knew it as well.

I shook off the close call and saw Han launch himself once more into the air. Sidestepping, I parried another punch. As he passed this time, I jabbed a stiffened thumb beneath his striking arm, into his armpit. *Let's see how you like being on the receiving end.* Now it was my turn to attack before he had a chance to regain his footing. I jumped, kicked.

Han spun backward and countered with a spinning back-fist that knocked me ass over teakettle. I panicked as the world swam before my eyes, and I rolled frantically away. Disoriented, I shifted blindly to cover where I thought Han would be coming from, as I scrambled to get my bearings.

My vision cleared in a second that took forever, just in time to see him coming in with a combination of techniques that turned him into a tornado of striking hands and feet. I barely escaped the flurry, gaining an intensely painful welt on my lower ribs—along with a burgeoning enlightenment.

There were an immeasurable number of fighting schools and philosophies, but most could be broken into combinations of a few categories. Strong or flowing, linear or circular, long range, short range, striking, grappling—all of those characteristics helped an experienced martial artist evaluate his opponent. So far, Han had almost exclusively used long-range, circular techniques.

I tested the hypothesis. Han spun backward once more, throwing the heel of his foot at my head. Instead of stepping back or to the side, I slid inside the technique and countered with an elbow to the back of his head.

On most people, this would have ended things immediately. Han rolled with the strike and came immediately to his feet, the only indication that I had even connected was a slight shake of his head. While I had apparently done little damage, that tiny victory lent credence to my idea and renewed my confidence.

Han attacked again. I needed to find out if he had any close-range techniques in his arsenal. *God help me if he does.* By getting in close, I would be more vulnerable to the big man's greater strength. He punched at my face. I raised an elbow to strike his knuckles, then shuffled closer. He tried to throw another punch, but this was my range, and I stuffed the technique before it could gain any power. Seeing what I was doing, he tried to step back to regain some distance, but I followed and smashed my elbow into his face—once, twice, three times before he staggered backward with a scream of rage and blood streaming from his broken nose.

Eyes widened in pain, the heavyweight still shook it off and attacked again. He was more cautious, more wily. He threw the spinning kick again, but followed with a knee attack, going for the shorter range. But I knew tricks that he simply didn't have experience with. I raised my own knee, driving it into his inner thigh, and at the same time, elbowed his nose again.

Bellowing in pain, his eyes glazed for a second, and I locked my hands around his neck, drawing him down into my raised knee before he threw me off with another sledgehammer punch to the ribs.

I hissed, feeling the sharp pain of a cracked rib. *Gotta end this now, or I won't last another pass.*

Without regard for the pain in my ribs, in fact, almost feeding on it, I jumped at him once more. Again and again, I worked at him, using every opportunity I could get to worry that broken nose. But the pain in my rib began to restrict my breathing, and I found myself rapidly weakening. Simultaneously, each attack on Han's nose only seemed to drive him into greater fury.

Maddened with the pain I had inflicted on his profusely bleeding nose, he drove forward like a frenzied bull. Gone was the cunning fighting machine. Instead, a man insane with pain and anger pummeled me with clumsy, but incredibly powerful punches.

I blocked and parried, but inevitably he got another one through, connecting with the cracked rib, and I screamed once more, blinking back tears and sweat. I staggered back, threw a blind kick with the toe of my boot and felt it connect with his inner thigh.

He barely slowed, but at least he was limping. He growled and threw another punch. I managed to brush past, trap his wrist, and pull him suddenly toward me. Off balance, he was exposed for the split second I needed to slam an open palm into his left ear, bursting his eardrum.

He howled from the pain. Again, I slipped past him, this time stomping the back of his knee hard enough to collapse the leg. He stumbled, and I punched him in the back of the head, right at the base of the neck.

Han dropped to his knees, and before he could get up again I locked my arms around his neck, pulled up, and twisted the bone of my forearm into the vagus nerve running alongside his carotid artery. Then I held on for dear life.

For three seconds, he heaved like a maddened animal. Five more seconds and his struggles weakened to a barely-felt pawing at my arm. Another five and he hung limply from the crook of my arm. I held for another ten seconds to make sure that he would remain unconscious for a bit longer. Finally, I felt safe enough to let him drop to the ground.

Heaving with exhaustion, I tried to straighten and gasped at the pain, but after a second or two, I managed a deep breath and forced my shoulders back. I tried to hide the throbbing pain that permeated my body as I took a few steps toward Larry. The crowd that had been deafening before was suddenly silent.

One by one, Larry's men began to lay down their weapons.

"It's over, Larry," I told him. "Let my boy go."

His eyes widened as he watched his troops surrender. Any sane person would have accepted the inevitable at that point.

Larry shot me instead.

No warning threat. No snarl of anger. No precursor at all. He simply pulled his pistol away from Zachary and shot me.

White-hot searing pain, more intense than all the damage Han had just inflicted, knocked me back to the ground. As I fell to the ground, I saw Larry's head jerk back, a crossbow bolt suddenly buried to the fletching in his left eye. There was no question of his living through that one.

Megan dropped the crossbow and ran toward me.

"I'm all right," I gasped. "Go get Zach."

She nodded and ran past me across the clearing to scoop up her sobbing brother. "It's okay, Zach. It's okay."

But it wasn't. From my prone position, I saw that Han must have regained consciousness just in time to see Larry's death. I yelled something at Megan, and she managed to shove Zachary away as the enraged behemoth tackled her. The two of them rolled around on the ground as I fought back the pain and dizziness, trying to get back to my feet.

Time slowed as I strained to brace myself with my hands and nearly fell once more to my face. My left arm didn't want to cooperate, and blood oozed from a hole in my shoulder. I tried again and made it to my knees. I reached back with my right hand and let fly the knife from my hidden leg sheath.

I watched as the knife tumbled end over end in slow motion, flying toward its target. On my knees, off balance, wounded, hurting like hell, I was surprised I hit Han at all. So was he. The knife hit sideways and barely nicked him, but the distraction was enough for Megan to jab a finger in his eye. Han screamed and twisted away, allowing her to scramble to her feet.

He followed, latched on to the punch she swung at him, and spun her around with brute strength. My senses still in overdrive, I could hear the shouts and feet running from behind me as Billy, Mark, and dozens more rushed forward, but I knew they were too far away. I watched helplessly as Han snaked an arm around Megan's neck and began to squeeze. I staggered to my feet, knowing I was closer than the rest of our people, but with the pressure Han was putting on Megan's neck, her esophagus was going to collapse before any of us could get there. I watched impotently as she managed to turn her chin into the crook of his arm. I cried a string of hopeless profanities as I watched him choking the life out of my daughter.

Megan bit him. As Han squeezed her neck, she dug her chin down into his arm and bit as hard as she could. Han screamed as she ripped a piece of his arm out with her teeth and spit it out. As he loosened his grip, she twisted her body to her right, slipped her leg behind him, slapped her left palm into his groin, and squeezed. For a brief second, he went slack with the pain, and she whipped her right arm back under his, then up over his head to claw into his eyes as she suddenly knelt and yanked his head back. The big man fell backward and landed with his neck squarely on Megan's bent knee.

He was dead before he hit the ground.

Senses finally dropping back to normal, I welcomed the darkness and fell.

EPILOGUE

Doomsday fell on a Saturday...

It's been more than two months since I first wrote those words.

Two long months of resting my cracked ribs, left arm stuck in this sling. I suppose I should be thankful. At least I can get up and walk into the field next door to watch as Megan teaches the morning self defense sessions. Still, it will be several more weeks before I'll feel healed enough to join them.

Some days I walk down the road to Mark and Jenny's house and watch as he hammers out his latest project on the forge. Sometimes it's a knife, sometimes a set of horseshoes. And sometimes we share a wry grin as he pounds out nails from whatever scraps he can find.

Poor Ken with his injured leg can barely get around. He can walk some, with the aid of crutches, but he tires easily, and I can see the frustration in his eyes at the slowness of his progress. It will be a bit longer before he's strong enough to make the walk to Mark's.

The world is different now. We don't have the pharmaceuticals that were once so readily available, and so we have to let Nature do her work unaided.

And we have to learn patience.

Jim comes by most days, and we all discuss the goings on of the town. We try to keep the topics light, but occasionally discussion turns to the uncertainties arising in our future.

For instance, we know now that our plan to store gasoline for the vehicles in town is likely to turn out to be a pipe dream. For while the gasoline may last another few years, we're finding that little things like oil filters, tires, sparkplugs, and a hundred other irreplaceable parts are rapidly wearing out. In another year, it's unlikely that there will be more than a handful of running vehicles left.

When the discussions take this turn, I tend to grow despondent. What will the future hold? What legacy will our children inherit?

But I'm generally an optimistic person by nature, and I write my spells of depression off to not having anything to do. Hence, this journal. It helps me keep busy and mostly out of Debra's way. Mostly, but not completely.

She told me this morning that she's pregnant. And in that mysterious way she's always had, she says it's a girl. I know better than to doubt her.

And I find now that I don't know what I was worried about. We may lose some of our old ways, some of the things that we once took for granted. But so what if we lose our cars? We'll ride horses for a while until we learn to repair the cars. And we'll be closer to nature than we were before D-day. How is that a bad thing?

It will probably take years before we figure our new balance between the past and the present. Eventually, we'll learn how to get the electricity running, how to manufacture the parts we need to get the cars running, and all the other things we used to know.

But for now, I have a way to hold the depression at bay, something to work for, to look forward to.

We're going to call her Amber.

ABOUT THE AUTHOR

The storytelling gene was inescapable. A father whose daredevil adventures personified the rebellious preacher's son, a Choctaw mother, and a veritable cast of characters in the family made for lots of "Did you hear about?" stories, as well as the inevitable oral histories.

Influenced by martial arts, trigonometry, *Star Wars*, and ice cream, Jeff finally decided what he wanted to be when he grew up—which should happen any day now—an author. His long-ignored and oft-lamented Attention Deficit Disorder notwithstanding, you hold in your hands the result of many years of patient writing, re-writing, research, and long hours at the computer.

Jeff's incredibly organized and intelligent wife's influence may be noted in this novel, but she in no way claims responsibility for any of the content, other than to say the story could use some "spice," which is what you would expect from a fan of J.D. Robb.

Jeff and his family live somewhere near Houston, Texas, with two "goggers," three kids, one grandchild, and Dead Tehya, the cat.

Half Past Midnight is his debut novel.

Note from the author: And that, dear reader, is what you get when you allow your wife to write your bio page!

Made in the USA
Lexington, KY
14 February 2012